ees

ats)

Seahorse Bay Books

First published 2024
Published by Seahorse Bay Books Pty Ltd,
www.seahorsebaybooks.com

ISBN: 978-0-6452611-0-3
(UK edition)

Note to Supervisor

I have started my field trip to the dimensions you assigned. I am finding it exceedingly peculiar here, but interesting. As strange as these dimensions are, I have found some specimens that are even stranger and I have chosen them as the subjects for my report. These specimens mostly run around on their tiny planets, thinking they are serious and important. They are all preoccupied with trying to make things out of bits and pieces that cannot go together, and then they wonder why they have so many pieces left over. They think they are unique and wonderful. I think they are wonderfully cute and amusing. Most amusingly, they think they are stuck in what they call spacetime. They have no clue that they are far more wonderful than they imagine.

First Observation

He watched the fire starting to eat the precious page. The sheet of dried plant fibre had fluttered away from the glowing centre, where his fingertips had let it go, coming to rest in ashes. Still close enough for a flame to nibble along an edge. Tasting. He wondered if it would have a taste for his words. He could still read most of what he had written there.

> Again and again. It keeps happening. One seer, two mystics, a hundred ordinary folk – all lost, days unmarked, on a forgotten quest. Then the day comes, for one. A day not foretold. On that day – awakened. Sight restored! And that one knew. Knew his Self. Self regained – as One, with Truth, of All. Wondrous nameless things now known. All that was known before upended, turned inside out, unneeded.
>
> Nothing could be the same again. Until ... it was. Oneness lost. Where? Where? Gone. Back – the old dim eyes. Lost again on tracks well worn. A flower on a field with no breeze. A bird in a land of no trees.
>
> That day, that hour, that eternal moment, it comes and comes again, that splinter of sight – to a hundred ordinary folk, two mystics, one seer. Comes and fades. For most. It was, but what was it – that seeing, that knowing?
>
> So the inexplicable is explained. Many ways explained. Clothed in rags. Or explained away: wild imagining; fleeting dream; sad delusion. Does it matter? Gone anyway. Lost again. Just a one-off. Perhaps. Perhaps. But for one thing. One thread. One tender thread through a hundred weaves – the same thread of light in a hundred rags. Truth unhid, waiting … wanted not. Trampled under a million filthy feet. Cast aside. Or taken and twisted where it has no fit. Taken, scrubbed in dust, tangled in tale and lore.

> Many times it comes – that splash of sight. Too many to pass by. How to find that joyous thread, so pure, so fine? How to unweave and see it straight and whole?

He thought he might know. He knew he did not know. Perhaps a bit. More than nothing.

Observation Series: **Foraging Behaviours**

<u>Summary of observations.</u> My specimens are always scurrying around looking for something. Amazingly, they have no idea what they are looking for is not what they want. They keep looking anyway and naturally, they do keep finding things. When they work out that they don't want what they found, they act surprised and make all sorts of funny little faces. Then, still not knowing what they really want, they just go back to their foraging.

Chapter 1

"And so, we may know there's a bunch of planets out there, whirling around all kinds of stars. Maybe some are even fit to have aliens scurrying about on them. But none of us has any idea how many of those planets are made of cheese like in the good ol' days, or if those aliens are made from sugar and spice."

Quentin's attempt at ending his presentation on a light-hearted note drew politely forced smiles from a few of his audience, and blanks from the rest. Only ten people had turned up for the conference session on exoplanet formation. Two had left early when they realised they were in the wrong room. He did not care about the small audience. He did not care about his lame conclusion. Quentin Narmast, astrophysics fellow at the Massachusetts Institute of Technology, was pleased – now he could add another conference paper to his resume. But Quentin's conclusion was wrong. One of those who had stayed until the end of his presentation had a very good idea of what aliens were made of.

He was called Conrad Lyzachootri on Earth, formerly known on his home world as $\{F4^3,F3^3\}$[1], or 27-8 for short. The conference marked the three thousand two hundred and sixty-third day of his assignment to this planet, pleasant but uneventful days spent diligently and proudly collating Standard Form Surveillance Reports – three hundred and twenty-six submitted so far – all glorious reports resplendent in each and every one of the two hundred and forty-three standard state-of-the-species indicator data points needed to calculate the Species Compliance Index.

[1] The set of the fourth and third numbers in the Fibonacci sequence, both cubed.

Making up the reports had kept him busy but his assignment here had offered no real challenges. Until now. Now at last, he was about to see some action. This was the reason he had left his home planet – to go places, do things, not to be stuck at home.

The brief had come through six days earlier. They said it was simple: recruit an astronomer for an Intervention Assignment. Conrad_27-8 had soon learnt that hiring an astronomer was not the same as hiring, say, a plumber, or a drummer for a band. He had been puzzled at getting no responses to his postings on Freelancer.com; he had found no listing for astronomers on Guru.com. His research uncovered plenty of clues on how to contact amateurs, but he needed a professional. Forced to widen his search, he had stumbled on that Boston Conference on Exoplanets. When he turned up armed with his stilted-awkward communication skills, wearing his transparent orange Fox Fluid rain jacket, his pi(π) t-shirt, his mustard Lycra bike shorts, and an air of confusion, he had instantly been mistaken for an attendee and waved inside. Once inside the conference, he sat through eight sessions, restraining himself from correcting speaker errors five times and rounding errors in computer statistical analysis twice, before he arrived at Quentin's. Quentin had a declared interest in the planets of other stars. Therefore, Conrad_27-8 concluded, he would be very keen to go to one.

Two days after the conference, Conrad_27-8 (as he now signed off his reports) was at the Kavli Institute on the campus of the Massachusetts Institute of Technology, the work address Quentin had given in his conference paper. He was systematically surveilling each of the six levels, accidentally giving the impression he was trying to find a meeting room. He had been down every corridor and into every room. Nothing had come of it except for some corrections and additions he had made to formulae scrawled on unattended whiteboards in three of the rooms – changes that later resulted in two prizes and a doctorate. He had not seen Quentin.

Convinced he was nowhere in the Kavli Institute, and not wanting to raise suspicions by poking around too much, Conrad_27-8 found his way to Forbes Family Café, across and down the street. Conrad_27-8 had calculated that, outside of Quentin's workplace, this was the alternative location with the highest probability of Quentin attending during working hours, and one that also had enough coffee to conduct the recruitment successfully. He saw that there were plenty of spare seats, but also sufficient groups of eaters, coffee drinkers, or just sitters to allow him to blend in, and he positioned himself to observe people as they arrived, while appearing to be occupied with the laptop he had brought. It had belonged to the previous occupant of this body, the human whose electrocution and subsequent departure from his body nearly ten years earlier allowed Conrad_27-8's consciousness to take up residence in it. After a fruitless two hours and forty-two minutes checking every arrival and eavesdropping on mundane chat, he became genuinely occupied with his laptop. While he was waiting, he could amuse himself with the game he had found on it. The game was called Trading on the New York Stock Exchange. He was good at it, much better than the previous occupant, so good that the people at his bank who at the start of his assignment had seemed annoyed about certain matters, soon became very friendly, constantly inviting him to 'special' and 'exclusive' events. He never attended.

"Of course, exo-planet formation can be modelled. I just don't have time to code the simulation software." It was Quentin. Conrad_27-8 had missed him coming in. He froze mid-click. Quentin and another person appeared to be walking directly towards him, Quentin holding a coffee, the other person a hot chocolate. Quentin was saying, "That's what you guys do," as he pulled the chair out from the table behind Conrad_27-8 and sat down.

From the corner of his eye, Conrad_27-8 saw the woman he was speaking to doing the same. Without moving his head, Conrad_27-8 turned to his left a little and leaned back to better hear the conversation.

Quentin was saying he needed it started *now*. The other person was saying she did not have Melissa available *now*, even if Melissa had somehow found herself, on and off, turning Quentin's hotchpotch formulas into simulation models for years now. The impasse brought their conversation to a halt. It was his chance. Despite his excitement, Conrad_27-8 turned slowly. He could have been trying to look casual, but it was because even after nearly ten years he was still not used to having arms and legs and he avoided any quick movements. "Hey, I couldn't help overhearing. Well, I suppose I could have, but I didn't." Conrad_27-8 smiled at Quentin and the person with him. They were both now looking at him, the woman mildly surprised, Quentin mildly annoyed. "Anyway, very interesting concept that – that simulation," he said to his potential recruit. Quentin glanced at Conrad_27-8, and then discovered his coffee cup had, at that exact moment, revealed a startling and fascinating new feature. He reached to inspect it more closely.

"Allow me to introduce myself. I am Conrad Lyzachootri, Director of Global Compliance Assessment." He was also the Acting Director of Global Affairs but felt it would be best not to overawe his potential recruit. Conrad_27-8 extended his hand according to the species norm.

Quentin was not really listening. "What? We have a department for assessing compliance now? Let me help you out then. For a start, don't wander around looking for compliance at MIT. You'd be better off trying your luck at a convention for Mexican bandits. Adios," he said, knowing that the conversation was not over yet.

The woman, who had not caught Conrad_27-8's introduction properly either, was looking at Quentin in a not-particularly-impressed way. Quentin saw the look. He was in a bind – if he did not get someone to do the software models, the Exoplanet Orbit Database study for his research project would not get done. He would then have very awkward questions about what the mounting expenses had produced for the department, and his fellowship renewal would not come along easily or quickly. What was more, he would never get back to the field of protoplanetary disk formation, where his interest really lay. So, he pressed Conrad's hand and said, "Quentin. Astrophysics Researcher."

"And I'm Tracey Iticant, Client Services Director in MIT IT Services." Tracey gave Conrad_27-8 a friendly smile and shook his hand.

Quentin looked at Conrad_27-8. Conrad_27-8 looked at Quentin. Tracey looked at them both looking at each other.

Conrad_27-8 said, "I am very pleased to meet you."

His gaze still fixed on Conrad_27-8, Quentin rested his chin on his hand and waited.

"OK," said Conrad_27-8, "I'll do this in one step."

"That would be great," said Quentin, hope renewed that this could be over more quickly than he had feared.

"I had been considering five steps, with two sub-steps at primary steps two and four. A most elegant arrangement, don't you think?" said Conrad_27-8 with a smile.

At that, Quentin and Tracey checked him over more closely. His outward appearance revealed nothing more than a middle-aged casually dressed man, like any of a hundred you might walk past in the street without a second glance. They glanced sideways at each other.

"One will be almost perfect," said Quentin.

"Almost. But … "

Quentin did not want to hear it. He had a point to make. "Sure. I find zero a much more 'elegant' number."

"Zero? Yes, it has some unique properties. But surely, zero cannot be considered a useful number in this case." Conrad_27-8 was confused. "Anyway, I just want to ask one important question," said Conrad_27-8, taking a deep breath to quell his nerves. "Here goes. As a qualified astronomer, are you willing to help implement the Galactic Council's policies in an assignment that would rank forty-nine on the Crossota Prestige Index?" Even after nearly ten years on Earth, Conrad still had a lot of work to do on the subtleties of introducing a contentious topic into a conversation with strangers.

Tracey said, "Did you say *Galactic*?" She saw that Conrad_27-8 appeared to be completely serious as he leaned forward, waiting, his face holding an uncertain, eager smile. Quentin was leaning back, smirking and rolling his eyes. He did not wait for the answer to Tracey's question.

"Well actually I'm not an astronomer, I'm only an astrophysicist." His ironic tone was an admonishment that being an astrophysicist was clearly at least two levels higher than any other kind of astronomer, on any prestige index you cared to name. "But of course, I want to help out," he said, now sounding overly sincere and leaning close to Conrad_27-8. "Who wouldn't? Maybe only someone who prefers not to chat with someone who makes a black hole look bright. But that's not me. No sir. I love launching my thoughts into a head where they can travel forever with no risk of encountering signs of intelligence. But, umm, you don't have something closer to the high nineties range, do you? On that prestige index."

"Quentin," said Tracey, subtly trying to dampen his belligerence. She had concluded that while the stranger was delusional, he also seemed to be trying to be friendly.

"But this is an off-world assignment," said Conrad_27-8.

"Ah – off-world. Perfect. You should have said that before. What else could I ever want?" Quentin leaned back, locked his hands behind his head, and looked at the ceiling. "Nope. Nothing. It's just what I want. And Christmas is just around the corner."

That did it for Conrad_27-8. Quentin had met all his 'desirable' selection criteria as well: he was open to an off-world assignment and he would support the Council's policies. He was glad that the skills and abilities qualifications for Council Agents, which in the Council's wisdom ran to one thousand and twenty-six items, were broad enough to be satisfied by a semi-sentient rock. So, no problem there either. He hoped the minor distinction between an astronomer and an astrophysicist would not be an issue.

"Excellent. It is all settled then. I can give you just what you want," said Conrad_27-8.

"Oh yeah?" said Quentin with mock interest. "So then, if I am getting my seventy beautiful virgins, they will all need their own bedrooms as well."

"Yes, but …" Conrad_27-8's voice trailed off.

"It would rank very high on the Hanky-Panky Satisfaction Index."

At the same time, Tracey was picking up her purse and positioning it as if about to thump Quentin on the arm with it. "You don't always have to be so mean," she said through her teeth.

"Fine then," Quentin said to Tracey, and then to Conrad_27-8, "where do we get on to your faster-than-light spaceship, Mr er …" Missing his cue, Mr er was looking at Quentin blandly. "Or do you just beam us up? Or do you have a wormhole in your basement that can whiz us across the galaxy, fuelled by a can of deodorant?" He sounded as if he was asking politely. That was Quentin toning down his sarcasm.

"Spaceship? No. No," said Conrad, who had no ear for sarcasm. "Your transfer will be completed by a single highly experienced Consciousness Transfer Engineer. She is really just a 'travel agent', if you like."

"A travel agent?" said Quentin. "I prefer to use American Express Travel."

"American Express Travel. They don't have access to the Galactic Consciousness Transfer Network, do they? Please, it will be better if we use our own people."

"Shame – all of those travel miles going to waste. And when we get to our destination, do these people of yours provide translation services or will we be speaking good ol' North American English which, as everyone in Hollywood knows, is the Galactic standard language?" Since it looked as if he wasn't getting out of this quickly, Quentin was wondering how far this guy's fantasy went.

"I was planning to cover that in pre-departure," said Conrad_27-8. "But I can explain a little now. You are misinformed about the Galactic standard language. The Council's language policy is for local languages to be retained, but improved in line with species advancement directives, with any change (of course) being subject to fair-use regulations and retrospectivity restrictions, along with heritage protection standards." Conrad_27-8 realised he was getting off track.

"But yes, speaking will take some getting used to. When a traveller's consciousness has reached their host-body destination, approximately ninety point two percent of travellers experience a level of disorientation between fifty-four and eighty-nine on Gilligan's Disorientation Index. Within a few minutes you should be able to physically operate the host body. It will take a little longer before you start to understand speech. But then you most likely will not be able to speak properly yourselves for an hour or two – after that you should have enough for basic communication with a native. It all works because speech is an unconscious learned behaviour. But we really should leave all of that to your pre-departure briefing."

Quentin was surprised. This delusion was not following any script he had been expecting. Even so, he had run out of patience for it. He said, "Yeah, let's leave it till then. You can cover the use of the escape slides at the same time."

Conrad_27-8 said, "When are you available to start pre-departure? The transfer is best done where you can be undisturbed for eight to ten hours. The traveller's normal abode is recommended."

"No problem, my apartment it is then. Anytime. Go away now. Bye," said Quentin, wanting Conrad_27-8 gone.

"Very good then," said Conrad_27-8, "I need to go and make the arrangements. I can have those done and be at your apartment at 6:15 this evening. I will have much more to tell you then. I will bring pizza."

"Sure thing. Go away," said Quentin.

Conrad_27-8 stood, then moved with care in the confined spaces between the chairs and tables. He nodded goodbye and started towards the exit.

"Don't forget to bring the ray guns too," said Quentin, waving goodbye. After Conrad_27-8 was out of earshot, Quentin said to Tracey, "Damn. I forgot to tell him to make sure he has a fistful of intergalactic credits. I'm all out." Tracey responded with an *I-am-trying-to-be-patient* look. Quentin went on, "Maybe I should alert someone that one of the Humanistic Studies experiments has gotten loose. Or, we could have a bit more fun with him. I'm almost sorry I didn't give him my address."

Tracey said, "I wish you'd stop having your fun with people. You should have a warning label."

"A warning label?"

"It should say *Open With Care*. Maybe not just you." She looked in the direction Conrad_27-8 had left. "Who knows what's really going on inside anyone's head? Is it a good idea to open it up? Maybe it should all stay shut away, like that mess you don't have to think about because it's stuffed in a closet – the one with the door that's falling off. Especially that guy's head – he was a strange one."

Quentin said, "Strange? Ha. I could give you strange." He was thinking of the current understanding of the universe as being mainly made up of dark matter and dark energy, not what we see and feel, so-called empty space being actually stuffed full of things called fields – whatever they were, then there was general relativity, or even special relativity for that matter, and he could go on. He just said, "There is more to this universe than meets the eye."

Tracey said, "OK. I should get going too. Um, did you bring that external Blu-ray drive you borrowed?"

Quentin said, "Mind-jumping galaxies, Wonder Woman, I left it back at the apartment."

Tracey said, "Oh, that's a problem. I need it tonight. And I have meetings for the rest of the day." She sighed. "Can I pick it up from your apartment after work?" It was going to be the easiest, quickest way to get it since they both lived in the same apartment block on Albany Street.

"Sure. Sure," said Quentin. "I'll be there."

After a moment's thought, Quentin said, "Kieran will be there too." Tracey knew about Kieran. He was Quentin's younger brother, a landscape worker in the MIT Grounds Services Department. A lot of people were uncomfortable with Kieran – they thought he had some psychological condition or mental deficiency. He had been with Quentin a few times when Tracey had bumped into Quentin in the food court. While Kieran looked and generally acted normally, he sometimes said strange things. Tracey had decided Kieran was harmless.

"No problem," she said. Tracey left, not for the kind of meeting she had let Quentin assume, but to visit her father in the Massachusetts General Hospital – he was in end-stage brain cancer. It was a visit neither she nor her father would welcome. Her father was not handling his illness well. At best he was cranky, at worst he fumed and lashed out at anything that was said or done. There were times she felt incapable of getting anything right. But through the long line of tense moments, Tracey was grateful for the time they could still have together, even though the idea of a pleasant visit was something she did not even consider. While he did not see it, it was plain to Tracey that after a lifetime of success and achievement, her father was for the first time facing something he had no control over at all. He was unable to do anything but express his unadmitted profound frustration.

Chapter 2

In another part of the Galaxy, Mist-on-Water was rousing herself from her breakfast to get ready. She was in no hurry. Even if she left after the sun was well risen, she could get to Sand-on-Stone's cabin and back before it reached its highest. She would be walking, as all the townsfolk did. She found her woven bag, the smaller one, and placed in it a few patties of ground grain, followed by a handful of dried fruit.

The village's inhabitants looked much like Earth's gibbons, a small ape from South-east Asia, but with shorter arms, more in the proportion of human arms with four fingers and a stubby tail. Their bodies were covered with short dense pale fur. They adorned themselves with multi-layered beads, pendants, and arm and leg bands. At a glance, Mist-on-Water did not stand out from any of the village's other older children. For the most part they were of robust health, fit from daily labour, cheery, with enough time to relax, entertain themselves or, for some, indulge in harmless mischief and practical jokes. Glances reveal nothing.

Mist-on-Water set off after saying goodbye to her mother, father, and younger brother. She ambled along a road paved with closely laid sandstone, past the few windy residential streets bordered with cabins of timber and stone, most of them set in a casual garden of flowers and vegetables, then out of the village and on past the farmlets that surrounded it. She saw her friend Clouds-at-Sunset working the family orchard and stopped and chatted for a bit about how the sap-suckers had come out early this season and whether it was best to send smoke through the orchard to slow their spread, or wait until the bluefire wasps came to feed on them. Clouds-at-Sunset had been contemplating this alone as her older brother, who was usually helping her in the orchard, was lying on his sleeping mat with a sickness.

Mist-on-Water took the turning leading to the high side of the village, called and raised her arm a few times to other friends as she saw them in their fields, then pressed on along the track leading into the forested hill country, up towards Sand-on-Stone's simple two-roomed cabin, for the final part of her education.

Before she had started her education, her parents had considered renaming her Fivequestions-at-Once. From her first lesson, she had thrived. Many of the children found it hard to decide on the two crafts that culminated their education. After completing their literacy and numeracy core subjects, they had several *grow-crafts* to choose from, along with dozens of *makethink-crafts*. But Mist-on-Water had chosen her two crafts nearly two years before she had needed to. Her *grow-craft* would be to farm, as those who knew her had expected. Nearly everyone in the village did that, anyway. She had chosen cultivation of fruit rather than grain because she liked the tending, the pruning, the keeping the trees free of parasites, and naturally, the delicious harvest. Choosing her *makethink-craft* had been more difficult. There was more to interest her there – the creative arts, performing arts, geometry, philosophy. Finally, she had set on arm and leg band design and painting. She was no genius, but she seemed to have a flair for it.

Within herself, Mist-on-Water nurtured an idea that she would not be long at those crafts anyway, feeling the first tiny pricks of a restiveness, a small, elusive itch for something beyond the normal villager life. The itch was aggravated by the thought that she had more to offer, more she needed to express, more she needed to do, than any place in this village would allow and that no normal village life could fully satisfy. But for now, that little nudge was an infrequent caller, usually dropping in when it was quiet, and then sliding away when the quiet was broken, rarely keeping company for more than a moment or two.

With her friends, her chores, her education, she was kept too well occupied.

After their two craft training subjects were completed, the final piece of every village child's education was one they all tried to get through as quickly as possible – dealing with the eccentric recluse up the hill. It was the one piece of their education they had no choice in, and Mist-on-Water had tried to wriggle out of it more than any before her. She disdained anything that did not serve what she considered some useful purpose and had decided nothing about this 'life training' sounded useful. It brought out the rebel in her.

The rebel rarely needed to come out. Usually, Mist-on-Water was good-natured and cooperative enough. She knew her own mind, was quick and inventive. It meant she made sure she was seldom coerced into anything. She cooperated because she wanted to, because she always worked out how to do what was wanted in the way she wanted to do it, in the way that made sense to her. It had to be that way, because in everything she was seeing links and connections, a bigger story that most other folk seemed to miss. She was canny beyond her years and could work it so that if others got their way, then she did too, with any compromises rarely hers.

With this 'life training', however, she could not take her place with the village adults until Sand-on-Stone had made her armband of graduation and awarded it to her. Despite her adeptness at, and persistence in, getting her own way, this was one of the rare occasions she did not. It irked her that there was no way around it. While giving in, she fully intended to convince the old fogey to give her the armband in no more than a few visits. She would use her talent for getting folk to see things her way.

Sand-on-Stone knew Mist-on-Water was on her way before she was halfway through the thick forest. He sat on a wide bench shaded by a sprawling old whitewood tree in front of his cabin and waited.

Mist-on-Water brushed aside the last of the branches where the trail opened to a flat clearing dominated by the whitewood tree, its outermost branches reaching to the eaves of the cabin. On the near side of the cabin an orderly patch of vegetables flourished. Behind it, a rocky outcrop rose as high as the roof. A small orchard, three rows of fruit-bearing trees, emerged behind the cabin on the other side, and a small field of grain occupied much of the rest of the clearing, following its irregular boundary. She had only been this far up the trail a few times, the last time more than a season before. She stood and took in the tree, the cabin, the vegetable patch, the field, all much as she remembered them. She saw Sand-on-Stone sitting on the bench under the tree, hands in his lap, head tilted forward, perhaps asleep. Mist-on-Water strode across the clearing, the sound of her feet, she hoped, forewarning her arrival. She stopped at the far end of the bench, next to the ashes from a fire not long burnt out. Seeing the delicate fluttering remains of a page at the edge of the ashes, she frowned.

"Well met, daughter," said Sand-on-Stone, raising his head and looking her over. All the village children were addressed as 'daughter' or 'son' by the adults.

"Well met, uncle," said Mist-on-Water.

Their speech combined about a dozen tones and several distinct lip-smacking sounds along with soft finger taps, slaps, or drumming made on their arms, legs, or anything else handy.

"How tread your mother and father, and your brother?"

"They walk easy."

"Good. I have not seen them in nearly a season." Sand-on-Stone's gaze went to a few clouds drifting past the hills on the other side of the valley. Giving voice to his thoughts he said, "Perhaps it would be better if I were a little closer to the village."

Mist-on-Water ran her fingers over a clump of long slender plants growing by her feet nearly up to her shoulder, selected one of the thicker and longer stems, and pulled it from the ground.

Returning his attention to Mist-On-Water, Sand-on-Stone said, "You have found good longleaf fibre there. It will weave into a strong twine for a carry bag. Is that your plan? Or do you plan to make a strong rope to tie me up so you can escape?"

"Yes."

Sand-on-Stone chuckled. "Then let us begin."

Mist-on-Water, still standing, said, "Certainly, let's begin. The sooner we begin, the sooner we finish. Can I ask a question?"

"Are you fearless enough for an answer?" said Sand-on-Stone.

"Fearless, you say? So-be.[2] How soon can I be finished here? And why should I even be here anyway?" When she had asked in the village about the time to be spent with Sand-on-Stone, no one had given her a clear answer. *Maybe just a few days*, they had said – she saw through the attempt to placate her. *Maybe a grey-moon cycle, maybe even a white-moon cycle. Maybe even longer.* On the reason why, the answer seemed to amount to nothing more than 'because Sand-on-Stone wants it that way'. Exactly the kind of answer that annoyed her. It seemed all the village elders respected Sand-on-Stone but apart from a brief stint with the older children, as they finished their education, he was rarely seen.

He usually only came down to the village for the major festivals, when everyone gathered. From time to time an elder would push through the forest to his cabin to discuss some matter. So, no real reason to be wasting time up there then, Mist-on-Water had decided. Especially since, gnawing gently inside her, she again felt the stirrings of a tiny unease, a hazy notion that the future she had planned might be missing something, something

---

[2] So-be – a local expression with a meaning that can range between "OK" and "If you say so."

unknown and therefore something she needed to spend time uncovering.

"Ah, straight to the point. Yes, we must hurry lest the river of time runs dry at our feet," said Sand-on-Stone with another quiet chuckle.

Mist-on-Water made sure her expression did not change.

"Why come here? Hmm," Sand-on-Stone went on. "The reason is simple: I can give you what you want. How long must you come? Of course, you will come no more when you have what you want. Why would you keep coming after that?"

"Because you can give me what *I* want? I don't need to do anything else?"

"Just accept."

"Accept what? What I want? Only that?"

"Yes. Only that."

Mist-on-Water thought this could be a trick. For a moment she thought about the response that had come to her, wondering if it were too obvious. She said, "And you will award me my band of graduation?"

"Yes."

"What I want is to be finished here. To go."

Sand-on-Stone said, "Say-you. This is everything you want?"

That small itch within Mist-on-Water stirred itself again for a moment. She thought, *What is it I want, really?* She said, "It is all I want that you have to give."

"Why do you think you know what I have?" said Sand-on-Stone.

"What else could *you* give," said Mist-on-Water, looking at the simple stone and timber cabin. Some crude iron and timber farming tools were propped against a wall and high up by the door, a bronze armband dangled from a string.

"Ahh, I have the key to everything. How else could I offer you what you want? Who knows what you could say? Maybe anything. Or perhaps you just want to learn the secrets of keeping the sap-sucker from your orchard?"

"What is this key to everything?" said Mist-on-Water, wondering how he had known about her talk earlier with Clouds-at-Sunset. Or was it just coincidence? Despite her intentions to engage with Sand-on-Stone only the bare minimum, she was starting to find herself drawn in.

"It is the key to knowledge, to truth."

"So-be. Knowledge of what?"

"Knowledge of all that is not."

"All that is *not*? Say-you. Wouldn't knowledge of all that *is* be a tad more useful? Living hidden away here, do you think you have anything new to tell me?"

Sand-on-Stone heard Mist-on-Water's gentle mocking but understood the intent of her ripostes was to probe, to test, not to cut. He said nothing in response.

Against her expectations, Sand-on-Stone had roused Mist-on-Water's interest. A little. This was not going the way she had planned, and despite what some of her older friends had said, Sand-on-Stone was not teaching mainly nonsense, not yet anyway. Strange perhaps, different perhaps, even with something to offer her perhaps. Sand-on-Stone's first lesson, if this was what it was, was not like the classes of the other teachers, ordinary village folk who happened to have mastered their chosen craft, but who spoke only of mundane day-to-day village matters. Mist-on-Water had a feeling that something about Sand-on-Stone was not so ordinary. Maybe he knew things that she could find interesting, or useful, or both.

She sat on the bench, on the edge, on the other end, as far from Sand-on-Stone as the bench would allow.

Observation Series: **Habitat Exploration**

Summary of observations. Even though my little specimens do not know what they are looking for, they sometimes embark on quite long journeys in search of it. Even though they have no clue whether what they want is over there, or right here, or that they might never find anything anywhere to satisfy them. I keep wanting to give them little pokes to stop them from wandering off.

Chapter 3

At 6:15, in his apartment, Quentin was rummaging for the external Blu-ray drive he had borrowed from Tracey, who was standing in the middle of his lounge room. The room was crammed with three couches laden with piles of recently washed clothing. Piles of papers and magazines sat on the rug among a basic telescope and different bits for it, meant perhaps as an attempt at decoration. The cables of a sound system ran across the floor and disappeared under some taped-up cartons. A coffee table displayed several books and two open packets of pretzels. An ironing board and a further assortment of displaced day-to-day household items told a tale of an owner who had other priorities.

Kieran, tidying up behind Quentin as he was upending things, was singing lines from U2's song *I still haven't found what I'm looking for*, but instead of the original's 'only to be with you', Kieran sang '*Only to know you true, only to know you true.*'

He was going on to the chorus, '*He still hasn't found …*' when Quentin said to himself, "He never gets the words right."

There was a knock on the door. "Do you want me to see who it is?" said Tracey.

"Thanks," said Quentin.

Tracey looked through the peephole to see Conrad_27-8, carrying a pizza box. She felt a twinge of guilt that the earlier exchange with Conrad_27-8 had gone this far, and opened the door. Conrad_27-8 walked in and looking around said, "Hello again."

Kieran said, "Hello. Nice of you to bring food."

Quentin was now standing next to Tracey, confused. "What are you doing here?" he said.

Conrad said, “It is time for your assignment. Six-fifteen.”

Before Quentin could work up a response, Kieran said, “What assignment, Quentin?”

Quentin drew in and let out a long breath and said, “Our screw-loose visitor here has selected me for an ‘off-world’ assignment.” He spat out ‘off-world’ as if to slap Conrad_27-8 with it. “An assignment that requires the rare and highly-sought-after skills of an astrophysicist. But not *any* astrophysicist. Noooo. He needs an astrophysicist good-natured and stupid enough to humour Captain Loontron here from the planet Asylum in the constellation of Call-Me-An-Idiot-9. Said astrophysicist would be me, of course.” He turned back to Conrad_27-8. “How did you find my apartment anyway?”

Before Conrad_27-8 could answer, Kieran, who had been looking at Conrad_27-8 intently, said, “You always say the universe is a very strange place. I see he is a part of it. Can we go too?” He meant himself and Tracey. He always included everyone.

“Hang on, Kieran …” Quentin started to say, now in a gentler tone.

But Conrad_27-8 had done some quick calculations and said, “Three agents? Three agents will be a very apt number. Our destination point already has a sufficient number of standby recipient entities available.” Quentin turned back to Kieran, who was looking delighted, and said under his breath to Tracey, “Well, how do we get out of this?”

Tracey was afraid this was not going to end well for someone, or everyone, and felt that twinge of guilt again. She said to everyone, “Look, I’m actually pretty hungry. Why don’t we have the pizza before it gets cold. And then we can talk about this.”

“Excellent idea,” said Conrad_27-8, “I can give you your pre-departure information at the same time.”

While they were eating pizza, Conrad_27-8 did most of the talking.

Conrad_27-8 started his pre-departure run-down by explaining that their consciousness would soon be transported to air-breathing, two-armed bipeds, similar to themselves – the host bodies (or 'recipient entities' as he called them). This was fortunate for them – these three newly recruited Galactic Council Agents – since it would make learning to operate the bodies relatively easy. Also, since their current bodies would obviously remain here, untended, there would be a limit as to how long they could stay away. They would need to come back every ten to twelve hours at most, ideally sooner. It meant they would need a number of transfers to complete the assignment.

Conrad_27-8 described the destination planet as having abundant vegetation, almost all safe to eat. Since their host species were herbivores, they should not have any concerns about food. The first real challenge for them would be learning to communicate. He explained that since talking was largely an 'unconscious competence' – you generally do not consciously control the sounds you make or even the words you say – they would need to approach speaking by just deciding to express the idea they wanted to get across. The host body's brain would know how to translate that idea into language and would speak, as long as there were no attempt at direct, conscious control. Understanding any speech they heard would be similar – pay no attention to the sounds themselves, and the host's brain would provide the meaning.

Conrad_27-8 wanted everyone to be reassured that he would be transferring with them, at least for the first time. However, they would also be meeting with the local Global Affairs Director who would assist them with the assignment. Along with that, each sentient being on the destination planet had what was called in the local language a 'minder', a quasi-symbiotic creature that was intelligent and devoted entirely to protecting its host. They were quite small – small enough to ride on the host – and invariably sat on one of their host's shoulders, nestled against an ear where it whispered warnings and guidance. The minders only spoke to their own host, never to another host, and never to one another.

Quentin had decided that not engaging would be the quickest way to get Conrad_27-8 out, so while Conrad_27-8 was talking, he had been thinking about his next steps on simulating planetary formation to refine his stellar evolution models, making use of the mounting data available in the exoplanet orbit database. He needed some results.

Kieran had been listening closely to Conrad_27-8's briefing, and Tracey found herself intrigued about what must be going on inside Conrad_27-8's head to lead to such a richly detailed delusion.

"How many questions do you have?" asked Conrad_27-8.

"Just one," said Quentin, looking at Tracey, "who calls 911?"

Conrad_27-8 started looking around for any sign of danger. He said, "Does your apartment not have all the required safety features?"

Kieran said, "You can't be safe when there is nothing you can be in danger from."

With a puzzled expression forming on Conrad_27-8's face, Tracey, looking at Quentin and indicating the pizza box and plates on the coffee table, said, "Can you help me tidy this up?"

Tracey and Quentin gathered the evidence of dinner and took it to the kitchen. She spoke quietly. "OK, what about this? The sooner we do what he wants, the sooner Conrad here can get to the point where nothing happens. He will come up with some equipment failure explanation, or whatever. We suggest he goes off to fix it, and you will be 'not at home' if he ever comes back."

"Or – we jump straight to the three-person, low orbit, boot-boosted, through-the-door weirdo launch." Quentin mimed his plan to make sure it was understood clearly.

The look Tracey gave him was enough.

"OK, we try your way first," he said.

They returned to the lounge and Tracey said, "Well Conrad, I think we're ready."

Quentin said, "Are you sure you brought the right galactic coordinates?"

Conrad_27-8 said, "For the travel agents, the address is as plain as the one printed on your driver's licence."

"Pfugh." Quentin had to start being more careful about leaving his wallet lying around open. He said, "Just get it over with."

Conrad_27-8 said, "Good. Step one is to position yourselves where you will be comfortable for several hours."

Quentin reserved one of the couches by flopping down on it, scattering some of the washing and folded his arms. Kieran said, "I'll get the yoga mat." Tracey took the other couch. Conrad_27-8 sat on the chair and Kieran returned with the yoga mat, unrolled it by the coffee table, and lay down on it on his back.

"Aren't you forgetting something?" said Quentin, looking at Conrad_27-8.

"No. I believe zero items have been forgotten," said Conrad_27-8.

"Your travel agent?"

"No. They work remotely, if you like. Now, step two. Simply relax and close your eyes. Try not to think of anything. I will give you a minute," said Conrad_27-8.

"Damn. I didn't put on my ruby slippers," said Quentin.

The room grew peaceful, with just the sound of four people breathing. Kieran started singing softly, 'He still hasn't found what he's looking for.'

Conrad_27-8 said, "Now, step three, the final step. Staying relaxed, draw all of your attention to a spot inside your head just above your eyes." Even Quentin, who was feeling a bit tired anyway, did this.

Chapter 4

Sand-on-Stone looked at Mist-on-Water sitting on the edge of the bench. She had shown she was bright and willing to listen, for now at least. It was time to find out how willing.

Sand-on-Stone stretched his arms, stood, stretched his legs, took a few steps towards his cabin, picked up a well-used mattock leaning against the wall, went back to the bench, and retrieved a small woven pouch from behind it. Mist-on-Water saw that the pouch was crammed full of something, but a string was drawing its top closed and she could not see what was hidden inside.

"Would you care to help me prepare some dinner?" said Sand-on-Stone.

"It looks like the grain you have ground in there will not take long to bake."

Sand-on-Stone opened the pouch, revealing dozens of tiny bright-orange balls.

"Ah – purple spot melons. They will be delicious. If you can get them to germinate." The finicky purple spot melon tested even the most gifted gardener.

Sand-on-Stone ambled to his food garden, dropped the point of the mattock in the soil next to a row of sweet twister beans, and pulled it along as he walked backwards, making a straight line. He went back to where his line began, heaved the mattock into the ground, and opened the loose soil, starting a furrow. He said, "You say you want to know something new? Could it be that even in my far-off humble little hut I have come to know just a few things that even someone who is very astute and well informed may not know?"

The question was not really seeking an answer, so Mist-on-Water said nothing.

"So-be, you are correct. I should not exaggerate. It could not be more than one or two new things that I know. Maybe it's fewer. But even someone who is very close to omniscient like – let's say – like you, even that one may not know them yet."

With a sigh of exaggerated patience, Mist-on-Water ignored his playful parody, waiting for whatever point he was coming to.

He went on, "Maybe I can tell you some things you don't yet know about you even? Yes, about you. But first, I have to tell you about The Source."

"The source? Which one? I know about them anyway," said Mist-on-Water, a derisive edge in her voice that she did not bother to soften. *Tell me some new things about me? We'll see*, she thought.

The 'sources' Mist-on-Water had dismissed were prominent in the Tales of the Talkers-in-the-Wind, the collected folklore that had been passed along by uncounted generations. She thought the tales, read from tattered scrolls, were pure fiction, made up long ago by elders sitting around their campfires at night dreaming up stories to answer the questions of innocent youngsters, lest they expose their own ignorance. Or to cajole them, as their elders had cajoled them, and as their elders' elders had.

It was easy for her to dismiss the tales. One lot of the scrolls was mostly about tribal wanderings, settlements, leaders, laws, troubles, and rituals. All pointless relics, Mist-on-Water groaned in her classes. The other scrolls took the sources as their subjects. They rose from the idea of the chain of cause and effect – seeds spring up as plants, rain and good soil lead to growth, crop pests make a poor harvest, and so on. For all the effects that had no cause they could point at – and there were many – they named a cause unseen. The cause for coming clouds, rain, storm, cloudless sky, drought, they named the Weather-Source. The force behind Earth tremors and the maker of soil and rock was the Land-Source. They named their sources thinking they were explaining everything. Mist-on-Water could never make them see they were confusing naming with understanding. She was not satisfied by that, and no one else should be either.

In all, eight sources were named: Weather-Source, Life-Death-Source, Land-Source, Water-Source, Fire-Source, Star-Source, Beauty-Source, Good-Fortune-Source. What were they, these sources? That was not made clear. They were alluded to as some form of beings, beings the common folk could not see, but beings of power, acting of their own volition since their actions appeared to be unpredictable. The appearance of these sources was never described. It was implied they had bodies, not flesh and blood bodies, but something less restrictive, albeit with the normal body parts such as feet, hands, tails, heads with faces.

With the writing, collection, and sharing of the tales, the dogma of the sources matured and oracles emerged who declared they had the ability to communicate with the sources, each oracle claiming an affinity for one particular source, or sometimes two. These oracles ensured each village preserved its carefully transcribed copy of the tales, nurtured the traditions, and had their time in each youngster's formal education.

The teachings about the ancient tribes put Mist-on-Water to sleep, but the other scrolls annoyed her to her bones. She seethed that the reasonable idea that everything had a cause was gratuitously and wilfully abused. It grated on her every time something unexplained happened and someone simply uttered the name of a source and was satisfied. It galled her.

Her lessons with the oracles or their novitiates went like this:

> She would say, "So, now I have learnt that the cause of last night's rain and this morning's fog was Weather-Source? No?"
>
> The oracle's novitiate, unsuspecting, would reply, "Yes."
>
> "Because Weather-Source was pleased by the dance of Life-Source?"
>
> "And the offerings. That is the word from the oracle."
>
> "So, now I understand how they came about – the rain and fog? Yes?"
>
> "That is correct."
>
> "So, the fog was not caused by the song of the HardKnuckledSpikeTop bird?" She was making up a ridiculous sounding name for a fictitious species of bird.
>
> "Pardon? What bird? What did you say?"
>
> "I say the fog this morning was caused by the song of the HardKnuckledSpikeTop bird. You can't see that bird, and its song is silent to our ears. Prove that I am wrong."

Sand-on-Stone, well aware of the teachings Mist-on-Water would have already received, said, "You learned about the sources? That's good. What have you learned?"

"That they are cold, surly, distracted buffoons, absent landlords plied with a rent they do not care for. If they care for anything, it is not us. If they speak any words at all, it is only to mock our troubles. Many call to them, they are not listening. While their domains are in ruins, they gambol about somewhere else. Any power they hold, they wield on capricious whims. They are disinterested, unjust, nasty. They are diligent only in authoring the scrolls of fear, they are the tone-deaf composers of melodies of torment. They are all of that, if they are anything at all. So, which one do you want to tell me about?"

"So-be. Quite a lot of learning already then." Sand-on Stone was taken aback by Mist-on-Water's vehemence. Nevertheless, he went on. "But of which source would I speak, you ask? Just *The Source*. But do not be misled. I call it *The Source* because we must talk of it. But it is a dilemma. What I am talking about has no name and can have no name. That is just the name I give it so we can start. We will talk of things that cannot be spoken, but we must start somewhere."

Mist-on-Water had been expecting more. She thought that Sand-on-Stone was no longer making sense but no flaws in his words were leaping out to her, so she held her tongue for the moment.

Sand-on-Stone gave her the pouch of seeds. He made a depression in the furrow he had started, then with a stick poked four holes in it, the corners of a square. Mist-on-Water placed a seed in each hole, pressing the soil down over it.

Mist-on-Water decided on her course of action. She said, "Please. Not another source. What is this about *talking of things that cannot be spoken*? If they cannot be spoken, then no point in speaking of them. That, or you will talk nonsense."

"Things that cannot be spoken – nonsense?" Sand-on-Stone was quiet for a time. Then he went on, "Think on this. You can talk of music. But do you have words that are true to that rare sublime melody that resonates deep in your being? We can talk of the entertaining plays of the travelling shows. But when a story speaks straight to your own life and stirs you to the core, are there any words that express that truly?" Sand-on-Stone watched Mist-on-Water as she pondered his words. He went on, "And then how do you talk of music to your friend who has never heard it? How do you explain art to your sister who has never seen it?" No answer. "No, it cannot be done. You can but point the path to the musician, to the dramatist, and speak poorly of the delights that may be found."

"Brrrhhp," said Mist-on-Water.

"And then, for something much greater than those, how will it be spoken of? We are just pointing to it. To how it can be found."

"Tell me then," said Mist-on-Water, "tell your tale. If you can. If you must."

Sand-on-Stone made a second depression further along his furrow and Mist-on-Water placed four seeds in it, covering them carefully.

Sand-on-Stone said, "First, a question. It is said that all the things we see here have not always been. Yes? They came from somewhere not known. Where? I tell you now, before anything else *was*, there was just The Source. Nothing else. Yes? So, all things were made by The Source."

"So-be." But her mind was already drifting. She'd had little interest in the dogmas of the oracles when it was so easy to find too many holes in them, too many flaws.

Sand-on-Stone leaned forward and spoke quietly, "But from what? From what does The Source make everything that is now? Before there was anything else."

"Unless you are going to answer that, this will be a very short story." She thought, *A good question, though. I should have thought of it.*

Sand-on-Stone did not give an answer. He extended his furrow almost to its full length and made two more depressions into which Mist-on-Water placed seeds. He said, "Everything that *is,* The Source made from its own substance. From itself. How else could it have been? This was before anything we see now was."

"So-be," said Mist-on-Water. There was a thread in this that more or less made sense to her, as it would to any of her species. They saw the world as continual comings and movings on, flowings from this to that over time. Everything that was here now had to have been something else before, and then something else before that, back a long, long time to when it all started as – as what?

Mist-on-Water said, "Say-you, this Source made everything from itself? And what was that magical source-substance?"

"Well, that substance is not truly known in our domain, in these three dimensions we see now. We see but the shadow here. No, not even the shadow. Perhaps only a shadow of a shadow. We call that shadow 'love'."

"Love is a shadow? And love is a substance?"

"Remember, we talk of things that cannot be spoken. What is seen with the eyes is seen but darkly. Love, the highest quality here, the most esteemed virtue, is a mere shadow of the true substance of … of … of The Source."

Mist-on-Water looked at Sand-on-Stone in the same way as if he had told her that the river water drifting past the village had all come from the tears of a giant wader duck.

Sand-on-Stone saw her expression and said, "So-be. Let it wait. That can be for later. Best if we just go back to The Source making everything from itself."

"Let's do that." The look she was giving him hardly changed. Sand-on-Stone turned back to his emerging melon patch, marking out two more furrows, giving seeds to Mist-on-Water to plant as he went.

"Just before, I did not say *The Source is making*, I said *The Source made*. Did you notice that? The creation of The Source is complete. It's complete, but it has no end."

"Much like this lesson?"

"You will ask: how could The Source create something that has no end? At some point it must have run out of … well, run out of itself."

"A better question would be how it can be complete when your Source forgot about all those things we don't have and still need and will need?"

"Very well, since you ask, our universe, with the stars way beyond the sky, beyond the moons, is very, very big, is it not?

"Big, yes. Bigger than most of the things in it, you could say. Even the really big, big things."

"How big though? I cannot tell you, but it has its numbers. All we see, the stuff of the universe, can be lined up for the count and that count will end, even though the numbers for the count are far beyond any we can understand. But the count for what The Source has made has no end." Sand-on-Stone looked up at the pale indigo sky, his eyes moving across the sparse still clouds. Then he slowly spread his arms wide, thrust his chest out and slowly swept his arms from side-to-side, twisting his torso, as if to demonstrate the unending count.

Mist-on-Water waited through his little performance, saying nothing, her eyes narrowing with scepticism. She looked at a tree on the edge of the clearing. She said, "What a compelling explanation." The tree she said it to looked no more compelled by it than she was. "So then, long, long ago, your source started its making from itself. This means everything I see now must be your source? And not the things I see? Or has your source been changed somehow?" She put down a little trap for him.

"No. The Source does not change. But you do not see The Source. Everything you see now is just a flicker on the face of time. Standing next to what has no count and no end, all you see is nothing."

"It would be very easy to go now." To her, all this was nonsense. But her trap was empty.

"And yet still you sit."

Sitting, Mist-on-Water wondered if this was going to be too easy. "That hopper beetle I see sitting on your ear, it is nothing?"

Just above his left ear Sand-on-Stone brushed away the hopper beetle that had landed there. "You call it a hopper beetle. I call it a veil. You can see it busy in my garden this morning, resting in the belly of the green-face bird this evening. We are folk seeing a thousand raindrops while knowing nothing of water. The fragile raindrop breaks against the earth and is gone. But the water is not lost. It becomes … What? So, The Source's giving is without loss. And what it gave, its creation, its substance, cannot be lost. No piece, not even the tiniest, can be lost.

Have you ever seen that? You can see it. Everything you see now is but fluttering veils cast over your mind. They are raindrops." His eyes held hers until she turned them away. "And yet you do want to see."

"Sooo-be," said Mist-on-Water, not understanding at all. She was grappling with the idea of giving without loss. There was something in it that reached to her. And what was that other seeing he was hinting at? Something radical, profound, unlike anything known or heard before. Was it worthy of her ear? In the end, what she said was, "Why should I care about it – your source? I can see it, you say. But I never have. What does it do for me, and what does it want from me? It doesn't even have any oracles, does it? None have ever come to the village."

"Yes, yes – good things to ask. Along with what you are afraid to ask."

"Afraid?" Fear was one thing she definitely was not feeling.

"Yes: if I and you are of one substance, what does that mean?"

Mist-on-water frowned. The question was unsettling, but that 'if' allowed her to not approach too close.

Sand-on-Stone continued, "But that comes later. We are only at the beginning of this tale, not the end. Perhaps it is enough for today."

Mist-on-Water saw that the sun now hung low in the sky and said, "I had better get back home. Walk easy, uncle."

"Walk easy, daughter."

Mist-on-Water hurried down the trail to her cabin.

Observation Series: **Physical Attributes**

Summary of observations. My tiny bumpkins think they are squeezed into just three of the dimensions here. It is because they have made themselves unaware of their connections back to trans-dimensionality. They are left with their amusing little antics – racing about, crashing into one another, falling over, jumping up again – all of that. Hilarious. They are trying to go back to being free. But they cannot let go of the three-dimensional blobs they think they are squashed into. And the whole time they wonder why they feel so trapped.

Chapter 5

Conrad_27-8, the first to be transferred, was the first to come to awareness. The body in which his consciousness was now ensconced was lying on its back in a bed, the bed curved up at the sides and topped with a thin mattress. The body's eyes were closed. He kept still for a few minutes while his awareness of this new host-body grew. He could hear occasional chirping and clicking sounds to his left. When he had a better sense of the extent of his body, and the locations of its parts, he tried opening his eyes. After some fluttering of his eyelids, squeezing and blinking them, his eyelids stayed open and he looked up at a flat, slightly shiny ceiling, creamy in colour.

With a bit of trial and error, he was able to move his head from side to side. Following that, he practised raising and lowering his arms and legs, bending them at the elbows and knees. Next he tried to sit up by pushing down with his elbows and tightening what he hoped were his abdominal muscles. After several attempts, he got himself to a seated position, just for a moment. Then he felt himself leaning to the right and his upper torso fell to the floor. The bed was low, so the fall left Conrad_27-8 with his head and a shoulder on the floor, and his legs splayed across the bed, his feet in the air. He swung his left leg towards his chest and collapsed the rest of his body onto the floor. Struggling to make his muscles do what he wanted, with jerks and spasms he wriggled and squirmed himself into a seated position, his back leaning against the wall nearest his bed. This was the second time Conrad_27-8 had done this consciousness transfer; it was going much smoother than the first time.

He looked around the room. He saw four identical beds, low, white, rectangular, the sides of the beds angling inwards to the base. Each of the other three beds held a creature like the one his consciousness had transferred to. The occupants had their eyes closed, and they were lying on their backs as he had been. They were slim, hairless, with pale brown skin coloured by irregular bands in shades of yellow and green, the skin having a subtle texture like smooth scales. Conrad_27-8 noted that one of the occupant's yellow-to-green bands of skin colouring were narrow, less than half as wide as those of the other two, which were like his. Their heads were dominated by a jaw that protruded under nostril slits but that had no distinct nose. The eyelids closed over large eyes that were set wide apart, tending towards the sides of the head. A long triangular earflap hung down to the bed. They all wore a similar loose-fitting garment of a thin and light looking material, slung over one shoulder and reaching to their thighs. Their garments were white at the shoulder, graduating smoothly to a different colour at the bottom – the nearest was a deep green, the other two were dark orange shades. They wore nothing on their feet.

Then he saw the minders for two of them, eyes half open, nestled into their hosts' thick necks, partly covered by the earflap. The minders were smaller than he had expected, he guessed about a third of the length of the host's head, scrawny with four short spindly legs ending with four toes, each toe with a single sucker at the end. The minders' legs were stretched outward, their toes spread wide as they grasped their hosts' necks with the suckers. Their smooth hairless skin was covered with intricate patterns in shades of grey and black.

He was too far away to be sure, but to Conrad_27-8 the patterns looked like fractal patterns. As he studied the closest minder, its skin pattern slowly morphed from one fractal pattern into another. Inspecting the minder skin patterns as best he could from where he sat, Conrad_27-8 was confident the pattern boundaries were a representation of what on Earth was known as the Mandelbrot set. He found that fascinating and perplexing. The Mandelbrot set is based on what Earth mathematicians call complex numbers, one part of which is the imaginary number '*i*' – a name given because it cannot be seen in the physical world, it can only be imagined. How could such a thing be found in nature?

Conrad_27-8 set that question aside to examine the rest of the room. The wall facing him had a translucent surface covered with swirling reds, oranges, and greens – apparently decoration – with three low shelves spanning it. The other walls were the same slightly shiny creamy shade as the ceiling. The hard, flat floor was beige with a subtle stone-like grain. The grain looked as if it were intended to be decorative. There were no other furnishings in the room. The wall to his right had a closed door, and the wall to his left had a window with what looked like glass in it. He could see it was light outside.

In one of the other beds, someone else was stirring, moving arms and legs, much as Conrad_27-8 had done earlier. Conrad_27-8 had no way of knowing who was in which body. He could not do anything much yet, beyond wait and watch.

It was Kieran who Conrad_27-8 was watching grow into awareness of his host body.

Each time Kieran moved, Conrad_27-8 heard quiet clicking and chirping sounds that at times seemed to be someone saying, "Quick-quick" and then at other times, "Look-look. Not calculated." He could see no source for the sounds, so he ignored them.

Kieran moved parts of his body by trial and error, much as Conrad_27-8 had done. After a few minutes he twisted his body out of bed, landing hard on his hands and knees. Pushing against the bed, Kieran rose to his feet and turned, swaying a little and catching his balance. Then he let himself drop back as slowly as he could, but without complete control, to sit on the low bed, his arms thrust down to the bed, stiff, holding himself up with a slowly swaying lean. Conrad_27-8, who still did not trust himself to try to stand, was for once a little envious of the benefits of being born with appendages. Kieran looked around and took in his surroundings, as Conrad_27-8 had done.

With the soft thud of Kieran dropping back to his bed, Tracey had opened her eyes. She started moving her head as if to stretch her neck and soon turned it to the side, looking at the other beds and at Conrad_27-8 leaning against the wall. Then she remained very still, head slightly to the side, eyes wide, staring, motionless apart from an occasional blink.

Quentin was the last to come to awareness. Opening his eyes, he looked down at his torso and started twitching his arms. Soon, each of his arms was grasping and clutching at the other, but with no coordination or accuracy. To Conrad_27-8 it seemed that he was trying to pull his own skin off. Then, with some determined but uncoordinated writhings and jerkings of arms and legs, Quentin managed to flip his body over so it was lying face down on the bed. He paused for a moment and then started jerking again, swinging and waving his arms and legs until his body was twisted across the bed, legs to one side, arms and head to the other, still face down. Stuck on his stomach and tiring, Quentin continued to swing his arms and legs about for a minute, much like a turtle stuck on its back, but in reverse. His minder, which had been scurrying around Quentin's neck and head as he thrashed about, making chirping and clicking sounds, sometimes clinging to the top of one of his ears as they flapped at the side of his head, was now straddling the top of Quentin's new skull. Its arms and legs were stretched out, its tiny fingers and toes spread as wide as they could go, the sucker on each tip pressed firmly to Quentin's scalp. Getting the same outcome as a turtle flailing about on its back often does, Quentin gave up and let his arms and legs go limp.

Kieran rose slowly to his feet, then with faltering, uneven steps walked over to Conrad_27-8 and grasping his arm, helped him to stand. Kieran pointed to Quentin and the two of them moved towards him, where he was still slung over his bed. He tried to evade them as they reached for his arms and legs, but with little coordination and diminishing motivation. Together, Kieran and Conrad_27-8 managed to turn Quentin over, so he was lying properly on the bed on his back as he had started.

Kieran said, "We have landed." He spoke with clicks, chirps, and different tones but Conrad_27-8, who had mastered the technique of not paying attention to the sounds, understood and was startled. He had not expected anyone to be able to speak this quickly.

"Quick-quick. Not quantified. Take care."

Conrad_27-8 heard the soft words in his left ear and realised then that he was hearing his minder. He had not noticed it there; he did not feel it clinging to him, nor had he noticed as it had moved about, which it must have been doing as he was hearing it speaking in different ears in turn.

Conrad_27-8 tried to say, "We must practise speaking," but all he heard were garbled sounds. After several attempts, he managed to get it out, one word at a time.

Kieran said, "Are you the … the tour guide?" to Conrad_27-8.

"Yes. Are you the expert in … in … suns?" Conrad_27-8's body's brain found no word for astrophysicist, nor did it seem to have any word for star.

Kieran said, "No. I am the expert in living things."

Conrad_27-8 then guessed correctly that he was talking to Kieran.

Conrad_27-8 turned to Tracey and said, "Are you the male?" thinking this would be the easiest way to distinguish between Tracey and Quentin. Tracey, who up until then had stayed very still, only her eyes moving, leaned her head back away from Conrad_27-8 and just looked at him and then at the others who were all looking back at her. She had understood the question. She opened her mouth, emitting a single long tone.

Conrad_27-8 said to her, "Remember, don't *try* to speak. Just put the idea you want to say in your head alongside the idea of speaking it."

Kieran went over to her, still a little unsteadily, and helped her to a sitting position. Unsteady herself, she swung her legs off the bed and sat more securely with her feet on the floor. Like it had for Conrad_27-8, it took several attempts for Tracey to get out the two chirps that were her first word: "No."

Conrad_27-8 said to Quentin, "Then you are the expert in suns." Quentin, emitting a stream of garbled sounds, swung a leg and pushed himself from the bed. Launching himself towards Conrad_27-8, he tripped over his own feet and fell. By reflex, his arms cushioned his landing and his face came to rest on Conrad_27-8's bare toes. Still emitting garbled sounds, Quentin scrambled to his hands and knees and rose to his feet, swaying and swinging his arms like someone who was trying to move in ice skates for the first time.

Kieran said, "You must familiarise yourself with the controls." Then together with Conrad_27-8 they took hold of Quentin again and guided him, most of his resistance spent, back to sit on his bed.

Tracey said, "What … what?"

Once Quentin was calmer, Conrad_27-8 said, "We have completed the transfer successfully. We are at the … the sphere called Allunda and our consciousnesses are now attached to the four assigned Allundrians. They are the only intelligent species here. You can see they are much more attractive than the bodies you came from."

Quentin and Tracey started taking in their surroundings in more detail. Kieran, lurching and swaying with each step, went over to the window. Conrad_27-8 watched his agents for any sign of transfer-mania – he had been told it was not uncommon.

Conrad_27-8 took the lead in making sure everyone knew who everyone else was. At the same time, they were each working on their motor control, moving arms up and down, flexing hands and fingers, standing, sitting, walking. They also practised speaking, starting with simple things like, "What have I done?" from Tracey or, in Quentin's case, "If you don't get me out of here, whoever left you unsupervised is going to regret it."

Each of them was still dealing in their own way with their 'this can't be happening' thoughts and slowly coming to terms with their situation when a voice from the door said, "A visitor has requested admission. The visitor's name has not been provided. Do you grant admission?" It appeared they had voice-controlled technology.

Before Quentin could even try to get out, "Not if you value your flimsy circuit brain," Kieran said, "Yes," and the door slid open, disappearing into a cavity in the wall. An Allundrian looking much like they did strode in, crossed its arms over its chest and said, "Always equality. Esteemed visitors, by the Mandates I will introduce myself: I am the Global Affairs Director here on Allunda. I bear the name HaaTiToTo of Nine Lake District. I give you highest welcomes, special agents."

Conrad_27-8 crossed his arms to HaaTiToTo and said, "I am Global Affairs Director (acting) on the … the … home place of the Agents here," waving his arm at the others. It appeared the Allundrian language had no word for planet. "We have an expert in … suns," indicating Quentin. "We also bring his colleagues. They will assist in the mission."

Quentin and Tracey, who were still sitting on their beds, said nothing, remaining as they were, alert, listening, and watching.

Kieran said, "Nice tunic."

HaaTiToTo said, "I trust your well-being is satisfactory?" There was no immediate response – they all just looked at him. "But I think you may still be feeling somewhat disoriented. And it will certainly take you a little time to get accustomed to your new body assignments. So, with your agreement, and in accordance with the Mandates, I will give you a brief orientation." No one objected.

HaaTiToTo began with a description of this planet they called Allunda. They had no word for 'planet', so the name was simply a literal translation of the truncated compound word in their language for the ground they stood on: 'all-under-the-sky'. Over ninety-eight percent of the planet's surface was covered by water, with the landmass located in a very narrow band circling the planet at its equator. The Allundrians numbered about twenty million. Most of this population was dispersed across just over two hundred main towns, all of a similar size, with around a hundred thousand citizens each, the towns spaced more or less evenly apart along the thin equatorial landmass. Clouds always covered the sky everywhere – the sun was only seen as a hazy disc behind the clouds.

The basics covered, HaaTiToTo was eager to move on to the subject of astronomy, but he floundered since the language had no words for astronomical terms. So, with speaking-permitted charades from HaaTiToTo drawing out occasional truculent and initially inarticulate help from Quentin, they invented their own terms. 'Look-sky-science' became the word for 'astronomy'. Quentin disregarded Tracey's suggestion of 'tube-stuck-on-eye-science'. 'Galaxy' (as in Galactic Council) was 'local-sun-group'; 'stars' were simply 'other-suns', planets were 'spheres-going-around-suns', or 'home-spheres'. By the end, Quentin, Tracey, and Kieran had improved their finer arm and hand motor control and their speaking to the point that, to another Allundrian, they looked and sounded only mildly inebriated.

"And now, I must confirm that the non-disclosure agreements, liability waivers, and species preservation accreditation certificates are in order." He turned to Conrad_27-8.

Conrad_27-8 shifted his weight from one foot to the other a few times. The silence became awkward. In the end he said, "Perhaps the formalities should be completed in line with local procedures, should they not?"

"Very well, then." HaaTiToTo turned to Quentin, Tracey, and Kieran. "You agree that to enable effective Galactic administration, the operations of the Galactic Council must remain secret. If you do not agree to this condition, say so now." He did not pause. "You also agree that your actions while here will be governed by the Species Preservation Regulations and accompanying Guidelines. There are forty-seven thousand three hundred and twenty-four regulations and three hundred and forty-five Guidelines, so I won't explain them all now. However, I will record your training accreditation in anticipation that you will familiarise yourselves with them and pass the exam in the next day or two. Agreed? Finally, you will agree that there will be no liability to you, by, in, under, over, or from any being, thing, or non-thing at any time. And, in any event, any liability shall be limited to the smallest amount of currency in circulation. Agreed?" Again, he did not pause. "Very good. Your agreements and accreditations are now a matter of record. Congratulations, Agents." HaaTiToTo paused to take breath. Quentin, Tracey, and Kieran were still just looking at him. Quentin was opening and closing his mouth, lips moving, but no sound coming out. Tracey's jaw was slack.

Finally finding voice and speaking so that just Tracey could hear, Quentin said, "That must easily be a new record."

"For?"

"For the amount of extreme stupidity, unparalleled nonsense, and blatant contradictions single-handedly combined in a single dialogue without any hint of embarrassment." Still quite foggy, as if he had just been woken from a deep sleep, Quentin had relaxed enough to go along for this ride, or whatever it was. He said to HaaTiToTo, "Thanks for your help, but we should be going along now."

"Certainly, I understand. You want to get started on the assignment. Your time is limited. We can cover that now." He explained that because of the continual total cloud cover, the Allundrians had no concept of stars or planetary systems, and naturally there was no science of astronomy here. The essence of the assignment was this: while the beings on this planet valued the sciences, the Galactic Council had noted that the science of astronomy did not exist. HaaTiToTo kept repeating how pleased he was that, for the first time, there was a real astronomer on the planet, and in turn Quentin kept trying to point out that, "Actually, I'm only an astrophysicist."

HaaTiToTo concluded by saying, "So, you see, there is no astronomy here, none at all."

Quentin, despite his field of expertise, said, "Fine, they have no astronomy and no astronomers, nor any of the various sub-species thereof. The problem is?"

HaaTiToTo's minder, which had been snuggled behind his left ear, closely watching and listening to everything, jumped up as if it had been pricked and started speaking in HaaTiToTo's ear in its tiny voice, repeating, "Importance. Importance. *Importance.*" HaaTiToTo said, "The problem is clear. The Galactic Council has passed a resolution that all planets under its oversight shall have access to astronomical data. I must humbly point out that I had a central and crucial role in the formulation and passage of that resolution. You see, I have some influence within the Council itself." He paused to allow his audience to contain their admiration. They sat and waited. "So, it was resolved: this planet is to develop the science of astronomy – it is essential, of course."

Quentin said, "Of course." He kept his gaze fixed on HaaTiToTo, who appeared pleased that the need for the assignment had been understood, then he said, "Essential for what?"

"For what?"

"Yes, the science of astronomy is essential for what?"

HaaTiToTo's minder looked alarmed and started bobbing up and down on his shoulder, giving his ear a tug each time he bobbed down. The minder put its mouth into HaaTiToTo's ear saying, "Listen – importance. Listen – importance. Listen – importance." HaaTiToTo spoke slowly, as if explaining something simple and obvious to a very dull student. "Every species must have a sufficiently advanced science of astronomy. It is essential to allow the work and edicts of the Galactic Council to be understood."

"Ahh – the edicts. Those would be readily accessed, I am guessing, on some remote Galactic Council world?"

"Of course, they are."

"And that 'work' – that would be its secret work?"

"Yes."

Before Quentin could say more, Tracey pointed to HaaTiToTo's minder and said, "I hope you don't mind me saying, but that thing looks a bit upset. Is it all right? Why is it doing all of that jumpy stuff?"

HaaTiToTo looked confused for a moment then said, "Ah, you mean minder. Don't worry about it. Soon, you will not even notice them. No one here pays any attention to anyone else's minder. We don't even notice them. You will forget about your own minder most of the time." Watching Tracey closely all the time, his minder slowly crept backwards towards the back of his neck and crouched down low, until it was barely visible.

Tracey's minder whispered in her ear, "Should not have said that. He will remember that."

Quentin said, "Before we get too distracted by the wildlife here, back on this astronomy business for a moment … Um, I hope you are not expecting this to get done quickly. Just getting proposals past committees can take forever."

"No committees. By the Freedom Mandate you can be under absolutely no restrictions. And as you are aware, your mission is restricted to no more than six, perhaps seven visits. Your time is limited."

Quentin tried to work out if the Allundrian was joking. He saw no hint of it. As diplomatically as he could, he said, "Didn't your second sentence there seem to be just a little forgetful of the first sentence – the one that came a tiny moment earlier?"

HaaTiToTo responded with a benign smile.

"Fine then, I just want to float a few balloons to start with."

"Float balloons? You want to float balloons? Balloons?"

It was apparent that the idiom did not translate. "Yes. You know, spherical structures made from polyethylene or some such, filled with helium, or hydrogen if you want more lift. But don't worry about that. First, I want to get the background here, maybe work through some options."

"Very good."

"Are there any optical devices for looking at faraway objects?" The lack of a word for telescope did not bode well.

"No."

"Any forms of flying transport?"

"No."

"Are any lights visible in the sky at night? Moons detectable by their gravity? Mountains high enough to break through the cloud layer? Cloud gaps at the poles, say? Vehicles confiscated from secret alien visitors?"

"No. No. No. No. No."

"Thank you. All good to know. I will get back to you with a detailed proposal."

HaaTiToTo, seeing there were no more questions, said to all of them, "Now, if it does not restrict you, we will have a brief tour outside, and at the same time you can work on your body control." Without waiting, he started towards the door, which was still open.

Tracey said, "Wait. I am … restricted." Turning to Quentin she said, "We need … we need to get back. Now." From the reactions she had seen from Quentin earlier, she was expecting him to back her up decisively. But he stood up slowly, looked around the room and out the window where they could see jungle-like vegetation, and said, "Aaar … Get back?" Then he surprised Tracey with, "We are here now. Let's look around a bit."

HaaTiToTo said, "You speak freely and I acknowledge your equality," and continued out the door. Tracey turned to Conrad_27-8 and said, "Why is he … talking like that?" But HaaTiToTo was already out of the door and Conrad_27-8 and Kieran were going after him, walking with varying but now reducing degrees of unsteadiness. Tracey and Quentin, both still pondering his words, trailed along behind.

"We go past the meal-room," said HaaTiToTo back to the others. The room opening from a door to their right was large, rectangular, and at least four times the size of the one they had just come from, with entrance doors on three sides and the other side clear like glass, overlooking an internal atrium. The off-white walls had subtle veins of beige and tan running through them. The ceiling was divided into rectangular panels; enough light came from several of them to make the room bright. A large low oval table dominated the centre. There were no chairs. Thin cushions, like the ones on their beds, surrounded the table. No hint of a kitchen was visible.

"Low table," said Tracey to practise talking.

"Maybe where they bring the midgets to eat?" said Quentin.

While they walked on down the corridor, HaaTiToTo gave them a quick summary of basic communication gestures. Opening and shutting the month quickly meant 'yes'. "The same as nodding on … our home," said Tracey to no one in particular. Closing the mouth firmly and narrowing the eyes squint-like meant 'no'. "The same as shaking the head," said Tracey. Holding the lips together and pushing them forward was 'maybe'. They smiled by dropping the bottom lip, showing their broad flat teeth.

Past the meal-room, the corridor turned to the right. HaaTiToTo went around the corner and led the group to a double door on their left. "Here is the dwelling's entrance. Are you ready to go out?" Above the double doors a narrow panoramic screen was apparently showing an image of what lay on the other side, at the front of the dwelling. Aspect ratio is nine to one, thought Conrad_27-8, checking the screen. As HaaTiToTo reached the doors and faced them, they slid into a wall cavity as the others had done. HaaTiToTo and Conrad_27-8 walked through the doors, followed by Kieran. Tracey and Quentin, still walking behind, saw that the screen above the door did indeed show the backs of

HaaTiToTo and Conrad_27-8 as they were walking outside.

The doors opened to a veranda that met a wide flat path made of a similar material to the dwelling's floor, but with a rougher surface. The path led away from the dwelling and joined a wider path, raised slightly, that circled a small grove of dense tree-like vegetation in front of them.

"A walkway?" said Tracey, again partly for practice.

HaaTiToTo opened and shut his mouth rapidly in agreement.

Spread around the circular central grove were several single-level dwellings like the one they had just left, each connected by their own paths to the larger encircling path. Between the towering vegetation they could make out dwelling designs that spoke of the builders' desires to produce structures that were attractive, as well as functional. Their roofs, made up of several flat sections positioned at slightly different levels, sloped gently to the outside walls which, while close to vertical, had a steep slope down to the ground. Rain would flow down the roof, then down the walls to grated drains at their base. Everywhere they looked they saw prolific vegetation growing in every space between the paths and dwellings. A light mist hung in the air. The sky was blanketed in light grey clouds, with darker clouds in the distance.

Crowding the circular area facing them was a forest of plants the size of very tall trees but with soft, smooth, dark-green trunks and branches ending in hand-sized, circular, flat, even darker green leaves. Like lily pond leaves, they all faced the same direction – up towards the sky. Yellow, red, and purple berries hung under the leaves in clusters of perhaps fifty or more. Other plants with long slender stems, even taller than what the visitors were thinking of as trees but with no branches, were crowned by long, thin, flat leaves that folded out like a narrow fan. Vine-like plants climbed the larger tree-like vegetation. Near the bottom of the trees, a form of moss was abundant, along with mushroom-like plants in many shapes. Some of the mushroom-like plants, topped with a yellow spheroid, were nearly as tall as the visitors; others grew out from the tree trunks rising like poorly stacked towers of white dinner plates.

High above them, at the tops of the trees, flew a multitude of chattering animals with skin membranes for wings rather than feathers. Shades of yellow were their predominant colour, with some markings of black, purple, and dark blue. Some of these animals flew under their own power but others climbed the vegetation, eating as they went, and after going as high as they could they glided down to a lower branch to start again. The group heard constant soft chirpings and clickings, broken by an occasional buzz as a fat insect flew past.

"It's beautiful," said Tracey.

Quentin was the first to notice the Allundrian coming from around the bend in the path, walking in their direction. In his ear his minder said urgently but softly, "Quick-quick. Protect-attack." Quentin nudged Tracey's arm and pointed at it. As she saw it, her minder sitting at her left ear said, "Look-look. Notgood-notgood," its words quiet enough that the others would not hear them clearly, or probably not at all. She said to the others, "Maybe we should get away from that … that thing, before it sees us." The others all turned to look at the oncoming Allundrian, close enough now that they were all in plain sight of it. It noticed their attention and as it continued along the wide path towards them, it veered slightly to the side of the path on which they were standing, apparently to approach them.

Seeing this, Tracey's minder said, "Look-look. What did you do? Notgood-notgood." Tracey felt self-reproach rising within her. As the Allundrian came closer, her minder kept talking, "Trouble now because of you? They know who did it."

Quentin's minder was saying, just for his hearing, "Quick-quick. Careful. Only one. Wait for chance."

As the Allundrian approached them, HaaTiToTo said, "Did I tell you about the Mandates? No? Oh – they are very important. They are the local laws here. Any law-breakers are dealt with severely."

HaaTiToTo turned to face the Allundrian coming towards them. Its skin had narrow yellow-green bands, like Tracey's. Conrad_27-8 formed a hypothesis that the narrower skin bands were characteristic of females of the species, with males having the wider bands. As the female reached them, HaaTiToTo crossed his arms over his chest and said, "See me. Always equality."

The Allundrian who had stopped in front of them crossed her arms over her chest and said, "See me. Always equality."

HaaTiToTo said, "By the Eight Mandates, I am named HaaTiToTo."

The Allundrian said, "By the Eight Mandates, I am named SiMiYah."

HaaTiToTo said, "My companions may offer their names, if it does not restrict you."

SiMiYah said, "No Mandate is breached. You may proceed."

At that, Tracey and Quentin simultaneously tried to make themselves inconspicuous behind HaaTiToTo but bumped into each other and staggered apart. Tracey nearly fell into something that looked like a large bunch of flowers hanging at head height, which she then pretended to take an interest in. Quentin stared at her with his jaws clenched. SiMiYah did not seem to notice. A plump purple bug buzzing around Kieran's nose had drawn his attention.

"I am named 2-7-8," said Conrad_27-8. SiMiYah gave Conrad_27-8 a questioning look but after the crossed-arm greeting, turned next to Tracey.

"I am named ChaShee," said Tracey, trying to produce sounds like her name while crossing her arms and giving an Allundrian smile.

"I am named KaaRon," said Kieran, also making sounds that were close to his name and smiling.

That left Quentin. He started making an attempt at saying 'Quentin' but the sounds were foreign to his body and all that came out was Ke-(spit)-(awk). His arms started shaking – just small quivers.

"How sorry I am. You have a micro-fungal infection perhaps?"

Relieved at being given a way out, Quentin opened and closed his mouth rapidly to indicate agreement, as they had been told earlier.

SiMiYah turned back to Tracey. She said, "It is nice to meet some new folk. Especially when you give a friend-smile on first meeting."

Tracey looked at HaaTiToTo but he was distracted, flicking the back of his hand at a small red and purple worm that had started crawling up his leg. Feeling she needed to respond, Tracey said, "We are pleased to meet you."

SiMiYah went on, "How pleasant you are. Your names are not like ours. You have come from a distant town perhaps? You are here visiting some relatives to celebrate *long-sleep*, perhaps?"

"Yes," said Tracey not trusting herself with saying anything more and thinking it would be the answer that might avoid the need for further explanation.

SiMiYah said, "How nice for you. It is almost time for *rain-meal.* If the Mandates allow it, perhaps you can join us for rain-meal, and we can talk some more. It may be a breach if you did not join us. Unless it would be a breach if you did join us." SiMiYah clasped her hands together loosely in front of herself and stood looking at Tracey, waiting for her to respond.

Tracey's minder said, "Quick-quick. Do not anger her." Tracey took a small step back, looking for some sign that SiMiYah might have heard her minder, worried now that SiMiYah might hold some hidden threat and also that she might get the group into trouble before they had even begun. She looked to see if anyone else wanted to handle this but they, perhaps advised by their minders, were leaving it up to her. "Which?" said Tracey.

"Which what?" said SiMiYah, smiling.

"Which breach would it be?" Tracey's senses were on high alert. With SiMiYah standing quite close to her, she heard SiMiYah's minder say what sounded like, "Look-look. Strangers here. Take care. Need know more."

"Ahh, you give a Mandate-response I have never heard before. This is difficult. Let me consider. Either or both or none, as you wish. Your freedom must be respected," said SiMiYah. "We must never forget those Mandates, must we? But sometimes it is so tiresome being reminded all the time. *All* the time." The last was more of a thought said aloud than a comment directed at Tracey. But when it had been said, SiMiYah's minder became agitated and moved quickly behind her neck from her left ear to her right and then back, chattering in each ear. SiMiYah went on, "Yes. Yes. I should say no more on that. For your safety, I invite you to join my clan at our rain-meal."

"For our safety?" said Tracey, her alarm growing. Conrad_27-8 and Quentin also started looking around for any signs of danger. Kieran was inspecting a plant covered with spiralling yellow and orange leaves that drooped to the ground.

"Yes-yes. It will be very safe at my clan's rain-meal," said SiMiYah, and then, "unless it is not."

His leg-ascending worm distraction removed, HaaTiToTo said, "Your invitation is in accordance with the well-being Mandate. We accept it, of course."

SiMiYah said, "We won't be able to get to my clan's dwelling using the GoOne I was about to take. We will need to use the community GoSome. I am not from this dwelling pod so I will need to return to my cousin's dwelling to borrow an access token. I will rejoin you here soon, if you have waited when I return." SiMiYah gave them the goodbye gesture, standing straight and holding her arms stiffly at her sides.

HaaTiToTo, Conrad_27-8, Tracey, and Kieran mimicked it back to her and she turned back the way she had come.

When SiMiYah was out of hearing, HaaTiToTo said, "She goes to get access to a transport machine suitable for the six of us. It is from the pool that is available to this dwelling pod." He indicated the dwellings that were spread around the circular grove of forest they stood next to.

Quentin watched as SiMiYah walked around the bend out of sight. Then he turned to HaaTiToTo and said, "Hello you. So, we are going to some place, possibly one we can never leave, to confront some more of these things, who may well have anti-us tendencies, to eat from a menu that we sort of hope does not include any of our body parts. Is that right?" He did not wait for an answer but went on, waving his arms, "What are you doing? Why did you accept that invitation? Is that a log in your head or are you just being friendly?" Then twisting his head towards his minder which had been chattering into his ear the whole time, he said, "I'm doing that. You can shut up."

Tracey had frozen, hoping HaaTiToTo did not carry any kind of concealed weapon, thinking that in his place, she would have been tempted to use it on Quentin. Conrad_27-8 also looked uncomfortable, fidgeting with his fingers, trying to recalculate the probability of mission casualties, but failing.

Kieran said, "KeNoTon doesn't know what he is looking for. What do the Mandates say?"

HaaTiToTo said, "The Mandates? To refuse the invitation would have been an attack on SiMiYah. The Mandates require all attacks to be defended. It could have become very difficult if we refused."

Quentin said, "So these 'Mandates' are the local laws, are they? Wasn't there some kind of 'no restrictions' Mandate?"

HaaTiToTo said, "Yes, that is correct – the Freedom Mandate. We must accept the invitation with no restrictions."

Quentin started waving his arms as wide as they would go, accidentally whacking Kieran across the side of his head with his hand and said, "No. No. No. If we *must accept*, that is a restriction? On us? Yes?"

HaaTiToTo said, "Do you attack the Mandates? Every attack must be defended."

Quentin said, "Defended … because the poor little Mandate might get a bruise, I suppose?"

HaaTiToTo said, "Yes. In addition, the Justice Mandate must be applied."

At this, Tracey failed to suppress an involuntary gasp. She said, "Justice? What kind of justice?"

HaaTiToTo said, "The Justice Mandate requires that every wrong suffered is reversed or corrected."

Quentin said, "Reverse the wrong that was said? How? Say it backwards?"

"Perhaps." He sounded as if he could have been agreeing to have lunch some time.

Quentin stared and said, "What? *What?* And of course, the 'no restriction' Mandate still applies to that too?"

"Yes."

Quentin leaned his head back slowly to look to the top of the foliage high above them, then after looking back down for a moment, he turned to Conrad_27-8 and said, "I used to think hydrogen was the building block for everything everywhere. But I was wrong. Here it's stupidity."

Conrad_27-8 said, "I don't think that theory is valid."

Quentin said to himself, "And our old buddy 2-7-8 here is all the proof I need."

Tracey said to Quentin, "Do you still want to explore? Let's just go back inside and get back home."

Quentin said, "The exploring I was thinking of was something nice and quiet where we keep to ourselves, not join up with a flash mob group tour. Not poking the natives to see if they shoot first. Weren't you the one who waved that thing down?"

Before Tracey could work up a response to that, she saw SiMiYah coming back towards them. She had only been gone a few minutes.

HaaTiToTo said, "It seems we will have to finish your assignment briefing after rain-meal."

Quentin said, "My assignment? About that. You see, those perpetual clouds could be a bit of a factor there. Makes that good old 'science of suns' a bit like looking for a black hole in a coal mine at midnight with your eyes shut."

HaaTiToTo responded with a look of placid confidence.

Tracey said, "You forgot *while wearing a blindfold*."

"Yes, that too. While wearing a blindfold. Just something to keep in mind."

HaaTiToTo said, "I understand what you are saying. The task is exceptionally difficult. I will speak to your Global Affairs Director about it." He said to Conrad_27-8, "It appears our goal of a science of astronomy for this planet will be nearly impossible. Even without the deadlines. I congratulate you on assembling a team with the competence to take on such a demanding assignment. It will be reflected in your next performance assessment." He waved away what he took to be Quentin's and Tracey's gestures of thanks.

When she was close enough for them to see, SiMiYah raised her hand to show she was holding a small flat white object, about credit card size, except square. Joining the waiting group, she crossed her arms and said, "Always equality."

Quentin said to himself, "I thought it was 'always freedom'." But most of the others, including SiMiYah had heard.

SiMiYah said, "Yes. Yes. All the Mandates must be upheld. Always freedom too. And always justice. And always clan. And al…"

Tracey interrupted and said, "For your freedom, you can stop."

SiMiYah said, "You are very kind again. I don't seem to meet folk who are very kind. I don't say folk aren't kind. They are. Of course, they are. A lot try to hide it, or something. But you don't." She looked at Tracey. Without waiting for a response, she went on, "And you have hardly even once reminded me of the Mandates. I do sometimes forget all about them. Actually, quite often. I usually just start doing whatever seems nice at the time. I know – it is very foolish. Everyone in my clans is always telling me I do not remember them enough. The Mandates. It will get me into trouble again, they say. But sometimes, just every now and then, those Mandates can be tiresome. Do you think so too? We are so grateful to have them, of course. I am not complaining. Thankfully, minder is always reminding me they are very important. I just wish they weren't so demanding. Yes, I know – we do have them to help us and, yes, it would be a disaster if we didn't have them. They do look after everything we need – our Mandates. And our bodies must be looked after, they need lots of attention. You can't get away from that. Just can't get away.

"Sometimes I feel like a spotted longreach glider stuck in a tiny cage. A bit silly, isn't it? Where am I trapped? Inside myself? My body is all I have, isn't it? Unless you believe there is a spirit that … that moves on when, well, you know. That's when you get away. If you believe that. Yes, a lot of people mock that, but I don't. I don't mind if you do believe it. The Mandate says you must be free to believe it, even though it is ridiculous. So I don't mock it. If a spotted longreach glider were born in a tiny cage, do you think it would know it was stuck? I think maybe it would have an instinct to fly. Inside it. So, it would be very confused. Don't you think?"

HaaTiToTo and Tracey opened and shut their mouths rapidly in agreement (Tracey started to nod her head but remembered the correct gesture before SiMiYah noticed).

"But do you know, one of my cousins, cousin OoLooGee, does keep some spotted longreach gliders in a cage. Their cage is a big one; they can move about. They get plenty of food. But they look miserable most of the time. Just clinging to some sticks she's put in there for them, looking glum. Then I visited one day and one of the walls of the cage had fallen off. But the gliders were still inside, clinging on, looking glum. It made me feel sad too. I don't know why. No Mandate was breached."

In a low voice, Quentin said to Tracey, "Maybe we should keep this one. She can talk enough for all of us."

A soft chime sounded at SiMiYah's side. She looked at her wrist and Conrad_27-8 saw that what he had taken for an ornament now showed two lines of purple symbols on the part that was flatter and wider. SiMiYah said, "We should be taking the GoSome to our rain-meal now," and started leading them along what they had thought of as a road. They now understood it was just a wide walking path that gave access from the cluster of dwellings to a larger two-level building. As she led them through clear doors, they entered a building similar in layout to a small shopping mall, with a large central corridor and doors, corridors and open rooms coming off it. In the background was the sound of pleasant rhythmic electronic music.

"Their technological and social development still has a way to go in this area," said Quentin, who liked to keep clear of shopping malls.

SiMiYah led them up a ramp to the top level which opened to a room a bit larger than the others. In all the galaxy, it appeared, a transit lounge could be recognised immediately. This transit lounge seemed too large for the thin sitting mats spread around sparsely, only enough mats for perhaps eight or ten. As they arrived, the lounge was occupied by two other Allundrians, sitting cross-legged. Overhead, just below the ceiling, running across it and outside the building, were two sturdy rails, cream in colour. They watched as a 'GoOne' was arriving, suspended from the rail closer to them. It was a simple pod, transparent except for the bottom, which was white. When the GoOne came to a stop, with its base level with the floor, the outer shell continued on through doors that opened in front of it, leaving its base and seat secured to the slight rise in the floor. Slouched on the seat an Allundrian was talking and gesturing. Tracey assumed he was communicating with someone using a device he wore on his head. The device began as a long plastic or metal finger wrapping around the back of his neck, flattening as it passed behind his left ear and coming to a point as it extended just in front of and above his left eye.

Leaving his seat, the Allundrian pressed his wrist against his ear and his communication device folded itself around his wrist. Tracey had noticed most of the aliens, including themselves, had similar devices wrapped around their wrists, or sometimes an ankle. She had taken them for personal decorations, like jewellery, but now understood they were pieces of communication technology. As he walked off, the base and seat of the GoOne followed the outer shell through the double door that opened for it. The two Allundrians who had looked up at the arrival had returned to their discussion as they waited on the next arrival.

"I will get our GoSome," said SiMiYah, and she went to a screen mounted on the wall to their right. On it they could see symbols, shapes, and images that changed rapidly as SiMiYah moved her gaze across the screen, blinking, winking, and saying an occasional word.

"This building is the resource hub for this dwelling pod," said HaaTiToTo while they waited for SiMiYah. "This room is the transport terminus. You can see the arrivals area on that side. We will wait here in the departures area while she uses the SeeDo. Our GoSomes will be here very soon."

"Will the vehicle's capacity be sufficient for all of us?" said Conrad_27-8, thinking of the single-seated GoOne he had just seen arrive.

"The GoSomes seat four, and they are joined together for larger groups. In a few moments, two GoSomes will arrive for us through that door over there." He indicated a large double door which closed around the overhead rail closest to them. "The seating assembly will move to the embarkation zone in front of us. After we are seated, the GoSome's shell follows the seats out and slides over them, ready to take us to our destination.

"It looks like SiMiYah has finished with the SeeDo," said HaaTiToTo.

"Tell me about these SeeDo things," said Quentin.

"SeeDos? Surely you have something similar," said HaaTiToTo. "These devices allow you to obtain information – the 'See' – and take actions – the 'Do'. We use them for everything."

"Now we are getting somewhere," said Quentin.

HaaTiToTo went on to explain that the SeeDos were everywhere, in every dwelling and public area. He also explained that most Allundrians also had their own BringSeeDo, the device they had seen the passenger using earlier. It was placed on the head, where it projected images onto the wearer's retina and emitted sounds into an ear. When not in use, it moulded itself to the owner's forearm, or for some, to their upper arm or calf. It was powered by the movements of the wearer's body. The larger public SeeDos were generally preferred, if one were around, being quicker and easier to use.

SiMiYah had stepped to one side of the SeeDo, facing the monorail. The doors below the monorail for departures opened and the base of a GoSome with its four seats glided along a recessed track in the floor, stopping in the middle of an embarkation zone marked in front of them. Joined on behind it was a second base and set of seats. For a few moments, no one moved and then Kieran walked to the front seat and sat down, saying, "I think this one knows where we're going."

Quentin said, "Wait. You don't know where we're going."

"Yes, I do. I'm going where this takes me."

HaaTiToTo said, "The destination has already been set."

SiMiYah, Tracey, and Conrad_27-8 took their seats and immediately, the front GoSome's shell slid out of the doors the base had come from and connected itself to its base, over the seats. Quentin and HaaTiToTo seated themselves in the two front seats of the rear GoSome. As soon as they were seated, the shell of the second GoSome slid out of the doors over the passengers, connecting itself smoothly to the base and seats. The GoSomes accelerated sedately along the monorail towards the doors opening to the outside.

Their GoSomes left the second level of the building and accelerated smoothly until they were travelling at around the speed of an Earth car in a city street. The vehicles still being elevated – higher than someone could reach them from the ground – gave them a good view all around. They had left the cluster of dwellings behind them and were moving through a large, perfectly square orchard. Trees bearing an orange fruit were planted in straight lines. In one of the lines, they saw a machine harvesting the fruit. They were travelling across the field's diagonal and past it could see more square fields or small farms, all the same size, all filled with perfectly straight lines of thriving crops or orchards, some with red, yellow, or orange vegetables or dangling fruit.

Beyond those fields, on both sides, they saw two more clusters of dwellings, both arranged in square plots the same size as the fields. Nearing the corner of the second field they were crossing, their GoSomes were again approaching structures. These structures were larger than the dwellings they had come from, twice or four times the size, with two or three levels. In the middle of this commercial looking tract, their GoSomes approached a cross junction and without changing speed, went along the track curving to the right. Here the monorail was busier. They were passing many GoOnes and GoSomes going the other way. With just her eyes moving, Tracey was checking out all the occupants. They all looked much as they did, very little to distinguish them, all about the same size and shape, all dressed the same way, the main difference being the subdued colours they wore. In the front of another pair of approaching GoSomes, like the pair they were in, two adults were sitting trancelike. In the one behind, four tykes were poking, pinching, standing, balancing, bouncing, wrestling, hanging. Tracey turned her head to watch that one go past.

Conrad_27-8 was fascinated by the order of it all – a town laid out purely with rounded squares, pods all the same size, some residential, some farming, others probably commercial, all interconnected by monorail tracks across the diagonals. He was getting a strange feeling he did not understand, an excited buzz. An Earth teenager would have explained the feeling to him as getting a crush. Behind him, Quentin was getting a different feeling – sleepy. From some hidden speaker, he could hear what they were saying in front. SiMiYah had been giving an enthusiastic non-stop commentary for the 'visitors from a distant town', alerting them to points that were supposed to be of interest as they went past, taking on the mantle of an informal tour guide. Quentin was inspecting the compact information panel positioned between the seats showing a detailed map, centred on the position of their GoSome, the map moving as it did. Among a row of symbols at the bottom, Quentin saw a symbol that his Allundrian brain told him meant 'mute'. Thinking he could have a private conversation with HaaTiToTo, Quentin tapped it and, testing, said, "Our arithmomaniac is pleasantly quiet. Has he fallen out?" From the GoSome in front, he saw Tracey turn her head back to glare at him. She said, "Who? What? Hush." SiMiYah's commentary had not paused.

Puzzling over the 'mute' symbol for any clue on how to operate it and seeing none, Quentin gave a brief sigh, closed his eyes for a moment and made a 'tch' sound. Then he saw that the symbol was now glowing. He did not know what had made it change but hoped they could no longer hear him in front.

"Interesting. I assume the Mandates allow us to speak privately now?" he said to HaaTiToTo.

HaaTiToTo glanced at the GoSome's information panel. "Yes, by the Mandates."

Quentin had set up his own private tutoring session about Allunda. It did not take long for him to confirm that HaaTiToTo could go on endlessly about his state-of-the-species indicator data points and the Species

Compliance Index, but despite being the Galactic Council's officially appointed Global Affairs Director for this planet, he knew next to nothing about the planet's sun ('it's up above the clouds'), geology ('we have rocks and soil'), atmosphere and climate ('it rains a lot'), planetary orbit ('probably has something to do with the two seasons'), moons ('not that I know of – what are they again?'), or anything else of scientific interest to an astrophysicist exploring his first exoplanet.

"Who would know?" he asked.

None of them. They did not wonder about any of that, not even the scientists. This was another confirmation for Quentin that they were all highly irrational and deeply disturbed.

After crossing the diagonals of a line of several commercial tracts, they came to another junction where their GoSomes took the track curving left. The track turned into another field, this one with trestled vines sprouting golden, delicate, frilly, lace-like leaves, and beyond it the backs of another pod of residences. No entrances were visible. While each design seemed unique, they were all variations on a theme.

The monorail entered the top level of the resource hub that serviced this cluster of dwelling pods. It was less than ten minutes since they had departed. When their GoSomes reached the disembarkation point, the base and seat stopped and the front outer shell kept going, sliding through double doors, leaving the seats anchored to the floor. Everyone left their seats and followed SiMiYah to the exit. Quentin, Tracey, and HaaTiToTo trailed behind slightly.

Their first journey having been uneventful, Tracey and Quentin were feeling less anxious.

Taking the ramp to the ground floor, Quentin saw that it went down further.

Quentin said to HaaTiToTo, "What is on the lower levels? I hope it's not the laboratories where they perform live dissections of alien visitors."

HaaTiToTo said, "They keep the common property down there."

"Common property?" said Tracey, wondering if Quentin would ever find himself in any situation where he might be tempted to exercise a hint of discretion or tact.

"Yes, all of the equipment and resources that anyone needs, or might need, but which they just use from time to time," said HaaTiToTo.

"No one can have their own things?"

"Of course they can. Having it otherwise would be a clear breach of the Freedom Mandate. But it would be foolish for everyone to have their own one of everything they might need. Hundreds of different things are kept here. Many are expensive and together they take a lot of storage space. If everyone were to have one of their own of all of the things kept here, it would be an enormous inconvenience and extra work for everyone – nothing but a waste. Think of something as large and expensive as a GoSome, for example. Used for only a fraction of a daypart[3], at most. Or even smaller tools and equipment that may only be used once in five, twenty, or fifty days. Almost everything is delivered automatically in a few moments via the underground service tube straight to the dwelling. Only a handful of very large items needs to be collected with a short walk from every dwelling's door."

"So, no restrictions on what someone can have?" said Tracey.

"Certainly not. None. Everyone keeps at hand whatever they are using every day, at least a few personal items, their own clothes of course, their BringSeeDo, furniture in their dwelling, their room decorations and so on."

"A few personal items? And this all works?" said Quentin.

---

[3] A daypart is a local measure of time – one sixty-fourth of a day.

"Of course. Otherwise, every household would be getting for themselves at least one or perhaps several of each of many of the hundreds of items here. Everyone would need their own dwelling to keep it all. Doing it that way or any other way would be crazy, yes?"

"Crazy. Certainly. You would know a lot about that," said Quentin. But he was thinking that all the community facilities and infrastructure seemed very well organised. Undoubtedly, getting the resource hub to work as efficiently as it apparently did would take some managing, helped along by a complex, reliable technology. Maybe these creatures were not totally stupid.

As they approached the exit, HaaTiToTo said to Quentin, "By the Mandates, I have some other business to attend to. I trust your rain-meal will be in accordance. I will rejoin you for your return consciousness transfer. Unless I don't." With an Allundrian goodbye, he turned back towards the ramp they had just descended from the transit terminus.

Quentin moved between HaaTiToTo and the ramp, blocking his path. He said, "Hold on. Where do you think you're going?"

HaaTiToTo said, "I go where I go by the Freedom Mandate."

Tracey said to Quentin, "Let's not make a scene."

Quentin saw that SiMiYah, who had walked ahead through the doors, was now turning back to them. "In accordance, then. Just don't forget the no-show penalty on the get-us-out-of-here Mandate."

HaaTiToTo was looking puzzled and was saying, "That's not one of the Mandates," but before he could finish, Tracey had pushed Quentin towards the door, using her shoulder to be as discreet as possible, her minder expressing the hope that she was not the one who would be the cause of 'a scene'. SiMiYah saw the stragglers were catching up, so she turned back towards where she had been headed.

Strolling from the resource hub building, Tracey noted that the light was getting noticeably dimmer. Like the one they had started from, this path circled a dense, lofty grove and from that, offshoots led up to dwellings fashioned in the same style as the one they had come from. Low, laden clouds drifted above them. On the path ahead of them, at least thirty paces away, three Allundrians, two adults and a child, were walking away from them up to a dwelling's entrance. They saw no one else out.

SiMiYah led them along the path, effortlessly maintaining a one-sided conversation about her younger brother who had changed his mind (in accordance with the Mandates, of course) about his career, about how he had been at the top of his class, had got exactly the job he wanted (very prestigious), had been very successful at it, but then had an idea about something he wanted to do more – completely different – so he retrained (did I say he is very clever?), and then he got a different job (it was just as prestigious), but then he thought of something else he wanted to do again, had to retrain again (it is lucky he is clever) and got another even more prestigious job until (guess what?) he did it all again, and again – he is up to seven careers now, and now he is looking into a totally different job again.

While SiMiYah rambled on, Tracey was thinking that HaaTiToTo had been right about not noticing her minder. Even though it was always offering a word, a thought, a judgement about every single thing seen, heard, or touched, Tracey found she had started not to notice her minder at all. No, it was not right to say she wasn't noticing, it was more that she had just become very comfortable with the arrangement. It was like being with someone who knew you so very well, they were always able to finish your sentences for you, except that with her minder, it was turned around – it was almost as if it was always able to *start* her sentences for her, that it knew exactly what she wanted.

SiMiYah turned to the same dwelling the three Allundrians had gone into earlier. They had almost reached the entrance doors when a large wet *splot* hit the back of Quentin's head. Immediately, he looked around but saw no likely source nearby, nothing above but the lumpy floating clouds. Hearing two more *splots* on the ground beside him, and looking again for the source, he saw more very large drops of water start hitting the ground.

"Fat rain," said Kieran, "very fat rain." In fact, the raindrops were the largest that any of them had seen – it seemed they could have been nearly half a cupful each. Moving to the shelter of the dwelling's veranda, they watched the rain slowly grow heavier until it chattered down steadily, noisily obscuring all but the closest and largest objects.

The drenching rain had begun as it always did, a thin band drumming in the fall of evening as it marched along the planet's narrow equatorial ring of land, a never-ending cascade chasing after the sunset, topping up the dams every town had in the high country, bringing cool air to the animals finding cover in the forest canopy, leaving behind soaked vegetation and an inky, moonless, starless, still night. They had made it just in time to their first rain-meal.

SiMiYah led everyone through the dwelling's entrance doors along a corridor and into a large meal-room, like the one they had seen in the dwelling they had started from. It also had a large, low, central table surrounded by thin cushions and mats. It too overlooked an internal atrium.

Tracey and Quentin were startled to see the room already occupied by nearly twenty Allundrians. Some were standing in groups of two or three talking, others were seated or reclined on the cushions and mats. A couple were using their BringSeeDos. A few glanced at SiMiYah and her companions when they arrived and immediately returned to what they had been doing. Kieran gave the arms-crossed-over-chest greeting gesture to the room in general.

Tracey and Quentin relaxed as they saw that no one was showing any interest in them at all. SiMiYah said, "These are some of my birth clan. The two over there talking in the corner are uncles. My brother sits by the far door with his spouse and eldest child." She waved at her brother who had seen her arrive earlier but now appeared not to notice. "Well, I can introduce you later perhaps." SiMiYah was still pointing out her relatives around the room, and having started with the closest was now on to the more distant – her other brother's wife's uncle's cousin – when three younger Allundrians appeared at the door to the right carrying large plates. The first was filled with large blue, red, lavender, and pink berries arranged with the colours in spirals and swirls. The next had slices of orange, green, and yellow fruits. The third had delicate frilly lace-like leaves wrapped together in a cone shape. The food was being collected from an adjacent room, the termination point for a service tube from the resource hub. As soon as a plate was placed on the table, the Allundrian who brought it went out and returned with another, until a good part of the table was covered with food.

"Now we must work out who will start," said SiMiYah to Tracey and Quentin. She took a long breath and released a sigh.

An Allundrian who looked older than the rest said, "Let us eat equally." There were sounds of agreement and some mouth nods.

No one moved.

Conrad_27-8 said, "I calculate the total food pieces available will not divide equally between those present."

"Freely spoken," said the older Allundrian.

"You *counted* them?" said Quentin to Conrad_27-8 in a low voice.

Encouraged by the Allundrian's response, Conrad_27-8 said, "Not only that, the number of food pieces of each food type will not divide equally between those present for any food type except that one." He pointed to a plate piled with slices of pink fruit.

In silence, all eyes turned to it.

"We must call for counsel," said one of SiMiYah's uncles.

In a low voice, Quentin said to Tracey, "What? They want to get legal advice on how to eat?"

As they watched, several of the Allundrians started using their BringSeeDos.

Quentin said, "What's this now? Most of them are getting their *own personal* legal advice? Is that their brains laid out on the table?"

Another older Allundrian said, "I seem to be the only one present with Mandate-Guide qualifications. I am only in my second placement year – just five more to go – but I offer my services. You may present your proposals to me for consideration."

SiMiYah said, "Perhaps we could just leave the number that will not be equal. We never finish everything anyway."

Her brother stood up and said, "Must you always interrupt matters you are not qualified to deal with? And don't forget you are under speak-exclusion."

Kieran had been watching an Allundrian youngster looking at a plate heaped with slices of pink fruit. Kieran said to him, "That one smells delicious, doesn't it?" All the eyes in the room were drawn to his arm as he reached for the plate and offered it to the youngster, who took a slice of fruit and ate it. Kieran also helped himself to a slice from the plate, took in the aroma with a deep breath and bit into it. There were some gasps and then silence for a moment as everyone absorbed what had happened. SiMiYah looked a little unsteady on her feet.

Then the larger of SiMiYah's uncles said, "Eat freely," as he reached for a plate of berries. Before he had closed his fingers on a handful, the others quickly repeated, "Eat freely" and rushed to grab whatever food they had their eye on, with a few forgoing the prescribed words and simply lunging at the food. With a victory to appetite, rain-meal had begun.

Quentin said, "It seems the stomach is mightier than the Mandate."

The Mandate-Guide locked his eyes on Kieran, walked around the table to him and as he got closer, said, "You can't … you can't …" When he stopped in front of him, fingers clenched, Kieran, with his mouth full, offered him a plate of berries. The Allundrian looked at the plate, opened his mouth, closed it, then turned and walked over to SiMiYah's brother. They started talking together in low voices, occasionally glancing across the table at SiMiYah and Kieran.

SiMiYah said to Kieran, "How did you know how to break the Mandate-lock?"

Kieran looked around and said, "There was no need to operate any controls. The doors were all open for departure, were they not?"

SiMiYah said, "Yes. No. You know, the Equality Mandate was locked in a deadly embrace with the Freedom Mandate." What she was trying to explain was that everyone was fully free to eat as they chose. At the same time, it had to be done equally. No one could be first or last, or have more or less. Conrad_27-8 had helped make their dilemma clearer than it usually was.

Kieran said, "I did not see a Mandate locking anything out, or in. I saw everyone wanted to eat and plenty of food ready."

"I suppose, if you look at it like that. No, I mean, we *were* stuck. Everyone knows about Mandate locks. They are always happening. The Mandates all serve us but getting them right – all of them – is tricky sometimes."

Kieran said, "The Mandates serve? I think they do serve as a good hiding place. Is that what you want?" Kieran's tone was light-hearted – he could have been talking about an interesting game.

"A hiding place? No, that's not how they work. I don't understand. Who did you say was hiding?"

"It's not a who, it's a what. And a why." Kieran gave a quiet Allundrian chuckle, a chesty warble.

But SiMiYah was distracted by what her minder was saying and said, "Yes, they allow *everything* to work. Without our Mandates it would be chaos. That is certain. They stop us from … from …" But her minder was hushing her, and she said nothing further about it. Instead, she said, "No, that is right. I don't really want to think about what would happen." Nevertheless, after a moment her thoughts went back to it. "But if we need them to stop something, what is it, I wonder? And yes, what is the reason? You know, I don't know. That seems strange – not knowing. Is it strange?"

Kieran said nothing, or at least had no time to speak before she went on, "It almost makes me wonder if everyone must be bad somehow, deep down, where no one sees. How could that be? I don't think everyone is bad, not bad deep down. How would they get that way? What is it then? You know I am a bit confused. And maybe it's not just me." She sighed. "Maybe there is a lot of confusion about. It's like being stuck in a bad dream where you have a feeling that something is not right, but you just can't see what it is. You are stuck with the dream, doing dream-thinking, everything muddled, confused, and you feel trapped. Is it too hard to get out?"

Kieran said, "Everyone is free to move about. The seat belt sign has been turned off."

SiMiYah said, "Free? Of course. But you could have been charged with a breach before. It was very brave."

Kieran said, "Everything in front and behind, left and right, above and below[4] has all the necessary safety features."

As they started eating, Tracey said to SiMiYah, "What was that 'speak-exclusion' about?"

SiMiYah said, "Oh that. Yes, I should have told you. I am sorry. Please don't be angry with me. It started before the last long-sleep. I made a Mandate-fault. Maybe a big

---

[4] He meant "the universe" but they had no word for that.

one. It was when I went with some of the clan for some entertainment after rain-meal. I was talking about the entertainment and the nice time we were having together. They were doing a play with singing. It was the SlinSloGenTor troupe. Did I tell you? Have you seen them? The performers were all very good. It was lovely. I was with my mother. I was very lucky. We had been invited by the Head of the Mandate-Council – HumBeTchTch. Do you know her? I know, very important. My uncle's wife's brother knows her. HumBeTchTch had invited SlinSloGenTor to do a personal performance. How could they say no? Did you know, before they became famous, SlinSloGenTor did two shows a day every seven days and then only one on the eighth. They worked hard, yes, very hard. But they are so famous now they can do whatever they want. They are in massive demand; they can work anywhere, anytime they want. For now, anyway. You never know how long it will last. Surely tomorrow someone else will be more famous. You know how it is. So, they keep going while it lasts.

"Do you know, SlinSloGenTor has been touring for over a year now? They have not been home at all. Not once. That is how popular they are. Isn't it good? One of them has a small child at home. He hasn't seen him for that long – over a year. He has to do it, you see. He must miss him a lot. To me, he even seems sad sometimes. You know like when sometimes someone looks like the Well-being Mandate is being very well satisfied but is sad inside. If you are looking, really looking, you can see that they are pretending. But he has to keep going, you see. I was thinking that it was a pity that he had to be away. It seems to be a shame. And we met them too, after the performance. It's true – we met. They were very nice. I think two of them were nice because that was part of the event – meeting some fans after the performance. You could tell – they did it because they had to. But I was talking to NolNenNoj – you know him, the outspoken one – as he was packing up behind the stage. I even helped a bit. He was happy to have a quiet talk. Just a normal chat. No slobbering follower stuff. He seemed a bit lonely, actually. I don't know about anyone else. After we met them, I was talking about it all with the others. It was such a thrill. But you won't believe this: I felt it was maybe just a bit sad too. I can't really say what it was, actually. Not properly. I was just talking about it. I was just saying that it was a pity that such talented folk had to be stuck, in a way. For me, anyway. Doesn't anyone else care about it? Is it only me? A senior Mandate-counsel was with us. He judged that what I was saying was in breach. I am not really sure which one I breached. But he is a very respected senior Mandate-counsel. He would know. He was very angry. Anyway, getting the Justice Mandate satisfied was very complex for that one. What was the reversal, or perhaps even the correction? Everyone had different ideas. I had just been thinking about things and talking. So, they argued a lot about who had been wronged. And I could not undo my talking. So, they decided to place me on a speak-exclusion. No one can speak to me unless it is for 'the necessities of day-to-day activities'. Everyone seemed to be pleased with that. I should have told you about that before. Are you angry?"

Tracey said, "I *thought* that everyone was ostracising you before. That is terrible." After a moment's thought she went on, "Besides, surely a breach has to be against someone or it is not a breach. On the other hand, isn't that 'justice Mandate' decision breaching the 'freedom Mandate' for you?"

SiMiYah said, "Oh, twisting Mandates! Yes, you are right. I wish I had thought of that in the hearings. I will speak to the trainee Mandate-guide about it."

Tracey said, "Wait a …" but SiMiYah had walked over to the Mandate-guide and started to talk to him, as if she had some good news to pass on.

The Mandate-guide said, "No, you are wrong. You do not have the training," stressing each word with a mounting volume.

But SiMiYah just kept on, talking more eagerly, now moving her hands and arms around for emphasis.

Speaking still more loudly, the Mandate-guide said, "No, this is all wrong. You must stop."

SiMiYah did not seem to hear and lost in her excitement, went on speaking, her gestures getting wilder.

The Mandate-guide shouted, "Stop!" Everyone in the room stopped talking and turned to SiMiYah and the Mandate-guide. Tracey started to make her way through the crowd towards SiMiYah. The Mandate-guide said, "SiMiYah, I am charging you with a Level One breach. You have four days to obtain counsel, assemble evidence in your defence, and be ready to petition for justice. Then you will be sentenced."

SiMiYah said, "But …"

"Yes?"

SiMiYah had a defeated, pleading look in her eyes as the Mandate-guide stood stonily in front of her. SiMiYah bowed her head slowly as Tracey reached her and then led her back to the others, through the crowd, everyone turning away as they approached, going silent as they drew near and then resuming their conversions in indignant whispers, concealing glances at SiMiYah's back after she had passed by.

Quentin said to Kieran, "We should have kept her mouth stuffed with food."

SiMiYah contemplated the Level One breach. The prescribed sentence was exile. It meant she would lose her livelihood as a HearTell integration designer. Not only her livelihood, but a job she got satisfaction from, as she worked with technical specialists across the town and from other towns to mould thousands of isolated HearTell electronic control devices into cooperative clusters – the intelligence behind the SeeDos that made life run smoothly for everyone. She would be cut off from her clan, even her closest relatives. Many of them she visited frequently, even though they rarely visited her. She would be eking out a subsistence living in one of the isolated shanty areas. Tracey did not know about any of this, but she could see that SiMiYah was distressed beyond words and her minder was saying she was obliged to help. Even if she was not obliged, she wanted to.

SiMiYah said to Kieran, "I need a senior Mandate-counsel for this. How will I get one in four days? They are usually booked up for years. Most of them will be starting their long-sleep now anyway. And what evidence can I get to put together a case?"

Kieran said, "No assembly is required."

SiMiYah's minder spoke clearly but quietly in her ear, "How? How? Do you know? Don't make it worse."

Conrad_27-8, who had been deep in discussion of the application of zero sum game theory to food consumption with Quentin, felt a tapping on his wrist. He looked down and saw his BringSeeDo showing symbols that read, *Meet me at resource hub. HaaTiToTo.* He said to Quentin and Tracey, "HaaTiToTo is ready for us to return. Perhaps we should be going back … ah … if the Mandates permit."

Looking at Tracey, Quentin saw she was relieved to have been offered a release. He himself felt that he had more than enough to mull over for now.

SiMiYah said, "I suppose you must go now. I will remember you when I am in exile."

Tracey said to SiMiYah, "It hasn't happened yet. We will come back tomorrow and help you work it out." Immediately, her minder whispered, "Was that wise?"

SiMiYah said, "Oh, will you? You will? Yes, maybe together we can fix this." But she looked glum. Holding her arms down at her sides, palms forward, she gave them the Allundrian farewell, saying, "The Mandates preserve you," and dragged her feet from the room.

Quentin, Tracey, Kieran and Conrad_27-8 found their own way back to the dwelling pod's resource hub and then up to the transit lounge where HaaTiToTo was waiting. There HaaTiToTo summoned two GoSomes for them and they started back for the dwelling they had come from.

On the journey back, HaaTiToTo told them about the Allundrian Mandates.

The Eight Mandates of the Allundrians

> Early in the recorded history of Allunda, the clan was the dominant social structure. Thousands of them wandered the planet's only landmass – the slender ring twisting around the equator. The clans were small, mobile. Ten or twenty mouths opened when they ate. Each clan roamed its own territory, an area marked only by landmarks named down the generations, territories that were slivers of dense forest rising between the brooding shores of the twin restless seas. Clans preferred to keep to themselves, meeting with intention only for the season of intermarriage. On some of those occasions, some seed of disagreement was planted, sprouting a crop of dispute, of prolific self-seeding strife, sometimes enduring for generations, even sporadically blossoming into lethal conflicts, conflicts at best placing a heavy, enduring burden on many a clan's resources, at worst threatening its viability.
>
> To stock resources for skirmishes and other times of need, the clans started to build permanent structures and, needing more resources than their number could offer, they formed complex loose alliances woven around small settlements. Even within their alliances many disagreements flared but, lest their tenuous new securities be lost, these they chose to quell, leaving them to abide as sniping grudges.
>
> Over the centuries, three of the settlements grew to be much larger than the hundreds of other small communities that had also sprouted. They became big enough to be called towns, having populations

of upwards of ten thousand. Centres of power coalesced within the three towns, as they attracted all manner of craft-folk, the learned, the wealthy, and the ambitious.

As the three towns grew larger, so competition between them grew. Their merchants squabbled over the fields of sweetpetal tree that produced copious resin that was harvested and processed and used as a key raw material in many manufactured goods. Their farmers schemed to include in their boundaries the richest groves of fruit and berry trees; their engineers placed competing claims on the hill gullies that could be dammed to hold the evening rains; their scientists guarded their own discoveries and emerging technologies and attempted to steal others'.

Swelling competition fed mounting tension and deepening suspicion, which in turn fed ever-more strident exclusion and palpable fear, which led to the day where the allied clans in two of the three towns prepared for battle. The clans of the third town, fearing that the winning clans, after they had absorbed the resources of the other town, would be too powerful a neighbour, decided it too would join the approaching conflict.

While the battle preparations were still underway, the venerable MahChBukCh, the leading merchant from the last town to make ready for the battle, sent requests to the leading merchants of each of the other two towns for a secret meeting. The three leading merchants met and agreed that a full-blown battle between the towns would be a disaster for them all. Using all their powers of coercion, threat, and blackmail, they forced the three towns' clan leaders to form a Council that would meet to attempt to resolve their disputes without combat. This Council became known as the Council of Resolution.

The Council of Resolution met for sixty-four days and sixty-four nights. Over that time, the disputes that had to be resolved were never able to be clearly stated. Nevertheless, the members argued, debated, formed alliances, squabbled, broke promises, gave impassioned speeches, betrayed allies, invoked lofty ideals, forgot agreements, and generally went from disorder to chaos and back. What did become clear to those present, and the only thing they did agree on, was that any battle between the towns would become a war between all the clans. They knew that a war, with every clan the enemy of every other, would be a disaster for all. On the last day of the fourth extension, in a moment of inspiration, the Council scribes removed from the many volumes of the record of proceedings up to that point, everything that was not agreed. The resulting single page became the Basis for Cooperation, also known as the Eight Mandates.

The minders played a central role in the final wording of the Mandates. Those present said that even that small amount would never have come about without their help.

The Short Statements of the Eight Mandates of the Allundrians are:

1. *Freedom.* Every restriction must be removed.
2. *Justice.* Every wrong must be corrected or reversed or undone.
3. *Equality.* Every inequality must be removed.
4. *Clan.* Every clan a citizen is in makes that citizen special, because those clans are superior to the ones the citizen is not in.
5. *Safety.* Every attack (or threat) must be repelled (or removed).
6. *Personal View.* Every citizen can adopt their own interpretation/have their own view on any

matter (and apply it however and wherever they want to).

7. *Purpose.* Every citizen has the right to a purpose (to give life meaning), one that they choose.
8. *Well-being.* Every citizen must seek and be provided the things he/she wants for her/his personal well-being.

As required by its Terms of Reference, the Council of Resolution circulated these 'Short Statements' in the three towns for ratification. Immediately, streams of delegations petitioned the Council for exemptions, inclusions, exclusions, variations, wording changes, word order changes, Mandate order changes, removal of Mandate order, and innumerable other vital matters. So, sixty-four days and sixty-four nights after the original Short Statements were circulated, they were followed by 'Clarifications' of several pages each, later bound together as the Book of Eight Mandates.

After the original Short Statements and Clarifications were produced, the Council of Mandate Oversight was established, with representation from each clan. The role given to the Council was to assist in the application of the Mandates. Each year since then, the Council had met for sixteen days to review and clarify the Book of Eight Mandates, with results recorded in the 'Volumes of Interpretations' for each of the Mandates. Despite at least the first fifteen days of every meeting being taken up with discussion on procedural matters, the assembled Mandate Interpretations now formed eight very large volumes, the smallest spanning over two thousand pages, and the largest – the volume on the Well-being Mandate – being the size of all of the others combined.

Now, over three thousand years after they were set down, the Allundrians universally acknowledge

> the Eight Mandates as fundamental to the welfare of every individual, every clan, every town, and the whole species. Since the Eight Mandates came into being, no town has risen up in violent conflict against another. There are disputes, of course. Any disputes must be brought to mediation. There, an independent mediator, assisted by accredited experts in the Mandates, convenes with the parties in dispute, each assisted by their own accredited Mandates experts, and works through the issue. These mediations are usually concluded after somewhere between twenty or thirty days to a few years, with a series of resolutions that are fully agreed upon and supported by all present, in the opinion of, and at the sole discretion of, the appointed Mandate experts.

HaaTiToTo was saying, "That gives you the basic background. Now, the enforcement process is where it gets complicated. Firstly …"

Tracey said, "Thank you. I think that's enough."

Conrad_27-8 said, "Actually, I am sure an ontological analysis of the Book of Mandates and the volumes of Interpretations, to identify the potential for rationalisation, would be well worth the time spent."

Quentin said, "Actually, no you aren't."

Conrad_27-8 blinked at Quentin, put on his BringSeeDo and was instantly intent on it.

With HaaTiToTo's discourse concluded, Quentin said, "In future, for the safety of your listeners, you should consider introducing your tales by using the words 'this is a long story', and to be totally accurate, drop the word 'boring' in there somewhere."

HaaTiToTo said, "No doubt, the Safety Mandate is to be upheld."

Tracey said, "Are you really going to listen to the acerbic little asides of Mister I-could-find-a-million-faults-in-a-flower?"

"It will be according to the Mandates."

Tracey said, "If you say so." Then she decided to ask another question she had been holding on to. "Does anyone here ever give a simple yes-no answer?"

HaaTiToTo said, "Maybe."

At the transit terminus, HaaTiToTo and Conrad_27-8 led them back to the dwelling and to the room they had started from. Tracey said, "Before we settle down, I … um … think I should visit the bathroom." HaaTiToTo showed her the way. She was hoping she would know how to use it when she got there. She did not want to have to be shown what to do. HaaTiToTo led her to a door which, on opening, showed a small room. Tracey went straight in and was thankful that the door closed behind her. The way to use the facilities was obvious enough. Although the spray of warm scented water and then the jet of drying air made her jump, she was finding them pleasant by the time they ended. She stepped to the door and it opened to Quentin, Kieran, and Conrad_27-8 standing in the corridor in a disorganised queue.

"I hope you haven't used all of the hand soap," said Quentin as he went in.

Tracey saw that HaaTiToTo had left them.

When they all returned to the long-sleep room, they lay down on the beds they had come to awareness in and Conrad_27-8 said, "Now the procedure to return is the same as the one to come here. Step one – make yourselves comfortable." He waited for a few moments. "Step two – close your eyes and relax. Empty your thoughts." After a few more moments, "Step three – focus your attention on a spot inside your head just above your eyes."

Quentin opened his eyes to the first light of dawn shining into his apartment kitchen. He stretched.

"Whoops. It looks like I nodded off." But he was wondering how his dream memories could be so lucid.

Even though his memories covered some hours at least, he felt fully rested. Quentin saw that Tracey was still also starting to rise from where she had been lying the previous evening.

Kieran was already up, standing in the kitchen eating cereal. He said, "I like Allunda. When do we go back?"

Tracey and Quentin looked at each other for a sign of confusion, question, denial, anything. Had they been hypnotised? What exactly had gone on? Had their pizza been drugged? It was unspoken, but they both realised that the other knew. What they remembered as being woken from a lucid dream had been no dream. Quentin's memories of their visit to Allunda flashed back, taunting his lack of understanding, haunting his casting for denials.

While Tracey and Quentin were still internally reassuring themselves that they were not insane, hanging their hopes on the fact that shared group delusions did not exist, Conrad_27-8, who was also already up, said, "That was a good start. We can continue tomorrow evening. I would like to progress the start time by prime number increments, if you will indulge me. That will make it 6:16."

Quentin was still too distracted by his own befuddled thoughts to respond with anything but a remote, "OK."

Conrad_27-8 said a cheery, "Goodbye" and left.

Chapter 6

On the second day of Mist-on-Water's lessons with Sand-on-Stone, she emerged from the trail to see him again sitting on the bench in front of his cabin, eyes shut. She crept up to the bench under the great low branches of the Whitewood tree and making not a sound, she sat on it. Expecting to startle him, she gave a sharp slap on the bench and called out, "Wake, uncle."

Sand-on-Stone sat unmoving, his eyes still closed. Mist-on-Water picked up a short stick and poked him in the side, saying, "Did eating your breakfast make you weary? Am I not free to go yet?"

Sand-on-Stone continued to sit for a moment, then he opened his eyes, turned his head to her, and said, "Free? Yes. When you see the bars of your cage are doors to a room with no walls, when your bird flies free of the air – then you are free. For now, you are free to not do everything you cannot do." He chuckled.

"Say-you." She was accustomed now to him coming out with strange words. Intent on her own course, she let them pass. "My older friends say you never gave them this lesson on your source. Do you give all the students the same lesson? Or is it different?"

"Yes."

"Which?"

"The same – yes. Different – yes."

"What?"

"Every student gets their education in the form that is best for them. There is one lesson, but many forms."

"Very good. Then I will take the form that is very fast." She was not yet in the mood for concentrating on any lesson, enjoying the fresh breeze on her face and gazing at the open yellow flowers drooping from the branches hanging low around their bench. Some greenface birds feeding on the flowers' nectar caught her eye and she watched them take their busy breakfast.

Sand-on-Stone said, "Do you want to continue from yesterday?"

Mist-on-Water said, "Why not? Yes, tell me your strange story. Perhaps it will be better than the after-dinner yarns they tell in the village. Those yarns are always about *the mischief that started when the stranger came to the village*, or *how the gorgeous guy finally gets the adorable girl* or some adventurer journeying into far-off lands. But make sure you give me a good lesson I can use." She was growing more confident. "Tales of other times, other places, may be interesting for a bit, but you haven't told me anything about here and now yet."

Sand-on-Stone said, "There is the story about the girl who asked, *how can I have everything now?* and then rushed off just as the answer was coming. Perhaps you would prefer that one?"

Mist-on-Water responded with a *look-at-how-patient-I-am-with-you* sigh and returned her attention to the antics of the greenface birds almost within arm's reach, fluttering about the tree's blooms waving in the breeze. One of the birds took hold of the petal of a bloom newly opened, precariously hanging upside down on it, chirping in sweet delight. The others rushed to it, crowding in, jostling for space, gaining, losing then regaining tenuous shaky toeholds, then all being thrown off and losing their prize as the whole spray of blooms jiggled in a sudden gust.

Following Mist-on-Water's eyes to the greenface birds, Sand-on-Stone said, "I see. Where were we? Ah yes, it was long ago, long long ago – The Source, the maker of everything. Not just the maker, the giver of its own substance to its creation.

"But do you know what the most important thing was? Life. The Source made life – beings that were the same as it was. The beings it made were beyond counting. And this is the amazing thing: they were not beings apart. The Source could not lose its substance, it could not lose itself. The beings were themselves but at the same time they stayed a part of The Source. They were all *in* The Source, just as The Source was *in* all of them, fully *in* countless beautiful beloved beings. Every one of them. Can you imagine such a thing?"

"It sounds very cosy. They had no problem with claustrophobia?"

"Yes, it is hard to imagine. But that was not all. They had the same nature as The Source. So, it meant that they too created as The Source created. Creating was The Source's delight and it was their delight as well. They too, had no limits. Their being was beyond measure."

Mist-on-Water said, "What did they look like? Were they like the giants that once roamed the land, if you believe the tales of the oracles?"

"No, it was very different then to now. Very strange."

"Strange? How?"

"This life – these beings – had no form; they had no shape."

"It gave them no shape? Why did your Source do that?"

"Two reasons I can think of. Firstly, they had to be as The Source was. Remember, their only substance was The Source. The Source is not bound to a form. Every form there can be is in it, but The Source is not bound to any of them. Like The Source, they had no form."

"That could not be."

"Not in this place we see now, certainly. But that place is not the place we see, the dimensions of that domain do not work like the dimensions we know." Sand-on-Stone continued. "Secondly, they had to be able to be a part – of anything, everything, relating to it, able to dance with it, to be the harmony to any melody. It was the will of The Source. For them to be without limit, across space, across time. Form, shape is limit. So, they had no form." Sand-on-Stone wanted to be sure she was following this. "So-be?"

"No."

"No?" Sand-on-Stone had expected some difficulty in understanding and he waited.

"No. Those two reasons you gave are just one reason – freedom."

"So-be. Perhaps just one reason then, seen two ways. Yes. They were completely free – completely free to be, as free to be as The Source." Sand-on-Stone realised Mist-on-Water had not only been following him, she had also been scouting around his words noting any stumbling on the trail. He would need to be more careful with his explanations.

But Mist-on-Water was not finished. "So, we are not talking about Life-Source then? I have heard some claim she gave birth to every species and gave to each of them one of her ten thousand faces."

"No."

"And we are not talking about StarSky-Source either? I have heard others claim that a day will come when time ends. Then he will put everyone who ever lived into a long line. Everyone will be lined up in order of how good they were when they were alive. The one who was most good will stand at the front, and the one who was most bad will stand at the back. He will make a magical sorting gate and line everyone up in front of it, in a very very long line, and he will say, *Behind this gate are the keys to the whole universe. Everyone who has been good and freely forgiven those who have been bad can go in.*" She looked at him for any objection.

Her telling lacked the justifying and prettying the oracles put on it, but the essence was there. Now, it was his turn to be patient. He put the tips of his fingers flat over his mouth to show he was waiting.

"But do you know what will happen then? When the magical sorting gate picks someone in that long, long line, the one last to go through the gate, the last one who was good enough, the one behind, the one who just misses out, will say, *But why do I miss out? The difference in goodness between me and that one I stand behind is too small to even find.* And the sorting gate will agree it is true. Every time the magical sorting gate picks someone in the long, long line, the same thing will happen to the last one to go through: the one behind who just misses out says, *There is no difference between me and that last one you let in. It is not just.* In the end, the magical gate will get annoyed by all the complaining and will only let in the one who is at the front of the line. Only that one will get the keys. But only because she can't complain. Everyone else will get tossed into a deep dark pit of turmoil."

"I haven't heard that part of the tale before. Are you sure it is from an oracle?"

"Let me finish. Guess what will happen next? The magical sorting gate will toss StarSky-Source into the pit as well, because he made a horrible gate that would not freely forgive everyone. This Source of yours, we are not talking about him?"

"I don't think the oracle for StarSky-Source tells it quite like that." Sand-on-Stone tilted his head.

"So-be, maybe I put in a few bits myself. But it is close enough."

"Only a few bits? Say-you. No to that one too, then."

"So-be. How did it all work in those dimensions then? You said it was different to here."

"You know how things work here, where we are: a birth, a life, struggles – big and small, joy, pain, victories, losses, a death. It is just the nature of the things we see. Who even thinks about it?"

"You forgot to mention tedious little tales."

"There, in the realm of The Source, the nature of things was very different to what we see now. It was more than just different, it was opposite, in a way. The nature of The Source was the nature of all. It followed, you see?" He put his fingers over his mouth, and waited. She waited too, giving away nothing. He went on, "It followed from their creation. Every living being was in harmony with every other living being. This had to be – every being was *part* of every other being. The Source abided in every being it created, and every one of those beings abided in The Source beyond time. They were one in all things, nothing separate, nothing but peace. The Source could not be at war with itself. They only knew peace. This is the first opposite."

"*Opposite* to now, say-you? That's a bit extreme, isn't it? I know what peace is."

"The second opposite is to do with giving. Giving was not like here. It was not giving away – it was not loss. It was increase. There, every part gave of itself to every other part, all of itself, just as The Source did. And so, giving, and in harmony, every part receives from every other part. Giving was no sacrifice. Once given to all, and received by all, nothing could be taken back – there was no idea for that – taking back. They did not have the ideas of *loss* or *take back*. If somehow those ideas had been offered to them, they could not have even understood them. They would have been complete nonsense to them."

"It's an alluring idea. I would certainly like to increase my harvest by giving it all to the bluefire wasps."

"The third opposite is to do with freedom. They were free be anywhere, to create anything, to know everything. They were not limited by time, by space, by weakness. Something known by one was known by all. Nothing was secret, hidden. Any place one could be, all could be. If they chose, they could be anywhere among all the stars, or they could be in every place, everywhere. There was no place they could not be. There was no effort. Anything that could be done by one could be done by all. Just to think was to create. Their will was done and once done, it stood beyond time itself. They had no obligation, no need, no lack, no conditions, and nothing done could be wrong or broken. Nothing died."

"Perhaps the problem with this dream is not with what you are saying, but with what you are not saying? Like not saying that there are other things you might want to be free to do apart from create? Rest and make merry perhaps?"

"All was joy far beyond words – complete unity, creation with beauty far beyond words, acceptance total. That was how it was for all that were breathed to life."

"So-be then, if any of that ever was, then yes it was different. So-be. I concede." She said this in a very non-conceding tone.

"Yes, there is much more to be told about that place, that time, but the most important thing is held in one word. Perfect. All that was, was perfect. All that lived, were perfect."

Mist-on-Water had never heard any ideas like these before. Despite her feigned dismissals, they did interest her. She liked to explore new ideas, probe them for flaws, decide whether they had a place in her ways of thinking, to expand the horizons of her mind.

Mist-on-Water said, "Can anything be so perfect?"

"Yes, it was all perfect."

"Say-you. Long, long ago all was good. And this is all that was? Nothing wrong?"

"Nothing could be wrong. Nothing could go wrong."

Mist-on-Water thought about the world she knew. She found it pleasant enough. Hunger was rare, but at the price of hard days in the fields. Yes, there were times of happiness, times that eventually drifted away to make way for times when happiness was elusive. Sometimes, words were friendly, but other times sharp, meant to cut. Much was good, but perfect? It seemed everything good had a companion. Beside it stood something broken, some problem. But nothing kept standing still.

Someone always came. Someone who happened to amble past this problem or that, saw it and with good intentions sought a better way. And over time, improvements, fixings – for an individual, for a family, or for the village. But for every little correction, for every small improvement, brokenness kept poking itself out in some other way or in some other place. Was there something deeper, some cause lying low unseen, one that squirmed out of every solution they had? A cause they had no correction for? No one could know. Too much was hidden. Nothing was certain.

One thing was certain. That final flaw, relentless, rarely spoken of. The creeping withering and final failing of the body thrust on them. Death. That ultimate breakage, unfixable, beyond improvement, and so pretended away until it demanded attention. Even then, she knew, they all stepped around that demand with platitudes and deflections. It had been that way with Mist-on-Water's other younger brother, whom she had delighted in, but who had fallen (*even that word hides the truth*, she thought) to the river sickness two seasons before. She had seen they knew no better way. Nor did she. She wanted a better way.

"If any of that were true at all, long, long ago as you say, something did go wrong, very wrong. What was it?" said Mist-on-Water. But she was thinking, *When he says what went wrong, the whole 'nothing could go wrong because it was perfect' drivel will be shown up as nonsense.*

"Ah, you have a sharp mind. Perhaps you will think on that question and find the answer. At the same time, you can help me prune the golden orb trees." Behind Sand-on-Stone's cabin, a small orchard of golden orb trees kept him, his occasional visitors, and a few families of black-toed climbers well fed for nearly half the year.

"So, it's a puzzle, is it? You challenge me? So-be." Mist-on-Water liked solving puzzles and was usually the first to find the answer.

While they were pruning the trees, from time to time Mist-on-Water suggested answers to her own question.

"Is this it? Some of those beings, students probably, strove to be accepted as the equals of their teachers. But their foolish teachers would not allow it. So, the students had a contest with the teachers to acknowledge their skills. Unfortunately, it turned out that the students were more able than their teachers and the whole inequitable social order disintegrated."

"An amusing start. But no. None of them were greater, with others lesser, not one there could do what any other one could not, not one came before any other, there was no first and no last among them. Perhaps your next answer will be more serious?"

"So-be. Here it is. There were a great number of them, yes? Countless, did you say? Then it was a shortage, not enough of something. They all squabbled over what they needed, in the dimensions of their domain, tugging, pulling at it until it all ripped apart."

"Say-you. There it is, but that is not it. You are right – they had no number. But remember also: their domain was without limit, nothing in it was with limit. There could be no lack there. A better try, at least."

Mist-on-Water frowned. They went on pruning.

"A rebellion. They were completely free, yes? Free to rebel, yes? A rebellion?"

"No. A rebellion must be against someone in charge, giving instructions, controlling. There was no such thing. The Source gave, it did not control. The Source's will was their will, their will was The Source's will. Nothing to rebel against."

More pruning.

"Some of them got together to make themselves special, better than the others. The others didn't like it and there was a big fight, a nasty fight between beings with unlimited power."

"Ah. Now you do test me. I will put it this way: there were no special distinctions there, no *us* and no *them*, not even *me* and *you*, not the way we know it. Here, folk are seen as separate. There, the idea *separate* was nonsense."

Back to pruning.

"Something came from outside and destroyed it. An enemy?"

"No. No enemies. Nothing could come from outside. There was no outside, nor could anything there be destroyed or even brushed with a tiny blemish."

She thought of her friend Clouds-at-Sunset's brother, who was still unwell. It had been a few days now.

"Some kind of sickness then?"

"No. Everything was eternal. Everything. There was no decay, no death."

"So, a mistake then? One, or maybe many, did something wrong and that Source was angry with them, or maybe the others were. It punished them. Like StarSky-Source."

"Not that. What wrong could be done? Nothing could take the slightest blemish, there was nothing that could cause angry words."

More pruning.

"So-be. It was good when it started but after a long time they tired of it, they didn't like the way it was, what they were doing. Like too much pruning. They grew restless, wanted something more, wanted to be something different, wanted to change, but they broke it all with their power without limit."

"No. They knew what they were. There was no more they could be, and what they were gave them deep, abiding peace, profound joy."

Back to pruning.

"An insurrection. Some of the beings wanted to have more power, to be in charge?"

"No. They all had all of the power of The Source. They could do everything The Source could do. There was no power they did not already have. And no being could tell any other being what to do."

"A secret then? Your Source had some secret that they wanted but it would not allow them to have. They tried to steal it or something and your Source banished them."

"No. No knowledge was forbidden, everything that was true was known by all."

"So-be. Then was it that they wanted something else they did not have?"

"Maybe you are going the right way now, but no. They all had all. The idea of *mine* did not exist. They moved freely across all of space. Every place, everything, was already theirs to know, to experience. When everything is freely available to all, the idea of *mine* made no sense. Their joy, the joy they shared with The Source, was in creating, not in having."

"Ah, I see it now. You say everything, *everything* was perfect. And then it all fell apart somehow. If it really was perfect, it could not have become imperfect. But you say it did – we have a paradox. But you cannot have a paradox. So, your story cannot be. You made it up to test me. Did I pass?"

"No, it is not a test. And I did not make it up."

Mist-on-Water decided she would offer no more answers until she found one she was sure of. The pruning went on with little spoken other than the words of the task.

She did have other words, for when the time was right. She did have a small trap of her own to lay, not a good one, a trap that any could lay, one that would be expected, looked for, and so would probably catch nothing. Even so, it might give a glimpse of the prey making its way around it. For a trap that would catch nothing, any time would do. "Before I tell you the answer to your puzzle, I have my own puzzle for you. Answer me this: how did your Source come to be? What was there before it?"

"The Source is not of time. Out of time there is no before or after. Out of time, before and after have no substance and so have no meaning. Time is a veil to seeing, letting you look on just two things. Through it you see the past – dead, a ghost, or the future – the shadow of a dream. Through it you see what is not." He shot a look of awareness at Mist-on-Water. "But perhaps you are too clever and have made me say too much."

When she took her leave for the day, Mist-on-Water still not had solved the puzzle.

Notes: Additional Species

Summary of observations. I suppose I should explain about the other species interacting with my cuties. I will spend some time on them, but not too much. I want to get back to my tiny dears.

Chapter 7

Conrad_27-8 was in his Earth home – his only home now – sitting on his lounge, eyes shut, his hands resting in his lap, palms up. It was nearly the time for his regular appointment with a Consciousness Transfer Engineer. He always made sure he was ready in plenty of time. As he waited, he let his eyes open for a moment and his gaze fell on the aquarium. He thought back to his home world, the recruiting ground for the agents of the Galactic Council. Back there, it was said it had been chosen as the recruiting ground because the population had the highest intelligence of all the known species. They emerged from the larva stage numerate, able to perform all the basic arithmetic operations (addition, subtraction, multiplication, and division) in up to eight digits of their preferred base-16 number system. By the time they reached the adult stage of their life cycle, every individual could perform advanced calculus and was proficient in thousands of complex algorithms.

They were bioluminescent. They could individually control hundreds of thousands of light emitters that covered their surface. It was the way they communicated. Communication was precise and efficient. Their discussions were also exquisite to look at. The planet they lived on was covered in water – there was no land at all – and water, naturally, was their home. To a human eye they would have looked like a very pretty jellyfish. The name they gave themselves translates as '65535ians' (which, even in its clumsy base-10 representation, any 65535ian child would instantly recognise as sixteen binary ones). The passed their days floating in the placid ocean, giving spectacular light shows and performing complex calculations in fluid dynamics as they worked out the best source of nutrition. They passed their time earnestly discussing contentious concepts of number theory, brilliantly solving problems in pure mathematics, and eating as gourmets. They had no predators or parasites or diseases. There was no work to be done, no cars to break down, no bills to be paid. Anyone and everyone was available for reproductive activities. They could produce and indulge in countless forms of entertainment, and they did. All in all, they led very boring lives. Floating, watching the shows, calculating, procreating, eating. Calculating, eating, watching, procreating, floating.

Boredom was the main reason Conrad_27-8's species was very receptive to telepathic contact from, and communication with, the Consciousness Transfer Engineers. During one of these chats, a Consciousness Transfer Engineer mentioned the Galactic Council and that it was having great difficulties finding agents – understandably. Any agent would need to leave the known comforts of home, would need to learn to control a strange land-based body that would have to interact with its environment and a multitude of other species in a world filled with confusing sights and sounds, navigate bizarre customs, endure days that were fast-paced, unpredictable, and possibly dangerous. There were a multitude of things the agent would be required to do, an exhausting list of places to go, unending data to collect and analyse. Immediately, by accident, the Galactic Council had recruited its first agent. Now, the Council had a full complement of twelve agents across the twelve planets under Council oversight, all 65535ians – the only source of volunteers so far, with Conrad_27-8 being the eleventh.

Conrad_27-8 brought his thoughts back to his here and now and looked at his watch. The appointment was forty-three minutes late now. As a species, the Consciousness Transfer Engineers were imprecise in their attention to time. It was decidedly annoying but Conrad_27-8 did appreciate that, for a Consciousness Transfer Engineer, being an hour early or late for an appointment was like being a few seconds early or late for him. He was still astonished that such a radically different species was able to mediate consciousness transfer for all the life forms they had attempted it on. They were happy to tell everyone they contacted everything about themselves. They made it into a very long story, reduced here to the maximum length that Quentin had been able to tolerate.

The Consciousness Transfer Engineers' home planet orbits an orange dwarf star, completing an orbit in just over two hundred and twenty-eight Earth days. Plants are the planet's primary life form, along with some insect-like fauna on the land and a plethora of primitive forms of the mollusc family in the seas. In the evolutionary battle for survival, one humble moss-like plant has taken ascendency over the land. *That's right, Quentin – a moss-like plant is the peak life form.* The name they use for themselves is the imaginative 'Us'. Elsewhere in the galaxy, their name translates essentially as 'Mossmians'.

Their beginnings many eons before were humble. The earliest recognisable ancestor of today's Mossmian was a mundane pebble-sized species of moss with a few thousand stems. With their evolutionary progress, this plant's average size grew through the millions and then through the billions of stems. Along with evolution driving the individuals' stem numbers up to and then beyond the billions, all interlinked, something changed. Sparks of awareness flickered. They thought, they knew themselves, they knew their needs. Physically and mentally, they had become the plant they now were.

With today's Mossmian taking several hundred Earth years to reach maturity, it was a relative giant. Fully grown, they were about two hundred metres across and two metres high, and after they reached their full size at maturity, they lived for many more thousands of years. A long life, but one not exactly lived in the fast lane. As the species grew in size, it also grew in complexity, developing specialised sensory stems that allowed them to be aware of their surroundings and gave them a form of smell that allowed them to detect locations of nutrition. As well as evolving these and other specialised stems, the Mossmians evolved to gain the ability to consciously control and direct their growth. By growing one edge of themselves and not replacing dead stems on the opposite edge, they could 'move', albeit it could take an individual some decades to visit a neighbour less than a kilometre away. Over their lifetimes, some might venture as far as a few kilometres from the spot the spore they had grown from had landed. Most went nowhere. In the planet's rich soils, sources of nutrition were abundant and simply by sending down shallow roots, the Mossmians took their fill at a leisurely pace.

But they were not the only ones taking their fill.

The giant moss-like plants had long been a dietary option for some of the planet's insects. So long that they had evolved means of defence. A plant was alerted to the presence of a predator through simple photoreceptor stems spread over its surface, giving it a primitive form of sight. Dealing with their lurking predator was another matter. To confuse or alarm their simple-minded predators, some of their stems had evolved to change colours, while other stems emitted deterrent odours. Other stems could secrete an organic acid as a defence. While these early defences worked, they were slow acting and often a plant suffered significant damage before it drove off a predator, a problem they had learned how to solve only relatively recently.

Being essentially immobile, the intelligence and self-awareness of these plants developed in a different direction to the paths taken by most intelligent life. They had no tools, no technology. Despite their physical limitations, the Mossmians developed an ingenious means to communicate. They used their specialised stems to develop a system of colour and scent signals. With this, they could communicate with nearby plants of their species – communication that was a mixed blessing. On one hand, it relied on line-of-sight and the direction of the wind. On the other hand, as a giant moss, vocabulary was limited, at least in the beginning, and there was not a lot to talk about. A silence had to last for at least a year before there was any sense of it being awkward. *"Something SiMiYah could learn from," Quentin had muttered.* Their thought processes related little to their bodies or environment – changes in those areas were close to glacial. Over time, rather than the incessant mundane chitter-chatter that beings on other planets wrapped around themselves as they drifted through their days, they became much occupied by philosophy and metaphysics. Over many generations, as they explored and experimented with their minds and consciousnesses, one of them stumbled on a technique for basic telepathy that allowed it to intrude on the primitive thoughts of its insect predators. It started with small mental pokes that distracted an attacker for a few moments, sometimes long enough for the insect to forget what it had been doing so it would fly or crawl off somewhere else. That one taught the others.

Over millennia, their telepathic techniques for predator poking improved slowly until a break-through event – it was when the most expert and gifted of them sent the idea 'nice year' (like saying 'nice day' for us) into his neighbour's mind. The neighbour spent most of the next five years wondering who that had been. With improvements in technique and with practice, the species replaced their clumsy colour and scent receptor stem communication with telepathy. This was the break-through development that launched a boom in their science of metaphysics. At the point where Conrad_27-8 was saying this to Quentin, Quentin said, "And they also solved the moss transport problem." Conrad_27-8 had been about to ask Quentin to explain that but had been distracted by Tracey exhibiting symptoms of a very sudden and severe cranial pain.

Up until that leap forward, for nearly three million years, the Mossmians' progress as a species had been sedate. However, the relatively short space of the next two hundred and fifty thousand years launched a reinvention of the lives of the plants as individuals, the blooming of social networks, and the discovery and study of alien life. It started from learning to extend the small mental pokes they had been giving predators. If the insect was distracted for a moment, or dozing, they learned how to poke in one of their own ideas, ideas such as 'maybe I will fly over there' or 'did I turn the lava over before I left?' It turned out that insects were easily influenced by the arrival of ideas like 'that might taste nice' or 'that spot looks cosy', so these predators soon stopped feasting on the slow-growing Mossmians and became miniature personal groomers, trimming dead stems and depositing nutrition where it could be absorbed. It was mutually beneficial. From there, the frontiers expanded rapidly. Soon they were in constant chatter between themselves, expressing and communicating subtle, complex concepts, advancing their knowledge and techniques of mental manipulation until the most recent startling discoveries.

Rigorously applying the scientific method, the Mossmians discovered that not only a thought or two, but a complete consciousness could be transferred from one 'Consciousness Capable Organism' (referred to as a CCO) to another. But transferring a consciousness between organisms cannot be done in any willy-nilly way; it must obey certain rules. After extensive experimentation, they developed the Seven Mossmian Laws of Consciousness Transfer. The First Law stated that a consciousness could be transferred from one CCO to any other, but only in one of two situations.

> The first situation: if the originating and receiving CCO's consciousnesses consented (this was a temporary transfer). For this kind of transfer to occur the receiving consciousness had to be in a state of non-self-awareness (such as being asleep) during the transfer.

The second situation: if a consciousness had vacated a CCO but the organism remained viable (called an unrestricted transfer). This vacation of consciousness invariably only occurred when the organism's death was imminent.

The second kind of transfer was the hardest. Good luck was essential. Timing was critical. They could only do it at the moment the body was on the edge of death, triggering the consciousness occupying it to vacate, but instead of dying, the body remained viable. It happened on Mossmia occasionally with the insect they called the flashstinger. The sting of a flashstinger was usually instantly fatal to the bugs it preyed on. When stung, the victim's consciousness immediately jolted away from its body. But on rare occasions, the victim's body survived the two seconds the poison was active and remained functional, but now with no consciousness. It looked comatose. That was when there was a small window to transfer a consciousness to it. While that window was open, a Mossmian could transfer the tiny, confused consciousness of a random bug to the flashstinger's victim – a slightly frowned-upon party trick. The Mossmians found they could transfer the consciousness from any organism to any other organism, even their own consciousness. Transfers of a Mossmian consciousness had only been done three times. Those first three 'mindonauts' had quickly withdrawn their consciousness from their target CCO, saying they could not tolerate the frantic pace of the sensory inputs they were getting. After that, consciousness transfer had been rarely done, until the discovery of the Galactic Council.

Recently (just over seven hundred years ago), a group of youngsters – Mossmian juveniles less than three hundred years old at the time – had been feeling bored. They had had nothing to do for seventeen years except play the same old telepathic game of dodge-em-insect with the same old insects. Then one of them came up with the idea of exploring the galaxy telepathically, searching for other sentient beings to communicate with. It was not easy. Their telepathic projection had to be narrowed and focussed to probe a minuscule part of the sky. Since they could not see stars, and only knew of them through the eyes of one species of giant insect, they were working blind. Over the course of a decade, with patience, the young Mossmians did find several intelligent alien species, species inhabiting planets having broadly similar biospheres. But the overwhelming proportion of individuals of those species shared a strong reluctance to welcome thoughts sent to them telepathically. They found few exceptions, rare, isolated individuals, until the 65535ians. The bored 65535ians were the first species they found that was generally receptive to telepathic communication with the Mossmians.

Soon after (just a few decades), the young Mossmians found another species willing to communicate. It was on the home planet of what was to become known as the Galactic Council. The species they found called themselves the Variants. They named themselves that way because every individual was born as one of a specialised sub-species – a particular variant. There were variants for all the specific roles in their society – the Food Producers, the Childbearers, the Designers, the Constructors, the Communicators, and so on. By luck, the Variant they had contacted was a Communicator – its function being to relay messages between the other Variant types. Making it all work were the Organisers. The Organisers were self-compelled to organise, just as, for example, the Constructors were self-compelled to construct. Collectively, the Organisers called themselves the Global Council, their mission to ensure nothing anywhere on their home world would be left improperly organised. When, through the Communicators, the Global Council learned of intelligent alien life, the Global Council immediately took it on itself to become the *Galactic* Council, again so that nothing should be left improperly organised anywhere in the galaxy. In the same way one might take on responsibility for preparing dinner, they had assumed responsibility for the orderly conduct and administration of a few hundred billion stars. Fortunately, not all those stars had life-bearing planets. In fact, the Mossmians had only identified thirteen so far with life, including their own, or with life sentient enough to respond to telepathic communication.

After the right number of properly convened meetings of consultation, the Galactic Council determined that, to provide adequate oversight, it would need local planetary representatives. But how could they do that? The local inhabitants were not suitable. They were almost all averse to telepathic contact, or for the rare individuals not averse, so far they had all had their own disqualifying peculiarities. The situation was only saved by the 65535ian volunteers – they were ready to serve anywhere. One of the Galactic Council's first official acts had been to formally engage the young Mossmian telepathic explorers as official and accredited Consciousness Transfer Engineers. Their job description also included providing the mind-to-mind telepathic connection service. This service would allow the planetary representatives to send reports to, and get directions from, the Council. The Consciousness Transfer Engineers would need to get the 65535ian volunteers to their appointed planet, starting immediately. The pace was frantic.

Less than a Mossmian year later, the first Council representative was settling in on her assigned planet. Employing the mathematical prowess of the 65535ians, and based on the populations of the other eleven planets and a range of other factors chosen for their obscurity, the Mossmians calculated that the Galactic Council would need approximately 219,154,533,553 representatives to be appointed across an estimated 3,834,342 (yet to be discovered) planets to achieve their Galactic goals. Noting that, up to that time, only a single 65535ian had been appointed as a Council representative, the Mossmians, again thanks to the mathematical wizardry of the 65535ians themselves, happily reported to the Council that the recruiting should be completed while there were still quite a lot of stars in the galaxy that had not burned themselves out, maybe even in less than ten billion years – that time being somewhat increased, of course, through the good fortune of the projected collision of our Milky Way galaxy with Andromeda in just four billion years. After that, there would be a lot more stars capable of accepting representatives and getting properly organised. Given their long life spans, the Mossmians felt none of this would be too much of a problem. The Council complained their task could never be done with fewer than two hundred and fifty billion agents, ideally recruited sometime the following week. Bitterly lamenting their budget restrictions, the Council was somehow getting by with an agent army that had grown to twelve. They put their astonishing successes down to their vast and supreme organisational competencies and gave themselves appropriate awards.

Occupied by this, the Council's young Mossmian Consciousness Transfer Engineers, now known to some as the Galactic Travel Agents, had been kept entertained for several decades and the Galactic Council had been carrying out its business with what its performance reviews declared as a great success. It had all the data to prove that, through its untiring efforts, the galaxy was not in the slightest more disorganised now than it had been several hundred years before – even if a few laws had been bent along the way. Not the important ones drafted by the Council – just minor ordinances such as the laws of physics.

It had been through some eavesdropping on discussions on one of the more scientifically advanced planets that the Consciousness Transfer Engineers had been surprised to learn that with their telepathic and consciousness transfer activities they appeared to be breaking a certain law of physics limiting the movement of things to the speed of light. This law had no organisational merit that the Galactic Council could find, and they started exploring avenues to have it repealed. Fortunately, they quickly found they did not need to bother. It turned out that telepathy and consciousness transfer did not operate in the four-dimensional space-time of physical perception, as specified in one of the clauses of that speed of light law. While the precise dimensional dynamics were never clear, they received advice that, under that clause, it was legal for interactions between consciousnesses to be instantaneous, not limited by that speed of light law.

But that was not the only law the young Consciousness Transfer Engineers were breaking. The Mossmians had no Global Council, no administrative bodies, no system of laws or social structures at all really. It was not surprising. Break and enter, for example, was somewhat impractical, as well as pointless. While they had no social structures, their philosophical musings left them with a clearly laid out set of ethics. All responsible Mossmians prided themselves on their 'proper behaviour' which mainly related to what they thought and said and somewhat to their interactions with other species on Mossmia. All Mossmians needed to conform to the rules of 'proper behaviour', or risk social exclusion. Excluded, they would receive no more telepathic invitations to philosophy parties where everyone just sat around (naturally) and chatted about the meaning of life for a few decades. They did not even serve drinks. Due to its harshness, this punishment had never yet needed to be applied. It had rarely even been mentioned, until recently.

Only a hundred and eighty years before, the activities of the Galactic Travel Agents had been discovered outside of the group. That juvenile prankishness had immediately (within a few short decades) become a source of deep consternation among the adult population. Then a decision was made. It was agreed that their amusement was improper, scandalous even, and that it should stop. The young Mossmians would have to comply. The Galactic Travel Agency was about to close.

Conrad_27-8 was not aware of that decision as he readied himself for the second trip to Allunda.

Observation Series: **Norms**

<u>Summary of observations.</u> These cute little guys have made up rules for themselves. They think they have good rules. They are not. They know what rules are, but they are clueless about what good is. They do not care. They think they can think anything they like - as if thinking it makes it true. Adorable but silly.

Chapter 8

Tracey arrived at Quentin's apartment just after 6:00. She'd had a typical day of meetings, reports, and emails – busy enough to push thinking too much about that night to the back of her mind. As soon as she came through the door, she said, "What was that last night? What are you going to do when he comes back? Assuming he does come back."

Quentin had spent a good part of the day thinking about those questions, and a few others besides. As a scientist, he had to go with the evidence. What the evidence pointed to was that something had happened, that something being most likely exactly as Conrad_27-8 had described it, and as their memories told them they had experienced it. He said to Tracey, "You may not believe this, but I definitely want to go along for this ride."

"What? Why?"

"It's obvious, isn't it? First-hand experience of an exoplanet! Anyone would give up their first supernova observation for that." By 'anyone' he meant anyone who was remotely interested in astronomy, even if that someone was only an astrophysicist.

What he did not say was that his career had taken a bit of a side-step, to put it mildly. Getting that stellar evolution grant had been an accident – everyone had known it would never get funded and he had only applied because he needed to be seen to be applying for things. But everyone had done such a good job of vehemently disparaging everyone else's pet project, instead of promoting their own, it had been the only one without impassioned detractors. He had got stuck with it, while his real expertise and interest lay in the development of protoplanetary disks. Now was his chance. Some inside knowledge could go a long way to fast-tracking theories that could put him at the top of his field. He went on, "But I'm as frustrated as a dog chained up in the middle of a hospital for lame cats."

"Frustrated?"

"Don't you see? No instruments. No calibration. No reference points. No actual data."

His head was bursting with a very, very long list of 'not knowns'. Starting with the basics: they did not even know how big they were. The size of an ant, or a tree? What light frequencies were they seeing? The colours seemed a bit off from the ones they knew. What was the planet's size, its gravity? What was the air temperature, even? What data *did* they have? Nothing.

"Oh," said Tracey, thinking a moment before saying, "but what will you do with the data when you get it?"

"It will go straight into the globally endorsed repository for all scientifically verified facts of global significance: I will post it on Fussbook, of course." He waited for Tracey to be amused by his little jest, but she was just looking at him blankly. "OK," he said, "obviously, the real story can never come out. The truth is I don't know yet what I will do with it, but we have a goldmine here and I want to dig a bit."

"I see."

"Why did you come back anyway?" said Quentin.

"Well, it's SiMiYah. I don't want to leave her in a bind. Besides, I have some research of my own it just might help me with. Not quite sure how," said Tracey.

"What research?"

"My father has glioblastoma multiforme. He's all bitter and twisted about it."

"He has a glowing-what?" said Quentin.

"Brain cancer."

"Oh."

"Anyway, it seems we *can* exist outside of our bodies in some way. There might just be a little footnote or maybe an incidental aside to your *data reference points* – footnote: *by the way, we seem to be a bit more than JABOC*."

"JABOC?"

"Yes, more than JABOC – Just A Bunch of Chemicals," said Tracey. "It's an expression my father uses. Maybe he made it up. He's not big on *superstitious religious nonsense*," mimicking her father's gruff tone with the last phrase. "Not that I am either. But I think there's something important in this."

"Hmm." But he had not really been listening. Tracey's enthusiasm for her discovery was not enough to deflect Quentin's line of thought from its fixation on *actual data.* He started making a list of data he wanted to get, organising it into categories of scientific disciplines.

At 6:16 a knock sounded on Quentin's door. Conrad_27-8 came in with Kieran, who he had happened to meet in the foyer.

Quentin was overflowing with questions for Conrad_27-8. He started while he was still walking in, "What's your story, anyway?"

Conrad said, "My story? I am in possession of zero stories."

"I'm talking about how you came to be Global Director of whats-its. Here on Earth. And you can throw in the tale about those Allundrian critters, while you're at it."

"Well, perhaps I can give you a brief overview for seventeen minutes and forty-three seconds before our scheduled departure. The actual departure time may be unavoidably delayed anyway."

Conrad_27-8 told the 'story' of the Mossmians and how, after the self-promotion of the Global Council on another planet (yes, it is another different one, Quentin) into the Galactic Council, they were appointed as the Consciousness Transfer Engineers, that this led to the recruitment of representatives to conduct operations 'in the field', and that no, he didn't know which star the planet of Mossmia orbited, or the star of the Galactic Council either, since he was not an astronomer, or even only an astrophysicist.

Quentin absorbed all of that for a time. "What about those bodies we went into? Did you find them on Airbnb, or what?"

"What is this Airbnb?"

"In our case, it would be Air Body 'n' Booty. Never mind. Just explain about the bodies."

"The Galactic Council's agent on Allunda found them. It wasn't difficult. The Galactic Council tasked the global director with cultivating the science of astronomy on Allunda. They have a few scientists who are researching what lies beyond their planet's cloud layers. But they are making almost no progress. The visible light of stars is never seen through them, even their sun is just seen as a brighter splotch in the cloudy haze that is their sky. So, they do not even know of stars. They do not have any propulsion system that will lift optical instruments high enough to get past their planet's cloud layers. They have recently detected radio sources in their sky and so the first steps in radio astronomy have been taken. Our agent contacted the scientists and showed that he was not from their world."

"How did he manage that?"

"He got a Consciousness Transfer Engineer to swap the consciousnesses of two sceptical but willing volunteers between their respective bodies."

"That would have got their attention, I guess."

"Yes. Just now the Allundrians are starting their annual hibernation period. Only it's for their hot season, so it's actually called estivation. Anyway, the four volunteers agreed to start their estivation a few days early to allow their bodies to be used while their consciousness is in this quiescent phase."

"Pretty trusting, aren't they?"

"Perhaps the money helped, too."

"Ahh, a fistful of Galactic credits was thrown in? I should have known."

"They call their local currency femto-units – each femto-unit is one 10^{-15th} of the base currency unit."[5]

"It doesn't sound like a lot."

"Well, there is only one piece of currency in circulation for the whole planet. Several hundred years ago, when they started up with electronic commerce, they decided to create a new global currency. They simply needed to work out how much of it to put in circulation. A simple deduction they could not deduce. They could not agree on an amount of currency that would be sufficient. For a while they thought they might need to circulate an infinite amount, to satisfy all the Mandates. Despite the Allundrians being otherwise highly rational, that was clearly nonsense. After lengthy efforts, they could not work out how to distribute an infinite currency across a finite number of holders. I could have told them in the beginning that it would not be possible. So, in the end they went with a single piece of legal tender, the minimum possible number. Everyone has it. They feel it satisfies the equality Mandate. They call their single piece of legal tender 'the unit'. Somehow they make it work."

"They have an equal share in a single dollar? What's the point of that?"

"No, no, not an equal share. Equality is satisfied because everyone accesses the same single unit. But everyone has their own quantity of little digital pieces of it – the femto-units. They earn them, hold on to them, and spend them, just like here."

"So, everyone thinks they've got a hold of their glorious dollar, even if there's not quite enough to go around. A disturbing tale, but not unexpected. No one thinks to wonder why their equality drivel doesn't extend to those good ol' femto-units, which incidentally would be the things that actually matter to everyone?"

"They don't seem to look at it that way. What you are suggesting would be impractical anyway."

---

[5] That is one millionth of a billionth

Quentin gasped. "I do hope you are not dismissing the ability of our distant galactic cousins to self-delude a gloriously impossible equality for themselves? Underestimate them at your peril."

Conrad_27-8 opened his mouth but was still working out how to respond when Quentin proceeded to his next question.

"Next. It was handy that the planet also has two genders, and that you managed to match us up with what we are used to."

"Thank you."

"No. It just seems a bit too convenient."

"I see, you are questioning it. No, the probability of that outcome was over eighty-five-point-eight percent. Even here on Earth, billions of years of evolution show that two genders for an animal species is the most effective number. It is the same on all the planets discovered so far, except one. We had enough pre-registered Allundrian volunteer scientists to get the gender assignment correct."

"Hmph." Quentin considered the answer for a moment then said, "And now, Tracey will cover gender anatomy."

"What?" Tracey's voice was a few semitones higher than usual.

"I saw you peeking."

"OK, I was just interested. Anyway, there's not much to talk about, from my point of view."

Quentin said, "Unfortunately, I have to say the same." It seemed the clothes were mainly decorative, not for modesty. "And what was that your Galactic Empire chum over there saying about *limited time*? What was he talking about?"

"Yes, I should cover that now we will be embarking on multiple transfers." Conrad_27-8 paused, unsure how best to explain it. "You see, over any sixty-day period the maximum number of recommended transfers is six. So, there it is, the limited time."

"Haven't you left something out?"

"I did? What did I leave out?"

"If I knew, would I be asking you? You left out the reason you have that little limit of yours. And how much they fine you – if you go over it."

"Oh. You could say it is for, um, for health reasons."

Conrad_27-8 now had everyone's full attention. The topic of conversation not being mathematics, he was uncomfortable. "Yes. After six transfers, a phenomenon we call *body confusion* starts to become irreversible. That's all."

"No, it isn't."

"What isn't? What isn't what?"

Quentin looked like a dog that had been told to sit for his dinner just when a slow fat cat had turned up and started to stroll around it, the cat all the while flicking the dog's nose with its tickly tail, a *not-all-that-hungry* dog with a cat-chasing compulsion. And that some invisible leash was still holding. Just. "This *body confusion* is what?"

"Oh, that. Yes. Well. It's when you come back. You start to confuse the lives of your departure body and your arrival body. You start feeling you don't fully belong in whatever body you are in. You get confused about which body you are, since you could be any of the ones you've been in. Something in your mind wants to tie your identity completely to a body. It no longer can. Not fully. But it keeps trying and trying harder and harder until it essentially seizes up."

Tracey looked uneasy. "How do I even remember who I am in that other body anyway? All my memories are in my brain somewhere, my brain back here."

"This is not an area I am qualified in. But it seems there is more to it than that. Maybe your consciousness retains access to them. For it, physical distance does not seem to matter."

Quentin dismissed it. "Six trips should be plenty for me anyway. Well then, back to your story."

Conrad_27-8's story was a simple one involving, he conceded, an element of luck. He had been one of the multitudes of bored 65635ians floating in the unbounded ocean of his home world. The calculations that he had once delighted in had lost their fascination, even foods that he had once regarded as the finest delicacies had started to taste mundane. Not only that, his previously enthralling hobby of finding proofs to what was known on Earth as the yet-to-be-proven Novikov conjecture had become stale. So, he had signed up as a stand-by representative for the Galactic Council. He had been chosen by ballot – a humiliating part of the story he had been deeply embarrassed to admit. The Council selected Earth as his assignment, the second most recent planet to have a representative assigned, its need being assessed as low due to the billions of pages of laws, regulations, standards, guidelines, edicts, handy hints, information manuals, tourist handbooks, policies, operating manuals, disposal instructions, timesheets, project plans, meeting agendas, progress reports, and so on, already in existence, a clear indicator of a society fixated on operating with brilliant smooth precision, of a planet skilfully organised to the smallest minutiae, of a species intent on the pure pursuit of order. Clearly, nothing could ever be going wrong there. Nevertheless, Galactic policy required that a representative be assigned.

Excited about the chance to add a new player to their game, the Mossmian Consciousness Transfer Engineers turned most of their attention to monitoring Earth. They were on the watch for a consciousness detachment event from a human body that was still potentially viable – like a flashstinger poisoning wearing off on Mossmia before cell-death started. It was like looking for a get-well card in a cemetery. They had to scan on average two consciousness detachment events (also known as deaths) per second for exactly this kind of detachment from a still viable human body. It required intense concentration.

According to Conrad_27-8, approximately 48.2944785 revolutions of the planet 65535ia after he had volunteered (or about ninety-eight-point four Earth days), the Consciousness Transfer Engineers detected the consciousness that had known itself as Conrad

De'Luttecroce of Boston, Massachusetts detaching from its body due to a misadventure involving a live electrical wire. In Conrad De'Luttecroce's case, a few seconds later a circuit-breaker tripped and stopped the electrical current, allowing his ventricular fibrillation to pass. The body, now no longer with the consciousness that had called itself Conrad limiting its awareness to it, was still viable, so the Consciousness Transfer Engineers transferred the 65535ian consciousness who called itself $\{F4^3,F3^3\}$ (translated here as 27-8) to it. With 27-8's consciousness attached to it, and with the electrocution event passed, 27-8 strained to move. The body gave a reflexive gasp, there was a single heartbeat, then another, and 27-8 started to learn to control the body locally known as Conrad.

The Galactic Council was extremely lucky with this agent. There were very few complications. Those that did arise, the agent dealt with efficiently and quietly himself. It could hardly have gone better if he had been trained. The late Conrad De'Luttecroce had been living alone at the time of his misadventure. Then he had just dropped off the radar for his few casual acquaintances. He had quietly slipped out of the freelance writing market. No one noticed. He never contacted his brother and vice versa. Since the blow-up over the loan, years before, he and his parents had not spoken. Several days after his transfer, Conrad_27-8's 65535ian body died from lack of sustenance and a return to his home could not be achieved easily. On Earth, Conrad_27-8 found he could make a very well quantified income by predicting, within an average margin of error investment analysts would call impossible, the next day's share price for all the stocks on the Dow Jones Industrial Average – predictions he used to play his *Trading the NYSE* game. 27-8's needs were basic, so he lived a comfortable, simple life, not remotely tiring of the endless variety of the planet that was now home. He had his work, he had his hobby too – his art – and he could combine the two.

Conrad_27-8 considered himself a fairly good artist. His medium, naturally, was numbers. He was particularly proud of his Standard Form Surveillance reports – works, he felt, that merited public exhibition. The reports needed data. That was his role – to get it. Clear. Simple. Not possible. No one on this planet would agree any of the data was correct. Flaws in definitions. Inconsistencies in interpretations. He could have easily found the correct data himself but that would have stifled his creativity. So, he made it all up, close enough to correct that no one would notice, but with an elegant series dropped in here, a careful randomisation there, a hint of a trend emerging over there, but then petering out over time. Nothing to alarm the Council. He made sure he did not make it too beautiful, too sensuous – someone would be sure to notice. He had settled into a routine.

Then had come the notification of the critical operation that the Galactic Council had turned to Conrad for. He was carefully selected partly based on his exemplary reporting record, and partly because of his complete success in not failing a single one of the training courses he had not bothered to take, but mainly because Earth is a planet that has more than enough astronomers, and he was the only representative they had there.

Quentin and Tracey were still struggling to grasp it all as the time was approaching 6:20. Kieran did not seem to be paying attention. He was singing The Beatle's *Hey Jude*, with the words not quite right, as usual:

"Hey, Jude …

… the figment you heed is on your should-er-er"

Conrad_27-8 had to stop answering questions about his story so he, Quentin, Tracey, and Kieran could make themselves comfortable for the scheduled transfer.

The second transfer was done the same way that the first had been, with the adjustment period after arrival taking just a few minutes. When they were all sufficiently reacquainted with their Allundrian bodies, they had to decide what to do. Tracey wanted to get to SiMiYah's dwelling. Quentin wanted to get access to the Allundrian DuckDuckGo, or even their Google if he had to. Conrad_27-8 wanted to offer helpful suggestions about the data Quentin should collect. Kieran wanted to go outside. One course of action would satisfy them all. They went out and headed towards the resource hub. It was bright outside; the smudge where the clouds were brighter was higher in the sky than it had been on their first transfer.

Entering the resource hub doors, Quentin looked over to the line of four SeeDos to their left. He nudged Tracey and said, "Can you give me a moment? I'm going to assess their level of social and scientific advancement, as revealed by the availability of League of Legends or perhaps Overwatch." He dragged Conrad_27-8, who had followed him to the SeeDo, back to Tracey by the ear, put her hand around his wrist, and told her not to let go.

Standing in front of the SeeDo, Quentin saw a central circle with a symbol in it that his body's brain took to mean 'all'. Radiating from it, on spokes, were about twenty other symbols. He put his finger on the symbol for 'information'. Nothing happened. Quentin said to it, "We come in peace. Take me to your master."

The SeeDo said, "Your instruction is not compatible. Do you want to contact support for assistance?"

Quentin said to himself, "This one must be using Windows."

He looked at the symbol for information and opened his mouth to try some other instruction but, his mind a blank, shut it almost immediately. At that, the 'information' symbol moved to replace the central 'all' symbol, and the symbols on the spokes now related to 'information'. Some of the spokes had their own sub-spokes with a symbol, an image or writing. With his accidental Allundrian equivalent of a nod, he had discovered the pre-schooler method of interacting with a SeeDo.

Quentin started roaming around the SeeDo information maze, sometimes getting to screens full of writing, and at other times bringing up lists and tables. From time to time he grunted and groaned as he made progress or went down false trails.

While Quentin was bumbling his way about the SeeDo, Tracey was watching the Allundrians as they went about their business – she still felt very disoriented here and wanted to better understand how things worked. One thing that soon became clear was that no one acknowledged anyone else unless they needed to. No one seemed to be interested in what anyone else was doing. There was no sign of anything like guards or security. Kieran was making faces at a child stifling giggles at the side of parents deep in conversation with one of the resource hub workers.

After several minutes, Quentin had had enough and went back to the other three.

"Find anything interesting?" said Tracey.

"A few things. I'll tell you later."

They went up to the transit lounge and Quentin showed off his newly acquired SeeDo skills by ordering their GoSome transportation. Actually, it was less his skills and more the intelligence built into the SeeDo which had identified his body biometrically as he approached it, and since the identified body was a resident of this pod, and therefore had full GoSome access, when he stopped in front of it, the SeeDo screen already showed a request for transportation with his last destination and number of passengers set. Quentin simply reduced the number of passengers to four and gave a mouth-nod to the *proceed* symbol.

Without incident, the Go-Some took them to the resource hub that accessed the pod of dwellings where they had eaten the rain-meal the day before. As they walked towards SiMiYah's dwelling, they saw her sitting on the ground on the edge of the central grove of vegetation, eyes cast down. Tracey said with a smile, "Hello. It is nice to see you."

SiMiYah looked up, returned a weak smile, and said, "Hello. You did come back. That is very nice of you."

Tracey said, "I guess your Mandate breach charge has not been withdrawn."

SiMiYah closed her mouth and eyes briefly in the Allundrian manner to indicate *no*. She said, "But I have found someone in my birth clan who is a Mandate-advocate. We can ask him to represent me."

Tracey said, "He is in your clan? Surely, he will help. Do you know him well?"

SiMiYah said, "He is my sister's husband's mother's aunt's niece's husband. We have never met. But I have made an appointment for 5400. I should be leaving soon."

The five of them took a GoSome to what SiMiYah called a production pod. It was laid out similarly to the dwelling pods, with a central circular area of dense vegetation. But instead of being surrounded by eight dwellings and the resource hub, four larger buildings of two or three levels looked over it. SiMiYah led them to one of the buildings and using a SeeDo inside the entrance, announced her arrival. She then led them to a waiting room that the SeeDo had indicated. As they entered, only two couples were seated in a room that had places for many more.

The wall at the front of the waiting area showed a list of names and room numbers. SiMiYah's name was on the list, but it had no room number. They sat and waited in silence. At one end of the room both sides opened to corridors. Occasionally a corridor let out one or two Allundrians. As they appeared, they all looked worried, distressed, or angry. After a few minutes, SiMiYah turned to the sound of a subtle tone and a room number appeared next to her name, the number pulsing slowly. SiMiYah stood and Tracey said, "Can we come too?"

SiMiYah said, "I only gave my name for the appointment. You should wait here. The Mandate-advocate might think you are involved." She went to the corridor on the right and turned into it.

Only minutes later, SiMiYah emerged from the corridor and walked to the four others who got to their feet. Her face was blank.

Tracey said, “Will he help?”

SiMiYah said, “He will help. But he won’t.”

“What? He will? He won’t? Why not?”

“Because of his fee. It is impossible.”

Everyone just stood, not knowing what to say.

SiMiYah went on. “He said the case will be exceedingly difficult.”

Tracey said, “But you did not do anything.”

“The Mandate-accuser thinks I did.”

“But you didn’t.”

“You can say that, by the Personal View Mandate. And he can say I did too, by the Personal View Mandate. He must have his own view, by the Mandate.” Naming it triggered a reflex in her to recite it. “*Every citizen can adopt their own interpretation/have their own view on any matter (and apply it however and wherever they want to).* Yes, we are lucky to have our Personal View Mandate. It is the most adored Mandate.”

Quentin said, “That’s what you think.”

Tracey said to Conrad_27-8, “Anyone can think anything about anything? Anyone can think something is anything now? Surely everything has to be what it is. It can’t be something else. If anything can be true, nothing must be.” She was hoping he would correct her conclusion.

He said, “Given a collection of contradictory propositions, the truth cannot be known. If they are all asserted to be true, truth is meaningless along with any assertions.”

Quentin said, “There you go. Exactly the reason we need that good old Mandate for not knowing the truth. There’s all the equipment we need to get into this game right there.” Quentin began miming the exaggerated use of a gaming joystick, staring into space, unblinking, jaw slack, then the joystick became a machine gun shooting at imagined aliens who managed to get off some shots, two of which thudded into him. Tracey's look stopped him from collapsing to the ground.

Tracey said, "What is hard about the case, anyway?"

SiMiYah said, "The Mandate-advocate will need his associates to allocate a lot of time to research. It will be very expensive. He must get all the evidence. He says there will be a lot. It is his view. He said that a lot. I think the Personal View Mandate could be his favourite too."

Quentin muttered to himself, "I'm starting to like that Mandate myself. It could actually be a good one. Yes – someone could take a view that all those other Mandates are garbage and ignore them. Or take a view they should just apply every other day. Or play opposites – my views on freedom and justice are opposite to yours (what are they again?). Not to mention that safety one. That could be a bit of fun. I might just remember it."

Tracey said, "What is his fee?"

"It is very high."

Quentin mumbled, "I beg to differ."

SiMiYah sighed. "You see, it turns out he is a collector. A collector of nuggets." She paused, searching for the right words, then looking away from them she said, "He set his fee … he set his fee at a full thousand-weight nugget of iron ore. He will accept nothing else. Even his minder was saying how good it would be, how much he needed it. How it was essential. How well it would satisfy the Well-being Mandate."

Tracey said, "A full 'thousand-weight'? Of iron ore? That's it?"

SiMiYah, letting out soft, mournful whimpers, said, "Yes, I know. Impossible. So, he says he will, but he won't. I can't do anything." She sat on the floor, rested her head between her knees, and wrapped her arms around her legs. She was occupying the smallest space possible while her minder wailed in its thin voice, though louder than usual, "Can't. Can't. Can't."

Moving away from SiMiYah at few steps, Quentin said quietly to Tracey, "A thousand-weight is about what you could conceal in your hand."

Tracey was confused but said nothing. Her minder was saying, "You shouldn't have encouraged this. I told you, didn't I? Now it is worse." Tracey thought it was probably true but at the same time it did not appear to be helpful. She said, "That Mandate-whatever is going to get well-being from some lump of rusty iron? What's the problem? Apart from the problem he obviously has?"

Quentin said, "I'm going to check some things on the SeeDo. I will be back in a daysplit."

Tracey asked quietly, "A daysplit?"

Moving towards the SeeDo, Quentin said softly in Tracey's ear, "It's about how long it would take something to fall from the ceiling to the floor. Don't take me literally – I just won't be long."

Quentin worked at the SeeDo for a few Earth minutes before returning. Tracey stayed near SiMiYah, who was not moving. Conrad_27-8 and Kieran discreetly watched the SeeDo over Quentin's shoulder, Conrad_27-8 offering the occasional helpful suggestion which Quentin did his best to do the opposite of.

Quentin found what he wanted and went back towards Tracey. Before he reached her, he motioned her to go over to him. Speaking quietly, he said, "This iron nugget doesn't sound too hard but it's not what you're thinking. On our home, iron makes up about a third of the crust, but here it's rarer than gold. And by the way, gold here is also rarer than gold, so to speak."

Tracey said, "Oh no." She looked at SiMiYah, still sitting apparently without hope, tracing a finger along the patterns in the floor, and her minder whispered, "You did that. Can you fix it? Can you? No."

SiMiYah's minder grew quieter. Quieter, but far from still. It moved about continuously but slowly, starting from behind one ear, crawling up to peek over the top of it, and then crawling back down behind it to reappear at the bottom of her other ear, whisper a few words into it, and then crawl up to peek over that ear and then back down to reappear below the other ear where it had started, tracing out a prostrate figure eight around the back of her head.

Tracey watched it make several circuits from ear to ear. Occasionally she picked out words it whispered – a few *can'ts*, a *never*, *not you* a couple of times. Tracey put her hand on Quentin's elbow and said quietly enough not to disturb SiMiYah lost in her gloom, "They say they help, but do they really?"

"Who says? Who helps? What are you talking about?"

"SiMiYah's minder. Is it really helping?"

"I haven't really noticed it." He was not interested, but with nothing else to do, Quentin watched it as it moved from ear to ear. "Right now, it looks about as useful as an astronomer conducting observations on a planet covered in clouds. Which is only marginally less useful than an astrophysicist doing the same thing. Is that what it's supposed to be doing?"

"They're supposed to provide 'warnings' and 'guidance', or something like that. But hers just seems so … so negative. It's making her give up all the time. I wonder if we could get it to help us out with this."

"And what is *your* minder *warning* or *guiding* you about that?"

"It's saying that I shouldn't because I don't know what I'm doing, which is true. But I don't see how this situation could get any worse."

"Yours sounds like it knows what it's talking about, at least. Sure, we could take some time out to coddle our foot-in-mouth prone sidekick here, or we could use the little time we have to do something mildly interesting, like single-handedly expanding the scientific data our entire species currently has on exo-planets by a factor of a hundred, or maybe a thousand, or maybe even a million." His voice grew louder with each number. SiMiYah raised her head to see what the fuss was about. Quentin froze and Tracey held her breath. SiMiYah saw them looking at her and dropped her head again.

Tracey said to Quentin, "Hush."

Conrad_27-8 said, "If I may suggest a correction to your quantification, you need …"

Quentin said, "No, you can't. Shut your orifice."

Tracey said, "I'm going to try anyway."

"What? Enlist the midget patrol? How? They don't seem to talk to anyone but their own scaly-skinned porter."

In response, Tracey took several steps to SiMiYah, crouched down, and said, "SiMiYah, do you mind if I talk to your minder for a moment?"

SiMiYah lifted her head, revealing a confused expression. "You want to talk to *my* minder? Why? Does minder talk to others? I have never heard of it. I don't even talk to minder. Hardly ever. But you can try anyway. Minder always listens. I don't care." She hung her head again.

SiMiYah's minder was crouched down behind her right shoulder, little more than its eyes visible, eyes flicking around at everyone in the room, peering at someone or something for a moment, then moving on. Tracey moved to her left slightly, where she could see the minder better. In a blink, the minder disappeared, moving as fast as a striking snake behind SiMiYah's neck. Alarmed at its reaction, Tracey took a half step back and saw that the minder had popped up by SiMiYah's other ear, crouching so low now that even its eyes were partly hidden. But they were still flicking over everyone in the room, dwelling on no one, not resting for longer than a moment. Every now and then it whispered into SiMiYah's ear, just a few words, sometimes maybe only one, too quietly now for anyone else to hear.

On an impulse, Tracey slowly reached her hand out towards SiMiYah's shoulder where the minder was clinging. Before her hand was nearly close, it was gone, to reappear almost immediately on top of SiMiYah's head. Tracey made a quiet soothing sound as she changed the direction her hand was moving to reach towards it again, even more slowly. Again, before her hand was close, the minder slipped away to hide behind SiMiYah's far ear.

Determined to get hold of the thing, she went after it faster and faster, then with both hands. It was no use. The faster she moved, the faster SiMiYah's minder got, never paying her any particular attention, avoiding her with no apparent effort.

Feeling the unequal pursuit, SiMiYah looked up and said, "You can't catch it, or touch it, or whatever you are trying to do, you know."

Tracey had had the vague notion she might have been able to pat it, or maybe rub its belly like a small dog and gain its trust. But it was clearly no pet – it was lightning-quick and, it would seem, extremely intelligent, so she gave up that idea. Wanting to at least have its attention, she tried to move as best she could to be in its line of sight. It was difficult: each time she shifted herself towards where it faced, it changed position to give itself the best possible view of the whole room. Eventually, Tracey settled for a position where she would loom the largest in its field of view, even if she were not central. It paid no more attention to her than to anyone or anything else in the room.

Tracey said to the minder, "Um, hello SiMiYah's minder, could I talk to you for a moment?"

The minder's eyes continued their flicking, as if she had not spoken.

Tracey repeated her question, speaking a bit louder and more slowly. The minder gave her no response, or any indication that it had even heard her speak. Tracey raised her arm so that it was fully in its line of sight. The minder's eyes might have flicked onto it for an instant but then they continued their unceasing vigil on everyone and everything. Tracey waved her arm up and down slowly, then more quickly. Still nothing.

"What do *you* think?" She was talking to her own minder. "How can we communicate with it?"

Her minder whispered in her ear, "Take care. Take care. You could cause a problem. Remember – it has happened. Maybe someone else should try. Remember –

many things, your fault – your brother. But I can protect you. Take care."

"Take care? Why?" But she was thinking about how she and her older brother had been estranged for over a decade now, trying not to remember how she had smashed his irreplaceable Sui Dynasty painted terracotta horse. She had picked it up to look at it when he had asked her not to. Dropping it had been a clumsy accident, but still all her fault. *How did her minder know about that? Or was it referring to something in the life of the being whose body she had, the one who was 'temporarily away'?*

With an effort, Tracey brought her thoughts back to SiMiYah's minder. "I am just asking how we can talk to it."

"That one is trusting you. Should she? Should she really?"

"Trusting? No, it's not." She was thinking aloud. "Oh, you mean SiMiYah. I'm talking about SiMiYah's minder, not SiMiYah. You see it – on her shoulder."

Her minder said, "Quentin sees it." Tracey looked at Quentin and, from his expression, knew what he was thinking. She said, "All right – don't say it. This is getting us nowhere. It's as if my minder doesn't even see SiMiYah's minder."

"Yes, you are quite correct as usual," Quentin said. "We have safely arrived at *nowhere,* if nowhere happens to be located somewhere where you can wait in a very long, very slow queue at the end of which they hand out large chunks of time which you promptly pour down a grateful drain before you exit. You are correct: that's exactly where we are. Nowhere."

"Then do you have any suggestions here, Mr *Good-at-criticising-but-not-at-anything-useful*, even if you are only an astrophysicist?"

While Quentin had been watching the whole futile exercise, his minder had been whispering, "She must be stopped. Stop this. No time. No time." Quentin, said, "Even a fully-fledged astronomer with super-hero powers might not be able to rescue you from this little wormhole you made and which is diligently sucking up every form of futility in the whole space-time continuum. But since you ask, here's a few ideas anyway. Maybe you could try miming to it – it might fancy a spot of comedic entertainment. Or. Perhaps you could draw little pictures for it. It might get a fatal case of split sides – that would stop it from getting in the way of your brilliant schemes. Or you could frighten it away by removing all your clothes. Or you …"

Tracey's minder whispered, "Quick. Quick. You are being found out. Stop him. Stop him." She lashed back at Quentin, "Or I could try assessing its interest in the post-mortem of a cantankerous *not-really-an-astronomer*." She felt she was floundering and powerless, but immediately regretted her outburst.

Tracey's minder was saying, "Made it worse now. Everyone's time wasted. Everyone's time wasted." Tracey's only thought was that her attempts to help SiMiYah were going nowhere near the mark and, as her minder had been saying, she had probably made things worse. Wanting an end to the recriminations, Tracey hissed back at it, "Don't you start trying to be helpful now. Leave me alone." Her minder stopped mid-whisper, letting out a long, soft, hissing breath, like a small puncture in a bicycle tube. At the same time, the Mandelbrot pattern covering its skin shifted, becoming more elaborate, the edges and contrasts looking sharper. Only Conrad_27-8 noticed that. After its skin pattern had stabilised, the minder resumed its periodic whispering in Tracey's ear, quieter now, but also a little more frequent.

Kieran, who was standing close to SiMiYah, heard her minder repeating, "Impossible. You can't. Not you. You can't. Not you."

He sat next to SiMiYah and tapped her on the shoulder. When she looked at him, he said, "All the required parts are included."

SiMiYah let out a quiet moan and said, "All required parts are included? But I don't have everything I need. Yesterday I needed things. I had to get them. Today I need a Mandate-advocate. Now I have to get that. Will I always be chasing something forever retreating just beyond my fingertips? Minder gives it many names. But I have just one for it: my need. I have to chase it. It can always get away. Just out of reach, it could taunt me there, but instead it charms with an enticing smile. It promises me it is an easy prize. Then no sooner do I think I have caught hold of it than it is smoke between my fingers, slipping away to lure me to it again. So, I play this game of catch-and-chase, catch-and-chase. It makes me so weary sometimes. Why is it never enough? Is there another way? Tell me, KaRon, if it's missing does that mean it is not a required part? No, as minder says: I can only accept my punishment. Nothing I can do about it."

Kieran said, "Yes. Nothing is what needs to be done."

"I don't know what I can do. Except get exiled, get banished from everyone. Just like my friend DahTiYahYah was exiled. I didn't know how to help him then. I wanted to. Yes, my minder is right – even he didn't know what to do either. Even though he is very intelligent. He is an expert geologist, you know. He knows where all the minerals are. All the polyatomic non-metals. All the silicates, the carbonates, the … the others. He was always out doing geochemical, sedimentological, and paleontological investigations. He was always telling me. Now he is exiled. Poor DahTiYahYah."

Tracey said, "What was that? What are you saying? Would he even know about iron nuggets?"

"Yes, even iron. He told me. But he didn't care about that, he was interested in crystal polymorphism. He was always talking about it."

"You did just say, 'even iron'?"

"Yes … oh … no. But he is exiled. Banished."

"You can't find him?"

"Ye-e-s, maybe he could be found. I know a way. But he is exiled. He cannot come to see us."

"Then we will go to see him."

"Go to an exile zone? Us? Do the Mandates allow it? An exile must not leave an exile zone. Of course. But they do not stop others from going to an exile zone, do they? Who would even want to do that?"

"It seems we would."

SiMiYah said, "I suppose I could check the records of the Breach Judgement Office to find out where he was sent. What, minder? Yes, yes, yes. But he may not still be there. Even if he is there, he may not know where to find real iron. Even if he knows, he may not help me."

"You could just check that. Unless you think you should stay sitting on the floor."

SiMiYah's minder was able to come up with several reasons why it would be better to stay sitting on the floor. But Tracey took her arm and helped her to her feet. SiMiYah led them back to the building's entrance and she soon had the SeeDo there flashing information faster than the others could begin to follow.

Speaking to herself as much as anyone else, she said, "There he is, or was." Then turning to the others, she said, "I have these coordinates from Four Creeks town. It is too late to get there today. I will try tomorrow. I suppose I have to."

Tracey, standing close to SiMiYah, heard her minder saying, "Try. Try. Is it any use? Is the exile zone dangerous? Maybe try. Try a bit. Not more than you are able. Just a bit."

Tracey said, "We will go with you tomorrow."

SiMiYah said, "You will? Really? We may succeed then. At least I will find out what it is like … being exiled."

At the production pod's resource hub, SiMiYah ordered a GoOne to take her back to her dwelling. The others took their own GoSome back to their dwelling. The journey was a quiet one as they considered the situation and listened to the very different advice they were getting from their minders, advice which revealed they always knew exactly what their host was thinking and were intent on guiding every one of those thought processes.

"It's a good thing it's Saturday," said Tracey after she had spent a few minutes lying awake. She wondered if their brains went through any of their normal sleep cycles between when they 'departed' and when they 'returned' to their Earth bodies. She did not remember any time spent asleep after their 'return', but then again, she never really remembered any passing of time during her normal sleeping. Recalling that she had some plans for the day, Tracey stretched, sat, composed herself, gathered the things she had brought, and with a few words left as quickly as was polite.

Walking towards his hospital room, Tracey half hoped her father would be sleeping. Then she could be with him for a spell that would, this time at least, be peaceful. His eyes were half-open as she came through the door and they turned to her without expression.

"Good afternoon," she said. He remained impassive. She realised it might not have been the best greeting. "At least I hope it won't be too bad." She leaned over and gave him a gentle hug. "It's nice to see you."

He grunted, a grunt that carried no meaning beyond acknowledgement of her presence.

She sat in the chair that had apparently been chosen to discourage lengthy visits, or to reduce the risk of comfortable ones anyway.

"Good afternoon, bad afternoon – they are just different mixtures of chemicals."

Here we go again, thought Tracey. At least he seems quite alert for the moment.

Her father was alert and, this being his first non-clinical company for the day, was not going to give up the chance of feeling like something more than just another patient.

He said, "Being nearly dead makes you think about things, you know." He was looking to the ceiling. Tracey waited, knowing that he had not finished. "Good afternoon, is it? Nice to see me, is it? But what does that mean? Is it true?" He waited for an answer. Not long enough for her to come up with one. So he gave her his. "This is what happened when you saw me. To start with, some photons departed from some light source, then some of them collided with the atoms that make up my body and clothes. Some of those photons got absorbed, some bounced off, different coloured ones. But I am getting ahead of myself. Of all those photons that were bouncing off me, a tiny proportion headed straight at the tiny areas in this room that are the pupils of your eyes. Those photons went through your corneas, got diffracted by the lenses in your eyes, passed through the vitreous body behind the lenses, and then went through eight layers in your retinas to get absorbed by molecules making up your hundred million or so photoreceptor rod and cone cells that are the ninth layer of both of your retinas. With me so far?"

Tracey had heard the gist of this talk before. She nodded.

"OK. So, then it all starts getting a little more complex. In simple terms, the photons hitting your retinal rod and cone cells cause them to emit chemicals back through those layers of different types of cells that the photons just passed through. Their job is to do their own version of Photoshopping so that the chemical emissions from your hundred million or so rod and cone photoreceptors can squeeze into just about a million optic nerve fibres, per eye. Those optic nerves are a piece of work in themselves. Suffice it to say, the cells in the optic nerve fibres send electro*chemical* signals towards some neighbouring neuron, and when they get there it posts its little messages via some neurotransmitters (they're a whole new bunch of even more chemicals), which go over to its neighbour.

"Now we are getting to the brain, where all the action takes place. Basically, we are talking about a massive number of brain cells – neurons, each of them with minuscule structures called dendrites and axons that send chemicals to other neurons, whose own dendrites and axons send chemicals, and on and on. Maybe a hundred billion of these things sending electrochemical signals and having chemical exchanges firing them up all over the place, all the time, as they get chemical signals from sensory nerves all over the body. Now, it is actually another bunch of chemicals that tells me how I feel about those chemical signals. You have your dopamine and your serotonin, your norepinephrine and so on. Then don't get me started on the hormones: adrenaline, cortisol, melatonin, the rest. Put the right ones together and you end up with *good*; some other mix gives you *bad*."

The look Tracey was giving him was neither good, nor bad, closer to *tolerant*.

"Anyway, somewhere in all that you have it: *you saw me*. That, at a very high level, in an embarrassingly simplified form, is what happened earlier."

"In all of that, I wonder, where is *you* and where is *me*? And what is my *nice*?" Her wondering was to herself.

"Sorry to say this, but everyone and everything you are aware of is just some *thing* touching some long chain of rods and levers, the first rod bumping the next which slides some lever until in the end inside your dark skull a bunch of switches gets flicked, dials get tweaked. We think our seeing and hearing and touching is what is real. But all we have is switches and dials. *They* are what seeing and hearing and touching is. *They* are what is real. The only place the father you know is, is in your brain, buried in those dials and switches. Everything you think is happening outside you is actually just in your head. Everything."

"But there is something outside. What's in my head doesn't come from nothing."

"What is outside does not mean anything. All JABOC out there – means nothing. It only means something in your head. Switches and dials. You decide what everything means. Everything."

"I decide? How? Are those switches deciding? Or is there more to it?"

"That's all there is. You and I – just a bunch of switches in the dark, not even any little glowing lights. What else could there be?"

He saw that he was not going to get any answer from Tracey. She was looking at the floor. In his mind, his words were echoing sharp, too harsh.

"How can a switch decide? How do they know themselves?" he continued. "How could those switches and dials be so amazing?" It was a whisper, almost a plea.

"They …" Her father blinked. Slowly. Then another blink. Longer.

She saw he was suddenly tired. She looked at the time and said, "Oh, look. I didn't know I had been here that long. I should let you have some rest."

With another gentle hug she left her father wearing a tired, thoughtful, puzzled expression.

Chapter 9

"Did you solve the puzzle?" Sand-on-Stone spoke loudly while Mist-on-Water was still coming up the track, pushing against the branches that crowded in on it. He was sitting on the large rocky outcrop behind his cabin from the top of which you saw the whole valley and the village it cradled.

Breathing heavily, Mist-on-Water emerged from the forest. "Is it a trick?"

"Gladly met, daughter. No, not a trick, but a difficult puzzle."

"Gladly met, uncle. Tell me then."

"So-be. Now, we are asking: How does what is perfect become flawed, horribly flawed? If the root of the flaw was in it, it would not be perfect."

"Agreed."

"Here is the answer: the beautiful life, the perfect beings that the Source created, those beings created with unlimited power to themselves create, had a new conception. It was an impossible creation – they created something new in a place where everything that could be, already was."

"So-be. And what was that impossible creation?" She did not expect an acceptable answer. She was sure he had planted himself into the corner of this field. She sat on the bench under the tree, not on the end. He too sat.

"It was an idea."

"Say-you. What idea?"

"Not."

"Not? Just *not*?"

"'Just *not*, you say. For them it was a revolution."

"A revolution? It sounds more like the start of an afternoon nap," said Mist-on-Water.

"Hmm. Having everything, the only thing they had no knowledge of, no experience of, was *not.* Not freedom. Not power. Not peace. Not joy. Not knowledge. Not eternal. Not us. Not The Source."

"So, they decided to create this *not*?"

"Yes."

"This impossible *not*?"

"Yes."

"Did any of them doze off while this was going on?"

"So-be. Remember, these perfect beings were one. They were one in having all knowledge, all power. They could make new realms, new dimensions. So to experience *not*, to know *not*, they created new dimensions of *not*, the realm of *The Not.* What do you think was in them? What could they create there that would be new? New, where everything that could be already was?"

"I suppose you will say: nothing?"

"No, I will tell you."

Mist-on-Water's face took on an expression of exaggerated patience. Sand-on-Stone went on, "Nothing, of course. Nothing was in them."

"It sounds useful. Is that where you found these lessons?" While sounding gently sarcastic, Mist-on-Water found herself interested. She was looking for flaws but, wild as all of this seemed, so far at least it had a thin rational thread running through it.

"It was nothing, but with a shape. It had a form."

"You can give *nothing* a form?"

"Certainly." Sand-on-Stone held his hands in front of him, as if he were holding some invisible object. He said, "Imagine a metal box, sealed so that no air can get in or out."

"Hmm."

"Now, imagine you put a hole in the box, then you connect a metal tube to the hole, then you connect the air hole of a forge bellows to the tube. Then you could pump all of the air out of the metal box."

"Perhaps."

"When you have done that – pulled all of the air out – then inside your box you have? Nothing. But *nothing* with a form, it has a shape – the shape of the box that holds it."

"So-be. Perhaps *nothing* can have a form." Her interest was drifting.

"Yes, they made new forms – *not-forms*. The *not-forms* they made were very, very complex. Much, much more complex and intricate than anything we see under this sky."

"Who cares? Something like that couldn't do anything. Your tale is starting to resemble a bird in a land of no trees."

"Everyone should care. Those *not-forms* are still lurking. Not far away. Close."

Glancing over her shoulder, she said, "I don't care how close your phantoms are. What can a nothing do? It must be boring, sitting around doing nothing. Which is obviously all there is for them to do."

"Some of them think. Some of the *not-forms* are thinking devices, *not-minds,* if you like. There is a multitude of them – they create *not*-thoughts. Those beings made the Not Realm, but they had no way of knowing what was in it. So, they made them, those not-minds, and put them in a new kind of life. This life was not the true life they knew, changeless in days beyond counting. It was small, fragile, transient, but able to perceive the Not Realm, and able to receive the not-minds. Then the not-minds knew that realm, in their own not-way."

"But you said they are close. Are you saying it is here? We are in your Not Realm?" Now he had her attention again, her sceptical attention. She searched his face.

The look he returned did not deny it.

She had to let this sink in. "So-be." It was starting to come together for her. This was his explanation for how perfection could fall apart. Mist-on-Water thought he ought to simplify his tale a bit, if he wanted to keep his audience interested. A bit of dramatic tension would not go astray either.

A flying insect landed on a weed between her feet. She wondered what it was thinking, if it knew anything. She flicked at the weed. She saw Sand-on-Stone had more to say. "What did your not-minds think about, I wonder?" She yawned. "Probably mostly about napping."

"They did not nap. They were very fearful."

She stopped herself from glancing over her shoulder again. "Who's afraid of them?"

"It's not others who are afraid; it's them – the not-minds – that are afraid."

"Now you want me to ask: *why?*"

"Their creators had to place in them a single true idea. Just one true idea, kept secret, hidden deep at the very core of their edifices of thought, painstakingly concealed deep, deep below every idea *not* true, never to be allowed out. But they had to have it. It was essential for their protection."

"If you are going to make this another riddle, I don't think I want to play."

"So-be, not this time then. The true thought they had was: *I must guard myself against any true thought – even a single one will undo me.* You see, the *truth* for those creations was as light is to the darkness. If light is allowed into darkness, the darkness is no more. It is not that darkness is a thing that has been destroyed, it is not a thing – it is simply absence of light. So, allowing light into darkness just undoes its nothingness. It was the same for those not-minds. If they allowed into their multitude of swirling, ever-shifting *not* ideas, any true idea – any idea that was not a *not* idea – it would start their undoing. So their creators gave them the *not* idea we would call *fear* to sustain them. The *fear* idea was the most intricate and slippery and darkly glorious of all their *not* ideas. Afraid especially for itself, it hid, moved, and hid again, kept on moving and hiding, its hiding places named a thousand times – sometimes *safety*, then *justice*, then *protection*, *prosperity*, *health*, even *us*, and countless others. But all those names were really just one name: *not fear*. Do you see its cleverness? A pretence to not be the very thing it was. Those hiding places were only made because *fear* needed to hide. Without fear there was no need for them."

Mist-on-Water stretched her legs and an arm. "So, nothing they believed or saw was true? Or really real? Is the mighty hero going to be arriving soon? To clean up all of this mess? Or at least save them from your tyrant?"

"Fear was no tyrant for those not-minds. They wanted it. It protected them."

Mist-on-Water struggled to imagine those confused minds trapped in their feeble parodies of life. "They must have been nothing but mixed up."

"Yes – the only things they knew were *not*. Mixed up? Of course. But fear made them deny what they were doing to themselves, to deny the truth, of course. All was a deception, a self-deception. Then, of course, they had to deny their self-deception. And so began the explosion of *not ideas* concealing, deflecting, projecting – a vibrant edifice of senselessness, deception, and denials. They thought this thinking made them safe."

"Safe? Doubtful. Not happy either, I'm thinking. At least they were not forced to listen to stale old tales about things that had nothing to do with them."

"Yes, you make a good point. Why would those not-minds want to be like that? They were aware of themselves. They could not possibly be happy. They could not even know what true happiness was. How could they find for their existence any meaning, any purpose? Now we are getting to the very heart of things. Your bird will soon be finding its tree. But think: their creators had succeeded. They had done the impossible."

"So-be. I suppose that was one job done, but those beings' time might have been better spent fishing. Perhaps that one was next on their list of things to do."

"No, the job was not quite done. The perfect beings, born of the substance of The Source, they themselves still had no experience of *not* – they still had no knowledge of *what could not be*."

"So, being sensible, intelligent beings, they gave up on the impossible?"

"Not quite. No, they did something even more brilliant with their Not Realm. They placed their own awareness inside those not-minds. Every single one of them. Every one of the multitude had made a not-mind and every one of them put their own awareness entirely inside it."

"Say-you. And the point of it all was?"

"It worked – the perfect beings created by The Source knew *the not.* Their only awareness was of their *not-minds,* minds attached to organisms in the Not Realm, organisms that grew, perceived, withered away, freeing the awareness to attach again."

"You are lucky I am very intelligent. Most other students would be following you like a hundred-legger leaf crawler hobbling along with ninety-nine sore knees."

"Let me end your torment then. We are nearly there. Those ancient beings now think they are lost even though they are really still in their home – their only awareness is of the *not.* Even though their days have no number, their not-thoughts say they are an untidy pile of dust waiting forlorn, helpless, for the next puff of breeze. They are in distress inside everything that gives them joy. Being the purpose for everything, they know no meaning. Still eternally perfect, they know only flaw. Still abiding in each other and in The Source, they know only solitude."

Now Mist-on-Water felt sorry for beings supposedly perfect. That annoyed her.

Sand-on-Stone went on. "They had done the impossible, but only in their awareness, not in what was. Even though they were aware of what was not, it had no substance – a bit like we are aware of dreams. But it was the *only* thing they were aware of, it seemed real to them. They no longer knew The Source, they forgot their true selves, they forgot their home. They were lost and confused. The realm of The Not was all they knew, and they believed in it. It was The Separation."

"That was when it all went wrong? It all got broken."

"That was when they thought they had lost their unity. In their awareness they had lost truth, knowledge, eternity, everything. But they had lost nothing, Mist-on-Water. Nothing was broken. It was just the *not-minds* they had made. They were telling them they were apart. They had created no way back for themselves."

"No way back? More than a small oversight for beings so intelligent."

"Here and now, perhaps. But there and then, the idea of undoing anything had never even existed. *Undoing* is a *not* idea, you see? It was inconceivable. Up until then."

"So-be, where was your Source-with-no-name while all of this mischief was going on? Out checking for bluefire wasps?"

"The Source remained as it was."

"It just forgot about all of its beautiful, beloved, lost beings?"

"No, The Source was their way out. The Source knew what they were doing, and that they were not giving themselves any way out of *not.* But The Source is substance. It could fill every part of the *Not Realm*, even the tiniest corner. It waited until they were ready to use it to return to their home, to return to themselves."

"So it all ended happily ever after, say-you? They found their way back and got free? Is that what happened to them, those beings? Those magnificent, confused beings with their *not-minds.* What about us? How did we get stuck in their *Not Realm*?"

"Now I will tell you something strange."

"At last, you warn me. But your warning for yesterday's dinner has arrived just as breakfast is being laid out."

"Consider the stars. I speak the truth: each star is a sun just like the sun in our sky."

"They are very tiny suns then," said Mist-on-Water, sceptical.

"Not tiny. Some are much larger than our sun. But far, far off. Far off. Further than can be imagined. Some of them have worlds. Some like ours, many very different. Some of those worlds have life."

"Say-you."

"On one of those worlds, the creatures are split in two, split in two but with one mind divided between them, a part in each, like the single stem that bears two beetle-wing nuts. When those creature-pairs are born, not-mind speaks from one creature; it speaks to awareness in the other creature."

"It has possibilities. With the right training, you could make a self-minding child. No need to tell her what not to do. Are you saying those beings are still trapped in their not-minds on that world by that distant star? Too distant to matter."

"Not just there. Here too. Here they still believe they are trapped. They believe littleness is trapping what is beyond limit, decay is trapping what is never-ending. Because they see so little. Think on it."

Mist-on-Water thought about it for a long time, and then she said, "You are saying it is us? They are us? Me? You? Can it be true? It can't all be true."

"Say-you?"

"It's too much. It's too extreme." She tried to imagine a life with no end – a very, very different way of living. "It scares me."

"You would prefer a simpler truth, one closer to your broken familiars? Alas. You hate what is broken, as you must, so you hate its source, whatever source that is, one you name or one you don't. You think that hate ugly and hide it deep." His eyes held her tenderly.

She felt he had wandered deep inside her, to places she had not been, had not known were there, that he was holding up a lamp, a single small flickering flame, seeing things there, and now she was seeing them too. "Some of it could be as you tell it. How can I know which of it is true?"

"Remember – I name things that are nameless and cannot be named. I tell of things that cannot be told. But I say to you – if any of it is not true, none of it is. True, as far as any fickle word can be true. Think on it. Search out my words. If you find one piece, just one piece, even the smallest, that could not be as I have told it, I will abandon the whole tale and you can have your freedom. Freedom from me, at least."

Mist-on-Water felt no need to give an immediate answer. She had none, anyway. At that moment, she was noticing how peaceful it was in this clearing in the forest. The silence lengthened. Mist-on-Water stood and stretched and realised she had been sitting still for too long. She took some steps towards the food patch, felt a loosening of her joints and then an urge to stroll around the clearing for a while and maybe clear her mind a bit too. She took her time and by the time she had completed a meandering circuit, Sand-on-Stone had risen too and was poking about in his vegetable patch, extracting the occasional ambitious weed. She said to him, "How do you know all of this? You may be old, perhaps even a dusty relic from my great-grandparents' time. But you were not there, so long ago."

"No, you are right. This dusty relic was not there. All I do is walk my path, and sift and weigh the knowledge I find set down beside that path by others who have passed before me. Set down along those paths are many knowings – here, one passed on from the times of the great-grandparents of your great-grandparents, there, another tenderly set down by some wayfarer who by chance passed by last season. Some knowings are large, some are small, some are pretty, some are plain. As I have walked my path, I have seen countless knowings set down on it. Many I pass by, but some have the look of a new meal waiting for my empty belly. So I take a taste, here and there. When I taste the truth in them – when it reveals itself, when it nourishes and sustains, if it endures – then I know I can tread the path more surely. Sometimes as I walk, I find some precious small knowing has grown in me, if it has been truth on which I supped. Some small knowing, the answer to some mystery. So, I too place it down on the path for some other wanderer. For someone weary, with a hunger in his belly, who may find the answer to his mystery."

Mist-on-Water understood Sand-on-Stone was not offering her evidence, that he had no proof, that if she wanted to measure the truth in his tale, she would need to do it herself. "It is a curious tale. I give you that. But what use is this to me now? My bird is still looking for a tree."

"Yes, what use is it? Something? Nothing? We shall see."

"Shall we? Perhaps I have had enough of your source-with-no-name."

"As you wish."

The agreement gave way to silence for a time. Then Mist-on-Water turned their conversation to the village, the latest news. They let their talk meander down other paths.

Seeing that their time was being poorly spent, Sand-on-Stone said, "Perhaps it is enough for today."

Mist-on-Water was happy enough to leave early. It would be Red Moons festival the next day and she had a lot of extra chores. "Yes. I will think about your strange tale. Maybe I will have questions."

"Walk easy."

"Walk easy to you too."

Emerging from the forest track and walking down the path towards the village, it seemed to Mist-on-Water that there were fewer workers than usual in the fields, and the normal village hubbub was subdued. Coming into the village, she saw small groups in conversation – three here and there, two over there, four further on. On a corner she saw her father holding his carpentry tool carrier, talking to another male. They looked sombre.

"Has something happened?" said Mist-on-Water.

Her father said, "Hello, precious one. Well, we don't really know. You know that sickness that your friend, Clouds-at-Sunset's little brother, Song-at-Dawn, has? It looks like two more here have it. A lad and an older aunt.

And Song-at-Dawn is getting worse. Some of his fur is falling out."

"What is it, this sickness?"

"No one knows. It hasn't been seen here before. The Elders will probably seek out one of the oracles for a consultation."

Observation Series: **Threats and Predators**

Summary of observations. My little sweeties are unbreakable. You cannot even take them apart. Yet they are afraid all the time. Sometimes they even think they are getting damaged, but they do not know it is only the camouflage they are hiding in getting removed. Lucky for them, they are harmless. I really want to take one home. It should not be too hard to look after.

Chapter 10

The next evening, Tracey, Kieran, and Conrad_27-8 were seated in Quentin's apartment. They faced Quentin, who was standing with his laptop balanced on his hand.

Quentin said, "My esteemed colleagues, welcome to this, the first international seminar on the planet of Allunda. Please restrain your applause." They were attentive but there was no applause.

After it became clear that the polite silence would not be broken, Quentin said, "Fine. Here is what I have so far. The daytime temperature on the planet at the current time of year is about forty-two degrees Centigrade, with the humidity always over ninety percent. It only goes down a couple of degrees overnight."

Tracey said, "What's that on a proper thermometer?"

Conrad_27-8 said, "Forty-two degrees Centigrade is one hundred-and-seven-point-six degrees Fahrenheit."

Tracey said, "What? With that humidity we should have been melting."

Quentin said, "I guess they evolved for it. And they have their *sleep time*, or as we would say, their hibernation period, except for them it's in the hot part of the year. They hibernate for good reason. In the hot part of the year, the temperature rises to over fifty-five Centigrade. It seems the planet's orbit is relatively elliptical."

Conrad_27-8 said, "Fifty-five Centigrade – that's one hundred-and-thirty-one-degrees Fahrenheit."

Quentin continued, "At least with the clouds, sunburn is not a concern. We were nearly three metres tall."

Tracey said, "Why do you have to be such a scientist? What's wrong with American units?"

Quentin said, "Weren't you born in New Caledonia?"

Tracey said, "That was a long time ago. I mean, not that long, but long enough. I mean, I was only young then."

Conrad_27-8 said, "I can convert that."

Quentin said, "But you won't." He said to Tracey, "It's about ten feet."

Tracey said, "Ten feet? I didn't feel ten feet tall."

Quentin said, "Finally, their gravity is about seventy percent of Earth's and their day is just under twenty-six hours long."

Conrad_27-8 said, "Seventy percent of Earth's gravity is approximately six-point-eight-six-four-nine metres per second per second. Would you like that in imperial units?"

Quentin said, "Cut it out or you're going to be known as 27-6."

Conrad_27-8 said, "27-6?"

"Yes, in memory of a couple of missing appendages."

Tracey said, "Anything else?"

Quentin said, "Plenty. Plenty of other stuff missing. Stuff I need to weasel out of them somehow. Not least, the thing you have all been wondering about too." He waited for someone to name that thing. No one named anything. "Yes, which particular star we happen to be taking our little field trip to. Wouldn't we all love to know that now? But we probably never will. I couldn't find any usable measurements of their sun's spectrum. Of course, they know nothing about any other stars in their neighbourhood. So, even assuming it is probably F-class or G-class, eliminating about ninety percent of stars in the galaxy – no doubt 27-8 here can confirm – that leaves us with just about thirty billion possibilities."

Conrad_27-8 said, "Probability theory is not a useful tool for this problem."

Tracey said, "OK. Interesting, maybe. But I don't see how any of that changes anything on the ground in Allunda. Are we ready to go?"

There were no objections. As they got themselves ready, Kieran was singing softly to himself Westlife's song *Safe*, the words slightly wrong again:

"How you gonna free your mind cos the dream you have ain't real?"

On Allunda, Tracey, Quentin, Kieran, and Conrad_27-8 took a now-familiar GoSome to SiMiYah's dwelling. She was waiting outside again, wanting to avoid the risk of difficult questions on what the five of them were doing. After the greeting formalities were over, SiMiYah explained that the exile zone her leading geologist friend DahTiYahYah, had been banished to was near the next town, a distance that converted to about two hundred kilometres away via the high-speed transit interconnector. A short stroll returned them to the transit lounge in the resource hub, where SiMiYah set their destination to a terminus on the outer edge of that town.

When their GoSomes had come to a smooth stop, rather than the resource hubs they were used to, they saw a simple terminus at the edge of a cultivated field. Leaving the GoSomes, the group stood on a wide flat path, taking in their surroundings. The path was bordered on one side by neat rows of a large bushy plant covered in yellow berries, some turning pink. On the other side grew neat rows of leafy plants resembling rhubarb, the long leaves purple at the base grading to dark green at the tips, spikes of pointy flowers shooting up from the centre standing tall over the leaves. In one of the rows a machine was working on the plants, tending them, or harvesting from them, or both. Conrad_27-8 snapped on his BringSeeDo and informed Quentin that they had covered the distance in sixty-three Earth second-order time units (meaning minutes), to the nearest time unit.

"Some in-flight entertainment wouldn't have gone astray," said Quentin. "And they forgot to send our flying plate transfer service."

Tracey and SiMiYah were several paces away, standing in the middle of the path. Tracey said, "Where to now?"

SiMiYah said, "Oh, let me flip you the map." Placing her BringSeeDo on her head over her ear, she made a few click and chirp sounds. The others put on their BringSeeDos, saw the message SiMiYah had sent, and inspected the map. It showed the GoSome terminus, the path they were standing on, their position on it, and a detailed representation of the fields on both sides, including the position of the machine at work a few rows of plants away. Beyond the fields, details became scant, except for a border marking the exile zone and the path which continued beyond the fields until it crossed into the exile zone.

Tracey said, "Do we have any transportation?"

SiMiYah said, "We will need to walk. I am sorry. I don't think any of the Mandates will be breached. Maybe the Well-being Mandate." She recited the Well-being Mandate, rote-fashion, as she had done hundreds of times as a child in class: "*Every citizen must have the opportunity to seek and be provided the things she/he wants for her/his personal well-being.*" Then, talking to herself as much as to anyone else, she said, "Do we need transport for our well-being? Maybe. If the Mandate-advocate needs an iron nugget for his well-being, then it is possible. Because well-being is not just physical, it is mental too. Everyone knows that. His well-being will be very satisfied if we can get one for him. He will have it forever and his well-being will be assured forever. Well, maybe not forever. But a long time. Probably. Unless … Unless, do you know, TraaCee, what happens sometimes is that you get something essential for your well-being, and it is very nice. Maybe even nicer than you were hoping – sometimes. Then one day, it isn't as nice for you anymore. Has it ever been like that for you? Yes? Maybe even just the next day, it isn't as nice as that moment you first got it. Even if it isn't broken or anything. As soon as the next day. The very next day. Yes? Huh? No, that is right, minder, it *is* good, when that happens, then I can get more."

While she was speaking, Tracey noticed SiMiYah's minder was getting increasingly fidgety. Still wanting to try to understand them better and maybe find a way they could be made to help, Tracey moved in close enough to

SiMiYah to overhear what her minder was saying to her. She had been expecting more, but its words were mostly, "Remember your need; remember body. That is importance."

Wanting to be empathetic, Tracey said, "Yes, what are we but our bodies?" Even as the words came out, they rang false in her ears. Her minder said, "Take care. Keep the secrets. Do not make it your fault." Trying to find a way both to be true to what she now knew as an agent of the Galactic Council (she winced inwardly at that) and SiMiYah's beliefs, Tracey went on, still feeling she was about to blunder, "So, of course, our body's well-being is ours. But does your minder know of any other way to be … to be …" but Tracey's Allundrian mind found no word for 'happy'. She was puzzled, then insight flickered. Wrapping around her she felt a heavy sadness for the beings here. Realising that SiMiYah had said something, Tracey pulled herself back to the conversation.

"Sorry, I was distracted. What did you say?"

SiMiYah said, "I said, to be what?"

SiMiYah's question dismissed the remnants of the gloomy thoughts that had started to descend. Tracey said, "Um … I mean, any other way to have well-being. Does your minder know of any other way to have well-being? A way that is more, um, *enduring*."

SiMiYah said, "I will listen. But first, I must give it a problem. What about this: I feel I need more well-being. I need help."

Tracey strained to hear SiMiYah's minder. She caught snatches, not fully coherent, like listening to a poor cell phone signal, chunks being dropped. What she caught was, "Listen: body need … body want … body know. Body you … body need … body want … body know. Many ways. It is all." A gist, not a solution. She wondered what important bits she had missed. She wondered if she had missed any important bits at all.

"Well, of course it is my body. It tells me what I need for well-being. And not just for plain old just-enough well-being. Not just so I don't starve and that kind of thing. It tells me about fun-times, real fun-times. They're wonderful – if I'm hungry, I could just eat grain every time. But my body tells me about a million nicer ways. I can have delectable fruits, aromatic spices, luscious creamy juice blends, and my favourite – sliced dawnflower melon stuffed with watermist seeds. You know it? Yes – truly divine. All of that, so much." SiMiYah glanced back to Quentin, Conrad_27-8, and Kieran who were still several paces behind them, to their left. "And you know, making a baby could be, well, some good exercise for a micro-daypart, or two. But it's not just that, is it? So much more. Yes, our bodies know. I don't know how. They can't think. I wonder how. And minder, too. Minder knows. Sometimes I think it would be nice if it wasn't all such a … such a … struggle. Is that it? The word? If we could just rest, if we could just have peace; and keep it. But then our well-being would just fritter away. What do I want? If everything weren't so … *limited*."

"Limited?"

"You, know: things, time, us. But it is silly to think like that. It doesn't work like that, does it? I do it sometimes – think those things, but minder helps me. Minder always tells me. Minder knows, doesn't it? Minder says it is all good, that there is no more, but then sometimes, sometimes … Minder works hard, poor thing. But then, you know, something else, like a gentle call, a faint light, serene – but what is it? Unknown, something unknown, reaching … and so I turn … then … just regret."

About ten minutes later, with SiMiYah still talking, the neat fields ended abruptly and the straight, smooth, flat path became a windy track, cracked in places, now rising and falling, entering a disarrayed, lush, overgrown forest, a celebration of jumping, gliding, and flying wildlife riotous high in the canopy. A dull light made it to the ground.

Tracey saw from her map that they were about a third of the way there already, but all their minders were getting more jittery than usual.

They continued along the track which, while not as flat, was still easy going. Had it not been for the jitteriness of their minders, it would have been a very pleasant long stroll. Rounding a long smooth bend in the path as it followed a low hill, they saw a small valley open before them. Dispersed around the slopes to either side stood several dwelling structures. They were made of the same material as the dwellings they were familiar with, but smaller, perhaps a third of the size, and their construction was not as perfect either, giving hints of less skilled builders.

Tracey heard SiMiYah's minder's words, louder than usual, "Exile zone now. Need help. Beware." It was very agitated and taking less care than usual in making itself inconspicuous. Tracey saw an Allundrian working in a small orchard below one of the structures. Before any of the others could object, she and SiMiYah started towards him and their presence in the valley became known.

The Allundrian in the orchard, hearing Tracey and SiMiYah's approach, turned to them and leaned against the tree he was working on, watching them approach. He was larger and stronger than any Allundrian they had seen before. While they were still walking towards him, he bent down and picked up a long knife – it looked ceramic – with a serrated blade.

When she reached the place on the path closest to the orchard worker, SiMiYah crossed her arms in the formal greeting gesture and said, "Always equality." The orchard worker placed the blade of the knife against a branch above his head, one as thick as a wrist, pulled the knife down in a single stroke, and made a clean cut through the branch. He said, "Always equality," but his minder was very agitated, darting from shoulder to shoulder, tugging at and shaking his ears with both hands while it whispered into them continuously and looked sideways at the visitors.

SiMiYah said, "We are visitors here."

Quentin muttered, "You don't say. Let's also point out that it's cloudy today."

It made SiMiYah even more nervous, but she carried on, "We are looking for someone. Can you help us? Do you know who is living here? Your orchard is bearing a lot of fruit."

The orchard worker said, "Visitors do not come here. Only exiles and vengeance seekers. I claim the Safety Mandate."[6] He moved back a step and to the side so that he was half hidden behind the tree he had been pruning.

Tracey said, "The Safety Mandate? Why?"

The orchard worker said, "Minder has already warned me that you will attack me and that I will need to defend myself. If you kill me, others here will seek vengeance."

Thinking aloud, Quentin said, "Seek vengeance? Which Mandate would that be, then?" In the quiet valley his voice carried better than he had expected.

Moving further behind the tree, the orchard worker said, "You are Mandate-trained, then? It is true, there is no Mandate that I can claim. Leave me alone. By the Safety Mandate I will defend myself. I will." The tall, strong, lethally armed Allundrian cowered behind his tree and stared wide-eyed down at the five visitors standing timid and deferential on the path below him.

Tracey said, "You have the Mandates here too?" She was not worried about her ignorance arousing suspicions here – everyone was ignorant about the exile zones.

"Yes, of course. What else will guide and protect us? They bring us everything, unless you breach them like I did seventeen years ago."

SiMiYah said, "What was your breach? Why were you exiled here?"

The orchard worker came out from behind his tree a little and said, "It was such a long time ago. It happened when I was working away from my hometown. I had met a beautiful lass there." He stopped for a memory, a memory of one long since gone. "We had started the

---

[6] Safety Mandate: "every attack must be repelled"

partner commitment ceremonies. Then I had to go back to my hometown for a bit. While I was away, she … she went with someone else. They went together a few times, this other male and her – no, several times it was. Then I found out what had been happening, what my partner had been doing. It was after we had done the clan link too. Then she told me about it. She felt bad. I wanted to know why. She said she had been lonely. She said it was because her minder was talking a lot about the Well-being Mandate. She was confused. She tried to tell me why. But she didn't know herself. I said I could never trust her. She was having – I suppose she has had – our baby. It must be grown-up now. I have never seen it. She ruined everything. I can never trust anyone again."

Tracey said, "I don't understand. Why did you get exiled?"

"She and her parents and I all argued. Then they claimed I breached the Justice Mandate. I hadn't corrected the wrong."

Tracey said, "*You* didn't correct the wrong?"

"Yes. When we argued I broke a family heirloom. It was a rare and ancient amulet tracing back to one of their birth-clan's tribal times."

Tracey said, "Oh. The amulet couldn't be replaced?"

"No, it was. I had to see a hundred archaeologists, but I got a replacement. It was the display case. It wasn't the same. They don't make them anymore. I know – nothing could be done after that."

Tracey said, "Exiled seventeen years for the wrong display case. I don't think I will ever get these Mandates."

Quentin said, "We are wasting our time with this pumpkin. Let's find someone else." Quentin was pleased that his Allundrian brain had found a word for pumpkin, one of his favourite vegetables – obviously, the vegetable here was not the same one, but it must be close. He felt he should try to get a taste. The others were looking at the knife in the orchard worker's hand. He was pointing it at Quentin, who was looking at the small plots of plantings round about, still thinking about pumpkins.

Kieran said, "Operating mistakes do not matter. You cannot damage the required pieces. Consumables may need to be replaced."

The orchard worker said, "What? What was that?"

Kieran said, "Nothing important can be lost. Anything lost was not important."

"Lost? Not important? The broken display case? Or my partner-promise? Which? They are not the same."

"Everything that is not important will go away."

"Well, of course. But you do not need to abuse me like that. It is obvious: nothing stays forever. Important or not. I suppose in a million years, none of it will matter. Or maybe even a thousand, or a hundred, or even ten. I don't know. If it won't matter then, why does it matter now? Quiet, minder, I want to talk to him. I want to know this."

Kieran said, "What really matters now always matters. What seems to matter now is nothing when you find what really matters."

"Nothing? It was not nothing. My exile is not nothing. It has ruined my life. My partner-promise was not nothing. I carry the scars every day. Deep, deep scars." With those words, the orchard worker slumped against the tree, as if his powerful limbs were suddenly too weak to bear his own weight.

"What you carry, you hold onto. What you hold onto, only you can set down."

"I am holding on, am I? How? Ah, you mean in my mind. Yes, of course it is in my mind. That is obvious, even for me." It was more his thoughts spoken aloud than a response for Kieran.

"It is as you choose."

"As *I* choose? I don't want to be like this. I hate it." He sliced off another thick branch. "It's not *me*. Minder helps me. Minder chooses. I want to be … to be … something else. *That* is what I choose. But I don't think I know what it is. Maybe I have never experienced it. I don't know how to choose it. Is there something else? If I want something else, why do I hold on to what I do not want? Minder?" But his minder had stopped still, still and silent, both tiny hands clutching its host's ear, burying its head under the flap. It was the first time Tracey had seen one of them unmoving, not talking, even for a moment. The moment was fleeting. Then it resumed its usual restless vigilance and it said, "He attacks. He attacks."

Kieran said, "If nothing can damage the important pieces, there is no attack. All operating mistakes can be corrected."

"You are confusing me. Maybe you should just go. Is it all really in my mind? All of it? I never looked at it that way. Where else can it be? I know my pain. I know I don't want it. But I have held onto it for so long. Was that a mistake? How can I stop?"

During the exchange between the orchard worker and Kieran, Quentin had wandered several paces along the path and was looking at the other dwellings to see if any of their occupants appeared.

The orchard worker said, "Who are you looking for?"

SiMiYah said, "His name is DahTiYahYah. I knew him five years ago. Then he was exiled here. It was a long time ago. He could be anywhere now. He was a leading geologist. Very clever. He probably knows how to find iron nuggets even. Maybe even knows where some are already. He probably changed his name too. It seems most exiles have to do that – clan honour, you know. I am sorry to have disturbed you. I will have to work out what I can do now. Probably nothing. I do hope your exile is revoked." She said the words, but felt it was a futile hope.

The orchard worker said, "He lives over there," pointing to a dwelling further down the path, on the other side.

SiMiYah said, "Who? DahTiYahYah?" She turned to Tracey, took hold of one of her hands, and hopping from one foot to the other said, "You found him. You found him. Let's see if he is there."

Except for Quentin, they gave the arms-at-sides farewell gesture to the orchard worker.

The orchard worker said, "Thank you for changing your minds about attacking me. May the Mandates preserve you." He watched them, still standing partly behind the tree, until they had moved a long way down the path.

As SiMiYah walked on, their encounter with the orchard worker still in her mind, she said, "Everything begins with fear."

"What?" Tracey had stopped and was looking at SiMiYah intently, concerned.

SiMiYah said, "Oh, sorry. I don't know where that came from. It just popped into my head. Minder didn't even say it. But is it right? Minder tells me the good reasons for the things it says to do. It always has some. Good reasons, that is. But just sometimes I get a feeling it is not that simple. Something is hiding behind those reasons. I will tell you – I have a little game I play with minder's reasons sometimes: I ask them: 'Why? Why, why, why?' You see, every answer gets another 'why?' And, do you know, when minder has run out, it always seems to end up with fear. Even when I think I have found a reason that is very good, very pure, if I look behind it closely enough it ends up having some *it-might-be-lost*, some *don't-want-happen*, something like that lurking behind it. It does make me sad. Maybe it is just me. You could try it. Maybe everything begins with fear."

"Surely not *everything*." But for the moment, nothing came to Tracey that would refute the idea. Her minder offered nothing; it seemed to be occupied with what might go wrong in the dwelling they were approaching.

SiMiYah went on. "Maybe I am all wrong on this. Our heads are filled with many thoughts, always coming and going, in and out. So many, many thoughts. Who controls them all? Where do they come from? Yes, minder, I know you give me many helpful ideas. But even minder, where do its ideas come from? My friend, RetWetFubFarn, works in the Tashex – you know, the exchange for town asset shares, where you can buy and sell your shares in farms and factories and all that. I just have a few holdings, but their prices are going up and down all the time. Up then down, then up then down again. I asked RetWetFubFarn why the price of my holdings kept going up and down so much, so often. Every day. All the time. The business is not any different today from yesterday, or this afternoon from this morning. Why should its value change so much?"

Conrad_27-8, whose more-than-adequate income on Earth derived from his models for profiting from stock market price movements, said, "The textbooks say the price is set by a function of the income stream, divided by the rate of return that can be obtained from assets of similar risk. But it is actually quite a lot more complicated. You see …"

"Precisely." She reconsidered. "I think. Well anyway, it was something like that. RetWetFubFarn told me that's what market theory says. But then the price should not be changing so much. He says the smart people know that it is really fear and greed that set the price. Fear – the fear of losing if the price looks like it is going down, and greed – the hunger for profit if the price is going up. But I think it is just fear."

Tracey had to ask. "What about that hunger for profit?"

"Is it hunger for profit, or fear of missing out on what everyone else is getting? Why? Because of fear of not being able to buy that iron nugget they want, or whatever it is. Why? Because of fear of not having their well-being? Why? Because … well, it's the Mandate. Why? I don't know that one. It must be why we have the Safety Mandate." She stated it by rote. "*The Safety Mandate: every attack must be repelled.* But it never really works. It just seems to make another one come. Is it even possible to be safe?"

She looked at her companions. None of them knew.

"Of course, I'm not usually noticing it – all that confetti of fear. Are you? Who would want to be afraid all the time? If we noticed, we would stop. I must be wrong. Minder never says this. But I keep looking behind some of my thoughts, at their *why*. Then I notice. When I do notice, quicker than a blink, minder has put up something else to notice. But when I'm looking behind fear – I see nothing. It's the start. Fear of missing out, fear of an end to a good time, fear of …" Running dry, she looked to the others for suggestions.

"Fear of condemnation," Tracey said.

"Yes, and fear of failure."

Conrad_27-8 had nothing to add. He could not quantify fear and shied away from it, convinced it had nothing to do with him. Quentin had not been listening. He had not seen any pumpkins, which had led him to wondering how they would get anything to eat here.

"It's the source. But what is its source? I don't know. There *is* a lot of it about, don't you think? Fear. Not real FEAR fear, not *I-can't-even-move* fear. Not that. It's all the dragging dour doubts, the sudden slaps of uncertainty, the piteous pleas of unease, the nipping nags of need, the whining what-if worries. They come in every shape and size. Once, one of my distant uncles could not go outside because he had anthophobia – yes, he was afraid of flowers. They cling to everything, everywhere – fears. Everything begins with fear. No one wants it that way, maybe they don't even know. But maybe you can see it if you look. At least we have the Safety Mandate."

Kieran said, "The Safety Mandate does not remove fear. The Safety Mandate reveals the mistake of fear."

Quentin, seeing nothing resembling a café, said, "Maybe you two could put on your smiley faces so we don't scare away our chum in there before we have even begun." They had reached the dwelling that the orchard worker had pointed to.

SiMiYah led them up the entrance path. Reaching the entrance doors, a digital voice said, "By the applicable Mandates, announce yourselves and your purpose."

SiMiYah said, "It is SiMiYah of BlueLake town and her colleagues. We are here to meet with DahTiYahYah." A few moments later, the doors opened and the voice said, "Proceed to the gathering room."

In the gathering room, DahTiYahYah was standing as they entered. He and SiMiYah looked at each other for an awkward moment before habit kicked in. SiMiYah crossed her arms on her chest and said, "By the Mandates: always equality."

DahTiYahYah gave her a wry look.

Then SiMiYah realised equality between her and an exile was not much in evidence. She said, "I mean … it is good to see you."

DahTiYahYah ignored the faux pas and indicated the sitting mats. "Please sit. I am afraid I cannot offer you resource hub refreshments here."

They sat. Barging through mounting layers of awkwardness, SiMiYah explained her predicament. DahTiYahYah listened carefully, saying nothing.

In the end, SiMiYah said, "Do you think you could tell us how to find an iron nugget?"

DahTiYahYah said, "I can certainly tell you where to look for one. Naturally, the known lodes where larger quantities could be found were exhausted many hundreds or thousands of years ago. But if you only need one, you may get lucky. The data is available if you know how to interpret it."

SiMiYah said, "I have only a few days. What would be the quickest way?"

DahTiYahYah said, "Wait just one daysplit. I will check something." He left the room, coming back a couple of Earth minutes later.

When he came back, he was holding an iron nugget. It was larger than his hand, irregularly shaped but more or less a flat oval with smooth indentations over its surface, like a piece of molten metal that had solidified suddenly. It was rust brown; nothing about it was attractive.

Holding it up, DahTiYahYah said, "I thought I still had it. This is from my collection. It is quite extensive, of course."

SiMiYah gasped, leaped up, and said, "That is exactly what I need. Can you tell us how to find one?"

"Perhaps, but there may be an easier way."

"What way?" In her excitement, for once, she was almost lost for words.

"I don't really want this one."

"You don't want it? We could have it? We could? Us? Me, I mean?"

"I think so."

"But it is very valuable."

"It's of no particular interest to me. Its rarity makes it a bit of a geological curiosity, I suppose. But it has no real geological significance."

"Are you saying – are you saying you will give it to us?"

"I don't want it. I am trying to reorganise my collection. This doesn't really fit. The collection is more to demonstrate a system of crystal classification based on crystallographic axes and other properties. This one was in my throwing out pile."

"We can have it then? With it I will get myself a Mandate-advocate. The one I have found – the one who wants the iron nugget – is very experienced. It is very good of you to help me like this. There must be a Mandate that you have excelled at. I can't think of which one it is just now."

"Yes. But first I need you to do a small thing for me. It is only so that I can satisfy the Well-being Mandate."

"You want me to do a small thing? I hope I can do it. I am not sure. It is small, you say?"

"For you, yes. You do know the clan head of 300-294-565 clan?"

"Of course. You know 300-294-565 clan is my paternal birth clan. We all know the clan head."

"Good. You just need to get her to revoke her Mandate-charge against me and that will lift my exile."

SiMiYah said, "Revoke a Mandate-charge? So you can return from exile? But no one does that. After all the time and expense of getting a judgement – why would they? But she is my clan head. Perhaps the Clan Mandate applies here. And the Clan Mandate instructs us: the members of the clan are special, and all must be upheld. My clan must surely help." Another thought was given to her. "No, that is right, why would she listen to me? Yes, I understand, I should not bother her, or maybe annoy her."

Tracey said, "We are so close, we can't give up now. I don't know what your minder is worried about. It cannot do any harm to talk to her."

SiMiYah said, "Yes, for most people talking does no harm. It just doesn't work that way with me. Sometimes." After a pause, "Often." Then, "Usually."

DahTiYahYah was looking at the iron nugget, turning it around in his hand.

The movement caught SiMiYah's attention and she watched the nugget as it moved, close enough to touch. She said, "I agree then. We will try."

Walking back to the transport terminus, Tracey said to SiMiYah, "What did he do anyway? To get exiled?"

"It was the clan head of my paternal birth clan. She published an academic paper about clans. Its title was 'Equally Special'. It was much admired by everyone. Except DahTiYahYah. He posted a dislike to it. Everyone was outraged. Specially all the ones who had admired it most. So, he was exiled for a double breach – the Safety Mandate and the Justice Mandate. Because she is a clan head – very powerful."

Quentin said to Tracey, "Hey. Let me make sure I have this right. First, the trusty Safety *and* Justice Mandate put away our rock-addled mate back there. Because presumably the dusty old Freedom Mandate has some clause in it prohibiting the use of any words that make sense. Now, we're bringing the good old Clan Mandate into play to loosen up the clan boss. What happened to this Clan Mandate thing for rock-guy? Why didn't his clan gang stand up for him? These guys ticked the Justice Mandate box but smashed this Clan Mandate to pieces at the same time. Is a Mandate a Mandate or not? You can't have it both ways. Oh, yes – and then his whole exile thing has to poke the Freedom one in the eye again. They must have done some fancy side-stepping on that one. Or should I just stop trying to see how any of this might involve rational thinking?"

Tracey said, "I'm sure it makes sense to them."

"Or … or, maybe they just kind of hope it makes sense as long as no one comes up with a Take-a-Tiny-Peek-and-Think-About-What-is-Going-On Mandate."

"They're making it work for themselves."

"Certainly. Just like giving your four-legged tail-wagger best friend the shiny promotional picture of his tasty dinner to eat is an example of 'making it work'."

At the terminus, they ordered a GoOne for SiMiYah and a GoSome for everyone else. When they saw the vehicles arriving, Tracey said, "Tomorrow we will talk to your clan head."

SiMiYah said, "Do you think I should just prepare for exile? Myself? Minder is saying that. It must be the way."

Tracey said, "Do you really want to listen to that?"

SiMiYah said, "Want to listen? Is listening to minder a choice? I wonder. Not listen? Why not? But yes, that is it – how will I get guidance? Does it matter if I want it or not, if it is what I need? Why don't I want it, if I need it? But yes, that is right: I – everyone – needs to be reminded about the Mandates. But why is there so much no, no, no; not, not, not?"

Chapter 11

Arriving back at Sand-on-Stone's hut early on the day after the Red Moons festival, Mist-on-Water saw that he was once again sitting high on the rocky outcrop behind his cabin. He was twisting yarn made from fibres pulled from longleaf plants. Walking up to the rock and beginning to clamber up it, she said, "I have found it. I should have seen it straightaway."

"Did you lose something?"

"Only my wits, perhaps." She paused as she tested her footing where the rock was smoother and steeper. "It is obvious: those *not-minds* cannot be here. Not with us. Not in us." She shuddered slightly as she spoke those last words aloud for the first time. The idea, flawed though it was, *did* discomfort her.

"Say-you?"

"I-say." She waited for Sand-on-Stone to ask her to explain her discovery. But he just kept on braiding his rope, his fingers nimble in silence.

"This is why: everything is not all just *not*. You are wrong about us being trapped in *not-ideas*. What about all the good things, and the very good things? Like my family, my friendships, good food, laughter, true love."

Sand-on-Stone gave her an enquiring sideways look when she said, 'true love'.

Mist-on-Water saw it and went on quickly, "What about all the beautiful things? You may have even heard about them – the music, the singing, the exhilarating story, the golden dawn bird, yesterday's sunset. Even if I see something not so good, have some *not-thought* as you would say, what about hope? Even when life is bad, very bad, just a tiny hope can carry someone along. It can take her through it. What about those thoughts? They cannot come from your *not-minds*. It's all just a fable."

"Ahhh –I see. You are correct." Then Sand-on-Stone added, "Of course."

Mist-on-Water smiled, pleased at herself. But it still left her with a lot of unanswered questions. She did not want to let Sand-on-Stone off this little hook without finding out if he had something else, something useful, to offer. She said, "Tell me what you think then. My friend, Clouds-at-Sunset, she has an older brother. We think he has had the sadness. He has had it for several days now. He is not quite himself, a bit mopey. He tries to hide it, but we can see. I was thinking about him and your *not-minds*. Does he want his sadness? It seems the answer is both 'no' and 'yes'. No: he does not like it. Yes: but he thinks it is right, somehow. Right to be sad. What do I tell him? Can we help? Now that your source-with-no-name is safely back with the children's stories, what do you say to that?"

"You are thinking you may let not-mind be of use – just for this one? So-be. But remember what I said: if part of it is not true, none of it is. But if it were you – with the sadness – what would you say the answer was?"

"I would say I'd fight it. I would defeat it."

"How would you know if you had won? Would you stand over the carcass?"

"There would be no carcass."

"Then it had no life. You cannot kill what never lived; cannot destroy what never was. You cannot fight *not-mind*."

"Because?"

"Try this. Hold your hands together like this." He held up his hands, fingers interlocked. "Tightly. No, tighter. Tighter, so you cannot pull them apart."

Mist-on-Water's hands were locked tight into each other.

Sand-on-Stone said, "Now pull them apart." Mist-on-Water gave him a scornful look. "Just try it. Feel it."

She tried pulling her hands apart, could not, and released them. "The point is?"

"What will happen if you keep doing that? If you keep trying to pull your hands apart."

"My friends will give me strange looks and stop visiting?"

"Yes. And your arms will grow stronger. Resisting strengthens. You tire and stop, but only to rest. You are not defeated. It is the same with *not-mind.* You may struggle against it. But each time you do so, what do you do? You feed it. The battle is a *not-idea.* If you set *not-ideas* against each other, they may slip away after a time, but there is no defeat. You leave them a little bigger. So, to fight *not-mind* is to strengthen it. It wants it. It needs it, that or some other kind of attention."

"What then?"

"If you do not want to make it stronger, disregard it."

"So, Clouds-at-Sunset's brother must accept a sadness hanging around his neck, teasing him like a little incessant nuisance sister, that naughty taunting sister not of his parents, but one he will always have?"

"Only until *not-mind* is no more. Until then, who cannot endure even the worst little sister? If you remember how little she is."

"You mean the *not-mind* that I have already proven is a shallow fiction?"

"Ah yes, back to that answer you discovered. That answer of all your good things. The ones you say disprove *not-mind.* Best to not be too hasty. The answer you found is correct, but not complete."

"Not complete? I know a lesson perhaps you should learn. It's called *when to give up*. Why is it not complete?"

"I'm not sure you're ready to teach that *when to give up* lesson. I don't think you have fully mastered it yourself. Would you try another little experiment with me? You might learn something from it."

"Another experiment? To learn something? If you must. That is why they lock me up here."

"First, please close your eyes."

She closed them.

"Imagine it is dusk, and on your face rest the last rays of the sun's warmth before evening falls."

She imagined it.

"Now, imagine that you have no sight, and you have never seen the sunset."

She frowned, wondering if she still wanted to go along with this, but she kept her eyes shut.

"Now, let me ask you this. The rays you feel warming your face are pleasant, are they not?"

She gave the finger taps of agreement.

"You like them? Those warm rays. They are good? During the cold night you will await their coming again in the morning?"

She affirmed all of that.

"Now, let me tell you this, you who have never seen. Even though you can feel its warmth, I tell you – you know nothing of the sunset until you have seen it."

Mist-on-Water opened her eyes. "So-be. *If* I could not see, I would not know it is beautiful. But I can see, and I do know."

"You like the golden dawn bird? Is it not the most beautiful of the birds as it stands majestic in the river shallows? And do you not also admire its reflection coming off the water?"

"Its reflection?" Mist-on-Water thought back to the times she had sat very still by the riverbank admiring the shy golden dawns. "No, its reflection is all distorted and twisted by the ripples. You may glimpse flashes of some of its beautiful colouring, but the reflection is nothing like the bird."

"So-be. I see. You are right again."

"I am?" Quickly, she turned her question into a statement, adding, "Of course." Her little jest drew no response from Sand-on-Stone.

"Yes, you are," Sand-on-Stone said. "You're telling me that if I'm not careful, if my gaze is set too low, what I see as good, wonderful even, might just be an ugly distortion.

A distortion of a beauty I have never known. Are you not telling me that?"

She had not been telling him that at all. She did not believe that she was seeing as distorted any of the things she felt were good. "A distortion? Like yesterday's sunset was? The one I saw?" Mist-on-Water felt she was on solid ground with that. Only someone who was delusional in the extreme could find fault in a glorious sunset.

"Yes, thank you, exactly like yesterday's sunset was."

"So-be. Distorted like yesterday's sunset was. I must be getting old before my time. Up here spending all my days with you. Because I have completely forgotten all my *not-thoughts* from it. Wait a moment." She paused and genuinely tried to think back to find anything that was negative about it in her mind at the time. Nothing. Nothing at all. So, she resumed her tone of gentle verbal jousting. "No, I cannot remember a single one of all of those *not-thoughts.* How distressing it is, forgetting something so important. But poor you – you must have to put up with that all the time."

"Yes, I put up with many things, but only so that I can learn the fallacy of the virtues of patience. That sunset yesterday – I saw it too – yes, it was exquisite. A fitting celebration of the life of the day. But I do remember it even now, yesterday's sunset – a jewel so blemished that its flaws overcame me." That surprised Mist-on-Water, but Sand-on-Stone did not wait for her to object. "Lovely for a moment, but now? Gone. Even if, as you say, my memory fades with the passing years, that sunset faded with the breeze. Its loveliness fled before my very eyes. My knowing of its beauty gripped the hand of something else. Its rushing demise too I knew. I knew it even as I watched. Was that a good thing? What about you? Did you want it to go? Why when this mind was knowing the one, was it also compelled to know the other? Why was that?"

Mist-on-Water said, "I pick you to answer that one. You're the one running this experiment."

"I wonder too, will a sunset come tomorrow, or some day after, look upon itself, remember the one, or the many, that came before it, and slink away, thinking itself lesser, unloved?"

Mist-on-Water remembered now that she'd had a fleeting thought that perhaps the orange in it had been just a bit too much this time.

"Then again, were other eyes looking out yesterday, jealous eyes, that said we must have that beauty? We want it; we want to be it. We must have it. We must paint it across our face. We must outdo it. Or everyone will stop wanting us. Then is your heart not heavy for that one? Where then was the unblemished joy in the sunset? How did it get lost?"

Mist-on-Water understood he was not really talking about sunsets anymore.

"It's something," she said.

"Something that's better than nothing. Better, say-you. Is better good enough? For you?"

She said, " You just want me to hate everything that I like, everything that is good."

"No, not hate it. But could it be that you discover that you are not satisfied with it? That you never will be. Not truly. Yes, The Source is still speaking to you, and still you are hearing. You see the shape of a jewel deep in your river, a jewel covered in mud and weed. Deep in your river, you glimpse this perfect, forgotten thing. Lest you dive in and look for it, not-mind says mud and weed are what you crave. I say they only obscure your true desire. If you look closely into the weave of all you call desirable, will you not see there but the fraying thread of fatal flaw? Then know you need not embrace those desires. They will try to rule you."

The mention of deep-down yearning tugged at Mist-on-Water. "Even if there is something else I yearn for, deep down, how do I find it? Even if my mind has some of your *not-thoughts* in it, are they nothing? Aren't they real? Do you want me to ignore the truth?" She did not wait for an answer. "So, Clouds-at-Sunset's brother – he must endure his sadness?"

"I don't think so."

"No?"

"I think not."

"Why not?"

"In and above and under all the flaws called beauty, music, the best of friends, all your cousins and, if you will allow it, even that *heroically-tolerated* parent – something pure blazes unseen, an untouched gift of something very good. Yes, Clouds-at-Sunset's brother sees those fraying threads so he can learn to release them and dive for the hidden jewel, in and above and under. It is a lesson chosen by the one ready to learn again. It is the lesson offered by a tender teacher rejoicing in every tardy student who shines beyond time, every student taking the lesson whenever he chooses and when he has finished it, he dismisses time itself."

Mist-on-Water was struggling, not with understanding what Sand-on-Stone had been talking about, but with finding it in her experience. "All of this is too much. You take me to the brink of something and tell me to look out. But it's too dim. It's too blinding. I don't know what's there. Something? Nothing? Soon you will tell me I can see nothing because my eyes are closed."

"I say only that if your eyes are closed, it's better to know it."

As she watched, Sand-on-Stone took three of his long, twisted yarns and started counter-twisting them to make a rope. It reminded Mist-on-Water of the ropes she had seen the fishers using back in the village on her way up. They had been making a drying rack. She said, "Do you know there is a sickness in the village? It hasn't been seen before. It makes you very weak, then your eyes go yellow and your fur starts falling out. Four have it now."

Sand-on-Stone started splicing off the end of his rope. He said, "What comes will go. The number of things that come is nothing to those whose days have no number."

Mist-on-Water was indignant. She stood up and leaned over Sand-on-Stone, fists tight. "Don't you care about this sickness? Many seasons ago there was a sickness down river in the village where they say amphora potters worked. It killed all the children and most of the adults. Everyone abandoned that place. Some said it was cursed. Some even blamed forest gremlins. Now it lies in ruins. The forest is covering it. I know. We went there to see. But not too close. Of course, there were no gremlins there. Could that happen to us?"

"What comes, comes."

"How can such terrible things be? What does your mighty source-with-no-name do about it?"

"The Source does as it does. Not more. Not less." He was showing no concern at all.

Sand-on-Stone's lack of empathy for a possible calamity made her more and more exasperated. She stamped her foot on the rock, not too hard. "Do you know I had another little brother before? He was lost to the river sickness two seasons past. Where is he now? Why was he taken from us? He was only small. I played *hide-me-find-you* with him every morning. Does his spirit roam about on the wind like the oracles say? Or is he no more, gone forever?"

Sand-on-Stone said, "Before I answer your questions, will you answer some of mine?"

"So-be."

He said, "Tell me, what do the small crèche children play with when it is your turn to mind them?"

Mist-on-Water was relieved to be talking about something more down to Earth. She said, "Nothing special. They play with anything. Sometimes we give them small round stones to roll, sometimes the carpentry master's off-cut pieces of wood. They play with many things."

Sand-on-Stone said, "So-be. When children play with the carpentry master's scraps of wood, do they build things? And then they pretend those things are real?"

"Yes, that is one of their favourite games. Except usually I need to help build something for them. A small village with streets and houses. Or a tower. It seems you may have actually seen children playing."

Sand-on-Stone ignored the gentle baiting and said, "Then what happens? In the end?"

"In the end, one of the younger ones usually pushes it all over."

"What? He destroys it all? Ruined? How could you let him do so much damage? Does not the older one get upset?"

They usually did get upset, often very upset, if the demolition was not what they had been planning, or if they had been planning to do the demolition themselves. She smiled and sighed at her memories of some of their overwrought antics. "Usually, one or two of them are angry. But what are you talking about? You know there is no damage."

"But think of their loss. A whole village. How can it ever be repaid? The younger children are out of control. What else could happen? Are some of them not in grave danger?"

"Why are you asking me such stupid questions?"

"Here is another question. The next day, or the next time they play, can they play with the carpenter's wooden off-cuts, making something new again? As if the previous calamities had never happened?"

"I will let you guess." She was finding it harder to be patient, just wanting him to get to the point.

"And when those children are bigger, no longer playing with the carpenter's wooden off-cuts, do they tell the tales of the grievous losses of yore, of their trauma?"

"They don't even remember any of that."

"So-be. Now we have it." Tugging down the length of his rope, Sand-on-Stone proved its strength. Satisfied, he started to splice off the other end.

"We do, do we?"

"Yes. You make sure the crèche-children you mind are doing no damage. None at all. Even though they think they are, they are not. Later, they understand that. If you are wise enough to make sure of that, would not The Source, creator of all things, loving every part of the creation, make sure it could not be damaged? Never. Even in the smallest way?"

"Say-you. Even if our little scraps and trinkets don't matter that much, what about our lives? I was telling you about this sickness before. Could it start taking away lives? Even many lives. They are not trinkets. What about them?"

"Do you ever dream, and while you dream find yourself anxious about something, or feeling lost, or even terrified of something in there – in your dream?"

"Perhaps." It was non-committal, but just that morning Mist-on-Water had woken from a dream where she could not find her home. The more she searched, the more lost she became, every place she went half-familiar, half-wrong. Her dream had held no terrors, but it had filled her with an ever-deepening unease. Until she woke.

"I do too," said Sand-on-Stone. "When I dream, my mind imagines it is somewhere else. It never imagines it is in my body, with its eyes shut, lying on my mat. It imagines another body, somewhere else, interacting with other bodies. Sometimes I know them, sometimes they behave in strange, inexplicable ways. In my dream I see many things, some familiar, some strange, some that my mind, when it awakes, knows could never be. In my dream many things are done, some by me, some by others. When I wake, I know none of it was done. But I never see myself dreaming or know my body lying there. And yet even though a dreamer knows not his body, does it not sometimes move about, does it not sometimes cry out?"

"My baby brother makes strange little noises and has twitchings in his legs and arms."

"Think of beings that dance through all the dimensions of space and time, casting off worlds and life itself with a thought. What sort of dream could those beings make? In their dream, could they forget themselves and imagine themselves tiny, frail sparks, come from a place unknown, a tiny glow an instant alone, an instant later gone forever? Even such a one's sleep-sent twitch has power far beyond what we imagine here."

Mist-on-Water did not know how to answer. She simply said, "Dreams do not matter."

"Even if they don't, do you not want to wake from your sleep?"

"But …" She did not finish, allowing her world to expand just a little. She knew that the old recluse was talking about just one way of explaining things. There could be many other ways, none of them having his elusive source or his not-minds. Was his true? She did not know. Nevertheless, something inside her was satisfied with this idea, for the moment, the idea that things that had once been grieved as a great loss would later be so unimportant they would not be remembered at all. Everything she touched, held dear, just playthings for the game of learning. Her best beads, even her armbands of merit, even the arms that bore them were seen playthings. Of no value. Their gain or loss of no consequence. Real value elsewhere, beyond decline. Even life itself. Especially life itself. He was saying that life itself could never be under the smallest threat.

What is my life then? Not the life of my body? Is this body I see not really me? Just seen as I see in my dreams? His ideas only uncovered a nest of questions. She was not satisfied with them, yet something in them, a soft whisper, had drifted down deep inside her and stirred something very still. That something had looked back in peace.

Then something else in her, standing guard in dimness beyond the far edge of her awareness, drew itself up, tugged at her attention, and set down its offering of well-trod thought, of familiar belief. Her mind moved to other matters.

The splicing of the ends of his rope finished, Sand-on-Stone slid down from the rock, tied one end of the rope around a small nearby tree, pulled the rope to its full length, and with the free end clenched in both hands, leaned back. The strands of the rope squeezed together as they took his weight and held firm. The rope had passed. Sand-on-Stone rolled up the rope and hung it from a peg high up near his cabin door, beside the copper armband. Mist-on-Water watched the whole process and wondered about Sand-on-Stone. She was finding it hard to pin down who he was, what was going on inside. She was not getting a feel for what he was going to do or say next, the feeling that she quickly got from the other villagers she knew and met, even the wandering traders and oracles. She felt she did not know who he really was. She wondered if it meant she did not really know who the others were either, the ones she thought she knew, despite her insights into their characters, her understanding of some of them better sometimes than their own was. Then she remembered her sense of not knowing who she herself was. How could she not know herself? At least it was not surprising that she could be having trouble getting a feel for Sand-on-Stone.

Mist-on-Water said, "I need to leave early today. There are extra jobs to be done, with four lying down with the sickness."

Sand-on-Stone said, "It is enough for today anyway. Probably too much."

"Yes, you are surely trying to swamp me with so many strange notions that I won't be able to find the embarrassing flaws in your little tale. It's not going to work. I can see straight through you." They both knew the last part was not true.

"If you find too many flaws, make a list. Then I can make sure I am better prepared for the next unsuspecting student." Bowing his head, he said, "Walk easy, daughter."

"Tread light, uncle."

In the village, quiet turmoil greeted Mist-on-Water. She soon discovered that another four villagers were showing signs of the sickness – two of them young males who had previously always been robust and healthy. That made eight in all afflicted now. It would not have been apparent to a stranger, but the normal rhythm of village life was faltering. The fields and crops were being tended by wives in place of husbands, brothers in place of sisters, cousins in place of grandparents. Some of the craft workplaces had closed earlier than usual, others had larger than usual piles of work waiting to be done, or pieces long completed still waiting to be taken away. On the faces that were usually cheery and content, seriousness and worry showed.

"Haya, Mist-on-Water. Have you heard?" It was her friend, Clouds-at-Sunset, calling to her from the other side of the main road through the village. She was crossing over to meet her.

"Well met. Have I heard what?" They came together in the middle of the road.

"The village council met this morning. They sent out runners to find the LifeSource oracle."

Mist-on-Water's village, resting in a shallow valley beside a lazy river, received about eight of the itinerant oracles over the course of a year. These itinerants made their rounds of the villages sprinkled along the river and presided over ceremonial events that came up every ten days or so in each village's calendar of rituals. The calendar called for a visit from most of the oracles just once or twice a year; a few were scheduled three times. But in times of special need, a message would go out with the traders or runners to arrange an extra visit. Most of the oracles arrived with a small retinue, tarried three or four days, teaching, conducting ceremonies, performing rituals, and then moving on.

If you asked today's village folk about the various 'sources' and the oracles attached to them, they would say they thought about them little, relied on them less. Most of what they wanted, they knew how to get – from their own labours, or bartered from someone else in the village, or sometimes from traders from the nearby villages. The economic system every individual was a part of was a simple one. It was obvious to everyone their staples were the result of their own or someone else's efforts, efforts they saw for themselves everywhere throughout their day. Farmers brought in the grain they then baked into bread. The seasons brought fruit that filled their bellies. Most households tended their own vegetables picked fresh for meals, fishers trapped the fish they grilled, sellers set up the market, and crafters worked timber, twine, clay, stone, iron or plant fibres for writing sheets, trading some of the more skilful craftwork with other villages. Very little arrived from somewhere else, where the labour or know-how or skill of its production was a mystery. Parents were often heard telling their children, "Getting what you want is a matter of give and take, not take and have." They were talking about their children giving up time, exerting themselves, carrying their share. The lesson did not take them long to learn. Everything they saw around them was teaching it.

Of course, idleness and indulgence were always quietly beckoning. Some worked hard for their larger, well-appointed cabins decorated with beautiful fresh flowers, or with extra pots or bits of art. Others were content with their smaller huts and more time for other things. Everyone found time or some staples to give to family or neighbours not so capable – the too young, the sick, or the infirm. The village council had enough volunteers for the occasional work and resources needed to develop and maintain the few community assets – the paved street around the plaza, the modest aqueduct. All did what they could or wanted to do – it was enough. So, with their give-and-take mindset ingrained, the villagers were self-reliant most of the time. They usually paid scant regard to the elusive, untamed 'sources'.

It was only when it came to things like rain (too little or too much), sickness, unusual bad luck, a lean harvest, or a poor catch of fish that they sought to gain favour from one of the sources. With varying levels of reservation, they turned to an oracle. The oracles were anything but reliable. While firm and clear on many generalisations, they usually managed, each in their own way, to squirm out of being precise about whatever the source-of-the-day wanted or was planning on doing or might consider doing if cajoled correctly. If someone cornered a careless oracle into an unambiguous declaration, the declaration ended up being wrong as often as it was right.

Different oracles also had very different ideas about the desires of these sources and how to influence them. Some said earnest petitioning was the way; others advocated offerings. Few village folk bothered to wonder how exactly these unseen beings got any benefit from an offering, or why some petition would persuade or motivate an otherwise disinterested source to take the action they desired.

Mist-on-Water was in that small number who asked the unwanted questions.

Despite blatant flaws and gaps in much of what the oracles said, most folk did not care enough to see the flaws, or they ignored them, or preferred an answer they liked to one they needed to test for soundness. A few folk approached the dogmas of the sources as interesting intellectual puzzles. Nearly everyone just went along with the ceremonies. At the very least, having some explanation for happenings that had impinged on their lives, or the hope of a say in future events, was better than nothing. At the ceremonial events there was some entertainment, a bit of socialising and merriment, and for the price of a small food offering or a simple ritual, it could not hurt. Most village folk, Mist-on-Water included, felt that they should go about their own lives as they pleased, and the sources could go about their business (whatever that was) as they pleased, just as long as that business did not cause the villagers any grief.

Of all the oracles roaming the region, the LifeSource oracle was the most enigmatic. She gave long speeches, uttering many words that sounded weighty and profound, but when taken together they eluded meaning, defied understanding. What she did convey, and frequently reminded them of, was that she was doing her best to explain the lofty message of the great LifeSource to them. After all, they were just simple village folk, were they not? For the most part, they agreed.

The one thing that the LifeSource oracle always made sure they clearly understood was the penance. The villagers waited for this part with some trepidation. For the other sources, when favour, insight, instruction, or whatever else was being sought, they generally required offerings, usually of food that oracles accepted on behalf of their source, burning a portion immediately and storing the rest in the trunks they all carried to be offered later. More often than not, the LifeSource seemed angry. The oracle pointed out many transgressions around the village – a poorly tended tree here, pests allowed in a small-food plant patch over there. Transgressions needed to be paid for; yes, sometimes with offerings, but sometimes it was harder – long fastings, unbroken vigils, arduous showings of devotion. Before long, someone always grumbled, or was not strong enough, or made some error. Then more penance was needed, the setting of which was carried over to LifeSource oracle's next visit. It was a never-ending cycle.

"The LifeSource oracle. This is a good idea?" Mist-on-Water did not bother to hide her scorn.

"They had to do something. What else is there?"

Mist-on-Water knew she had no answer to that question. She admitted to herself that she understood little of how the world worked. Too little. While the others gazed on the good but looked aside from the decline and death waiting for everyone and everything, she let herself see it all. She, who was the quickest to glean the hidden motives and desires behind the superficially innocent daily exchanges around her, admitted she did not understand if the story of the world was the simple but ignored one of stone becoming dust, or if there were some other story. If there were some meaning beyond sparks of beauty beaten out by brutal decline, demise, decay. The village council had done something because they could not do nothing. Did it even count as something? Sand-on-Stone always talked of some *thing* at the root of everything, of *every* thing that is, something unseen. It was a thing so well hidden that, try as she might, she had not yet found proof of it anywhere. If there was some *thing* that stood behind everything, should it not be obvious? Of course, Sand-on-Stone would have some explanation for it. Maybe he wanted to become a new oracle. But even if his explanations were better than the ones the oracles had, they were not final. Every answer any of them gave kept spawning more questions.

Mist-on-Water knew that almost everyone accepted that there were questions they did not have answers to. She did not accept it. Not for important ones, anyway, like the ones Sand-on-Stone had so many words for. Then again, if his words were true, his answers were worth remembering.

If only she could be sure of them.

Observation Series: **Unexpected Behaviours**

<u>Summary of Observations.</u> I am supposed to note any unexpected behaviours. But almost everything about my cuties is unexpected. They do not do or think anything sensible. These critters even think certain individuals in their wacky society are more important than others. They think this because they do not know what is important. And they do not know that *all* the pups are needed for the pack to be complete.

Chapter 12

The next evening when Conrad_27-8 knocked, three then two times at the door to Quentin's apartment, Tracey and Quentin were discussing tactics.

Getting up to let Conrad-27_8 in, Tracey said, "I know you don't really care about SiMiYah but I think we owe it to her to help."

Quentin said, "Hey, don't drag me into your little guilt trip. I don't remember promising any refunds. I don't even remember any cash being exchanged."

Tracey said, "So our heroic interplanetary only-an-astrophysicist is ready to pack his toothbrush and check out?"

Quentin said, "Whoa there, lassie. Not so fast. I still want to try to get something scientifically useful from that merry band of lizard-skinned pinball brains. It should be easy – I already have *some* data from their SeeDo access points. There's *loads* more." He cast his eyes at Conrad_27-8, who was wincing and putting his hands over his ears. "It's just that I'm starting to get pulled outside my area of expertise. I could get data on the planetary geology, meteorology, technology maybe, or even biology. But *you* need to watch yourself. With those loopy Mandates and their *do-I-have-an-idea-for-you* minder sidekicks, your sweet homey social services project will likely make the seven-billion-dollar Microsoft Windows phone look like a huge winner."

"What Microsoft Windows phone?"

"Exactly. Seven billion down the gurgler."

"I just want to try. Are you sure you want to go back? You're not exactly a pile of smiles when we're there."

"Me? I'm as happy as a homeless mutt that's been adopted by a butcher."

"And then keeps getting sent on holiday to his vegetarian sister. But you may have a point about those minders. I'm not sure about them anymore."

"What do you mean?"

"Well, they *seem* helpful, but … I don't know. Their help just doesn't seem to help, no matter what they say."

"You could be right. It may be that they're just a little too attuned to their owners. Take yours: it's always twisting itself up over non-events. And you're happy to accept the eternal condemnation befitting a glorious, awe-inspiring, supernova stuff-up for every one of those non-events. And poor old Kieran's must be off in dreamland most of the time. Hardly notice it."

"Maybe mine is a little too ready to roll a guilt carpet up to my doorstep. But I wouldn't say yours is any better. It's always got its dukes up, spoiling for a punch-up. A little bit one-track, if you ask me."

"Not necessarily. Just because mine is one of the few to have a clear view of what's going on, and is ready to respond, you don't need to feel threatened by it."

Conrad_27-8 said, "Thirteen minutes to departure."

Quentin said, "And him too. Even 27-8 here's minder is always trying to get everything to tally, down to the thirteenth decimal point. Gets all het up if someone uses naughty words like *some* or *loads*."

Too late, Conrad_27-8's hands rushed back to his ears.

Tracey realised this conversation was going nowhere. "Are we all set for this trip then?" she said.

"Given the restrictions on luggage, I don't have any more to pack."

Kieran seemed ready. He was singing U2's song *One*, the words slightly wrong again:

"One life … we get to forgive each other, forgive each other."

Tracey said, "Good. Can we say we have a good plan of attack for our impending sojourn? We are ready for action?"

Gently pressing for everything to be nicely organised, for everyone to be working together more or less, and knowing that it was not, and they were not, Tracey was hoping for an agreement on something, even if it was a small one.

"No." It was a chorus. *At least we're in unison on something*, thought Tracey.

They went anyway.

When Tracey, Quentin, Kieran, and Conrad_27-8 arrived on Allunda, it was just after noon. With the Allundrian day being nearly two hours longer than an Earth day, each time they made the transfer and arrived, it was earlier in the day. They met SiMiYah outside her dwelling, as they had arranged. She greeted them, pleased to see them again, but without enthusiasm for the task that lay ahead. Her clan head lived in one of the adjacent pods of dwellings, just a short walk down the path in the opposite direction from the resource hub. It led to a park where the corners of four dwelling pods met, a tranquil park filled with water features babbling quietly. It had three other exits. The exit they took from the park led to a pod of dwellings arranged in the way they were familiar with – a central circular grove of dense vegetation surrounded by eight allotments with single-level dwellings, all with their own subtle variations in colour and design.

Turning to the left where the path met the ring path around the grove, SiMiYah led them to the second dwelling, announced their arrival, and as instructed, led the way through the dwelling to the gathering room. There they waited, standing or sitting on one of the thin mats. The three walls without windows were almost half covered by SeeDos, two of them showing what could have been tiers of scrolling newsfeeds, the other one showing waves breaking against a rocky shore, a wild setting yet somehow calming.

A voice instructed them to proceed to the business room where the clan head discharged the duties of her role. They entered to see the clan head of SiMiYah's paternal line sitting on a thin mat behind a low oval-shaped table. On each end of the table was a platter bearing food arranged in striking patterns. Behind her, two shelves ran along the full length of the wall, sparsely decorated with sculptures, the largest one a representation of a family tree with copper inlays. Others were perhaps awards. She had no special garment or adornments of office. She did seem older than most of the Allundrians they had seen, a little thinner, a little paler.

The clan head said, "I remind you of the protocol. As a clan member, you have the right to a hearing. I see you bring associates or colleagues. They may attend but they must remain silent unless you elect to adjourn for counsel."

That suited Quentin and Conrad_27-8 perfectly but Quentin still muttered, "Yes, and here we have another example of your freedom Mandate at work improving your community." Quentin remembered Kieran and quickly looked over at him to see if he had taken in the instructions.

Kieran had his back to them, examining a SeeDo that occupied the complete wall opposite the clan head. It showed an elaborate, interactive family tree. Quentin thought he had most likely not been paying attention, and even though the clan head was not physically intimidating, he did not know what other kind of power she might wield. Tracey had taken in the rules of conduct and wondered how she would be able to help SiMiYah, if she needed it.

SiMiYah said, "Let it be seen that 300-294-565 Clan reigns above all. I pledge my allegiance to the clan." It was a ritualistic greeting.

In response the clan head said, "The clan's honour is assured. No other clan can approach our excellence."

Muttering, Quentin said, "Clan 300-291-325? Doesn't really roll off the tongue, does it?"

Conrad_27-8 said, "It's 300-294-565."

SiMiYah was barely aware of the quiet chatter behind her. Her full attention was on the clan head. "I trust all is well in the clan's ranking, my Madame Primary."

The clan head said, "The clan retains its pre-eminent position, of course. We crush all that oppose us, we squeeze them into slime. We rejoice in every victory. Look at this latest score." She spoke every word with fervour, her passion blazing as she raised her arm towards the SeeDo, fist clenched, part invitation, part victory salute.

SiMiYah studied the SeeDo behind them where the clan head had indicated. "Ah yes. Poor old 453-452-786 Clan lost out very badly again." Against the clan head, her enthusiasm was a little subdued.

Quentin, who had moved to the window, said to the view outside, "Ouch. Is that the dismembered carcass of the equality Mandate decaying out there in the gutter?"

Tracey, hearing him muttering again, went over and stood by him, so she might have some hope of subtly getting him to restrain himself, if needed.

SiMiYah said, "You have lifted the clan to a most enviable position, my Madame Primary."

The clan head said, "It is as expected. I trust you are bringing another chance for us to gain another glorious victory over the others."

Kieran, still studying the intricate and no-end-in-sight family tree, said without turning, "Who are the others?"

Tracey, Conrad_27-8, and Quentin looked at Kieran and then turned their eyes quickly to the clan head. The clan head gave no sign of having heard the question. She said to SiMiYah, "Tell me, which clan will we contest? We will smash them down the rankings."

SiMiYah gave potential contests some thought. She came up blank and said, "The contest to smash them down the rankings? No, there will be no contest."

The clan head said, "You are right – which clan it is matters not – we will crush them easily. What we need to start with is the event that we will score from. When was it posted? I will work out who to bring into play, and our tactics."

SiMiYah said, "The event? Yes. The scoring event." SiMiYah's minder was holding her left ear and giving its advice in a continuous stream. "Perhaps I do overreach. Wait, I need to explain about the event, no I mean about what we want to talk about. It … It …"

Tracey had walked to SiMiYah and sat beside her. She said quietly, "Would you like to take counsel at this time? We may need to clarify the tactics."

SiMiYah said to the clan head, who had started tapping her chin rapidly, "We should confer. Will you grant a short recess?"

The clan head said, "Yes. Yes. Attempts to score against us are mounting again. I must attend to them." She waved them off to a door that led to a smaller recess room.

In the recess room, Tracey said, "I am not following this. How is some kind of clan battle going to get the clan head to release DahTiYahYah's exile and get us the iron nugget?"

"How? Yes, you are right – it is tricky. Clan heads only know how to win victories for the clan. It is all they care about. And DahTiYahYah's birth clan is Clan 525-244-725, one of our fiercest rivals.

"His exile was a serious loss of face for his birth clan, who suffered a humiliating scoring penalty. Not only them, all his clans. I don't remember how much it was exactly, but it was a lot. It even made the daily clan contest highlights when it happened. Yes, it did. A big setback for their clan rankings. It would have made everyone in of all of his clans very sullen."

"All of his clans? How many clans is he in?"

"Well, more than most, as I remember. I will need to check." She went to the SeeDo that was in the room, already showing the same clan explorer tool that Kieran had been interested in earlier. After some rapid swirlings and flashings on the screen, she said, "There it is – his full list. The total is three hundred and fifty-six. He belongs with three hundred and fifty-six clans. Not extreme, but more than most. Of course, his links to some of them are a bit remote and also some of them are very large, like his birth town clan (763-711-175) and his School Sector Alumni clan (725-580-806). Even an exile event would not have been a big setback for those. But some of the smaller clans went down a long way in the rankings. A few of my acquaintances were downcast about it for days. They didn't want to talk about it. Like HaChaHooCha who I work with – he had to put up with taunts every day at first – he's in DahTiYahYah's geologist clan. Some of his co-workers are in the oceanographer clan – they try to contend against a geologist any chance they get. Those oceanographers would bring it up whenever there was a dispute, or even just a chance encounter. It totally undermined his credibility. He couldn't do anything about that – the exile had nothing to do with him. And here you can see the approval point losses for all his clans. Ooh, I didn't know it was that many."

Looking over SiMiYah's shoulder, Tracey said, "The approval point losses?"

"Yes, it was one of the bigger losses for that day."

"A lot of points were lost." Tracey's confusion was growing, but she didn't want to show her ignorance of something that apparently needed no explanation to the inhabitants here.

"Probably just those idiot referees, as usual," Quentin said to the ceiling.

With some more rapid eye movements and occasional short voice commands, SiMiYah highlighted the score breakdown for DahTiYahYah's exile event. She said, "Yes, of course, the raw classification measures for the event were highly negative. Look at all the areas that had extreme lows – aesthetics, skill, knowledge, intelligence, creativity, entertainment, and on and on. The event posting algorithm set those. Then, the event is fed to the news lists of everyone who will likely be interested. That was nine hundred and eighty-six thousand, four hundred and fifty-four individuals the event went to. Let me see how many 'looks' the event had. Well, there you have it all – the tallies for 'looks' and the 'responds'. It got a lot of attention. A lot of attention. That is why the exile cost so many points for his clans."

Conrad_27-8 said, "Interesting. A somewhat crude creation, but not without some of the innocent charm primitive works such as this can offer. The actual algorithms could easily be reverse engineered from this data. Well, I could do it easily, anyway."

Quentin, who had been walking about oozing impatience, stopped next to Tracey and spoke in subdued tones to an imaginary audience: "Now folks, for those who have joined us late, we already have one contestant lying in a crumpled mess in the corner. Wow, look at that will you, smashed beyond recognition. Poor thing. But fortunately, we can go to the replay and get the identity of that unsuspecting chump. Now we see it. Ouch. It was the equality Mandate – never had a chance. It started with a simple pass to rational thinking, and rational thinking just put it straight on the deck. A clear foul. With rational thinking totally out of the play, the poor old equality Mandate just walked straight into a speeding flock of frolicking nonsense and never even saw what hit it. There you have it folks, ga-ga thinking has been elevated to heights never seen before here in the goo-goo talk sports arena."

Tracey turned her head to him and gave him a long cold stare.

Quentin said, in the same subdued tones, "Well folks, it looks like we are out of time for tonight's update. But stay tuned – you will be the first to hear about any breaking developments, here on the comedy-sports channel. Before we go, we will meet a bunch of intrepid explorers who stumble into a maze made up of the finger pickings of a thousand slimy snot-flinging clowns, and hear about why they don't just go straight back to what they should be doing." He put his pretend microphone in front of Tracey, who swatted his hand away.

Tracey said, "If we just get through this one meeting, we'll have plenty of time for your stuff. It shouldn't be that hard to convince that clan head, or whatever she is." She was trying to sound a lot more confident than she was.

Quentin said, "In case you hadn't noticed, all of these things are comfortably crazy."

"Of course, they're a bit strange to us. This is a different planet, remember. They have their problems too. It doesn't mean they aren't trying to improve."

"I have some more news for you: these guys aren't reading any self-improvement books. They don't even think they have a problem. They're happily gorging on the sweet insanities baked into their loopy Mandates, enshrined no doubt on tablets of playdough."

"Wait on. Those Mandates aren't too different from philosophies that a lot of people agree with back home."

"At least those people have the decency not to turn their lewd predilections into both an admired art form and a highly respected branch of the sciences."

"Are any of us so different from them?"

"Do we have a lot of crazies out there? Probably. But again, at least most of them aren't glorying in it and plastering it all over wall-sized screens."

Their whispered conversation had been getting louder and now SiMiYah, who had been deep in her own thoughts in the far corner of the room, turned towards them.

Trying to find a way to get back on topic, Tracey said to SiMiYah, "I wonder how DahTiYahYah's exile 'scoring event' impacted the score of your clan head. You know, over all the other clans that she belongs to."

"You mean like a personal overall score? Yes, I don't know of anyone who has looked at a scoring event like that. Of course, not everyone follows the scores as much as they should, but even the most casual clan members review the scoring and ladder positions of their closest clans a few times a day. Or more often if some big scoring is happening. The clan status navigator does not have that capability directly, but I know how to correlate the data. I helped design the data feed consolidation, you know."

SiMiYah had the SeeDo twirling and flashing information again as she continued talking, "Now, here are all our clan head's memberships. A very large list naturally. I will just get the scores for that exile event. There. Now a simple tally. Oh."

"What?"

"Well, even though our birth clan got some score from it, she lost out quite badly on clans that she and DahTiYahYah both belong to. There are nearly a hundred. Overall, she lost eight hundred and seventy-eight points."

"That could be it then."

"What could it be?"

"We can show her that if she withdraws DahTiYahYah's exile, she could regain the points she lost."

Quentin sat on the floor next to Conrad_27-8, leaned against the wall, and said, "Say, is that TraaCee over there actually trying to have the conversation I appear to be hearing?"

Conrad_27-8 looked at Quentin, then at Tracey and SiMiYah, then with confusion back at Quentin. He said nothing.

SiMiYah said, "It is as you say. The points would probably be regained – it would depend on the responses to the post, of course. But even if the clan head's points improve, it would not be a gain for the clan. That is all anyone cares about, especially her. No one even knows what their personal score is. Your clans' scores are what matters. They *are* your score. But it is not just your *score*. It is your *protection*. Minder knows."

Quentin's impatience got the better of his reluctance to becoming an active party to something that on its best day would be less than pointless. He said, "Let me see if I can help with this little 'recess' we're enjoying. Would that be all right?"

SiMiYah gave an uncertain confirmation, opening and shutting her mouth once, very slowly.

"Now, just to assist our thinking, I will take things step by step, and I will even ask some questions that might seem to have very obvious answers. But it just might trigger a different way of looking at the problem. Agreed?"

"Agreed."

"Good. If I have it right, in this little game, you try to gain points for your clan by spreading around all of the good things its members are doing, and then you try to get your opposing clans to lose points by spreading around all of the bad things they're doing?"

"Yes. You are correct."

"And the prize for winning is? Two nuggets of iron ore maybe?"

"There is no winning. Just going up and down the rankings. When your clan goes up its rankings group, everyone else is envious. Members of opposing clans will resent the success – sometimes with verbal or even physical violence. But when your clan goes down its rankings group, well it is embarrassing. Your minder will always tell you about that, so that you are ready."

"It sounds like you lose both ways. And what your minder wants you to be ready for is, of course …?"

"Ready to deal with the derision."

"Naturally. And with all the hundreds of different clans everyone belongs to, at any given time, lots are going up, yes? So, all good. But wait, lots are going down too. Not so good. On the other hand, don't forget, lots are going up. Must make it tough to work out if you're winning or losing."

"Ah, yes, I see what you are saying. You have a strange way of looking at things sometimes. Not very sensible. But of course, a few clans are much more important to you than the others, as your minder will helpfully inform you."

"Especially those that win well?"

"Yes, and more importantly, those that lose. They need you to work harder to help improve their performance."

"But then when you work hard at it and the clan goes up the rankings again, everyone can celebrate."

"Yes. Unless you are just regaining lost ground."

"What about the clans at the top of their rankings groups?"

"No one wants to be in one of those."

"Of course not. Because they are top." But Quentin's sarcasm was lost there.

"Exactly, the only way to go is down."

"So, second is good then?

"No."

"Let me guess. Because it is only good if you gain rankings, but if you are second and your ranking improves then you will be top?"

"Obviously."

"And then your ranking can only go down."

"Obviously."

"Now, if someone were looking at things in a strange way, then being bottom must be highly sought-after. The only way to go is up."

"No, everything you are saying is strange, just as you promised. Of course, going to the bottom rank is the worst move down. If it happens, the period of mourning is much longer than any other move down, bar one."

"Bar one?"

"Bar the move down from top."

"The move down from the ranking no one wants is the worst?"

"It is the top ranking, after all."

Mostly to himself, Quentin said, "There must be some way to beat this system." Then he saw that everyone was looking at him expectantly. He had the germ of an idea. "So then, another question you may find strange: what would happen if someone worked out how to be mainly in the winning clans?" Quentin glanced at Conrad_27-8 for a hint that he could solve that particular equation, but he was showing no sign of interest. Quentin's glance turned into annoyance. He continued. "Would that be of value?"

SiMiYah looked startled. "Just be in the winning clans? That would be very nice." She laughed, one of the very few times they had heard the sound, like a soft gurgle. "But how would you get to be just in winning clans? As you know, when you get cast into a clan, you are in. That's it. Maybe I know more details about the technology than you do, more than almost everybody. I help with its maintenance, you know. Let me explain – I will try not to be too technical. Mostly your clan casting just happens because of where you have been, or what you have been doing, what you like to eat, who you have been with, what you do in your leisure, and in your work, and lots more. All of that – from the day you are born – everything about you. It is all collected. Some days a new clan comes and another day a clan goes, but most just stay. One day you will get put into a new one, another day you get taken out of one. Most clans you will never get into, and most of the clans you are put in, you never get out of. The clan infostore keeps track of it all. It's very accurate."

"It sounds extremely complex. Something that complex must have its limits, its flaws. A little back door? What about them?"

"Well, yes, it is very involved. And very accurate. You can try to clan-jump for higher rankings. Many do, just about everyone probably. It often happens when there is a new clan and it starts doing very well – maybe it is a new food, or some SeeDo entertainment or game or something – and so it seems like everyone in the whole town starts doing the things they need to do to get cast into it. Maybe they like doing the things, or maybe it is just to get into the clan, like you say. Of course, it happens. But there are not many of those clans. No important ones. Not really. Not for long. Maybe for a day. Unless minder says. Minders know, minders tell. But minder knows *all* my clans, it makes sure I know about every one of them that is doing well. But more importantly, it makes sure I know about every one of them that is doing badly."

For a moment Quentin was lost for a way to respond. His single, tiny, possibly-bright-idea had fizzled dismally. He said, "And everyone wants to go along with this game?"

"Of course. But how can you call clan rankings a game? They are critical. It is from your clans that you know who you are. You, me, everyone. Without your clans, you are lost. With them, you *belong.* You need to listen to your minder more. I know being in all our clans makes everyone fight all the time. Not big fights, just little fights: the dagger word, the crusher look, the clenched thought. Do you notice it? Do you know I actually don't want to fight? I don't like it. But some do – they like it. Or maybe they just think they do, but they really want something else. I just want … I want to be …" But she found no way to finish her thought. "Anyway, with our clans we can all be together – all of us in the clan. You don't want to be alone, do you? That is the worst thing. I know. But it is strange that to be all together, in our clans, we all need to be apart – apart from the other clans. It sounds wrong – being separate so we can be together. I wonder sometimes if there is another way. But our minders know. They know all the clans, all the rankings. Do you want to hear about my nephew? Once he did it. What you are saying. Once he almost did it. Do you want to hear about it?"

Quentin's attention had drifted soon after SiMiYah started talking, but her unexpected pause jarred him back to her last words. He said, "Does the egg want to hear the recipe for omelette? Of course it does."

"Well, once my nephew TeDitTeDot was very excited. It was last year. I don't know how he did it, but all of his important clans were near the top. They were all doing very well. *All* of them – his personal top eight clans, *all* near the top of their rankings groups *at the same time.*" She paused a moment to let the enormity of that sink in, lost again for a moment in the marvel of it herself. "He was ecstatic about it. He was telling everyone, of course. Then, guess what? Everyone seemed to just turn away from him.

Even his clan-kin, even his friends. Exceedingly strange. No one came to see him anymore; he was even made unwelcome at walk-eats if he casually tried to join one. He told me all of this, so I went to him for a quick walk-eat. He told me all about it. I said, if only there was a clan for everyone who had their clans near the top of the rankings. It would not have many clan-kin in it, that clan. But you would be safe there."

Tracey said, "How did all of his rankings protect him then?"

"Yes, I know what you are thinking. It is very dangerous, very radical. You must be careful. We cannot say it, but I know you are thinking: *are those rankings just a distraction?* I think it too sometimes. What is really important is the clan, not the ranking. That's what the Clan Mandate says." She recited it as she had countless times in class. "*The members of a clan are special, and each must be upheld for the sake of the clan.*"

Tracey said, "So if it's not really about the rankings, what is it? Am I cast into all of my wonderful clans for some other reason?" Her words gave her an uncomfortable twinge that she was being deceitful. She did not feel any of her clans were the slightest bit wonderful, or the clans her Allundrian host body had, at least.

"Yes. No. I don't know. You and I, all of us, we all need to be made safe somehow, safe from *the others.*"

Tracey did not like the sound of that. "The others?"

"Yes. You know, the ones outside. Not us. The ones *outside* our clans. The ones *apart* from *us.* The others. The ones who are not our clan-kin. We need to know who they are, what they are doing. That's what it is. Minder speaks."

"I am not your clan-kin."

"You must be in some of my clans." SiMiYah turned to the SeeDo.

"Not any important ones. Am I one of the others?"

"It is true. Like you say, you are not in my clans. So, you are one of the others. But you aren't. It's wrong. I don't want it. I only need my clans if I am apart, if I am not safe. But the only reason I am apart is because of the clans, all the clans. My food clans, my work clans, my talk-to clans, my work-with clans, your clans, their clans … This is all confusing me. Yes. Sorry, minder, it is safer to listen to you."

A voice announced that SiMiYah was instructed to return to the clan head's business room to finish the appointment.

Tracey said, "So, we don't know how to get your clan head to revoke DahTiYahYah's exile?"

"No. We should go back in to her now. Maybe we could just ask for it."

When they returned to the business room, SiMiYah said, "Regrettably, we have concluded that we cannot show you an important scoring event for the clan. But I do have a special clan-kin request for you."

The clan head sighed. "So many requests. What is it?"

SiMiYah held her hands in front of her, palms up. She said, "I need you to revoke DahTiYahYah's exile. Then I might be able to get a Mandate-advocate. I am in great need of one."

"Revoke the exile. Why would I do that? No. Now leave me. There is much to be done."

SiMiYah's shoulders drooped and her arms dangled loosely at her sides. She turned and with a feeble sweep of her arms, signalled to everyone to leave.

Not caring much if she was being listened to or not, the clan head said, "You know I have no choice but to uphold the dignity of this office. Yes, yes – it is my dignity as well. I am needed here. Yes, yes – a good question: where else would I be wanted? How can I even know if I am wanted? But this office bears heavily down on me – such a wearisome prize. Must life be such a burden? Yes, yes – even if I escape it, what do I have left? Perhaps nothing? Does it matter? I leave behind nothing I really care about. Must I keep on? Yes. No – I do not want to keep this up. I endure it for the clan. But how much longer must I?" They had all paused to listen, not knowing how, or if, to respond.

On the SeeDo, Kieran navigated the family tree to the clan head's entry and expanded it to show her face and a long list of details about her. He said, apparently to himself, "Every part is essential for proper functioning. But before any part can function properly, the packaging must be removed."

While they turned again to leave, the clan head was still saying to herself, "So much to be done. Too much to be done. It smothers me. Is there no way out?" Then she said more loudly, "Wait. There may be a way."

Everyone turned back to face her.

"You know my duties as clan head of our birth clan are very prestigious. But I have had the honour for seventeen years now. I have come to the time where I choose to pass on the title. But my successor, the next-in-line, DooDiDiDoo has not been ready to accept the honour. You know him, I think. If you can convince him to take up his succession as clan head of 300-294-565 clan, I will revoke DahTiYahYah's exile for you." She looked at the SeeDo behind her and one of the entries close to her own on the family tree expanded, showing a face and a long list of details about him. "That's the heir to the title of clan head – my nephew. You should meet with him – it may require quite some discussion."

SiMiYah said, "Yes, I do know him. A bit. Ask him to take on the mantle of clan head? He will be very excited. Surely that will be easy. Not too hard. Even I can do that. Of course I can. But what could go wrong? What do you think?"

Tracey and the others did not know what to think. Their minders were warning them to keep quiet.

Chapter 13

It was the eighth day after the first case of the unknown sickness. The morning arrival to the village of the LifeSource oracle and her retinue brought with it ripples of disruption to routine. Both of their pole barges needed room to be secured, to the grumbles of the fishers; their shelters had to be set up in the best part of the clearing set aside for guests of the village, displacing some travelling traders; their stores needed to be replenished with food, mostly the perishables but also some of the non-perishables. A few acquaintances were renewed. The odd worn or damaged possession was repaired or replaced. Welcoming formalities were completed. Villagers of influence, or who wanted to influence or who needed another to be influenced were received or sometimes put off until later. General village folk who had petitions to make or who requested counsel were told which morning or afternoon they could attend, and this was recorded.

This LifeSource oracle had a largish retinue – her partner, two of her grown children, a daughter-in-law with a small baby, and an errand-youth who was on call for any jobs to be done or assistance to be provided. They all played their own parts in getting themselves established, with the casual ease that comes with something many times practised.

After the oracle and her retinue had spent the morning settling in and then the afternoon dealing with the first flush of visitors, the village council convened in the evening to formally brief her on the reason they had requested her attendance. At that time, the eight Council members included two healers. The more senior of the healers told the LifeSource oracle about the sickness, about how it had first appeared, then about the next case two days later, then about the next two cases in the following two days up to the present. Now, they had eleven villagers in various stages of the illness, with none having yet recovered. The LifeSource oracle told the elders that she needed to visit those with the sickness so that she could divine what had stayed the LifeSource's hand in bringing healing up to now.

The following day, the oracle visited all eleven villagers who had contracted the illness, asking about their activities in the days leading up to the onset, examining their homes, food plots, farms, or workplaces, gathering further answers from those who lived with them. She asked about their work or studies, about their blood relations, and about who they walked and sat down with. At the end of each visit, she burned aromatic plants and sat, eyes shut, chanting as the smoke filled the dwelling. In the late afternoon of that day, the oracle asked the head of the village council to convene a village meeting so that she could reveal to them what she had divined.

As the sun was easing down to almost touch the hills behind the river the next day, over a hundred of the nearly hundred and fifty who lived in the village and the surrounding farmlets waited on the clear ground under several very large whitewood trees. These were by far the largest trees in the area, having stood longer than memory on the low flats between the village and the river. Mist-on-Water was standing near the edge of the crowd with Clouds-at-Sunset and her older brother. All the village elders were there, talking quietly among themselves, pleased that the turnout was good, a little apprehensive about what they might hear. The other villagers were relaxing after their workday and chatting in small groups. Two young boys sitting by the river sang lines from some of the popular village songs, practising their harmony, laughing when they got it wrong. Some younger children played a game rolling stones in the dirt. Sand-on-Stone was not there.

The LifeSource oracle did not wait for, or need, an introduction. She approached the whitewood tree nearest to the village, went to a strong low branch at waist height, climbed onto it, raised her arm in greeting, and said, "Folk of the village of Three-fishes-leap, I greet you." The response was a half-hearted murmur.

She went on, "It would be better that I were coming at happier times." After the more enthusiastic scattered murmurs of assent had faded, she said, "Let me tell you about this sickness that has befallen you."

Someone near the front of the crowd said, "Yes, LifeSource oracle. And how to have it taken away from us."

"Of course. But first, you will remember our revered LifeSource is the author of diversity beyond counting. How greatly she blesses us. But as well as diversity, she decrees an order for things. So it comes that every life is made different, but some are made the same. All must be tended after their own nature. I tell you, news of your sickness has reached the folk of the village of River-bends-twice. They talk there of a trade embargo, to prevent contamination."

This was news only a few village councillors knew. Consternation settled on some faces.

"They bear you no ill feelings. But they think of what is prudent. I see that since I was here last, some of the redberry fruit trees remain ill-tended. We all know this saddens LifeSource. We must never forget that we cannot take unless we give. It saddens me too that I must talk to you about the longspike weeds allowed into your fields …" The oracle's discourse meandered about, touching on a host of further affronts to LifeSource, affronts that the LifeSource benignly tolerated because she understood too well the deep ignorance of the perpetrators, but for which amends still needed to be made. Next, she bemoaned their lack of worthiness to receive the bounty LifeSource poured out on them every day and that surrounded them, lamenting their lack of gratitude to the LifeSource, who had brooded over them since birth. As she spoke, many of the villagers barely recognised the corrupted place she was describing as their own abode. Others were nodding and acceding to feelings of remorse. The hills had just hidden the sun, the light was dimming, and a cool breeze was drifting off the river when the oracle drew her address to a close.

"I have spoken to you of many failings that trouble our noble LifeSource to her core. But these are not the source of the sickness that has come here. And so – and this bears down heavy on my heart – I must tell you of a vision that has been cast upon me, a vision not of the failings I have already spoken of, copious though they be. No, it is a vision of a host of iniquities– a host of iniquities even more grievous than all those others."

The gathering, which the whole time had been listening carefully, respecting the LifeSource oracle's every word, became very still.

"More grievous than all of them, I say. Because of them, the unstainable purity of LifeSource can no longer endure her unceasing watch over you. There are moments when she can but turn her face from the festering sewer of iniquities that abides here and at those times, when she looks over you not, entry is permitted to this punishing sickness that afflicts you. The glorious LifeSource has uncovered for me the dark byways trodden by miscreants among you. She has revealed them, and yes, not only that, she reveals the paths to your deliverance." The silence was abrupt. She slowly scanned the crowd below her, moving her head from one side to the other, her eyes unblinking, her gaze starting with those closest and moving further back in long, wide sweeps.

The tension grew until someone towards the middle of the crowd shouted, "Who do these iniquities lie with?"

LifeSource oracle turned her eyes to the speaker, held them still for a single long, slow breath and said, "They lie with the fishers." Towards the back, in the part of the crowd nearest the rickety jetty that poked out into the water, the stillness of the gathering was broken as several villagers shifted about on their feet. It was where most of the fishers were standing. Many eyes turned in their direction. The fishers lived a little outside the village proper, three throwings of a pebble away. Their dwellings, simpler than most, stood on the riverbank where there was a small rise. They had only small food gardens, poorly kept, sparse in harvest. All or most of their catches they traded for other food and staples in the village. There was rarely anything left over even for small luxuries. Some said they were lazy and indeed, compared to many of the others, the fishers' workday was slow and without strain. They also favoured WaterSource over LifeSource when homage-dues were given.

Another voice, not of a fisher, said, "How can you say it is them? What have they done?"

"I will tell you. I have visited every one of the eleven that the sickness has cast down."

One of the village elders said, "There are two more today."

The LifeSource oracle ignored that, saying "All of them, every one I tell you, is a fisher or has some tie to the fishers." Whispered words and quiet chatter sprouted across the gathering. It was true, two of the sick were fishers. And nearly all present realised they, or someone close to them, had had some recent dealing with a fisher. In their parents' time, the fishers did not belong to the village. They had different ways and were kept apart by an invisible fence. In many of them, fear turned back to its work on that half-forgotten fence, to refresh, strengthen. Only the group of fishers stood still, alert, uncertain, wanting to fade away, not wanting to give any hint of guilt, aware that many eyes were discreetly turned to them.

The voice that had called out earlier said, "Did they not fish today, as they did the day before, and the day before that? What is it that has changed?"

Another said, "You heard LifeSource oracle. Everyone knows the fishers keep themselves outside of the proper cycle of festivals respected by the rest of us. Who knows what strange and offensive rituals they keep secret in the dwellings they build apart from ours. We have all heard the stories. Who knows how long the offences have been going on? You have heard it. LifeSource has been patient. And now we are told our boundlessly wise LifeSource's patience has reached its end. So, *we* have to pay the price for benignly accepting those outsiders, sharing the bounty of our fields, letting them have the handiwork of our crafters, when we should have been making them do their fair share."

A new voice called out, "Perhaps they can work our fields. Let our children catch the fish. They can already catch as many fish as the fishers do anyway, just playing or for sport." This last claim was not true, but few cared to note it.

Yet another voice, speaking at the huddle of fishers said, "They are not part of us. They are not like us."

The oracle said, "Sadly, they do not take up their share of the burden. You are generous and they exploit it."

A voice said, "Maybe they have been too much in the study of idle Wakes-For-Bedtime." That drew a few cautious laughs. Idle Wakes-For-Bedtime was a potter whose real name was Laughter-at-Sunset. He was known as idle Wakes-for-Bedtime because after the midday-rest meal when his pots had been fired, he frequently made off discreetly to a quiet place until he was found dozing by some customer. He spent his free time fishing and often sought out the fishers for their tips. He had been sitting against the trunk of one of the trees, asleep of course. Hearing his name, he stood abruptly, dislodging several small twigs some practical joker had been placing gently on his head. There was more sniggering.

Only a few were vocal – the rest would have let things be, just as they had in all the days leading up to this one. After all, they were seeing, talking with, or trading with fishers all the time. But even so, when they did, they saw not a villager, but a fisher. They were not their brothers, their sisters, their cousins. So even the ones who stayed quiet had no thought against the mood that was growing.

The LifeSource oracle said, "Listen to my words. I hear you utter much that is true. They are their kind, you are your kind. They are not your sisters, your brothers, your cousins. They are not even your neighbours."

Mist-on-Water said loudly enough for her voice to carry to the oracle, "Is that really true?"

The oracle said, "Who questions me? I have knowledge from beyond. Do I hear a child speak? Let those who have learned the ways of LifeSource speak. Let the adults speak."

She might have let it rest but being called a child goaded Mist-on-Water on. "From beyond? From beyond what? Never mind, I am sure your answer will only be understood by yourself and not even by the wise adults here. Being but a simple child, I simply seek to be educated on who my brother is. One brother I had is gone now. Now, Clouds-at-Sunset here is like my sister. Her brother has the illness." Mist-on-Water put her arm around Clouds-at-Sunset's shoulder. "What other brothers and sisters could I have that I do not even know yet? Yes, too many times I bicker with them, but when I let go of that anger, I know they are a beautiful gift … the most beautiful gift. Could even a fisher be one? My sister or brother? Is there some hidden twine that binds us all?"

The oracle said, "They are they, and we are we. That is all. Those matters are not for children. I will give you all a small piece of the knowledge I have, but not too much – more you could not endure. So, mark well this foretelling: the suffering from this sickness has not passed. Its troubles will touch every one of you. Deep angst will consume many, cold fear will creep into the heart of every one of you, you will not know who will next be pierced by the talon of disease. None among you will know what to do. So-be. Neglect this at your peril."

At this, murmurings of concern spread through the crowd, but Mist-on-Water said to Clouds-at-Sunset,

"That sounded impressive, but did she just tell us anything we didn't already know?"

Clouds-at-Sunset's only response was a frown.

The head of the village council, who had been standing to the side near the branch the oracle was sitting on, took a few steps towards her and said, "What does LifeSource require? What must we do to be free of this? How can we be brought back into her favour?"

The oracle said, "You parents, you give up your best food for your children, so that they can grow strong. You farmers, you cast down the seed from the strongest plants, so that next season's harvest will be bountiful. You lovers, you search out the thing most precious to you, to place in the hand of your beloved, just to see a smile dancing on her face. It is the same way with LifeSource. She is pleased to give you the best of her gifts so that you may grow to be strong in life, like her. We, in our gratitude, we all give up our homage-dues for LifeSource. And so LifeSource is pleased with us and in her gracious way, LifeSource blesses us."

"It sounds more business transaction than gracious blessing," Mist-on-Water grumbled, but with enough wits to ensure no one heard.

"But these times are not the usual times. The blessings we seek are not the usual blessings. The homage we need to make is not the usual homage." The oracle paused to allow the weight of her words to settle, to let the villagers prepare themselves. "Now I must pass to you the word gracious LifeSource has spoken to me.

"She says to you, you farmers, you must give one part in five of your last season's harvest – the grain stored, the fruits dried, the nuts collected." She paused and said, "And, from now, one part in four of the fish caught." The farmers, always less cheery than most, their faces creased from ceaseless strain and eyes hardened from tarrying long on the fickle sky, looked grim. The council records told that last season's harvest had been good. But that was half a season ago. Much had already been consumed and traded. One part in five would reduce their stores dangerously.

The oracle had been expecting that these long-suffering farmers, true to their kind, would take this new burden in their stride, as they did with the unforeseen trials that every other day dropped at their door. Some would probably have a harmless grumble later. She said, "But to ease any burden, we can take this in many parts, just a part each time we come back here." There was no response from them beyond a few heavy breaths and the grim set of their brows. Many of the fishers steeled their gaze with anger, stirred more by injustice than from the fish they would forfeit. Knowing they would find vanishing support from the high-siders, the ones compelled to unleash a curse strangled it in taut throats or trapped it between clenched jaws.

The pattern set, the oracle continued. "She says to you, you crafters, you must make homage-dues of five of your best works; we will select what is worthy." At this there were some gasps. Some thought of the many days of painstaking labour that had gone into each of their best works. Others were thinking of their favourite pieces, pieces into which they had poured all of their skill, their talent, their gifts, pieces that amazed and delighted all who saw them. They had never been given a price, and were never intended to be traded. But, bound by the precedent they had passively assented to, still no word was spoken. Many eyes were cast down. The oracle relaxed a little. She knew she was asking much of these villagers. While their dismay still stayed any words on their lips, she said, "I say to you, you will all rejoice come next season when this illness is just a dark memory." The oracle turned to the Village Voice, the head of the village council.

The Village Voice, still shaken by the decree the oracle had passed to them, said, "We have heard the words of LifeSource and we are thankful for them."

Really? We are? thought Mist-on-Water.

"The council and LifeSource oracle will meet in the morning to plan the collection of this homage-due. Walk easy this evening, all of you."

Habit summoned a subdued smattering of the usual 'walk easy' response. With only the very young retaining any energy, individuals or small groups began making their way back towards their dwellings. No one rejoiced in having found a path to escape from the pestilence that assailed them. It seemed they would be compelled to exchange one burden for another. They had been hoping it might be less weighty, at least.

Watching the slow dispersal, the LifeSource oracle was grateful for her ability to gain the village's consent to such a burden. Very few others, if any, could have extracted such an onerous homage-due, with almost no resistance. She did feel sympathy for the villagers. But it would be for their own good. She was confident that LifeSource would restore her gifts to the village quickly after they had made their homage-due pledges and began releasing them to her.

Observation Series: **Physical and Psychological Needs**

Summary of observations. My funny poppets do not know what they need. They keep trying to attach parts of their habitat onto themselves, or sometimes they even try to stick themselves onto parts of their habitat. They think it will make them better. They do not know that they have no authorised accessories and all the required parts are included. I wish I could pat them and make them all calm down.

Chapter 14

Leaving the clan head's business room, SiMiYah's step had a bounce to it. She said, "We may be able to get all of this done now. I'll find out what cousin DooDiDiDoo is doing." She pulled her BringSeeDo from her arm, pressed it against her ear, and it unfolded around the back of her head, under her earflaps. On one side, a wire-thin arm projected past her eye. After some eye movements and blinks, she announced that DooDiDiDoo's status showed he could be contacted.

She said, "Please excuse me for a moment. I'll just have a quick see-talk with cousin DooDiDiDoo." A few moments later she was talking, appearing to be looking at someone who was not there, and arranging to meet. Tracey surmised that the BringSeeDo was projecting an image of DooDiDiDoo into her pupil.

While SiMiYah was busy, Quentin said, "His name is DooDiDiDoo? His biggest challenge as clan head will be suppressing mass outbreaks of sniggering any time he's introduced."

SiMiYah took off her BringSeeDo, collapsing it onto her right wrist. She said, "Because we have clan head business, he will share a walk-eat with us. We just need to meet him at the entrance of building six in business pod 4-1 in hub 2-4." She walked quickly out of the dwelling. As Tracey and Quentin trailed behind, they gave Conrad_27-8 an enquiring look to see if he could offer some explanation of 'walk-eat', presumably some local activity that they had no experience of.

Conrad_27-8, who had been carried along by his own train of thought, misunderstood their questioning looks. He said, "I agree, the nested rectilinear coordinate system of addressing would be a very welcome improvement at your home. As an incidental benefit, all your … your… very large town things would all need to be torn down and rebuilt properly to accommodate it."

Tracey did not bother trying to correct Conrad's misunderstanding. She mimed sipping coffee at Quentin and then held her hands in front of her, palms up in a human gesture of questioning. Quentin responded with a human shrug.

From the resource hub, SiMiYah took them on a short GoSome trip to another resource hub connected to a business pod where DooDiDiDoo worked in a small team responsible for managing the town's hydro-electric power supply.

A different style of architecture greeted them at this business pod. Here, while still clustered around a central circular grove of vegetation, the buildings were larger, had two or three levels and, taking up more space on their allotments, were more tightly packed together. Their tighter spacing only left enough room between them for a narrow path bordered by slender vegetation that reached above the roof lines. The most common plant had clumping stems like bamboo but with hand-size circular leaves branching off horizontally. Spread along almost the whole lengths of some of the stems, from the ground to above the rooftops, bunches of deep red berries dangled. The five walked along the central ring path until they were nearly a third of the way along it. Despite their clear mission, they walked slowly with an air of uncertainty. A single Allundrian exited the building they were approaching. They all recognised DooDiDiDoo from the picture they had seen in the clan head's business room.

The greetings DooDiDiDoo and SiMiYah exchanged were formal, without warmth. SiMiYah introduced her companions and DooDiDiDoo gave a cursory response.

"Our walk-eat will need to be quick. I have another visitor soon." He reached up to a low branch of the tree they were passing under, where several bunches of yellow berries hung, and pulled off one of the largest. One by one, he pulled off and flicked the berries into his mouth. SiMiYah picked a small bunch of crimson berries from a bush they were walking past.

She said, "The venerable clan head of our 300-294-565 birth clan sends her greetings to you as well." Her voice carried a cheery, carefree lilt.

"Yes, yes. The venerable clan head of our 300-294-565 birth clan has sent you to meet with me. I wonder why would that be now? Why doesn't she just link up with me herself over a quick see-talk?"

SiMiYah said, "Our clan head had a backlog of postings she needed to attend to. She has a very desirable proposal for you. But she thinks it may take some time to discuss it."

"She has a proposal? Desirable, is it? And very generous, no doubt. She must be making the Personal View Mandate work overtime to say that." His tone made it clear that he did in fact doubt that the proposal would be generous. "What is this proposal then? She does not still want to offload her clan head mantle, I hope."

SiMiYah said, "*Give up* her clan head mantle? She would have to pass it on to you as next in line. Would that not be a great honour?"

"So that *is* it. An honour, is it? It would be about the same honour as being invited to appear before the whole clan to demonstrate with the orifice intended for releasing waste how to suck up a hundred unpeeled orange spike berries. How did you think I would suddenly welcome something already many times rejected?"

"At last, someone who talks my language," Quentin said to Kieran.

DooDiDiDoo picked some berries off his bunch that did not look to his liking and flicked them away.

SiMiYah gave no answer to DooDiDiDoo's question. She was looking flustered, her fingers fidgeting with themselves. Speaking to herself, she said, "It is an honour, isn't it. Unless by the Personal View Mandate you have another view. Anyone can, can't they – have any other view. Then it isn't an honour. Or, is it? Yes, I know I should not have thought it would be easy."

DooDiDiDoo, still inspecting his bunch of berries, was not listening. Tracey turned to him. "Excuse me. If I can just ask a quick question: what would be the biggest drawback for you of being clan head?"

DooDiDiDoo looked at Tracey as if she were an annoying and distasteful bug that had appeared that instant and said, "Well for a start, the clan levy that funds the role is a pittance. It is enough of a struggle making do with the miserly pay I get for my work here as a hydro-electric overseer. The job needs finely honed technical skills, but they pay for minions. I would have to give up my position here. How does she expect me to live? Without extra income, I would be thrown into a miserable subsistence existence."

"And what else?"

"That's enough. No, I would be breaching the Well-being Mandate too."

SiMiYah recited it, a reflex groomed through every one of her years of schooling: "Well-being: every citizen must have the opportunity to seek for, and gain, the things she wants for her personal well-being."

DooDiDiDoo said, "So there you are: forbidden by Mandate. I must get everything I want. It all has a cost. Nothing more to talk about." He looked pleased.

Kieran said, "Everything is included. Credit details are not required."

SiMiYah said, "Yes, yes – I agree completely. Everyone must have their well-being. It cannot be neglected. Although, I must admit that I do sometimes – neglect it a little, just a tiny bit. I shouldn't, I know. No need to. There are so many things we can get for well-being– all that nice food, all the different kinds of entertainment, maybe the masterwork of art, maybe the precious metal, yes, iron even. Yes, many, many things. If you don't make sure you have enough, you won't have your well-being. You must make sure. You must work at it. Well, well-being is not really work, is it? Just getting it

– that's work. You know the saying: 'It's the price you pay for your time of play.' I do admit it: I neglect it sometimes. Sometimes I think I will just forget about it – not do it, or even …" She stopped speaking and looked about. Then in a whisper, she said, "Or sometimes I even think: maybe do I even want them – my well-being things?" She stopped and waited for the reaction. DooDiDiDoo rewarded her, his expression wavering between shock, contempt, and anger. She went on quickly, "But only sometimes, not often. Not enough to breach the Mandate."

DooDiDiDoo said, "You sound as confused as a three-fingered simpleton trying to count to four. Surely your minder is not saying it?"

"No, minder is not saying that. Minder is groaning about it all. Poor thing – it's doing everything it can. My way of thinking about things is just too muddled for it. But anyway, do you know, sometimes what I think is this: do I really want to hear all its words about how I need to get this and that? So many words, all the time. *All* the time. Get this, get that. From someone. Then from someone else. Someone else who has to lose some of her well-being things to me. Which violates the Mandate for her. So around we go. How will that Mandate ever work? It's always a battle. Some peace would be nice. Some quiet. What? I suppose so. I suppose if I did pay more attention to the Well-being Mandate, as minder says, and made sure I had the things it says I want, I would get my peace and quiet. But I tell you, minder would have to stop worrying first."

DooDiDiDoo said, "It worries because it knows."

"Yes, it does know. It knows that every one of those well-being things has its own little needs and wants. All those nice things I keep in my dwelling room, those useful things I have in my work pod. They need to be looked after. They are always breaking up, wearing down, getting lost, getting taken, needing cleaning, fixing, filling up, or emptying out – just lots of fussing over. But I do need them, don't I? It's funny in a way – sometimes I wonder if those things need me more than I need them. Or do we just need each other? I don't know. It sounds wrong."

All of this was puzzling Tracey. To her, the Allundrians had seemed very unmaterialistic. Their personal property was scant.

DooDiDiDoo dismissed SiMiYah's doubts. "I know what I need. I need my fento-units. They get me the things I want. They get me the things I like. One day even," he cast his eyes over SiMiYah and the others, "hopefully, a better class of annoying meddlers."

"Well yes, of course they make me feel nicer too, those things. That's funny too, you know? Those things I like are just some bits of polymer, or traces of copper, aluminium, silicon, maybe engineered into a micro-fibre-reinforced resin casing. Much like us – just a fantastic concoction of chemicals. It seems a pity. Sometimes I look at those well-being things and I ask them: how do you give me a nice feeling? What power do you have? What is that feeling, really? Minder likes it – minder tells me it's good. Don't worry – they don't answer me. Not yet anyway. But I want to know: where does my feeling come from? Is it in them?"

"What you really need to know the answer to is this: do you have any way to make me feel I should continue this walk-eat? What *I* know right now is that all your talk is less useful than a washroom for a fish," DooDiDiDoo said.

But SiMiYah was absorbed in her own thoughts and DooDiDiDoo's question did not break into them. "I know this is muddled, but I don't think my nicer feeling comes out of those *things*. So, I have a strange idea: could it have already been in me all the time – that feeling? Is it already inside me somewhere, somehow, trying to get out? But I'm too wound up to let it, too bound up with something that is not here, with me. When I get that something, I just relax a little bit. Not too much. Then a little bit can come out – a little bit of feeling nicer. Not too much. I'm getting very muddled. I'm not even completely sure I know what I want. Actually, not even half-sure. Minder is trying to straighten it all out for me. But minder thinks my questions are wrong. I ask: can my well-being things really make me feel nice? But minder says: your body needs them, it likes them. Then I think: but a body doesn't know anything. But minder says to stop it, so I go and get them. And then they all turn into wayward children, running off and getting lost, or insisting on their own way, or doing something I don't want. This is twisting my mind; it throbs and aches. Do minders hurt?"

DooDiDiDoo realised she was no longer talking to him and said to no one in particular, "I don't need this nonsense. She would need to be twice as smart to get to stupid."

"Minder heard that." SiMiYah was angry. "But I have a question for you: what do you do when the visitor comes? You know, the visitor that comes. Yes, it always comes. If not this day, another day. Another day comes and brings that scorning visitor. *They are not enough*, it scorns. All those things for your well-being, all your flimsy femto-units, they don't work anymore – on that day they are not enough. You can try to keep shoving them into some emptiness inside you but after they have all gone in, it's still there. A dark hole doing one thing – hiding the black lips kissing you with hard words. What do you do then?"

DooDiDiDoo had not been expecting her outburst and only responded with a look of confused innocence.

If SiMiYah's indignation had flared quickly, its burnout was swifter. She turned away and looked up to the forest canopy. In a monotone she said, "I think it's hopeless. Everything. Nothing is right. Nothing is good." And then, "I don't want to go on." She stopped talking and left them trapped in silence.

As she stood with them, exposed in her doubts and vulnerabilities, no one moved. Tracey could not think of something to say that would not sound trite. She looked to see if Quentin would take the lead for once. Quentin was thinking they were so far off track that they would need an atlas to find the place to get a map that showed where they could start a trip to get them somewhere near where they wanted to go. Conrad_27-8 too was squirming in the face of a problem he could not, for now, put a single number to. Kieran was listening to the silence. DooDiDiDoo had pulled his BringSeeDo from his upper arm, snapped it over his ear, and was engrossed in it.

Trying not to look at SiMiYah at the same time as trying not to look as if they were avoiding looking at her, they all watched her for what might come next. SiMiYah did not appear to be at all self-conscious or awkward as she softly hummed a whimsical tune to herself.

Tracey had a desperate thought and moved her head to catch DooDiDiDoo's eye. "What about the service to your clan? Would you not be greatly thanked and praised if you freely gave your service to the clan, making an honourable sacrifice for them?" Even before she had finished saying it, her minder tut-tutted that it was the wrong approach for this individual who appeared to enjoy being cranky. She had to agree.

"Oh, so you think I would like to have the thanks and praise? That would be my compensation?" DooDiDiDoo's tone was laden with derision. "Excellent idea. Then I will be able to eat thanks for breakfast and praise for rain-meal."

Even he had seen through it in an instant. Tracey was clutching about at nothings, reaching for a new angle to hook his interest. There must be something, but she did not know enough about him.

SiMiYah said, "I'm sorry we wasted your time."

DooDiDiDoo grunted, turned, and started a brisk walk back to the building he had come out of.

As he was nearing Kieran, Kieran was reaching up to a large, yellow, bell-shaped fruit hanging at head height. He plucked it, bit out a chunk of the flesh, and held the fruit up to reveal a cluster of dark purple seeds. Mouth full, he said to DooDiDiDoo, "Ah! Look at this. Here are countless generations waiting to flow out of this one fruit. Right now, it is embracing just a few seeds, sleeping. But it has not yet found its purpose. Its purpose is for an ever-increasing abundance of life to flow from it – countless generations. All it can do is look inside, see its seeds, and release them, even as they sleep. If it will pay that price – the price of releasing the burden it bears – it will reap the abundance it has given."

DooDiDiDoo stopped mid-stride and said, "I know what you mean. My aunt KamSoKamToo needs to be a bit like that cloudseed fruit. She is very wealthy, but she's seized my shares in the BlueLake town farming collective. She has complete power over them as trustee for my brother and me. She seized the trusteeship after our parents died in the earthquake of '54. She should release those seeds she's keeping from us. They are ours. We never get any of the income – she just reinvests it. I can make those seeds grow just as well as she can. But she's always saying that the capital must be put to work. Between us, my brother and I own sixty percent of the collective now."

Tracey said, "It must be a big responsibility for her to take on for you."

Quentin muttered, "But what a win for that equality Mandate." No one heard him.

"So she always says. Of course, she gets her generous *trustee fee* to compensate for the heinous burden of having to read all the income statements – the poor thing. But she is already very wealthy – she doesn't need that income. She should give me my owner-units. I would manage them properly and still make them grow. Especially when her twenty-five percent *trustee fee* stops. I would be getting a good income."

"Good enough to live on? More than your miserly pay?" That was SiMiYah asking.

"Certainly. If she did do that, I would be able to take on the mantle of clan head. And my clan battling would make that old git look like a puff of cool air. Yes, that's true. I could forfeit my job."

"You say you would agree to that?"

"Yes, clan head HumSumSon will have what she wants. But aunt KamSoKamToo is a hard nut."

"KamSoKamToo. Of 24-9 quadrant?"

"That's her."

SiMiYah gave a little jump and looked as if she were about to embrace DooDiDiDoo. He leaned away from her. She said, "I know her. We are related. She's my cousin, twice removed. We get on very well. Sometimes. I can talk to her. She will do it for me. She will give them to you."

Tracey, twisting her head trying to look at her minder but failing, was hissing, "I know." To SiMiYah, "Let's not be too hasty. Let's hear what she has to say first."

SiMiYah dismissed her concern. "I can do it. Then you can be clan-head."

DooDiDiDoo said, "I am willing to serve the clan. If I get my BlueLake farm collective owner-units."

SiMiYah crossed her arms over her chest to DooDiDiDoo, a gesture of thanks.

"Very brave of him too, to sacrifice that mundane tedious job he hates. I guess it must satisfy the give-it-up-in-the-name-of-science Mandate." This time, Quentin's interjection was loud enough to be heard. They all pretended they had not.

SiMiYah said, "We can present your case. I am sure you will be very appreciative."

"When you arrange for me to get what is mine? How I will dance and sing for you. If there were only more who were as generous – everyone would be able to have … well … they could actually have what they have. What an inspired idea."

A chiming sound came from DooDiDiDoo's BringSeeDo. He said, "That is all I have time for. Let me know how you go." He gave a quick gesture for goodbye and without waiting for a response, turned back to the building he had come from, walking quickly, muttering, "So, we get to have what's ours. How excellent."

Watching him walk away, Tracey said, "All the pieces seem to be falling into place. It's a shame that has to be one of them."

SiMiYah said, "What? The pieces are falling over? What, minder? Yes, what she says is right. This is getting too difficult now. I need to get DooDiDiDoo's farming collective owner-units to him for him to accept the clan head mantle so that clan head will revoke DahTiYahYah's exile so he will give us the iron nugget the Mandate-advocate requires in exchange for taking my Mandate-breach case."

Quentin said, "The hip bone's connected to the knee bone, the knee bone's connected to the toe bone, the toe bone's connected to the thigh bone, the thigh bone's connected to the …" While he was chanting his jumbled anatomy lesson, SiMiYah pulled her BringSeeDo from her wrist and clicked it over her ear.

She announced that DooDiDiDoo's aunt was not available to meet until the next day. She said, "Yes, I know. We are running out of time." It was to her minder.

Tracey said, "There is still enough time."

SiMiYah said, "She said there *is* still time. I can go and see cousin KamSoKamToo tomorrow. I will go as early as I can."

"Not too early," said Quentin.

Tracey was toying with an idea for their next trip – a way to do things differently. Maybe a better way to deal with all the obstacles that were appearing at every turn. Despite the encouragement she had given to SiMiYah, she too felt they were running out of time.

Chapter 15

The morning after the LifeSource oracle had given her speech, Mist-on-Water walked up the erratic track to Sand-on-Stone's cabin earlier than usual. She emerged from the forest to see Sand-on-Stone bent over in his vegetable patch, making something with long, straight sticks. He had four sticks, each as thick as three fingers, spread evenly in a straight line and pushed deep into the loose soil, each standing as tall as Mist-on-Water. About a third of the way up an end stick he was tying a thinner stick, longer, long enough to cross the other uprights. Mist-on-Water went to the other end of the cross stick and held it level, up against the far upright.

She said, "You missed the gathering with LifeSource oracle."

"Well-met to you too. I was tending my white-stripe melons. I hope that LifeSource approved."

"She didn't approve."

Sand-on-Stone, surprised at her certainty, pulled the knot in the longleaf fibre tight and looked to where she was squatting.

"It has started. I started it. They are starting to conceal them – the things they don't want the oracle to take," Mist-on-Water said.

He took two longleafs from a pile at his feet, went to the next upright and holding the cross stick against it with one hand, stretched out with the other so Mist-on-Water could take the longleaf from it.

"So-be. We have a rebellion. What if LifeSource finds out?"

She started tying her end of the cross stick. "She won't. For the same reason she didn't approve your melon tending – there is no LifeSource."

Sand-on-Stone mused, *LifeSource or not, there is an oracle.* "The oracle knows about the last harvests from the village records."

"So-be. There is not much the farmers and orchardists can do. But the crafters can. They all have things they keep, and want to keep keeping, things they enjoy. And the fishers – they slink through the marsh when they see her coming. They will never pay, or they will just send her the stink-fish they usually throw back. She blames them, but she can't make them pay."

"You convinced them all to do this – all the ones who can?"

"Not all. Some are too afraid. When there isn't even a LifeSource to be afraid of. Or they don't have anything special. Like the potter – he doesn't care. But the paper maker had a big store – it is much smaller now, almost nothing. And some others – I could see them thinking about it. There is no reason for them to lose so much."

Sand-on-Stone tightened the final knot holding the cross stick to the third upright. Mist-on-Water picked up another long stick and held it against the uprights, about a third of the way from their tops, while Sand-on-Stone tied it, going more quickly with the help. Then they tied a third long horizontal near the tops. "The oracle must have given them a reason – a good reason."

"She says it is the good act of sacrifice." Still thinking about the previous evening's village gathering, Mist-on-Water said, "What about your source-with-no-name? What sacrifices does it require? What way has it made for someone to get what she wants?"

Sand-of-Stone made a quiet grunting sound deep in his throat. It could have been a soft groan. He said, "It is the same sacrifice that the singer, the musician, and the poet make."

Mist-on-Water considered that. "You mean, all of the time the singer devotes to practising and improving her voice, learning the song and the words. And the long tedious hours the musician gives up to mastering her instrument, or the days and nights the poet forfeits searching out elusive lines?"

"No, I mean the joy the singer must endure when he and the audience delight in his song, the happiness a musician playing one of his favourites is forced to accept when a passer-by dances to the melody and rhythm, the faces of wonder taken to places new and fair that the poet is compelled to witness as he sends forth his lines." Sand-of-Stone saw that Mist-on-Water's face bore the look of one offered a good price in the market for something she had not come to buy and neither needed nor wanted. He felt he was losing his sale. "It is the sacrifice of giving without losing."

"That is no sacrifice."

"Say-you." With the trellis all tied, Sand-on-Stone started to tighten a few loose knots. "What is it then – your sacrifice?"

"So now it is my turn to educate you? So-be, I will then. But I will tell you of not one, but two sacrifices. One a sham, and one true."

Sand-on-Stone was now systematically checking the trellis, tightening knots, and pushing down on the uprights. "Two things named once. You will confuse me."

"Then pay careful attention to me, uncle. Even you may be able to grasp it."

Sand-on-Stone picked up a thin, hand-sized, smooth, flat stone, went the bench under the whitewood tree, sat and waited, attentive.

Mist-on-Water said, "Good, you are ready." She stood in front of him, looked to the sky for a moment, and said, "The first kind is the sacrifices all the oracles of the sources counsel us to make. Each oracle puts it inside her own special little story, but they all go the same way: the pick-a-name-Source is wonderful, see how she or he has given us this and that? Yes? Good. Now to show your gratitude or devotion or to keep it going or whatever it is, you must offer sacrifices. Don't you see – it is just a trade? It is coercion to settle a bargain never made. The oracles want to make this trade something special by giving it a special name. This trade is not true sacrifice. How can it even be just? An obligation never asked for, never agreed to. If I did the same, I would be called an extorter. It makes me angry."

"So-be. A sham sacrifice – just a trade. Yes, I think my old mind is slowly grasping your difficult ideas."

"Take care that your mocking does not damage this poor vulnerable student. I am the only one you have, you know."

"So-be, I will try to preserve your delicate, timid nature." He smiled to himself at the thought of Mist-on-Water being either delicate or timid, then continued. "But perhaps the deception that angers you is just a flimsy wisp that collapses against the first sally that your anger might throw at it. How carelessly your 'sham sacrifice' holds up its mask. With a glance it is easily known for what it is. And yet how many of us here trust and seek the corpse of loss, draping it in fancy beads, so a sham is celebrated even as it stands naked and pleased beside its coyly dropped veils. Will you wrench from them what they grasp for, from those who, with their grip still firm, will wake one morning to feel nothing in their fingers?"

"Even if they want it, it still makes me angry."

"Tell me then, daughter, what is the other one – your true sacrifice?"

"The true one is good. It is when you give up something even if you are not compelled to, even if you are not asked to. It is when the mother goes hungry so her child may eat. It is when the youngest brother makes some bad error, say a very bad error where justice calls for him to take a punishment he is too young to bear, and then the stronger eldest sister says it was her, takes the blame, and takes the punishment. It is when a powerful evil is defeated, no matter what the cost."

"This is good?"

"And noble."

"To be celebrated?"

"To be honoured." Mist-on-Water was very sure of herself.

"To be desired?"

"To be cherished. Like all that is good and noble."

"Say-you. Do you remember the times you looked after the tikes in the crèche?"

"Not this again. Perhaps your memory is failing you, uncle old-timer."

"What is the price they have paid you, to keep them safe?"

"I will levy the price on them when I am head of the village council. They will pay dearly." She said it with mock menace.

"You should leave the poor humour to me – I am much better at it," said Sand-on-Stone. "How is it that you were forced to this burden – your time in the crèche? Are you being punished?"

"You know it is one of the village council works. They organise the things that benefit many."

"So, not being punished. And no reward either? Such a lot of work."

"It is something we share – the ones who do it. The ones who choose it as one of their tasks on the village roster. For some of us, yes, it is a burden. For all of us really, at times. Sometimes I like it, but much of it is hard work. It is demanding, wearing, tiring. I do it because it is needed. The infants need us."

"Then do you say you make a sacrifice, even if it be your true sacrifice?"

"Some of it is in there, I suppose. And what about you?"

"What about me?"

"What do you say?"

Sand-on-Stone stood and walked back to his vegetable patch. Using the thin flat stone he still had in his hand, he loosened the soil around a tiny black-spot berry climber seedling, no larger than his thumb, that had self-seeded in the tilled soil. Lifting it with wispy roots encased in a clump of crumbly soil, he said, "I say you embrace the ideas of *not*."

"I embrace what is good and noble."

"Hunger is good? Conflict is to be sought? Errors are noble? Without such as these you will not have this sacrifice you seek."

"You scramble my words. Is it not better to give, than to turn aside?"

"I can see in this true sacrifice of yours also what you deride. It too is a trade."

Watching him take his delicate package to the vegetable patch, Mist-on-Water thought about his words. She said, "So-be, perhaps one loses, and another gains. But the loss is by choice, not a trade. There is no exchange. It is a loss borne freely and gladly."

"Ah, still a loss say-you? For our noble sacrificer? Why does he do it?"

"No, there is more than just a loss. Perhaps, you are going to say it is still an exchange – an exchange for feeling good, proud even, or for the honour of the humble bow before the praise, or the warming of the thanks. Those may be there. Why not? But there is more. Is there not a turn towards something new, a reach towards something better, can you not see an embrace there with something pure and good?" She was pleased that she had been able to get this out. It had been a burden growing on her mind for the last season, but she had not felt there had been anyone who would understand. Or care.

"Do we now arrive where a thirst may be quenched? Or, I wonder, are we here just to watch the river flow by?" Sand-on-Stone had posed the question to the stone in his hand, so Mist-on-Water gave no answer. "The ones who are holding back from the oracle – are they embracing this pure and good?"

"They only have two ways – keep giving her what she has not earned, or give up her nonsense for something better."

"Who tells them what is better? You? Don't they care about the wrath of LifeSource? Did you prove she does not exist?"

"I didn't need to prove it. They know what makes them happy, they know what they value. I only had to remind them. They did not even know I was doing it."

"It reminds me of a story."

Her eyes narrowed. "This story does not involve the village crèche, I hope."

"No. It is not even this village. Another village, not too far." Sand-on-Stone had dug a small hole for the seedling, placed it in it, and was gently pushing the soil around the root clump. "A young lad in that village had just finished his education. He was lucky because in that village there was no old hermit living up the hill they had to waste time going to."

"Tell me the name of it. They may take me in and let me graduate there."

"This young lad had not chosen his craft yet. He could not decide. So, he used to help the oldest auntie in the village by tending her vegetable garden. He was very good at it. That garden had the biggest, sweetest, juiciest, most perfect vegetables in the whole village."

"Why would he do that? What about his own family's vegetable patch?"

"They didn't like the way he did it. He had his own way. He used to collect all the food scraps he could find, especially the fish scraps. He was forever collecting them and mixing them and piling them in piles and turning the piles while they rotted. It was all quite smelly, and it attracted every crawling and buzzing insect. When one of the piles got to its smelliest, he would put it around the vegetables, or dig it into the soil, along with all the crawling and buzzing things. But the old auntie did not mind because her vegetable garden was at the back of her cabin, and she could no longer smell very well."

"That old auntie was very lucky he would do so much work for her."

"Yes, she knew that. So, she let him have any of the vegetables from the garden, of course. He tended her vegetables, and he had the best vegetables in the village, and he was happy."

"Good. A nice short story for once. Does this mean I can leave early?"

"Then one day, an old fisher uncle asked that lad if he would tend his vegetables. He had seen him taking the scraps after the filleting and he knew about that old auntie's vegetable garden – the best in the village. Everyone in that village talked about it, in the same breath as they laughed at his – the worst. It could not even really be called a vegetable patch. The plants in it were always either dead or dying. The old fisher uncle said the lad could have all the fish scraps he wanted – it would save him throwing them in the river – and he could eat any of his catch too, if he would tend his vegetables. The lad agreed and soon the old fisher uncle had the second-best vegetable patch in the village. The lad had all the fish he could eat, even the tastiest, along with the best of the best vegetables, and he was very happy."

"He's going to have trouble tending those vegetable patches when he starts his craft."

"It was not much work. You know how it is. Those vegetable patches are not large. Once the ground is worked, once the seeds are placed and their food dug in, once the weeds are cleared, once the new plants are tied, or not, most of the time they just do what they do, growing away. He did not need to come by often. He made sure little problems were fixed before they became big ones. So, not much work, until one day a farmer asked him to make a vegetable patch for her. She could grow grain, but she could not grow vegetables. Barely. She had given up on them and when she wanted any, she had to go and see what was at the market. She envied everyone else who could go out and get exactly the one they wanted, fresh, just a few steps from their door. He agreed and soon she had every type of vegetable thriving just outside her door. She was very pleased with the lad."

"Let me guess. She let him have some of her grain. Now he has all the grain he can eat."

"No, she did not. She gave him her farm. It was the biggest and best in the village. It was excellent cropping land, already cleared, land that every season gave good crops. It was far too large for her. Her family had grown up and left to go their own ways. She had other farmers come and work it for her – ones just starting out on small farms, or whose crops had failed, or who bartered a share for their labour. She gave it to him so she could just live in the cabin and visit her neighbours and have her vegetables."

"What? She gave him her whole farm. The folk there give away farms? I definitely need to find that village."

"Yes, he had the whole farm, plenty of workers to work it, his favourite fish and all the best vegetables, and he was very, very happy."

"Until …"

"So-be. Have you heard this story already? Yes, he had all of that until the day one of the village councillors decided to move in with the lass from the cabin next to him. She wanted them to settle and start a family. The two of them were perfectly matched. They both liked the same things and disliked the same things. One thing they both hated was working outside in places like vegetable patches. Since he had moved out of his cabin, the councillor said the lad could have it, if he set up a vegetable patch for him and his new family – not too close. The cabin was quite bare and empty, but with his vegetables, his fish, his farm and new cabin, the lad was very, very, very happy."

"What, it's cabins they are giving away now? Is there anyone left in that village who does not have a most excellent vegetable patch?"

"I'm glad you asked. One day, one of the craft masters – she was the best master in the whole village – she was extremely busy, so busy she always missed the times for planting seeds in her vegetable patch. So she asked the lad to … well, you know the rest. The crafter was so delighted with her vegetables she filled the lad's new cabin with her best crafts, and the lad was very, very, very, very happy."

"Getting to be quite a lot of vegetable patches to look after, now. Even if they do most of the growing by themselves."

"The lad did not mind. He had other things to think about. There was an especially important event coming up – the council elections. The villagers who did not have one of the lad's vegetable patches felt they were missing out. They said they would vote him onto the village council if he set up a council-run vegetable patch, not too big, just for growing his speciality – purple spot melons. Then they could all share them. He agreed. So, he was voted onto the village council. Now the lad, even though he was still young, with his new status as a village councillor, was much respected and envied, with his large farm, his cabin filled with the best craftwork and on its table, the best fish and vegetables. He was very, very, very, very, very happy."

"About time for him to choose his craft, I think."

"Now he started getting invited to all the dinners, all the parties. Every evening, he dined and was entertained, with many friends there, some very special. He was an admired councillor, had his good farmland, slept in his nice cabin filled with many fine things, kept tending all those vegetable patches – and also a new one – his own. And he was very, very, very, very, very, very happy."

"Not needing to listen to tales that have no end would have been a big part of that."

"Then one day, an oracle came. He was an oracle for LifeSource. The oracle saw all the lad's flourishing vegetable patches, the lad's way of growing getting the credit. The oracle said, *they are not being grown in the way of the traditions, without the right homage – it was not right.* The lad did not know how his vegetables could be grown any better. He asked the oracle to show him some better ones, so he could learn. To the lad's surprise, the oracle became very angry."

Mist-on-Water tapped her forehead. "Oh, I see. This is the *Better Not Go Against the Oracle* story. I should have known."

"The oracle announced that LifeSource shunned the lad. Any who associated with him would be cast out of her favour too. No one wanted that, even if they were not sure about LifeSource. The lad was expelled from the council, the farmer took her land back, the councillor would not let him live in the cabin next door, the craft master demanded her crafts back, the fisher would not give him any fish. But the oracle said the lad had to keep tending all the vegetable patches until he learned the right way."

"What did he do?"

"What could he do? The lad was no longer welcomed to dinners, he had no farm, he had no cabin filled with the best craftwork, no fish, no friends to eat with, everyone sneered at him, even his family would not speak to him. He was forced to keep working those vegetable patches. They did not even let him eat the vegetables – their vegetables. All he did was spend his time with his smelly scraps tending all those vegetable patches. Then …"

"Then?"

"He was very, very, very, very, very, very happy."

"What? How can he still be happy? He has lost everything. He has nothing. He should stop working all those vegetables."

"None of those things – not the fish, not the farm, not the cabin, not all the craftwork in it, not the village council status, not the merry parties, not even the delicious vegetables – none of them were what had been making him happy."

"So-be. Having lots of possessions and influence do not make you happy. Everyone knows that. It's what everyone says. You did not need to tell me such a very, very, very, very, very, very long story."

"Say-you. *Everyone knows it.* Yet everyone who hears that story thinks at the end that the lad will be unhappy, that it needs to be fixed. Even you. What do you really believe?"

"So-be. A clever tale then. Cleverer than the oracles' little fables. A tidy little trap there. But the net seems to have a hole. Why would that lad still be happy working with those smelly vegetables? Do we not say it is friends or family, being safe and free, seeing a better future – they are where happiness really comes from. But he had none of those. How could he still be a hundred times very happy?"

"It was what he had been doing with the vegetables."

"Ah. So, the source of happiness is digging. Digging while swimming in a swarm of bugs. The bent-beak bird must be ecstatic."

"Did you say, *The Source*? I wasn't going to bring it up again. But since you have raised it yourself ..."

"I need to find a way to keep your source-with-no-name out of it."

"You already have that way. There are only two ways to live here in time and dust. The first way is the way that releases the quiet echo in you, that expresses the tender glimmer – the echo of the laughter of The Source, the glimmer of your hidden self. That echo can sound anywhere; that glimmer can shine on anything. That is one thing you can do. If you know how. The lad had found that way, with his vegetables. Doing *not* is the other way. That way he kept discarding. He made no sacrifice."

"And if they had taken away his vegetable patches?" She already knew what he was going to answer but felt obliged to take this walk to the end.

"He would have been even happier. He would have found that the way he had with his vegetables, he could have with anything, anywhere, with anyone."

A glimmer. It itched. It teased. Mist-on-Water felt it. She wanted to scratch it. She could not reach it. *Hidden self? Fanciful. But that itch. What is it? What can I do about it?*

Observation Series: **Conflict Resolution**

Summary of observations. Sometimes my scrumptious tykes have squabbles among themselves. One of them does something and another one wants it undone. That is right – it wants the other one to turn back time. Even they have worked out that this is impossible. It does not stop them from wanting it and even trying to make it happen. Duffers.

Chapter 16

Tracey and Kieran arrived at Quentin's apartment building together.

As Kieran let her into the apartment, Tracey was saying, "They are all just doing what their minders are telling them to do. Like slaves, almost. Maybe we could try to get them apart. Then we would be able to talk to them without those minders interfering." Quentin was standing in front of them as they came through the door. "What do you think?" Tracey asked him.

Quentin said, "Certainly. Yes. But I do not think we will be ready to attempt something that challenging until we have mastered discourse in analytic philosophy with the more intelligent decorative pebbles in your pot plants."

"Have you found out anything about them from those SeeDo things?"

"I don't think that even their expansive databases extend to your decorative pebbles."

"No. The minder things."

"Ahh, of course. Let me check." He took a step to his laptop sitting on the bench, placed his hand on it, and stared at the ceiling for a moment. "Hmm. No. Haven't quite got to that one on my list, not yet. But I will. It is sitting just under two slightly more urgent tasks: *How to fake being interested in aliens that are as useful and exciting as white on white wallpaper,* and *Investigating the care and feeding of weirdly distasteful critters not mentioned in Harry Potter.*"

"Fine. I'm going to start up a little research project of my own then."

"Make it a quick one. I want to wrap up my investigations this trip. I seem to be getting a dose of that body confusion fraction brain was talking about."

Each time they came back, they had all felt it, hardly noticeable at first, but growing. Last time, Tracey had taken several minutes to re-orient, had had a panicky feeling that she was in the wrong body, or that her body was the wrong place for her, until she accepted the thoughts that followed: it was the right place. She had to remember this body was hers and was her.

Tracey said, "What about that Galactic Council astronomy mission thing you're supposed to be doing?"

"Don't worry about that. I'm not. Our sitter has either forgotten us, or he's very good at delegating."

Three knocks on Quentin's door followed by two more told them that Conrad_27-8 had arrived.

To Kieran singing America's *A Horse with No Name*, with his usual own take on the lyrics, they settled themselves for their transfer.

I've laughed through the desert on a source-with-no-name …

Quentin thought, *what is he doing?* At the same time, Tracey was wishing she could carry a tune that well. Then Conrad_27-8 told them to clear their minds, ready for departure.

Meeting SiMiYah at the front of her dwelling again, Tracey said, "Always equality. I am looking forward to meeting your aunt."

Quentin said, "And *always get it over with* – the Mandate that should have been. Maybe it's not too late to slip it in. I too am looking forward to seeing your aunt, or at least the back of her. Does she live far from here?"

With a look of slight confusion, SiMiYah said, "She resides in the 24-9 octant. You are not long in our town, are you? Have you been to the 24-9 octant before? It is the octant where the very wealthy live. Her dwelling pod is not the *most* exclusive, but it is still very prestigious." She had started walking towards the resource hub as she was speaking.

"Making everyone else equally envious, thanks to the equality Mandate, of course," said Quentin, trailing just behind her, not caring if no one heard, or if everyone did.

"Of course," said SiMiYah, giving an immediate reflexive response to a question that had an answer so obvious, that for her no further explanation was called for.

Quentin looked at her. She gave no sign that she was being anything but sincere. He gave a human shrug, body language that would have mystified SiMiYah if she had noticed it.

"I suppose you know what these octants are all about?" Quentin said to Conrad_27-8, not really caring, but also, goaded by his minder, feeling uncomfortable with a gap in his knowledge.

"Yes, it is very simple. That is one of the benefits an advanced society enjoys, once it is intelligent enough to organise itself properly."

Quentin ignored the feeble attack on his species and waited for the information that he knew Conrad_27-8's minder was insisting he provide.

"As you have seen, groups of dwellings are organised into rounded square allotments. They call them dwelling pods. They are all the same size and shape. Each dwelling pod has eight dwellings, with a resource hub attached at one corner. The dwelling pods are always grouped in fours – the four quarters of a larger square. They call that a dwelling quadrant. Around each dwelling quadrant are the farms – eight of them, each the same size as the dwelling quadrant. They call each farming area a produce unit and the eight of them are a produce octant. So, an *octant* is simply a three-by-three grid of eight produce units, with a dwelling quadrant in the centre."

"Thank you. I'm glad I asked."

His irony was lost on Conrad_27-8. "Don't mention it. I am glad to have provided some interesting information."

"Yes, I have some very interesting information. Now I have established that it is possible to experience relativistic time dilation at normal walking speed."

"What?"

"That's right. With the assistance of our brief chat, our short stroll has felt like it has dragged on for at least a day."

Arriving at the resource hub, they turned towards the transit lounge ramp.

Tracey felt the mood was a touch dour. With a cheerful lilt to her voice, she said, "That didn't take us long."

Understanding what Tracey was trying to do, SiMiYah worked at a smile while her minder adorned it with a nervous tinge, saying, *Yes, here now. Are you really ready now?*

The Galactic Council agents-at-large had been wondering what the 'prestigious' part of town would be like. Their first impressions were underwhelming. At a quick glance, from the outside the dwellings looked very similar to the ones they had already seen, perhaps a smidgen larger, with the allotments sized for six dwellings in the pod, rather than the eight they had seen everywhere else. Then they started seeing other differences, but subtle ones. The gardens were individually themed, resembling to Kieran's eyes traditional Japanese gardens. Here a gurgling water feature, there flowing sculptures blending so well they were barely noted at first, and over there a small casual moat embracing a quilt of colourful rounded pebbles intricately arranged. The plants were subtly different too – more exotic perhaps – the flowers larger, or more copious, or shaped more delicately, or their colours more brilliant, or their patterns beautiful. The plants themselves were distinctive as well – this one impossibly slender, some over there with elaborate geometric shapes – clearly carefully pruned bonsai-like, or maybe they were shaped as art. Others had unusual leaves, or no leaves at all, just green lace-like fans, or long twisting bushy filaments, dense and dangling.

The surface of the path they were treading was different too – slightly spongy, softer underfoot. Other things were no different – the dwelling designs and materials, along with their cluster around the familiar central grove of trees and vegetation. They still had to walk the path that circled the central grove and gave access to each of the six dwellings.

"How many dwellings to a pod did you say a well-organised society has?" Quentin said to Conrad_27-8 as they followed SiMiYah.

Conrad_27-8 said, "Yes, I am dismayed too. It is a great shame that they have marred the elegance of their town in this way. Perhaps this aberration will be corrected later." His minder was repeating, *Incorrect. Incorrect. Eight, not six. Eight, not six.*

At SiMiYah's cousin's house, they were instructed to go to the gathering room. Entering the room, they saw it was like the one where they'd had their first rain-meal on their first trip. To Tracey and Quentin, that seemed like weeks ago; to Conrad_27-8 it seemed like precisely four trips ago. A large low table, surrounded by mats, commanded the centre of the room. Where the other tables they had seen were white, or shades of cream or occasionally pale pastels, this table had a deep lustrous surface artfully decorated by delicate veins that resembled fire. Tracey found it very striking and was fascinated at its wispy fiery veins that flashed, gleamed, and glowed as she shifted her head the tiniest bit. The impression was of a living fire trapped just below the surface. The room also had several elaborate decorations standing out from the walls, cleverly mounted to give the impression they were floating by the wall. Concealed lighting above and below served as spotlights on each piece. They were clearly abstract works of art, their shapes and colours complementary but at the same time subtly provocative. Like the table, Tracey thought them stunning and wanted to spend time studying them to fully appreciate their artistry.

However, she could not dwell on them. The room's only occupant before they had entered, seated on a mat by the table, was studying her visitors. SiMiYah and her cousin exchanged greeting formalities, with hesitant hints of affection offered by SiMiYah not noticed by her cousin, as far as Tracey could tell.

SiMiYah extended the introductions, saying, "And these are my colleagues." She introduced each of them, getting a quizzical look when she gave Conrad_27-8's name – he was still going by 'two-seven-eight'. They each exchanged formal greetings with cousin KamSoKamToo, Quentin restraining his expression of impatient scorn to an affected over-sincerity, its undercurrent of mockery completely lost on the Allundrians.

Cousin KamSoKamToo said, "How fare your clans?" It was a habitual question, not really expecting any edifying response.

SiMiYah gave the usual answer, "In accordance." That meant 'in accordance with the Mandates'. After an awkward pause she went on, "Yes, and we saw your nephew DooDiDiDoo yesterday. He asked us to send his greetings too."

Cousin KamSoKamToo grunted and said, "Him. I didn't know you knew each other. I hear of him more than I care to. Let's move on to the matters at hand. The work must be done. Your meeting request said you have a proposal for the 24-9 Produce Collective."

SiMiYah said, "Yes, but it does involve DooDiDiDoo."

"But he is only a hydro-electric controller, not a HearTell integrator. Not an iota of logistics experience either. He has no skills we want. Essentially useless. And in saying that, perhaps I compliment him too much."

Under his breath, Quentin said to Tracey, "Attention now, musicians, this piece is in the key of …" He blew a discordant raspberry. "And we are starting on this note …" Then he made a game show 'wrong answer' sound. Tracey leaned one shoulder against the wall and let the other slump as she looked at her feet.

SiMiYah was not aware of Quentin's comments. She said, "Oh. We were hoping you might release the Resource Hub Collective shares you hold for him in trust. It is just seven hundred of all those one hundred and three thousand shares I know you own and manage. You wouldn't even notice the loss of that twenty-five percent trustee's commission in your income."

Conrad_27-8 said, "Actually, zero point one six nine nine percent is a detectable amount in a properly monitored set of accounts."

Cousin KamSoKamToo jumped up and said, "You thought that he could be given his shareholding?" She lifted her arms up in front of herself and held them out there, arms and hands stiff and straining as she searched for words. "You thought that might happen? Did you also think it might not rain this evening?" The latter was extremely improbable since it had rained every evening in recorded history.

SiMiYah said, "I thought … Wait … I know. I thought …"

"What could make you think that I would want to do that? Are you as useless as he is? Do you know how useless he is? I even gave him a chance in the business when he was younger. He managed to excel at two things. Just two – incompetence and irresponsibility. He made a complete mess of everything he touched, or forgot to touch, or was too lazy to touch. A complete mess. And then I had to fix it all up myself. He couldn't even do that. It was maybe twenty years ago, and since then he asks for another chance at least two or three times a year. Does he think my memory has leaked out through my toes? He still wants to claim his inheritance while I can still kick him."

SiMiYah said, "He has surely changed a lot since he was a youth. He is only asking for what is his. He should be able to enjoy it."

"Do you think I enjoy throwing away valuable assets like garbage?"

Kieran said, "Are you enjoying your anger?"

"Yes. What? Enjoying it? I don't do it for enjoyment. The work must be done. Someone must act responsibly. It was wrong. Someone must pay."

SiMiYah said, "I know. I understand. It's the Justice Mandate." It seemed she could not help reciting the words of a Mandate, every time one was named. This time it was the expanded version. *"Every wrong must be corrected by being reversed or undone and its perpetrator must be scolded or exiled to deter future perpetration and will also be compelled to undergo behaviour alignment."*

Quentin said to Kieran, "Did she just say *scolded*? Are they serious?"

Tracey did not like the sound of *behaviour alignment.*

SiMiYah had not finished. "Yes, I know, it is very important. Without the Justice Mandate the wrongs being done would be like the cloud of yellow-back wasps buzzing around overripe orange spike berries. Hundreds, no thousands, no millions of them. Wrongs, wrongs, everywhere." It was clear that SiMiYah felt strongly about this. Did I tell you about my older brother TaTumTaTa?"

"Here we go." It was Quentin.

"He was hosting a social event for his co-workers – it was at his dwelling. Then one of his co-worker's children broke a string on his guitar.[7] Of course, justice was required. Everyone agreed. Then it turned out everyone didn't. Agree, that is. One wanted the child to earn the fento-units to buy a new string. But you actually have to buy a set of eight – you can't buy just one. So, there was a big dispute about what would happen with the other seven. Someone else wanted the child's parent (who should have been supervising it) to get replacement strings, and have them professionally replaced and tuned. One even said that TaTumTaTa should be the one to be scolded for allowing the guitar to be touched by the poor traumatised child. She started the behaviour re-education for TaTumTaTa on the spot. Someone else said the guitar

---

[7] SiMiYah was referring to an eight-stringed musical instrument similar in appearance to an Earth guitar.

shouldn't get even one new string, but the broken one should be fixed. That idea was discussed a lot and it was almost agreed on until TaTumTaTa pointed out that it wasn't possible. Isn't it good that everyone is very fervent about the Justice Mandate? Not good that they were all fighting, I suppose. But good that they all wanted justice so much. Even if it is so hard to do. They still tried and kept on trying. All except TaTumTaTa. This is a bit embarrassing, but it was late in the evening and they were all still clattering, clashing, clamouring about justice and then TaTumTaTa said he didn't care. Can you imagine it? What was he thinking? I don't know either.

"It was as if no harm had been done after all. He had been livid when it first happened. It was very strange, don't you think? I asked him why – why he said that. He said that the more they argued – his friends and workmates – the more they were in dispute, the more they split themselves apart, the smaller his guitar looked. Yes, he said it actually looked like it was getting smaller and smaller while he was looking at it. It was getting tinier and tinier and then so tiny it was like he could not see it all. He could only see all his friends and workmates working with the minders to put up ugly fortresses between themselves. Luckily, *they* still cared. Wasn't it strange that something that fixes everything as well as the Justice Mandate does was so … so damaging?

"Yes, yes minder. Not damaging. No, not strange. But I say it was a perfectly complete mess." She looked around for any sign of disagreement. There was none, so she continued. "And then there are all the other wrong-doings, all the wrong-doers. You know what I mean … everyone who is not doing what they should – what I know they should, who is not doing what I want, who keeps doing what they should not – what I don't want, who keeps saying the wrong thing, or hasn't said the other thing, who is looking the wrong way, or who's breaking, or not making, who's keeping or should be keeping but isn't … you know, *them.* Maybe not major crimes, but so many. A thousand times a day. Against me. Against everyone. You and I must have justice for every one of them. Or you and I will have to carry all those wrongs. It is countless, the missed justice. I don't know how we go on when so much justice is just ignored. How do we bear it? I see it everywhere, all the time, for everyone. We all walk around, frowns tightening our faces and our guts, everyone splurging in the market of judgement, exchanging the coin of bitterness for the cloth of failure. How can we even do it – go on without getting all our justice? I don't know. Sometimes it seems when I don't get my justice, it hurts me more than those wrongs ever did. Minder remembers. Minder remembers everything. It forgets nothing. It keeps reminding me, grinding me, grinding me down, long after the Mandate call. Minder keeps remembering for me. Sometimes I just want to forget about it. That's strange, isn't it minder? It's not that way? No, we can't forget about it. Yes, where would that end up? If we forgot about some of it, we might think we could forget about all of it. Where would that end up?"

"She hasn't even started with transport rage." Quentin, who had been sitting against the wall, eyes shut, and could have either been listening to her with deep concentration, or dozing, was ignoring the fact that here all transport was automated.

Cousin KamSoKamToo had been watching and listening to SiMiYah closely. She said, "Since you feel so strongly about our venerable Justice Mandate (no need to re-state it, my dear), I have something to suggest. And I may even reconsider that business about DooDiDiDoo."

SiMiYah said, "Yes. Anything."

In unison, Tracey and Quentin said, "Wait." Tracey added, "You can't …" before she accepted it was too late. Then she turned to Quentin, to watch speechless frustration, dismay, impatience, and disbelief pushing each other aside for prominence on his face, until frustration and a late starter, resignation, shared the victory.

"Good. It should be a simple matter for you. You seem to have a knack for getting others to listen to you," KamSoKamToo said.

"Certainly. What is it, this simple matter?" SiMiYah oozed all the confidence of someone about to jump into a dark pit she could not see the bottom of.

"Do you see my SoCaPi sculpture over there?" Keeping her gaze fixed on SiMiYah, she waved at a sculpture cleverly mounted to appear suspended in the air, shining bright in a corner of the room where the lighting was subdued. About a third of the height of an Allundrian, rotating almost imperceptibly, it was illuminated from several angles by concealed lighting. Predominantly a deep lustrous silver, at its edges hints of gold, amber, and sepia bloomed and shifted as slowly as it rotated. It was an abstract rendition of an Allundrian tree, the branches thin, very fine, triangular in cross-section, but with smoothed edges, intertwining briefly, sensuously, before they spread and narrowed to impossibly fine tips.

"It is very nice. Yes. Very nice." The more SiMiYah dwelt on it, the more it was captivating her. "What about it?" Her voice was hushed as she held her gaze on it.

"If you look carefully, you can see that the tip of one of the branches is broken off."

SiMiYah looked over the tips of the branches closely, and then she saw it, a tiny sparkle on the end of one of the branches, where perhaps half a finger length had been broken off. "Oh. Yes, I can see it."

"I know who did that. But I can't prove it."

"I see." Her uncertain tone revealed that she did not see at all.

"Yes. It was my master arts director. Not my current one. The one before. I had to … well, let me be frank, I had to terminate him. He was just impossible – always falling behind in his work. Even completely forgetting to do things sometimes. He could not be permitted to go on. Wealth must have *some* privileges. So, there it was – two messy tasks for me, two completed. Master arts director terminated – check. Carcass disposed of – check."

"Terminated?" Tracey gasped the words involuntarily, quietly, shocked. "You mean …"

"Yes. A messy business. He started well enough, but he left behind – and let me be frank again – he left behind what can only be called a very unsightly carcass. But I needed justice. Even if I had to cut up the whole carcass, dispose of the pieces. But once he had been terminated, it had to be done."

"He was *falling behind* and so you … and then you … you cut up the carcass?" Tracey took three small steps backwards. Her eyes were wide, staring. SiMiYah was wallowing in confusion, her eyes moving between cousin KamSoKamToo and Tracey. Even Quentin looked alarmed. Conrad_27-8 had started recalculating the probability that their mission would involve casualties. Kieran was studying cousin KamSoKamToo thoughtfully.

"Of course. But after that, while he was moving all his detritus out, he broke my SoCaPi sculpture. So petty. So spiteful."

"*After* you cut up the carcass … he was moving out?" Tracey realised she was missing something.

"Yes. Now I need justice. Both for my SoCaPi and for the body of work that miscreant was responsible for. You call it a body of work." She glared accusingly at Tracey who had not called it anything. "It was no body of work. It was a festering carcass, what he left behind. A putrid shambles. Just rid me of it, I told them. Incise it from my collection, I said. I had to. But of course there were some pieces I had to keep, the most excellent ones, well, almost all of them really, but they are all moved about in my collection now. Definitely moved. So, it is like it is a totally new collection." She gave her visitors a brief scan for any hint of disagreement. She saw none. "Now, just a simple confession, that's all I want."

"But I didn't call it …" Tracey did not finish as comprehension dawned.

"It is all you want? Will it stop your distress? Can you forget the Justice Mandate?" Kieran had asked the questions.

"Yes, a simple confession, it's all I want. So everyone knows the truth about him. It will be a start. It was a mistake to even appoint him. Now, my reputation is nearly in tatters. Everyone knew. Everyone. Do you know what happened then? Of course you do. Everyone does. It was a total disaster. Nearly the end." Cousin KamSoKamToo was clearly struggling to hold back her mounting distress. "What happened was … everyone … they all started …" She had to pause again to compose herself before concluding, each word a burden, "They all started talking." She caught a breath, seemed unable to release it. "What am I to do? What am I to do?"

While Tracey and Quentin were still waiting for the announcement of the calamity that had befallen her, Kieran said, "The only thing you or anyone can do here is free yourself from the judgements you send. Because mistakes can do no harm. You cannot be harmed."

"I? Be harmed? Of course I can. But not by that dolt, not by ones like him. I will not allow it."

"Who do you allow then? And why?"

"Who? Yes, who then? Who then?" Cousin KamSoKamToo turned away in thought. "Indeed, why would I allow *anyone* to harm me? No, I won't. I don't. I am stronger than all of them. I can deal with anything they throw at me."

Kieran spoke softly. "Maybe even stronger than you know. Is the mountain harmed by wafting puffs of breeze snuffed to nothing? The mountain need not heed any puffing breeze, it just goes on. Unless it thinks itself one of the wispy clouds it sees all around it – the wispy clouds that flee the stroke of the sightless breeze."

"What a strange idea. Yes, yes – enough of this. Minder reminds me." She fixed her gaze on SiMiYah.

"What?" SiMiYah had difficulty finding voice.

"Get that confession, and I will release DooDiDiDoo's trust to him. Good riddance to it. Can you do that?"

"I can. I will. Many thanks, cousin." SiMiYah had not the slightest idea of how she could get that confession.

Outside cousin KamSoKamToo's dwelling, SiMiYah detached herself from the others, put on her BringSeeDo, and started a see-talk conversation with someone who Tracey assumed was cousin KamSoKamToo's former master arts director. It did not last long.

"What did he say?"

"He said: Am I available? Of course I am available. Everyone knows I was terminated. Yesterday, he said, after I awoke, I simply could not do a single thing all day, I had to …"

"No, I mean, will he see us?"

"Yes, he said we can see him anytime. I think we can have a walk-eat and then go to his dwelling pod. Or perhaps we can get some food from one of the food dispensing points in this resource hub and then take the GoSomes. Or perhaps we can take the GoSomes now and then eat at the next resource hub. Yes, minder? Yes, or perhaps if we do eat, her master arts director may end up going out somewhere before we can get there. Huh? And also, he could change his mind about seeing us. We should go now. What? No, that's right. We don't want to appear too eager." SiMiYah started walking to the resource hub.

Whatever happened to 'we can see him anytime', Tracey wondered.

Dropping behind to Quentin who was dawdling several paces to the rear, Tracey asked him, "Is this all right with you? No smart ideas?" She preferred him to approve of what they were doing, to the extent that was possible for him.

"All right? Of course it is. How could it get any better? This all seems to be working out splendidly now. If I have it right, when we get our ornament culprit to confess to his heinous crime, cousin KamPiKamPi back there …"

"It's KamSoKamToo," corrected Tracey.

"As I was saying, cousin KamPoKamPoo here will give good old DiDooDooDi … DoDoDiDi …"

"DooDiDiDoo," suggested Conrad_27-8.

"Yes, him. She will hand over DooDiDooDi's trust account. And then DooDiDooDi will generously but humbly accept his coronation as clan head, allowing the current holder of the prestigious mantle to revoke the rock-head DahTiYahYah's exile, at which point, said rock-head will rummage through his rubbish bin and yank out his stinky iron ore nugget so SiMiYah can drop it on the toes of the almighty Mandate-advocate, who in gratitude will float the idea past some of his buddies that maybe she need not have her membership privileges to this den of writhing insanity revoked in retaliation for the unspeakable crime of thinking too loud. Yes, a very splendid outcome, so far. Questions do spring to mind, but I will restrict myself to a very small number. In fact, I could try to keep it to just one question."

"While there is still an element of subjectivity, I agree, that one should not be considered a large number." Conrad_27-8 wanted to contribute.

Quentin turned to Conrad_27-8. "Regarding the actual number of questions, I have some bad news for you."

"Bad? How bad?"

"Very, very bad."

"I don't understand." Then a possibility dawned. "You don't mean …"

"Yes, I do."

"Don't say it."

"I'm going to."

"Please."

Quentin ignored the plea. "That number – it will be an approximation."

Conrad_27-8 went pale and placed one hand on the wall to steady himself.

Turning back to Tracey, Quentin said, "My first question of an unknown number is this. Do we know how many acts this little farce has to go?"

Tracey gave a human shrug, saying, "We don't have much time left anyway. Does it all have to make sense if we get what we want in the end?"

"Maybe. On the other hand, if it doesn't make sense, how can we know what we want to get in the end?"

They kept on going to wherever it was they were going to.

Chapter 17

"It has begun." The prickly seed of angst planted in Mist-on-Water at the village meeting with LifeSource oracle had sprouted into a thorny fury, a fury she did not care if anyone saw, and that those she met were cautious to keep away from. Stopping where Sand-on-Stone was crouching with his back to her, she saw he was making a new handle for his mattock. Sand-on-Stone looked up from his chiselling and gave her an enquiring look.

She did not wait for the question that might be coming; she had not finished. "They have started taking things. It is not right. It is not fair. Why does everyone just let them? Help them, even? The sickness has fallen on thirteen now, probably more since yesterday morning's count. And then last night, old Aunt Petals-on-Wind died. Everyone is bound up in fear. Will all those homage-dues really help? No one has the answer to that. I don't believe LifeSource oracle. She does not know how far this sickness will go. *In the hand of LifeSource*, she says. Bird droppings served up as sweetmeats! Everyone nibbling on them. So, they have started extracting their so-called homage-dues from us. Now everyone groans under two curses. She wrongs us. She should be the one made to pay."

"Do you want this to smother your joy?"

"Oh, is your source-with-no-name coming to fix this wrong, is she? How?" She glared at Sand-on-Stone. Sparks were flaring in her eyes. "Which one am I supposed to be taking joy in: LifeSource oracle slinking off with the finest of our finest, or those who whimper through the day and expire before the darkness passes?

They are not even following my plan – hardly any of them. *Too risky*, they say."

Sand-on-Stone who, on any other day, she would have clearly seen was innocent of both counts, was for the moment the only target for her ire.

"Source-with-no-name will not fix any wrong. But forgiveness takes them all away," Sand-on-Stone said.

"Old Aunt Petals-on-Wind died last night. Who will go tonight? And tomorrow?"

Sand-on-Stone had no answers to those questions, so he stayed silent.

Mist-on-Water's anger was ebbing now, leaving behind a sulk that she embraced with tender resolve. "Who is at fault in this? Not us. Yet we are being punished. LifeSource should be getting punished. I will not stand and do nothing." Then, standing in the stillness, for an instant, she saw exactly what she was doing and knew she did not want it. But before her insight had taken hold, it was gone. The prickly mood that she had pulled over herself surged back, standing a firm surly vigil.

She stood firm but the stillness tugged her. Her thoughts went back to the half-seen insight she had had. I don't want to feel like this. Not really. But how can I help it when all of what is happening is happening? I can't ignore it. Why must we just endure it? She said, "I will work out what to do and tell the village council."

"And they will do what you tell them?"

"I will make them."

"Mist-on-Water against the whole village council – not a very even contest."

"So-be. They can get help if they want."

"Must you be the one to act?"

She knew where this was going. She could pull this weed before it had even popped up. "If there were a proper source-with-no-name, or a source-with-any-name, she would do something about those wrongs. If there were one."

"I can only talk of The Source. I do not know of the others. But The Source never does anything about nothings. You, though, you can stop doing what you don't want."

"Nothings? So, this could-be plague is nothing? What about the oracle's theft? How can you say that? Have you already forgotten everything that I just told you?"

"I think I remember you spend some time in village crèche."

"Not that again."

"Are there times when the young ones make something, working very hard, with all of their abilities? Then, when they finish, even though what they make is poorly done, they are very pleased with it?"

"Haven't we been through this already?"

"Is it not wonderful, this quiet impulse to create. Even in ones so very young. They want to create. Where does that come from? Do they all not have it? Did you put it there for them? Did you teach it? No. And yet it is there, a gentle compulsion to create."

"Must I really play this game again? So-be. Yes, they make things. Until an even younger one, or sadly, even an older one sometimes, comes along and breaks apart what the other has made. A not-so-gentle compulsion, that one."

"But remember, a not-so-gentle compulsion that you, in your wisdom, can see as less than calamitous."

"Perhaps I can see that. But the calamities are very real to my little tikes."

"So-be. Very real. And not just that. Is it not often, in the little games they play, that their imaginings confound you? The things not there, they see so real, so real the little ones get lost in them, lost in passions for them, seized by those things which you know are not even there. And later they will know it too. Amazing, confounding things, the little minds they have. But I distract myself. Back to that calamity: then what?"

"Then what what?"

"Well, what do you do about it – you the demi-source of that domain?"

"What do I do? After one comes and breaks apart what another has made? If I tell the culprit she did wrong and must not do it again, would that be wrong of me? Even if I want to tell the other it does not matter, to her it does."

With one hand, Sand-on-Stone lifted the new mattock handle he had been shaping and turned it around, dangling it from his fingers. He found a spot that needed more work and positioned it for his chisel.

"I was thinking of bringing forth another matter, not of villains and victims. But since you have made the invitation so tempting …"

"Actually, I am sure that invitation was sent to you by mistake." Mist-on-Water's desire for her surly vigil was draining away.

"Regrettably, I am already at this party, elegantly adorned with my best armbands and beads. Now, I must unwrap the host-gifts I have brought for you." He picked up the shoulder bag that was on the ground beside him, peered inside, then reached in and pulled out a bunch of invisible objects, a bunch nearly too big for both his hands. Fingers stretched wide, he held them out to Mist-on-Water. "Here they are." With the barest tilt of her head, she looked sideways, down at his empty hands. He said, "They will help you with those infants going berserk. Some offerings for you, oh mighty demi-source."

"You think the village council resembles an unruly crèche? Perhaps there is still some hope for you. But your gifts look a bit mouldy and stale, like that thing on your toe."

Wiping his toe on the ground, Sand-on-Stone said, "Here is the first one." He balanced his pile of invisible gifts on one hand and with the other, picked one off the top and offered it to Mist-on-Water. "You could make the culprit fix it – what he broke. Or make him give some compensation."

"It can never be fixed – not back the way it was. Some of the other carers give the wronged child some treat, a consolation, but that does not stop the naughty one from doing something bad again. Aunt Petals-on-Wind cannot be fixed. Even with long wakes."

"So, not a good gift, as you say." He tossed it over his shoulder and selected another invisible gift. Turning it around, he said, "You could keep the culprit away then, where he can do no damage. Then it would not happen again."

"Another poor gift. It's a bigger nuisance to keep apart those toddling tyrants and their toys. And usually their play together is good. Until one of them does … something. You can never be sure which one it is going to be. Or what they will do. After, she might never do it again. All that nuisance for nothing. In the village we cannot keep the sick ones apart. They need help. They are not making the sickness. But keeping the oracles out – that I like. Except they will just go and do their mischief somewhere else. No, I won't be responsible for that."

"So-be, you are not happy with my offerings. What do you do, oh demi-source? What do you do about those tiny tyrants?"

"Sometimes it is a penalty. Set some price they don't want to pay. Even if it is just the sharp word of condemnation, the hard shoulder of rejection. Sometimes it's the only way. They pay that price, and they learn."

"It seems harsh for ones who know so little. Is it the only way?"

"Perhaps you want to admonish me if sometimes I tell the aggrieved child to bear her loss bravely, to be strong and accept a patient sacrifice. I also explain to the culprit it is not good to break things. And I will teach that she has upset the other child. Also, not good. If she is old enough, she will need to apologise. For others, a time apart is needed, until they calm down. But where is the culprit for this sickness?"

"When you admonish the culprit for the wrong, when you set the price, when you make him declare his wrong, what do you teach him?"

"Not to do it again."

"And that in your crèche realm there are crimes and criminals, criminals that perhaps even include yourself, the delinquent demi-source in their little world?"

"I do not say that." But, annoyingly, he was right.

"Because that destruction he wrought – perhaps a whole block village levelled – is real? And important?"

"I do not say either of them."

"And yet they are there. Behind all the rest. Crimes and criminals declared. Even though you also know nothing done in that crèche makes for real harm. The morning's squabbles are gone with lunch."

"Hrrrg." She was usually the one pointing the fallacies held on to by others. She did not like finding some in her own hands.

"So, you don't want any of my offerings?"

She had never felt that her answers at the crèche were good. They changed little. Even as those tikes grew out of their toys, oftentimes their games stayed the same. "You can tell me what is wrong. But what about how to fix it? What about how to stop all that trouble?" Her words stopped. She looked uncertain. Then it came out. "I may be in trouble."

"What trouble?"

"It's LifeSource Oracle. She has been asking about me. Questioning the village elders, and others. She pretends it's just conversation. But now she knows who my parents are, what they do, where I live. She may know or suspect what I was doing – telling folk about what to do. She may be planning something She is crafty. She has influence."

Sand-on-Stone stopped working on the mattock handle. "So, I consort with a little criminal, do I?"

"It's not me. It's her." Mist-on-water was affronted. She folded her arms and clenched her fists.

"Exactly what LifeSource Oracle herself would say."

"Say, and be wrong." Mist-on-water stamped her foot for emphasis.

Sand-on-Stone looked to the sky, "And many others would say it too."

"They would not." Mist-on-Water was fuming now. She kicked at a stick on the ground. It went skidding into the vegetable patch. "I do nothing wrong."

"Nothing? Not even a little bit?" Mist-on-Water unclenched her fists but her arms remained folded. Sand-on-Stone said, "So-be. Even you do little wrongs. Wrongs against all manner of folk." He paused to watch her frown grow and fade. "And those folk are always doing little wrongs against you, are they not? Countless things that should be different, or better." He chuckled, "Little wrongs everywhere, too many to count. Your day is full of them. They are the real problem. Because they are legion."

Mist-on-Water did not refute it.

"Tell me then – do you really want that? Why do you want them – so many crimes and criminals, culprits and victims?"

"When a wrong is done, when something is not right, I want to know what and who."

"Ah – it is to protect all your little crèche toys. But do you? Too soon they are gone. Then forgotten."

"What else can I do? It's better than nothing." The words were out before Mist-on-Water had time to consider them. She thought, *in the end, it is very close to nothing.*

"Unless there is something that can never be lost. Something important that can never be blemished."

"Something important can never be blemished? It's your source, is it? Say-you. What do you call Aunt Petals-on-Wind's flesh, now quietly rotting? A pleasant garden, is it? A pleasant garden of decay? Did she plant it? No. Now she has reaped it. Who can do anything? She can't. The source of that, whatever that source is, is grotesque." She was angry again. He was missing the whole point.

"At last, we flush out the real culprit." He slid the iron mattock head down the handle, inspected the fit, and slid it off again.

"One who cannot be dragged to the village council. Or anywhere." Mist-on-Water tightened her jaw. "A do-nothing source, teaching nothing in her crèche, drowned out by the din."

"The Source cannot do anything that will teach what is not, that will teach that what is of no importance is momentous. The Source teaches freedom – it says you must let yourself be free of every complaint. Of every little gripe against everyone and everything, that which keeps your attention away from all that is truly precious. You are asking what you can do. That is the only thing you can do in this crèche of life. Such a small thing, yet not a small thing – setting aside a thousand ways well learnt, long known, trusted, and familiar. Leaving the path that has led nowhere. Easy to learn. But needing practice."

"Free myself of every complaint? I would need to not see what I see." She was sure he would agree that was ridiculous.

"Another correct answer."

"One I don't want. I don't want to make myself blind, to stop knowing." She wished she knew what she *did* want.

"You will need to see differently."

"Seeing is seeing", she said. But Mist-on-Water was thinking about seeing differently.

"Say-you, oh, demi-source of your glorious crèche-realm, all those children content there, seeing in their playthings all they need, until they see the invader come, disrupting, destroying – such wrenching losses. But at least they can see them."

She let a long sigh be her answer. *So-be. I do not see what they see. I see more than they, not less.* It would be an answer. A strange one. One easy and hard. She could not think of a better one. But only if everything he had said were true. She needed to know the truth of it. "So-be. Let her show me then, your source-with-no-name. I have not heard her. Could it be she is a little timid? One day perhaps, she will speak to me. Or is she too shy? If she speaks, I may listen. Until then I will keep my crimes and criminals."

"Is there no place for forgiveness?"

"Which kind?"

Sand-on-Stone raised an eye-brow. "There is more than one?"

"Yes. There is the kind where the criminal says she says *so sorry* to the victim." Mist-on-Water's *so sorry* dripped with insincerity. Then the victim must stop being angry. Mist-on-Water, hands-on-hips, glared at him. "How is that just?" She snorted. "The other kind is where the victim just has to say *it doesn't matter*. Even when it does. Even if the wrong-doer doesn't care. If it didn't matter, the victim wouldn't need to say it. It's all a lie."

"Exactly. That's the forgiveness I mean. It is when someone does something. Something some eyes of flesh say is bad. But the someone with those eyes knows all is well, and so does not need to say or remember anything. That is forgiveness."

"That's lying to yourself."

"Yes. Unless you have learned it is your eyes of flesh that are lying. Lying to yourself."

"Say-you. Tell me: that different say of seeing – who has ever done it? Who has found it? Even the old aunties do not speak of it. Are they still looking? Or is it just that it's hard to do something that cannot be done?"

Sand-on-Stone set his chisel and sliced some fine slithers from the handle. When he was satisfied he slid the head over it again. He inspected the fit – it looked snug. He walked to his small vegetable patch and gave a few test swings. The handle passed. Sand-on-Stone gave it a happy pat. Looking to the sky, he said, "If some old auntie told you, would you believe it?"

"I may."

"You should never believe it – what she says."

"What? Then I should not believe you either."

"Nor me either. Do not believe it. Not until you yourself have found it and can tell of it."

"What is not there, I will look for forever."

"And yet it seems to me that you do feel a hole, a void, something lost, or if you will not say *lost*, something to be found, at least. You sense a call. There is no one who does not hear a whisper of something more, that thing not known. In time, that one, he will find it. Then he will know what not to do."

"So-be. But what does she do until then? There are so many choices."

"First, you must believe you need to learn."

"Believe? Learn what? Perhaps I do. Will it be what I want? I don't know. I don't think I like this puzzle."

"Would you like an easier puzzle?"

Sand-on-Stone went into his cabin and almost immediately came out with a large thin slate under one arm, and the other hand dangling a drawstring bag. He placed the slate on the ground, revealing a grid of fine lines etched into its surface, and emptied the bag of small, smooth, black-and-white pebbles next to it. They were the pieces of a game everyone played, but few mastered. They played through the whole afternoon. Sand-on-Stone was a good player, but Mist-on-Water won more games than she lost. To Sand-on-Stone, the games had no beginning and no end, they flowed together, a free flow of patterns, of tension and release, of embrace or distance, aligned or alone. All fascinating patterns. Nothing won, nothing lost.

The fading light announced their last game. Mist-on-Water hurried down the track back home before the best footing was lost in dimness.

Observation Series: **Individual Differences**

<u>Summary of observations.</u> Every one of my treasures wants to be unique and special. They think it will make them more wanted. At the very same time that they all want to be special, every one of them wants to be treated the same as all the rest. If only they could see how adorable they are already. Most of them have no hint that they are manifestations of The One or that they are sparks of Essence. It is not surprising that they never know what to do.

Chapter 18

"It can't be done."

Quentin had been lost in his thoughts as he and Conrad_27-8 waited for SiMiYah and Kieran to organise some food at this new but *just-like-all-the-others* resource hub, so he had not noticed that Tracey was back from the SeeDo doing whatever it was. He thought he had missed part of the conversation. To disguise his confusion, he just said, "It can't be?"

"No. We can't get these minders away from their hosts."

"Hmph. At the risk of extending this conversation even further past its expiry date, there must be a way."

"Yes, it has been done in the past, a long time ago by scientists, anatomists, I think," Tracey said. "It seems they were a bit rogue. Of course, it isn't that difficult with a few simple tools. They ended up enclosing their subject in a net and pulling a band up the net between the Allundrian and its minder to restrict where the minder could go. Then they had the minder trapped in the net. Quite easy, really."

"As a scientific endeavour, the experiment does sound like a pile of fun. And I have to put up with mundane entertainment like, say, watching a couple of galaxies collide. Even if that does last a little longer. Why, oh why, did I ever settle for being just an astrophysicist?"

"Then they separated them – the minder and its host – they put them in different rooms, or something. Then a strange thing happened." Tracey paused to give Quentin's curiosity a chance to kick in. He was looking at the corner of the ceiling. Sighing, she said, "The minders lost consciousness. Completely. No way to wake them. But the hosts - the hosts couldn't think properly. They didn't know themselves. They started thinking they were everything, and nothing. No matter what they did, it all ended badly whenever a minder was taken away from its host."

"That is strange."

"Yes, but the point is: we can't force the minders apart from their hosts. We can't stop their interference."

"The demise of Plan A then. A pity. Especially since there is no Plan B." Quentin did not bother to feign disappointment.

"What if they stopped listening to them?" Tracey gave voice to an idle thought, not one that she felt offered any hope.

SiMiYah and Kieran arrived, each carrying a tray of food. It looked like their first rain-meal together, except with smaller plates and serves. Tracey wondered at how much they had been through since then. *Had that first meal really been just four trips ago?*

Tracey had been hoping that the master arts director's home would stand out from its neighbours as some sort of artistic showcase. She was disappointed. From the outside at least, apart from two smallish stone sculptures (*cast-offs?* she wondered), it looked much like all the others. Concluding that the master arts director could not indulge in the same way as his affluent clients could, she suspected that inside the dwelling it would be similarly mundane.

In the front of the dwelling an Allundrian sat, legs crossed, on a large, low, flat rock surrounded by an ankle-high dense carpet of fern-like plants reaching up just below the top surface of the rock. Their delicate fronds bowed and waved together in the faintest puffs of breeze, a slowly rolling miniature sea of green. The gentle sea gave way only to the rock the Allundrian sat on, a smooth humble island, beige with thin dark sedimentary bands.

He stared into the distance. He could have been in a trance.

"May all be in accordance," said SiMiYah hesitantly, reluctant to disturb the stillness.

"All doings in accordance," was the immediate automatic response. "I thought you might get here a bit more quickly. What? Yes, that's right: not that it matters anyway. Nothing matters. I'll never get my seat on the Council of Global Union of Arts Academies now. She quashed that." The others all realised this was the master arts director.

SiMiYah introduced each of her companions. The master arts director, remaining sitting, inspected each of them for any aspect of note or interest and, seeing none, kept his responses to the minimum formalities, which while polite, were at the same time casually dismissive. Tracey suspected that if he happened to pass any of them in the street tomorrow, he would probably not recall how he knew the vaguely familiar face. At least they found out his name, one that it seemed everyone was too embarrassed, or too angry, or too disinterested to say – ChiBelTra.

"We have come because I need your help."

Tracey winced inwardly at SiMiYah's forthright approach.

"Opening a gallery, are you? Or setting up an exhibition pod, perhaps?" ChiBelTra deftly mingled colours of scorn, exasperation, and misery through his words.

"No. It is what we talked about – KamSoKamToo's SoCaPi sculpture." SiMiYah added tentatively, "The one that is broken."

"The broken one. Yes, very amusing that."

"What are you saying? Amusing? But it is priceless. It *was* priceless."

"Priceless? Perhaps. And yet a price was given, and taken."

"Yes, a great price, thrown away, when you broke it." She gave him an accusing stare.

"I did not break it, but I know who did." He looked back at her calmly, untouched by her condemnation.

"Who broke it then?"

"Why should I say? She can go on believing I did it. It is very funny." He gave an Allundrian chuckle, pleasure in his eyes.

"What is funny about it? I don't understand how you, of all people, can say that."

"It is funny because, only I, of all people, can say that."

"What are you talking about?"

"Will I tell you? Perhaps I will. It is funnier shared. Before I tell you, answer me this: why does KamSoKamToo care that it is broken?"

"She cares because it is a beautiful masterpiece. It *was* a beautiful masterpiece."

"It is beautiful craftsmanship, yes, but that craftsmanship is no masterpiece."

SiMiYah was stunned. She could only say, "Everyone thinks it is. Everyone."

"Who cares what they say, those everyones. What do you say?"

"Me? Well, perhaps I don't know much about art, but I know that that SoCaPi piece is good. I know it is very good. It *was* very good. At least it is very good now. It still is. Before it must have been perfect."

"Even though you never saw it before it was, as you say, broken?"

"I think it is very good. Even now."

"If you know little about art, how do you know what is good art? Or even what *was* good art. Art you never saw?"

"The broken bit is very tiny. It is very hard to see. Probably hardly anyone would see it. I had to be told to look for it, very carefully. So, I do see the master work in it. It is just that now I know it is broken. I know it. So that mars its perfection. For me, anyway."

"You know it is broken, do you?"

"Yes, I saw it."

"Most amusing."

SiMiYah had forgotten she was here to get master arts director ChiBelTra to agree to a request, and frustration at his nonchalance was overwhelming her. "What is amusing about it? Do you get some guilty pleasure in breaking great artistry? Did it make you jealous? Was your vengeance on KamSoKamToo satisfying?"

"I tell you again: I did not break it."

"Tell me then, if you did not break it, who did?"

"SoCaPi."

"What? SoCaPi? The artist? You are lying. How do you know? Why did he break it? Was it an accident?"

"He broke it to give it meaning."

"What are you talking about this time? What meaning?"

"When the tree was nearly complete, after all of its fine, sensuous branches had been fully formed, it was beautiful, but it had no meaning."

"No meaning? It had no meaning?"

"Yes, no meaning. How many people have come, looked, seen the exquisite workmanship, admired it, and left? When they come, they believe they will see a perfect sculpture. They expect it. So that is what they see. They do not find that it has a tiny broken splinter, the single broken splinter that sheds a tiny spark of light. They do not see that just one branch lets out its tiny light; that it seems to be sharing out its life. This is what makes it a masterpiece."

"How do you know this? Are you lying?"

"After I saw it, the tiny piece broken off, I went to SoCaPi, and he told me. He was very pleased. I was the first to see it. Or perhaps the first to see it and then to ask him about it. You can ask him."

SiMiYah saw that what he was telling her was true and she let it lead her to a new insight. "The tiny speck of light is the life of the tree. Yes. You can see it."

"Yes. And after you have been looking at it for a time, it asks a question – that tiny light."

"What question?"

"Hmm. Shall I tell you? Or perhaps you should listen for it yourself."

"I am listening to you. You said you would tell me."

"As you wish. I listened to that tiny sparkle SoCaPi told me about. It took some time but then I did hear its question. The question I heard was: why is just one branch broken away? And then, I saw it. I saw what the tree would be if it freed itself of every one of the myriad tiny, fragile branches it so adored and clung to."

SiMiYah saw it then too. She gasped. "Yes. Yes. The single tiny sparkle would be a countless multitude, all joined together, a dazzling blaze of glittering fire. No, not dazzling, that's too harsh. No, it would be a radiant beacon of life. A new hope. It would … it would …" She gave up. What she saw for that instant she could not put words to.

"A meaning worthy of a masterpiece, you think?"

"But we must tell cousin KamSoKamToo."

"Tell her what? Who broke it?"

"No. Yes. No. No, that it is not broken, that it is … it's … completed."

"There is no Mandate for it. Let her believe that I did it. Unknowingly, she declares that I am a great artist. I know I am no great artist. It is amusing in so many ways. But she knows nothing, SiMiYah."

SiMiYah said, "It may be that my cousin KamSoKamToo has her faults."

"Oh, so there is some question about that now, is there?" Quentin mumbled. Tracey kicked his ankle.

But now SiMiYah was back on her mission. "She has some faults, but she does not need to suffer over nothing. She shouldn't. She should understand that what she has is so much nicer even than what she thought. She should know that. Why should her false secret torment her?"

"Would that not be justice, in accordance with the Mandate? For her many faults?" ChiBelTra had no leaning to let her off that easily.

Tracey said, "It seems too cruel a torment that she does not know what she has is the equal of any; more than the equal."

"That's it. You are very clever," said SiMiYah. Tracey looked mystified. SiMiYah did not notice. She went on, "The Equality Mandate: *Every inequality must be removed.* That's why we must tell her. She does not have equality if we don't do it. Poor cousin KamSoKamToo."

"Poor KamSoKamToo, did you say? *Poor* KamSoKamToo?" ChiBelTra looked bemused.

They were all struggling with the idea that the word 'poor' somehow belonged with KamSoKamToo: rich, influential, ruthless, in all appearances in want of nothing.

Tracey started saying, "That's not what I meant. I meant …" But she realised anything she said would probably just spur them further down this unhelpful detour. "Oh, forget it."

SiMiYah did forget it. She went on from where she had left off. "Cousin KamSoKamToo. We cannot treat her any differently. Because Equality Mandate makes us all the same. Even though we are all different, we must be treated the same. It is the Mandate. It is not easy, sometimes, but we must do it."

"Yes. Especially when we can shove the Clan Mandate into it too, so everyone can be special. Equally special." Quentin's feigned innocent saccharin enthusiasm was not lost on Tracey, who wondered how hard she needed to kick his ankle this time to wipe away the angelic smile stuck on his face. "And on top of that, we can all have one of those nice art things to make us properly equal." He was nodding and smiling, feigning happiness at the thought. "By the Mandate."

SiMiYah said, "Yes. For Equality, you can have one too."

Quentin doubted it. "I suppose I would need to cough up quite a bunch of fento-units."

"Of course, you would need to pay the standard art price of fifteen fentos, I think it is. Or is it fourteen?"

"Hmm. Isn't it amazing that everyone of us can buy a masterpiece for slightly more than the price of a flavoursome drink?" Quentin was sarcastically pointing out to SiMiYah that she must have misspoken on the price.

"Well, yes. All thanks to the Equality mandate. All art work must have the same price. Fifteen fentos. Or maybe fourteen."

Quentin could sniff out a catch like a dog could sniff out a cat. He said, "That reminds me, I need to sign up for a couple of dozen masterpieces tomorrow. Should have them in no time."

SiMiYah said, "Yes, you should do it soon. You just need to be in the queue. Unless ..."

"Ah ha. That's the one – the queue. And then – *unless*?"

"Well, yes. It depends on what you want. For some artists, their masterpieces have quite a short queue. Or even no queue."

"No queue. For a masterpiece. I'm shocked."

"Of course, the work of some artists is not wanted as much. Because… Well, because … You know what I mean. I really should not say it. Your minder will tell you. By Equality."

"No, I get it. Some of the artists might be pretty *poor* artists. But they have to all make *masterpieces*. By Equality, that is. And what about the *better* artists? Or even the *best* ones?"

Hearing those words spoken out loud shocked SiMiYah. They were all but forbidden. Few had ever heard them spoken by another Allundrian. Minders, on the other hand, said them frequently. Wide-eyed, swallowing a gasp, she tried to hide her shock, saying, "Yes, the queues for some may be longer. It depends. I don't know."

"And would you know about that not-broken piece you poor cousin has?"

"The queue for that piece will be very short. Naturally."

"Naturally. Because …" Quentin hoped for a very short answer but knew that was unlikely.

"Well mainly because... Well, the artist may decide not to do another one. By the Mandate. Or probably will decide. For a long time, that is."

"How inconvenient. Or is that 'how convenient'?"

SiMihYah gave no sign of having heard Quentin's question. "Or a very, very long time. You know what I mean. By Equality. They can decide that. No point in being on a queue then."

"So. Quite lucky the old cuz turned up first for that one she has. All for the price of a couple of drinks."

ChiBelTra added, "And the queue activation charge, of course. Nearly a million, that one was."

"Now we have it. Isn't it great to see that Equality Mandate working so well for our artist folk. Even if some say they are just a pimple on the butt of society."

"Yes, it does work well. But not just for them. It all works the same for everyone. By Equality."

"So, some kind of queue, a step to the left, a jump to the right, a couple of optional let's call them *service fees*, and everyone is delirious. Equal, I mean. Equal."

"Yes. Even me. The single labour rate makes us equal. Of course no one can live on it. Luckily I get some special work allowances. Not just me. You get yours too. Different ones, because of what you do. For me, I get my travel allowance. Even though I never need to go anywhere. Then there's the grooming allowance, the no on-call compensation allowance, the exercise facilitation allowance, the de-stress and re-stress allowances, the reading and meeting allowances, the … oh there's more. I forget them. No one is the same." She slapped her hand over her mouth. Too late, the words had already tumbled out. "I mean …"

Nearly everyone stared at her blankly, unsure why stating the obvious had embarrassed her. ChiBelTra was no longer paying any attention. He was intent on pruning individual leaves from a small plant with tiny secateurs.

SiMiYah had to fill the silence. She said, "Everyone is not the same. *No minder, I'm going to say it. I don't care.* We cannot be the same. Not even twins. I am not the same as that SoCaPi artist. I cannot do what he does. And he cannot do things I do. Only minder knows which one is … is … b-better." She paused at the shock of hearing herself say the taboo word. Her minder's head was buried in her ear. Absently, she said, "Yes, minder. Sorry, I mean we must all be equal."

Quentin snorted. "So there's our answer. It means you and your buddy who you will soon be equally exiled with, must both equally have an iron nugget. Then you won't. Be exiled, that is. Problem solved. Check." He marked a check in the air.

SiMiYah grimaced and looked at her feet. She said, "And it means I must live in a town equally with everyone else and not be exiled." She gave a quiet whimper.

"Check again." Quentin made another air-check, emphasised with a flick of his wrist at the end.

"And it means I can revoke DahTiYahYah's Mandate-charge equally like our clan head can.

"Check to that, too. And you can get to be the clan head, too. Don't forget that."

"Yes, it means I have an equal chance of the honour of being clan head as DooDiDiDoo."

"And guess what? Another check." Quentin's air flourishes were getting larger with each check.

"And it means my wealth must equal that of rich cousin KamSoKamToo."

"Might have some flow-on effects, that one, but check anyway."

SiMiYah, arms at her sides, turned her palms to face Quentin – the equivalent of a human shrug. "I know what you are saying. It can sound silly sometimes. But we do need the Equality Mandate. So everyone gets fair treatment. It's not fair if someone is treated badly because they are different."

With another flourish, Quentin slapped his forehead. "Of course not. The same treatment for all, I say. We can't have anyone being *special.* Despite what that funky old Clan Mandate demands."

"We can have special but not if it is going to be bad for someone. Good special is … well, good for them."

Quentin was tiring of this. Almost as an aside he said, "And thereby, bad for everyone else?"

SiMiYah hid her face in her hands. "I don't understand how it can work. None of us are the same. It can only work if the … some *essence* of what we are is the same for all of us. And the differences we all have don't matter at all."

Kieren said, "If that were true, the Mandate would not be needed."

"But is it true? If not, the Equality Mandate would be a good thing. If …" She finished with a sigh.

Tracey said, "If?"

SiMiYah groaned. "If it wasn't useless."

Conrad_28-8 said, "Need I point out the rules of this game are self-contradictory? The game will frustrate everyone playing it."

"Frustrate? No. It is beyond frustrating. I don't know what I should do. Everything I do turns out wrong. Does it mean I need to predict the future? But I can't do that. Even minder does not know. Hush, you. Yes: minder is very clever. Minder always finds something to do, even if it is nothing, but even minder cannot know everything. How can I know the right way to do something? Everything is all messed up. I just want it to be nice. I try. It's always too hard. Now I am going to be exiled. Everyone I know, everything I have, will be gone. I will be no one; I will be nothing. Yes, I know you will help, minder, but sometimes it doesn't help."

"She sees it," Tracey said under her breath to Quentin.

"I need help. I can't do it myself. I tried, but I can't. Who can tell me what to do?"

Very gently, Tracey said, "Who says you can't?"

SiMiYah looked to the ground. She started to turn on the spot, her feet making small, slow steps. "What if … I wonder, what if … I just ignored minder for a time. A bit.

What do you think, TraaCee? You are intelligent." It was shared in a conspiring way, as if she could keep it secret from her minder, which was clearly impossible. Her minder simply whispered quietly in her ear, so quietly even she barely heard it, *"Cannot."*

Tracey turned to Quentin. "Maybe she is onto something. With the minders. Do you think?"

"If what she has been talking about made any sense to you, your dirty little secret is safe with me."

"Well, at least she thinks I'm intelligent."

"Then her dirty little secret is safe too."

SiMiYah stopped turning. She had come to a decision. "I will just go and tell cousin KamSoKamToo the truth about her sculpture."

Tracey looked dubious. "Yes, but then she won't give DooDiDiDoo his inheritance for us, will she?"

There was a thoughtful pause. In the end, SiMiYah conceded, "Probably not." Another thoughtful pause. "But … but if she gets her whole collection commended, if she gets a very rare, very privileged commendation, she may."

"She didn't agree to that. What are you thinking of, anyway?" Based on their last experience with cousin KamSoKamToo, to Tracey it sounded like a high-risk gamble.

SiMiYah ignored the question and walked back to ChiBelTra, still sitting on his rock, still intent on his miniature pruning. "If we get you your admission to the Council of the Global Union of Arts Academies, do you think you could arrange for your friend SoCaPi to announce a special commendation for cousin KamSoKamToo's collection?"

"An amusing idea. Of course, he would be happy to do it for me. He has always praised it – the work I did for her. Would it choke her? It may be most entertaining to see that: her gagging on recognition of my talents, on recognition of me, the one she turned away from like vomit. Let me think on it for a moment." He closed his eyes. Before anyone had been able to wonder how long this thinking moment might last, his eyes were open again. "Yes, quite amusing. Why not. Let us say I will."

"You will?"

"Yes. I will."

"Cousin KamSoKamToo may even take you back."

"Why would I want that?"

"At least you would be doing what you want to do."

"My admission to the Council would take care of that." But he sounded as though he was talking of an event that could never happen. His hand waved, a gesture that could have been taken as dismissal, either of SiMiYah's suggestion he could be taken back, or of his visitors. The parting formalities were brief, ChiBelTra having no interest in further conversation, his visitors also feeling they had achieved as much as they could.

Tracey made herself wait until they were a good distance away from ChiBelTra on his rock. "What have you done? Is this a minder idea?"

"I know what I am doing."

"How can you get him admitted to the Council of the Global Arts Union? Even if you can, that will take time anyway. We have very little time." Tracey did a quick calculation. "You need to nominate your Mandate-advocate by tomorrow."

"My great-aunt BaBaBaBaDah is the head of the Global Union of Arts Academies. She and my mother are very close. She is very helpful. She lives in our dwelling pod and eats with us for most rain-meals. I have been hearing about the games they play in there, in those academies, their schemes and tricks, since I was smaller than a pink bean sprout leaf. I know exactly how to get ChiBelTra in, and quickly."

"At least your great aunt is convenient. So, we are going to see her now?"

"No. I am going to tell cousin KamSoKamToo about her sculpture."

"I suppose you have to, because of the Mandate."

"The Equality Mandate? Yes, if you say so, because of that too."

Tracey's minder was still tossing out doubts and she gave voice to them. "But can the Council admission be done quickly enough? Even if it is done tomorrow, even if everything falls into place and we get him in, surely your Mandate-advocate will need time to review your case, to plan your defence, to gather witnesses and evidence. Won't he? I know his is no minor matter, even though I don't really understand any of this."

SiMiYah said, "Come on. Soon we will see great-aunt BaBaBaBaDah. She is very helpful."

They started on their way again, as if, it seemed to Tracey, out for a pleasant stroll.

Straggling behind, Quentin said to himself, "Today's episode has been brought to you by the casual slaughter and dismemberment of the Mandates Equality and Justice. They gave themselves willingly."

Chapter 19

"No one knows what to do." Mist-on-Water had come to her conclusion.

She had been sitting for a long time at the base of the rock that loomed behind Sand-on-Stone's cabin, sitting and crouching behind an invisible fence she had set up, her silent mood swaying between livid helplessness and calamitous distress. Sand-on-Stone was still working his vegetable patch, pulling weeds, as he had been when Mist-On-Water had stomped out of the trees and flung at him her news that three more villagers had died, including Clouds-at-Sunset's little brother. She had shouted it partly in grief and anger, partly because she had taken the direct path to her rock, passing Sand-on-Stone at some distance, and he would not have heard her at normal volume.

At her words, Sand-on-Stone had stood, watched her take herself to the rock and then, sensing her invisible fence, continued his task, watching her discreetly from the distance.

"No one." She said it again loudly, so Sand-on-Stone would hear that she had more information to prove their world was faulty, ailing, failing, that a remedy eluded even the wisest in the village. It was the first opening Mist-on-Water had made in her fence.

"Is anything being done?" Sand-on-Stone started walking towards Mist-on-Water so he would not need to shout.

"Everyone is doing their own version of pretending to themselves that they are going to the highest authority, pulling the right lever, applying the correct tool, but they don't even know that no one and nothing is in control."

"No one is in control?"

Mist-on-Water felt she had made that point clearly enough. She did not elaborate. Sand-on-Stone reached the rock and went to the spot he knew, the one that let him sit leaning against the rock with his head back, in comfort, a couple of steps away from Mist-on-Water.

Sand-on-Stone said, "So, am I just a tender leaf, one day basking in the sun, the next dismayed to find myself torn away by a passing fluky gust of wind? Or am I a busy hopper beetle, laying her eggs in the log that is stacked for the fire?"

"Both."

"Nothing to be done, then? By anyone?"

"Nothing." She drummed that thought into place in the ranks of a parade of evidence of powerlessness she had assembled, neatly in formation, for her own inspection and approval. She was making her inspection and dispensing approvals until she came back to newly enlisted *do-nothing* and had to stop. Mist-on-Water was not one for doing nothing, not for long. She also decided that, while others might be fully inept and toothless, when it really counted, she did not belong with them. She decided to yank her new enlistee, Miss *no-one-can-do-anything,* out of her parade. She said, "You just have to judge what to do."

Sand-on-Stone twitched a nostril at her. "You know what to do? About this sickness?"

"No, I don't know. I just told you that. No one does, no one can be certain. But I can work out what I think will work, what might work. I can find a plan, even if no one else can, even if all their plans are stupid."

"Are your plans always as good as the one you had when we started? The one that had you escaped long ago?"

"My new plan involves chaining your ankle to a stake in the village crèche, so you can learn a thing or two in there. Then you will no longer burden your students with silly tiring questions."

"It could work, that plan. At least the horde of rampaging children would have something new to bounce on, poor frail me. Or is that your real plan?"

"As well as the bouncing, there would be target practice. Wouldn't you feel good to be of some use at last?"

"Could I truly aspire to a cause so worthy? But do you have any plans for this sickness?"

"I know some things about it. Yes, four have died. But one seems to be nearly better. LifeSource oracle says it is because they are fishers, or they associate with the fishers. But nearly everyone has some dealing with a fisher from time to time. It tells us nothing."

"Is there anything special about the one who is nearly better?"

"Moons-in-River? Everything is different about him, and nothing is. The more I look, the more I find, especially things that are different. He is just like everyone else. He works his family's grain fields, eats the usual things, except for a few things he doesn't like as much, takes the water from the spring, goes around the village like everyone else, talks to many, nothing unusual. But there are lots of things he has been doing that others haven't. He ate some foods that some of the dead ones didn't, he didn't eat other foods that some of the dead ones did, he took no special remedy. Yes, and the dead ones' homage-due gifts, if we must talk of that. Some of those had already been given, others had been set aside. He has not yet given his, but he has put them aside. There is no pattern. It must be something."

"Something, but you do not know what."

"Something, or some things. There are too many things, too many villagers, too many villagers doing too many things, too many villagers not doing too many other things. Who knows how all these things work together? Who can predict it?"

"Perhaps this problem is not for you to solve."

"I must decide, or it will be decided for me. The village council think they know how to decide. And all the others too. They all think they know what is needed, what is good. If a tree in their orchard gets the blue branch fungus, they lop the branch, even big limbs. But now their orchard is being blighted and they are flicking at twigs. They say they do what is needed, that what they do is right. But they are just collecting twigs and throwing them in the river. It all floats away. It means nothing. They do not like what I tell them."

"What do you tell them?" Sand-on-Stone worried at the answer to come. He knew Mist-on-Water trod very close to the edge sometimes with her views, very close to the edge between the slippery soil of grudging tolerance and a chasm of indignation, caring little if she toppled in.

"They say we must all work together on it. They tell us we must all expect the best, no complaining, we must be confident. Why would they say that? They only need to say it if there is something wrong, if there is something to complain about, if there is something to worry about. They are only throwing dead flowers around the dung heap. They say *don't look at the dung heap, look at the nice flowers.* But they only put dead flowers there because of the dung heap. They don't like the dung heap, but they don't know what to do about it, so they put dead flowers on it. So, I tell them they have found a dung heap and they are rolling in it."

"Who can promise a plan that will not fail? You?"

Silence. Not one clacking bird. Not even a breeze in the trees.

Mist-on-Water felt the silence was speaking against her. She settled her head on the stone behind, her gaze resting on trees on the far side of the valley, where they met the clouds. "Perhaps we should separate them, the sick ones, letting just a few tend to them. Some sicknesses pass from one to those who are close to them. But then, how to cure the sickness? That is the real need. We must find the way to cure them."

"And when you choose your plan, will you be certain it will work, this plan you will find somehow? How will you know if it will make things worse, or if it will just be wasted?"

"If I knew everything, I could be certain. But I don't. No one does. But I do know some things, and I can learn more. My plan will use what is known, not wander after foolish wishes and giddy guesses like they are doing now. I want to do something, the best I can find. Everyone else is."

Sand-on-Stone relaxed his head back against the hard stone. "And all you know – is it enough? Enough that you will need no guesses, giddy or otherwise."

Mist-on-Water raised her head and turned to Sand-on-Stone. "I won't do nothing. There are no instructions for this, are there? Your source-with-no-name has none. In that story, the one you say others told, we have cut ourselves off – from her, from one another. Maybe that part is right – sometimes I do feel cut off. The oracles are our ears for the other sources. But your source-with-no-name has no oracle. Your source-with-no-name just let us cut ourselves apart. Its precious creation. Just a little careless. Where was it – out taking a pee? Even if your absent-minded-source sent me some morsel of guidance, why would I take a nibble? There would probably be an ingredient or two missing, or salt confused with sugar."

"Yes, there are those who have seen it. In some domain beyond time and space, we turned our awareness away from all knowledge, away from that place where there are no questions, to a new land where there are no answers. But that split did not happen without the participation of The Source."

"What? That source-with-no-name knew? She knew what they were doing? And didn't stop them?"

"The Source knew? Of course. Before that split there was complete unity, full communication. Nothing was known by one. Everything was known by all. The Source and all the perfect beings it had drawn from its own substance knew everything together. Everything one did, they all did together. *Stop what they were doing*, you say. But in that place, there was no stopping of doings."

"So then, your perfect source was … she was … complicit. I seem to remember it was something of a disaster, their foray into that strange twisting of time and space."

"The Source did its part. And remember: no harm has been done."

"It joined in making the whole mess?"

"It did its part."

"Are you trying to make this as painful as possible for me? I'm not in the mood for it." She gave him an intense dark stare. "Tell me then: your source – its part was what?"

"You will remember that the beings worked it so their awareness was sent to dwell in not-minds attached to feeble organisms so they could experience the *not*. But the beings in those not-minds did not know who or what they were. So, they gave the not-minds and organisms they were attaching themselves to a name: *myself*. But of course, that was a false name. The Source, author of truth, gave those organisms their true name. It named those organisms *learning tool*. From The Source they became the means for the *not-minds* to take lessons in truth, a means for the *not-minds* to learn what they were, to learn where they came from, to learn how to release themselves, when they were ready, to learn the truth of the *nots* they called their desires, to learn how to discard them. The Source gave the means to release every eternal awareness grafted into a *not-mind*, to release them back to the single forgotten joyful desire they had known before, together with The Source."

"Brrhhp. That could not work. I will tell you why. You say those beings had their new *not-desires*? *Not-desires* perfectly guarded by their fear? But now they are supposed to go back to what they can no longer want. Why would their *not-minds* want what they cannot want? Your source could not take it away from them because, I seem to remember, it had no way of taking, only giving. And they had to be free, too. Remember that. I must be learning this lesson well. Now I can almost make as little sense as you can."

"You are mostly right. Of course." Sand-on-Stone turned to his side and gave her a quick wink.

Only mostly? thought Mist-on-Water. Her indignation made her listen very closely to Sand-on-Stone's next words.

"You are right about this: the working of this way back is hard to find, but it can be done. Let me try to explain. Everything is built on something. Even the *not*-minds are given form by what truly is – the substance of The Source. Those beings did not, could not, take away or in any way diminish their true selves. It was still there, unchanged, but hidden. Their *not-minds* had just covered over their knowledge of themselves, their knowledge of everything. Their *not-minds* hid everything true under layers and layers and then more layers of *nots*. Those *not-minds* are a noisy, bustling, chaotic market of *not-ideas*, each *not-idea* calling out attention to itself, much shouting, much tugging at wrist, tapping at elbow, cajoling, each one straining to push to the front, all promising emptiness in the guise of satisfaction, all smiling, naming just you their secret special friend, all assuring you they will always fill the emptiness of *the not*. So, the not-minds make their not-realm a market. There is much for sale in there but all steeply priced, and outside … outside its shabby booths, nothing." He rested his back against the rock again, looking to the clouds. "Ah, but The Source – The Source calls that realm a room of lessons. Because one thing the not-minds do well, in their flimsy frames, is learn. They need that, so they can know of this never-before realm. Even not-minds can learn something is missing. They can learn that what is pressed on them there is not for them; the not-emptiness can never meld to their true selves. So, they can learn again. Those not-minds can learn they are not *body*, not little, not alone, not fading, that the hopes they forge are cages of empty promises trapping a self that has no need. Then, yes, they start to see their wondrous, dark, immaculate, tangled edifice of flashing *not-ideas* as chaos, that chaos of *not-ideas* colliding and morphing at every junction in their vast *not-mind* labyrinth, contrived to distract and mislead. It is then a visitor slips in, creeps past the sentries of that baffling riotous bazaar, whispering a hint: release. And so, the seeking begins. The seeking for another way. The seeking for their true desires, their true purpose, their true selves."

Mist-on-Water let out a loud breath, vibrating her lips. "I've let you meander about with this like a geriatric turtle,[8] but now you seem to have toddled off into an entirely different valley. You were going to tell of your source's way of release, remember? If you drop your seeds on soil barren and cracked, there will be no crop."

"That way – that other way they seek, the one strange to them. You were right before – they do not really want it. In fact, even while they sought it, half-hearted, they feared it. Even if they start looking for it, if now and then they pass by it, they will not know it. When they see it, they will misunderstand, look away, walk on. Not yet theirs, the mind for it. So, The Source's part was to send a guide to show the way, to place in their arms what they do not know how to pick up. Then they can learn that the wants of their not-mind fail them. The guide whispers words foreign to the realm of the not, bewildering to not-mind. Words of reunion, of return."

"That way – it is the way back? There is a way back?"

"Yes."

"I suppose you will tell me you have this guide. A scroll giving instructions, is it? Is it in your cabin?"

"The guide is no scroll. When those beings made their realm of *not* and their not-minds, The Source released another life from itself." Sand-on-Stone leaned his head back and slowly pulled his hands down his face. "Words fail here. They fail everywhere, I suppose. This life, it was … it was another awareness. That awareness could go into that nothing realm where The Source was not known. That awareness joined each of them there to perceive the

---

[8] An aquatic animal similar in slowness to an Earth turtle

nots they were seeing, but without being deceived by them. At the same time, that awareness still perceived the true dimensions which they no longer could. It was their teacher, their guide. The Source gave it to them, gave it into their not-minds, every one of them. They learn and it teaches. It teaches the way back to the true realm, the realm of truth."

"And by *them*, you really mean *us*?"

"If you like."

"Not particularly. But so-be. And the name of this guide? What is she called? Is it you?"

"It is not me. It too has no name. It cannot fit into a smattering of sound."

"So-be. Does this unnamed guide know more than LifeSource oracle then? What does she say about our sickness?"

"Do you mean the one in the village?"

"Of course – the one that has killed four for no reason. Can your *guide* tell me the reason? Can your *guide* give me a cure?"

"Yes."

That was unexpected. Mist-on-Water had been expecting what she usually got from the oracles – the nimble side-stepping, the languid adroit weaving of pretty words, a feeble weave that frayed in haste at her first well-aimed poke. "Say-you. And yet no one has told me about hearing from this *guide*. It seems this *guide* is a little coy. Or very coy. Not very helpful in a guide, Where is she hiding?"

"I can only tell a little about it – The Source's guide." He paused, tapping his fingers together, repeating a broken rhythm. "Do you happen to remember the times that you looked after the children in the crèche?"

"Not again. I should have known. I take back my question."

"It is too late, I hold your question captive for interrogation. But no, it is not the crèche again. As a teacher, I am just doing my duty of playing nasty tricks to make sure my student is awake. You know I must."

Nasty trick or not, it had pulled Mist-on-Water from her dark mood but left her still armed with her keen detection, her incisive inquisition, her calm defiant resolve.

"I will tell you about the folk of the Walkup-Walkdown village."

"The Walkup-Walkdown village?" Mist-on-Water sounded dubious.

"Yes, the Walkup-Walkdown village. It is far from here, but not too far. Those villagers had built their cabins on a small plateau near the base of a mountain range, cabins squeezing around a brook that gurgled from a crack in the mountain rocks, a never-ending trickle of fresh clean water, rolling down through a belt of dense forest, where the thirsty trees drank it all. That little brook never reached the fertile plain below. Now every day, those villagers had to go through the forest to work their fields and orchards, but the forest was dense and treacherous. Things lived in there, shrieking things that rushed and clawed and snapped if disturbed. Other things known only by their alarming calls; yet other things that had stings, one sting enough to creep through flesh and bone, slow, quiet, eating away, wasting; other small, swift, scurrying things that darted in packs with slashing teeth, a hole sliced in arm or leg or back, the pack gone before the first blood came, before pain burst out. Even the plants there warred against interlopers, vines tripping and ensnaring, thorns tearing sinew, trees dropping branches to bar the way. But, there were tracks through the forest down to the plain, five tracks in fact, that could take the workers safely to their fields."

"Best stick to one of those tracks, I'm thinking."

"Yes. Did I say the tracks were safe? It was not quite that they were safe. One day a track might be safe, another day it might not. If a track was safe one day, if might not be the next. Another one would be safer. So, each day they had to decide which track to take, which would be the best one."

"You did say this was a true story, didn't you?"

"It is true enough. Do you want me to get to the end of it?"

Mist-on-Water gave quick finger taps of affirmation.

"The village had three seers who parleyed with the spirits, who communed with the unseen, who gleaned the portends, who passed on their hidden knowledge when choices needed to be weighed. Each morning, the seers counselled the workers on which track would be safe to go down that morning."

"I am guessing that those seers are not actually this *guide* of yours, this *guide* of your source-with-no-name."

"Correct – as usual. Let me continue." He shifted his weight against the rock. "The seers did not always get it right, it seemed. Sometimes on the chosen track, the workers startled a lone resting predator, but usually they came off not too badly; or they stumbled on some hiding beast, not the worst kind; or some other mishap befell them. Perhaps worse things were awaiting them on the other tracks on that day, perhaps not. They did not know."

"Still not seeing any useful-looking *guide* hanging around anywhere."

"No, neither am I. Perhaps this is the wrong story. Let me finish it anyway. It may have something in it." Sand-on Stone rested his head back against the rock. "Now, where was I? Ah yes, the tracks. Every time the villagers took the track that the seers had marked, going down to their fields and orchards, they sang songs and chanted chants, rowdy uplifting songs and battle chants. Their songs and chants were to confuse any fierce creatures that might be lurking near the track, and to ward off spiteful spirits that might be passing, even forest gremlins. They were very superstitious, those villagers.

"At the end of their day, work done, when it came time to go back to their homes, they did not have the seers to advise them. Those seers were still back in the village. Tired after their toil, wanting home, craving rest, the workers did not have anyone to tell them which track to take. But ages past someone had found a way. They just started singing one of their songs. It was always the same song, just one song, a very old song. When they started singing that song, their limbs stirred, their toes found new energy, their legs seemed to hear some call, and the workers simply went up the track that their legs took them to, all of them going together. With their feet following an unseen guide, the fallen logs on the track became steps up the hill, the sudden calls of the forest beasts no longer startled them, the sounds of claws and teeth rushing at them rarely arrived. They just faded back into the forest.. They kept singing their 'Going Home' song as they went up the track, in different keys and changing the rhythms and harmonies to keep it interesting. No one knew who had made it up. This is how it went." Sand-on-Stone sang the song, his voice faltering at times. The song sounded old; it echoed of distant lands.

Mist-on-Water listened patiently. "So-be. It is catchy, I suppose. I will try to remember it the next time I need to get from my fields at the foot of a mountain through a nasty forest to my village. Shouldn't you have told the story about the song that can cast out the sudden plague of earaches that befell the village youths on the brink of finishing their education?"

Sand-on-Stone rewarded her with a half-smile.

"Wait. I think I have the start of a new plan now. We will get you to sing to the sick ones. That would surely drive the sickness away, if we can keep the patients from cutting off their ears first."

The half-smile turned half-frown.

"So-be. Let me sum this all up now. First you tell me your source-with-no-name has made some guide. Now you tell me a story where the guide seems to be a pretty song. But now I am hoping that even you would not be suggesting the answer to our sickness is to brighten up and sing a cheery song. So where is this guide you promise? I am still not seeing her."

"Yes, the guide is unseen."

"Say-you. So now we have a guide-who-hides. Perhaps it's a good complement to a source-with-no-name."

"Unseen is not the same as hiding."

"What about me, what about the other villagers, where do we find this *guide-in-hiding*? What is she doing? Does she have *a song* for the sickness?" She said *a song* as if it was the most foul, contemptible, inadequate thing imaginable. "I don't accept that."

"Don't you want it? To know what to do, where to go?"

"Not like that. It's just a superstition. A sad delusion. I. Will. Not. Accept it." She glared at him and her nostrils flared.

"Good. Correct."

She fixed on him a withering stare that said *this had better be good.*

"I am pleased I could not lead you astray. That story gives the wrong answer. To the Source, you are never in the wrong place or the right place; nor is the way you are going ever right or wrong. It is only your thinking – that is confused. It needs guidance away from that. The guide is the path from confusion to truth."

Mist-on-Water sat very still, quiet. Listening. Eyes moving, slowing, scanning, seeking. Speaking quietly, the softest whisper, she said, "I see any guide-in-hiding. Is it behind your cabin?"

"You hear it. It is a bird always singing. But there is a choir. The choir sings with the notes of *not.* The bird sings not a single note that the choir does not turn into a chord in its own key. The single tone called unity becomes the minor chord of specialness, augmented with the note *us*, diminished by *them.* The vibrant rhythm of eternity splutters, stuttered in day and season, the droning dirge of an un-eared cantor counterpoints the melody called love. Yes, hard to hear in that raucous rabble. No, you will not hear that bird, if you do not know to listen for it, if you do not know what to listen for, if you do not try."

"Ah, the voice conveniently lost in the ruckus. I should have known. Does it not know it needs to shout when the room is crowded? Say-you? But now the time has come for me to give you your exam." Mist-On-Water said it with her best solemn master-crafter instructor voice. Her playful words were disarming, a camouflage; her intent was destruction.

"My exam?"

"Yes, to see how your teaching is progressing, to find out if you are getting the benefit of our lessons together, or if extra work is needed."

"So-be. Perhaps you should have warned me of its coming. I have not had a chance to review my work, but I will do my best."

"Here is your first question: if your guide-in-hiding knows every need I have, and if this guide has made a path for me, for everyone, to freedom, joy, peace, the way out of fear, why does it not tell me, or tell someone, anyone – I don't care – how to deal with this sickness? Certainly, it is a place of fear that we cannot escape. Where is this path of escape? That's your first question. Good luck with it."

"So-be. Can I have a moment to prepare my answer?"

"You will lose points for wasting time. It would be a pity to have to fail you."

"So-be. So-be. Then can you pretend, for a moment, that I am a guide, even an excellent guide?"

"Now that may be too difficult, even for me."

"Thank you for trying anyway. Now, what is a guide, but one who teaches the way?"

"Perhaps one who shows the way? A shame – your first mistake so early in the exam."

"Bo! Unleg it. You may be right. Yes, you may go the way a guide shows you without learning it. A guide need not teach it. Sit-on-it."

"There's no need to start using bad language." She had never heard him say the mild 'back-kneed', let alone the eyebrow raising 'unleg it'. "It is only a few points off for that one. Don't lose heart yet."

"So-be. But please remember, these words I hobble along with are cracked crutches. They try to pull apart what is one. The Source, everything, just one." He made a new start. "Guiding, learning, growing, teaching – are they not all toes coming out of one foot? Anyway, I did make a mistake," Sand-on-Stone said. "I should ask: what would The Source's guide teach to a being who has all knowledge, her knowledge of all things just misplaced for a time, her knowledge even of herself covered over? Yes, that is it."

"You seem to have forgotten that I am the one who has set this exam. I am asking the questions here. Nevertheless, let's review the start of your answer: it appears you're saying I know all things? Somewhere? Somehow? But how convenient this witness you have dragged in, this forgetfulness. I would question it, but I think I already know all its answers: *I don't remember.* This witness cannot support your case. It has nothing to offer here. Remove it."

"Please let it have a few small words before it slinks away: only because you have forgotten can you hold dear promises of loss, can you embrace a world you fear, can your trust fall on frail flesh."

"A poor testimony. I know what is plain to see. I see the sickness. I see family, I see friends. I see my fingers dancing to my whim, I smell the scent of my arm, I feel the fur on my leg, I hear my feet snapping twigs as I walk along. Is it not all a marvel? I know what I am, this day, the day before, the next. I have not forgotten anything."

"Say-you. Yes, you know. But not everything. Who can fathom the wonders of our flesh, our breath, the pulse of life? In your not knowing could there not be something greater, a Self you do not see? A Self that should you see it beside your fleshy wonder, would in an instant turn you from fawned-on flesh. Not a marvel now, but a fleck? Leg and foot you see, yet how often is this question posed: *who am I?* And how many answers will you find, perhaps as many as the days that come, perhaps as many as the tongues that speak of you. Why should that thing you see be so hard to find? How could there even be a question there? Everyone knows you, do they not?"

"No one knows me. They can believe what they like. I know what I know."

"So-be. Now, to continue my answer I must go back to my pretend-work, return to my duties as a pretend-guide. Let me see." Sand-on-Stone paused in thought. "Yes, perhaps we will try it this way. Let us say a rock comes to me believing it is a leaf and fears the puffs of breeze, thinking they will carry it away. Am I to teach it how to tie itself down? If the river comes believing it is a grain of sand and fears the rain, thinking the drops will wash it away, am I to show it how to build itself a roof? If a tree comes believing it is a drop of dew and fears the rising sun will slowly waste it away, am I to take it to a cave that it can hide itself in? No, better that the rock knows it need not strain against the wind, that the river knows it is born of the rain, that the tree knows its life is from the sun. Only then can they be their true selves. So it is with the guide The Source has given. The guide will not take the thread of your dread twisted around a lie and weave you answers from that. It will not give you any answer that by words unsaid affirms for you this lie. Your dread must first be unwound, the lie laid bare and then seeing truly, you will dismiss torment and lie together, unwanted both."

Mist-on-Water sniffed.

"But it will do nothing that affirms for you the demise of the body you know now is your demise. Or that lets you declare you could be broken, become faulty or lose anything in the smallest way. Or that your days could not be beyond counting. Or that you are alone, apart."

"Say-you. So-be – enough of these games. I know there is some truth in what you are saying. Everyone has doubts. Everyone grows weary of them. Everyone casts their line for answers but pulls in confusion. Could there be a better way? So-be, tell me. I don't want to be confused. I have had enough."

"Listen then. When in every angry shout you but hear a call of distress, a distress you can answer with quick relief, when every stranger who approaches with brow set to test your guard, you embrace as your precious lost brother suddenly found, when in every flap of sagging flesh you but see a veil to protect your sight from your sister's radiance, then you will remember, and remembering, all your chains, all weariness, all torment will fade to peace."

"What about the torment of this sickness that guide-in-hiding has not helped us with? Does she not know about it? Can we not tell her? Does she not care? Can she do nothing?"

"Its care is the care you have for the children in the crèche, distraught over their broken creations. You do care about them, don't you? Even the unruly ones?"

"I care. I speak and I act. Perhaps not very well, but I try. But has she tried? What instruction has she sent? What can she do? Tell me, or you fail this exam."

"I don't need to give you that. You already have it within – not within your body, but within the bounds of your consciousness. If you search quietly within, you will find many, many things. But you will have found what the guide has given when what you have found brings nothing but peace."

"Or. It could be that no one has given anything right. Not you or anyone or anything. And you are not writing down any answer for this question in your test."

"So-be. The Source's Guide gives the same answers as you do in the crèche: you may offer words of comfort to the distraught child, but words, I think, the child refuses to start with. You may try to teach the culprit, a teaching he does not want, I would guess. You may even like to rebuild what has been broken, but you cannot do that until the conflict has passed, I think. But then as you watch conflict passing out the door, as often as not it is taking the hand of interest along with it, it seems. The child who decides the answers he wants – he may ask, but he is not listening. What will he hear?"

Mist-on-Water usually met any question with an answer, a good one, quite good. But of late, as she had been seeking the company of better answers, better than good. Deeper, truer. None had been coming. This time again, no answer came. Not deeper, not truer. She only said, "That guide-in-hiding of yours needs to speak up a bit."

Sand-on-Stone sighed. "It has no need to shout, to push in, to entice, to nag, to excite – it alone rests in truth forever fixed. Its only way is to offer; it is mine to accept. It can be found in many messengers, some seen, some heard, but bearing one message: *all must be released.* That is the single task it gives to you."

"Even if release lets me perish, writhing in pain, groaning in distress, sprawled in the dust, weary, weak, and broken?"

"Those you are not free to do, but you are free to imagine you do them, as you are free to imagine you are the sum of your limb, your gut, your breath. You are free to cower before the whining wind whipping specks into your eyes while a power far greater than all the stars and worlds abides in you. You are free to lament the decay of what was never you while the forever-you blooms without end. You are free to clutch at tattery trinkets of brittle twigs while everything that ever was, is and will be is held out to you. You are free to imagine you are free being that which can never be free. But there is a better way to be free."

"And what would that be? To keep dreaming those fantasies everyone has, but even a limp-mind is not addle-witted enough to believe in?"

"Believe? Yes, you are right. Only believe as you find. You will seek what you desire. Examine what you want. Do you have it? Do you know it? Only you can look for it."

Sand-on-Stone had opened the gate to a thistly, unworked paddock.

Mist-on-Water decided not to enter. "You look at this, now. You have squirmed away from the question I have set. I asked: what is the reply of your hiding source-guide? Can you hear it? This is your last chance to tell me. Your time is nearly up."

"Its first reply is this: decide. It is the only thing you do here. Decide if you will keep following not-mind, or if you will stop. Decide if you will take the other way. *It is an easy way, but craftily hidden. Hidden among many other paths, but those other paths, they all lead back to themselves.*"

"There is too much in this. How can I even begin?" Forgetting to mark the exam she had set, she slid down the rock and walked to the edge of the clearing, where the branches reaching over her seemed to make her world smaller, simpler. With her mind teased with questions taking her to yet more questions, her feet took her further into the simplicity of the trees. Her questions came along for the walk. *Is this really all there is? If there is more, how can I find it? And why is it so hard?* Still grappling with her questions, she emerged from the forest and was surprised to see that she had meandered to the edge of her village, on the down-river side. She had come too far now. Her next steps would be to home.

Observation Series: **Their Goals**

Summary of observations. I am a bit sad about this. My cuddly muffins do not know what to do with themselves in these dimensions. They are forever getting bored and frustrated. They are often asking themselves what their purpose is. The answer is obvious. To get back to where they once belonged. I know I am not supposed to, but I even suggested that to one of them. He made a song about it.

Chapter 20

The sky had turned a shade darker. Were the ever-present clouds a touch denser than usual? The brighter part of them, where the furtive sun gave itself away, was lower in the sky. Despite the dimness, the air felt warmer on her face than it had a few days earlier. Tracey guessed it was mid-afternoon. At least these little discussions were not taking too long. It was better than most of the meetings she endured back home. Although equally unruly in their meanderings, they were far more tedious, going on and on, before ending up nowhere. She thought that here, they were getting somewhere. She hoped so.

"Here we are," said SiMiYah. They were standing on the path leading to the dwelling of SiMiYah's great-aunt, the head of the Global Union of Arts Academies.

"Difficult to argue that one," said Quentin, keeping a safe distance from Tracey. Only Conrad_27-8 heard him.

SiMiYah approached the entrance and the double doors opened for her, without the usual *state your business* challenge.

"She will be in her workroom," SiMiYah said without breaking stride and turning down a passage to the left.

"She's expecting us?" Tracey was still nervous about going into these encounters poorly prepared. With this one, as far as she knew, their preparation was not so much poor as totally absent.

"No, but she likes me to come by anytime. More often than I get a chance to, actually. I haven't come by for a while so she should be very eager to talk. We may even have to stay the night. You will have no choice – she will find some Mandate for it. You will enjoy it. She is an excellent host. She is very helpful."

"No." The problems the idea of staying could bring added to Tracey's nervousness and her voice was tinged with a panic she tried to quell. "We can't stay the night."

"No?"

Tracey thought quickly. "Remember your Mandate Breach hearing? There is a lot we have to get done before you will have your Mandate-advocate for it."

Before SiMiYah could respond, they had walked into a room with a single occupant to one side who was sitting on cushions facing a SeeDo. To the other side was a low table surrounded by cushions, and in the opposite corner, someone had made an untidy pile of several crates beside a similarly untidy rabble of sculptures in diverse styles and materials.

SiMiYah said, "Great-aunt BaBaBaBaDah, may all be in accordance."

"Ah, SiMiYah, it has been too long. And you have brought some others with you. They are friends? Or maybe some work colleagues? How pleasant."

"They are …"

"They are not some artists you have brought to see me, are they?" Great-aunt BaBaBaBaDah straightened and stiffened, wary, aloof.

"No, not artists. We …"

"Yes, but enough of that, tell me all about what you have been doing."

It was an invitation SiMiYah could not decline. She touched on a few recent events at her work and passed on some snippets of family gossip, which brought her to the drama of the recent family rain-meal. From there, she stumbled into her long, detailed story of everything that had happened since, punctuated only by occasional *Oh dear*s from her great-aunt.

When SiMiYah finished with, "And so now we have come to see you," Great-aunt BaBaBaBaDah expelled a final *Oh dear*, and then silence fell as they waited for helpful Great-aunt BaBaBaBaDah to take the initiative. SiMiYah had not asked her great-aunt to have ChiBelTra admitted to the Council of the Global Union, but her plea would have been no clearer if she had.

Great-aunt BaBaBaBaDah said, "But you must stay for rain-meal."

"Certainly, we accept, in accordance. But it's a little early."

"Of course, we will not start it now, but one must make plans. Meanwhile, you can tell me about everything you have been doing."

"But I just …"

"Yes, yes – I know, you have been working, seeing people, troubles here and there. But tell me about everything else. What has been fun, exciting? I want to hear about that, my dear. You went to an exile zone, you said. Were there dangers everywhere? How did you manage to escape it? It must have been thrilling there, not like here: the same day after day after day, routine stacked on mundane, bland piled on dull."

"Dull? But you are the Head of the Global Union of Arts Academies. It was always your dream. I am excited for you. You have fully satisfied the Purpose Mandate: *Every citizen has the right to a purpose, as they choose.* Think of everyone else, so many, so many who long for what you have, to sit where you sit, so high, knowing they will never reach it." SiMiYah was not thinking of them, she was wishing she were more like her successful great-aunt.

Quentin was feeling his internal pressure building to imminent-supernova levels and strained to hold it in. *So many will never reach it? What about the AS THEY CHOOSE bit of your fatuous little Mandate?* But despite his minder's enthusiastic goading, the moment passed and his annoyance collapsed in on itself, a fading white dwarf, a minnow in its constellation, almost invisible, sitting unnoticed, grumpy and feeble.

"Yes, I have my purpose now. My days are stuffed full of it. My frantic, draining, empty days."

"Empty days? What?" SiMiYah was confused.

"Did I say empty? Yes, minder, silly of me to actually say it, but I am stuck now, aren't I? Minder thinks that maybe I need a bit more excitement, you know. Minder also thinks I need to keep this prestigious, safe, stale title I have. And with it, the squabbling puff cakes in their supercilious queue leading to my door, with their polite squeezing past and pious shoving, eager to pour their dronings into my ear day and night. And then minder tells me I need more excitement. After all these years, I despair of ever getting what it wants. Is minder broken, do you think?" She broadcast a mechanical smile, a habit, empty of any pleasure, mirth or contentment.

"Minders don't break. That is silly." SiMiYah had never heard the idea expressed before. "Isn't it?"

Great-aunt BaBaBaBaDah turned her attention to SiMiYah's companions. "And what about you? Are you doing anything exciting here? SiMiYah says you are not artists, at least. Are you scientists? Engineers? Are you building some amazing new machine to see beyond the clouds perhaps, are you about to discover the elixir of eternal life?" As she spoke, she scanned Conrad_27-8, Quentin, Kieran, and then left her gaze resting on Tracey. This was fortunate because she did not notice that panic had frozen Quentin, seizing his breath, leaving only his eyes free to flick towards the door.

Tracey was startled to find herself made the centre of the conversation. "I – we – are not from this town. We are only visiting. Relatives. Nothing exciting. Sorry."

"Ah yes, another town. They are all the same, aren't they? Never mind, you can keep chasing your purpose, whatever it is. Just be careful not to catch it."

SiMiYah said, "Great-aunt, I don't understand. Why are you talking this way? Why are you asking about this excitement, danger even? Surely you are not looking for that?" She was tempted to add *at your age* but thought better of it.

"What I am looking for? It seems you are too polite to say *at my age*. But *at my age*, I have found many things. I have fulfilled the Purpose Mandate many times. Now, look, I have an enviable collection of shipping containers littering my floor and when I am not delighting in those, I promote obscure pieces of art whose purpose I can only guess at."

SiMiYah said, "But what about all of those artists you have helped? Everyone says you have done wonderful work."

With a flick of two fingers, her great-aunt dismissed it.

Kieran, who had been examining the jumble of visual arts in the corner of the room, said, "The purpose of all of these was given by their makers?"

Great-aunt BaBaBaBaDah looked at Kieran and then at SiMiYah. "Do you know, folk come to me and say: how wonderful it must be to help all of those struggling gifted artists, so they can craft their brilliant works, so they can cultivate their talents. But I tell you: everyone is creating something. Not just artists. When an artist creates her piece, she knows what it is for. After she has created it, will it choose its own purpose? *That* would be silly." She gave a sniff and half smile. "And everyone else. Everyone else is creating many things, in her work, in her family, when she is with her friends. Some of those things they can touch, but most of them she leaves in their minds. Her friends take what she has made with them when they go – in their minds. Everyone is making things. But do any of those things go away and decide what they are going to be for? Of course not. Their purpose came with their making. We are fortunate to have the Purpose Mandate. We are the only ones who have no maker. So, by the Mandate, I choose my own purpose. I make myself. Or is it minder?"

"How, I wonder. How will I choose?" SiMiYah was thinking about what purpose she would choose in exile, forgetting how close she was to escaping it.

"But you have already chosen. It's easy. It's what you like to do, what you want to be. Of course, getting to do and be what you want may not be easy, but we have the Mandate." Her great-aunt looked perplexed at needing to explain.

Again, Quentin was amazed and frustrated that this apparently highly intelligent being could say it without a hint of sarcasm, without her tongue dropping off. He was tempted to ask Conrad_27-8 to help her work out how to put two and two together, how to see their ambitious Mandate hid no purpose of its own, let alone having one for anyone else.

SiMiYah pre-empted any arithmetic lesson. "And yet … and yet … No, you must be right. There are many things I want to be. Minder is always pointing them out – the things I am not that I want to be. Even though, thanks to minder, I already am many, many things. I'm a HearTell integration designer. I do like it, mostly. I'm friend to DahTiYahYah, RetWetFubFarn and TraaCee and I have my ani-graphs – you know those moving drawings. I make my ani-graphs change with the expressions of whoever is looking at it. You want to see one? No – no, they are not very good – it's just a hobby. But are they really the purpose the Mandate wants? Minder thinks so. Still, there's something, tugging, snagging, dragging me. Sometimes I feel I am adrift, lost, only hidden currents carrying me, drifting, unaimed, uselessly stroking out to find the beach of a shoreless sea. When does it ever end? Always more to be. What I want to know is: is this all I am here for? But *that* is a silly question."

Now Tracey was confused. "What's silly about it?"

"Well, it's silly because … well because … who is going to answer it? It is like when someone asks: *is it meant to be*? Lots of folk ask it. But something can only be *meant to be* by someone. So, when someone asks: *is it meant to be?* (or maybe she doesn't ask but she just says *it is meant to be*), she is really saying: *does some kind of greater being mean it to be*? Which is very silly, because everyone knows there are no other beings anywhere, nowhere else even for other beings to be, and obviously no greater beings. Everyone knows that, except the foolish ones who say there are."

"I see." Tracey herself had, at times, grappled with that question: *is this what I am meant to be*? She had not been able to find a final answer; one that kept on being right. But she had not seen the unstated assumption behind it, either. She had put it on the pile of things to think about later.

Quentin's level of agitation was subsiding a little in the presence of reasonably sound logic, even though there was no evidence that that logic was at risk of being applied to any topic of scientific merit.

"But of course, they can say it by the Freedom Mandate, and by Personal View. They can say that there are some beings we don't see, who we don't know about, somewhere. But I don't. So, who am I giving my question to? Myself? Do I keep asking myself a question I don't know the answer to? That is definitely silly. I can make up any answer I like. Who is to tell me if my answer is right or wrong? What? I do it? Do you mean you, minder, or me? Then I decide what I am here for. I make my own purpose, but did I make myself? Or is there no purpose here at all? In the end it all fades to dust. So, yes, minder, it is silly. No, I won't ask it anymore, but I feel lost."

From over by the pile of sculptures, Kieran said, "Are you lost? You need to know the way home. Then you will know what to do."

SiMiYah tilted her head, but her minder knew there was something it had not understood and was quietly repeating, *"Not. Not. Not."*

"Home." Just one word, but Great-aunt BaBaBaBaDah made it into a place impossibly far, forever gone. "My home is in my studio. It was. The studio I had. It is gone now. It would be hidden under dust if it wasn't. It has been so long."

"But that is wonderful." SiMiYah's cheery side had sprung forth again. It faced a wall of blank looks. "You can just get yourself a studio again. Go back to doing your visual sculpture. It's your answer."

"I cannot do that. I am Head of the Global Union of Arts Academies."

"You can easily leave that title. Let someone else do it."

"No. I can't. There is my contract."

"Your contract. What does your contract say?"

"Like all contracts, it is complex, with many binding clauses, but the most important is that, if elected, I must continue in my role for its full term."

"But your terms are only one year. The next election is coming up soon, straight after long-sleep. If you get nominated again, you can decline it."

Conrad_27-8, who had put on his BringSeeDo, said, "I see you were first voted Head of the Global Council of the Arts thirty-two years ago. Over the three hundred and fifty-three-year history of the Union, your tenure has now exceeded the previous longest tenure by twenty-nine years. In thirty elections the vote for you was unanimous, in the other two years, two of the more befuddled Councillors had forgotten which election they were voting in; they had nominated and voted for an obscure sculpture. That means that, during your tenure, that piece of sculpture has had the second highest number of votes. According to the bylaws, it would become acting head, should you be unable to discharge your duties."

"That's right. I am always elected. They don't want anyone else. There is no one else. There hasn't been for thirty-two years."

Thirty-two years previously, as one of the smaller, little-known Global Unions, the Global Union of Arts Academies had come to the point where all of the natural candidates for its head had, in succession, been elected, and after taking the role, they had almost all, each in their own way, quickly forever excluded themselves from a future term by guiding the flailing Union to infamy, destitution, chaos, disgrace, neglect, and most heinous, public indifference. Most had bumbled to their peculiar failing in a single term. Those less competent with their programme had needed two. At that rambling meeting of councillors, BaBaBaBaDah's name had come up in side-chat about a recent exhibition that had been successful, rare in those days. The secretary, who had not been paying full attention, thought she had been nominated as head. There being no other candidates, BaBaBaBaDah was duly elected. Then, in BaBaBaBaDah's time, year on year, the Global Union of Arts Academies' prestige had bloomed, its influence had exploded, its public profile had blazed brighter and brighter. It had become a Union of high esteem, aspired to. The Union had found that thirty-two years earlier in their stumbling, they had fallen over one of an extremely rare species, an endangered species that had a sense for art, could make a shambolic administration work, could play the politics, but most importantly one who knew how to get folk to need something they never knew they wanted. She shone as head, and when she shone, she threw a light that made them all look good, important. She made them everything they wanted to be. Now those who sat on the Council were not about to let her go easily. Not while she gave everyone on the Council what every one of them wanted. They had caught her, and they were going to keep her – as was their right by the Freedom Mandate.

"Someone else can do it. Maybe not as well as you. Just decline the nomination."

"I can't decline a nomination. It's in the contract."

"Get a Mandate-advocate – an elite grade. They can get anyone released from any contract. They know the ways."

"I can't be released. I've already had the brightest of the most qualified Mandate-advocates go over it. They all said they could do it, but I haven't been able to get a single one of them to do it. The contract says I can't engage a Mandate-advocate to contest the contract."

SiMiYah blinked twice in surprise. She said, "The contract says you cannot engage a Mandate-advocate to contest the contract?"

"It says that."

Quentin said, "I need to get whoever drew up that contract to do my next tenancy agreement."

SiMiYah was not listening to him. "There must be a way out."

Quentin muttered, "If there was a way out, it would be marked *Enter Here*."

Internally, Tracey heard a distant alarm start to ring.

"Yes, there is always a way. The only way is for someone else to engage the elite-grade Mandate-advocate to get me released from the contract."

"Someone else can do it? But I know an excellent elite-grade Mandate-advocate. He always wins. He has already allocated a service time-slice to us – a conditional allocation."

"It's allocated before long-sleep?"

"Yes, it's before long-sleep."

Every time someone spoke, it made Tracey more worried about where they were going. She said, "But wait," and was ignored. SiMiYah and her great-aunt were intent on their mission. They were beyond distraction.

"It may work. But there must be clear evidence that I have not been involved in engaging the advocate. The payment trail must begin and end with you. You can get no consideration of any kind from me. Nothing in return. Ever."

Tracey, feeling this was carrying them to a place that she definitely did not want to go, said, "Maybe we need to talk this through a bit first. Don't forget what we need, what we came for."

SiMiYah said, "Minder always knew it would be hopeless. At least Great-aunt BaBaBaBaDah will have the Purpose Mandate satisfied."

"Again. Like all those other times? Like all those other pointless times?" Tracey didn't care that everyone heard the lacings of bitterness. "I know you are pleased for your great-aunt, but everything we have done now all seems so pointless."

Kieran said, "Our purpose is to go home, all together."

Tracey said, "Yes. Soon we will need to go. It will be too late for you."

But SiMiYah turned to her great-aunt and went through the steps that would take them to engaging the Mandate-advocate.

Great-aunt BaBaBaBaDah said, "It should work. There is little time. I will start now. I will put ChiBelTra's name to the vacant seat on the Academy Council. The others will agree soon." She turned to the SeeDo and with some blinks, winks, and a few short sounds, ChiBelTra had been nominated for the vacancy. She knew that despite his recent disrepute, most of the Council members would accept ChiBelTra's nomination, because it was from their head. The other council members would accept the nomination simply *because* of his recent disrepute. It would probably be unanimous.

Tracey went to stand by Kieran, who was still inspecting the jumble of artwork closely. Quentin and Conrad_27-8 joined them. She said, "This could take a while."

Conrad_27-8 said, "We should be leaving in no more than twenty-seven thousand of this world's time units."

"Are you sure? Not twenty-seven thousand, three hundred and twenty-one point two?" Quentin's attempt to wind up Conrad_27-8 was wasted.

"You could be correct. But without precision regarding our return journey timings, regrettably it is not possible to determine the required departure time exactly. And I have made allowance for only foreseeable minor delays, not for any major delay that could be caused by one or more highly improbable, but possible, catastrophic events. In the case of such an event, we will miss our departure window and risk irreversible dissociation from our originating organisms. More importantly, we will be late for our debriefing with HaaTiToTo."

"Thanks for another cheery thought." Sharing her unhappiness made Tracey no happier.

At the mention of HaaTiToTo, Quentin's stomach sank. It was a reunion he had been trying not to think about.

Tracey stood with the others, apart from SiMiYah and her great-aunt, but her attention was on them and their progress. For now, while the two of them waited, they were exchanging the latest news on what different family members were doing.

A chime sounded. With a glance at her SeeDo, Great-aunt BaBaBaBaDah said, "There it is. The nomination has been ratified. ChiBelTra is a member of the Council now." Before her great-aunt had finished saying it, SiMiYah was connecting to ChiBelTra.

From there, Tracey was startled by the speed and ease at which it all fell into place. SiMiYah had waited for word back from ChiBelTra to say that he had explained to cousin KamSoKamToo what had happened to her SoCaPi sculpture and the news of the special commendation for her collection. SiMiYah also reminded KamSoKamToo of her promise for DooDiDiDoo to get his trust fund and was next speaking to DooDiDiDoo, letting him know he needed to accept the title of clan head. As soon as she got the notification on her clan rankings feed that there was a new clan head, SiMiYah checked DahTiYahYah's citizenship status. His status showed clear: he was no longer exiled. With the revoking of DahTiYahYah's exile, she had a long talk with a very excited DahTiYahYah who, while they spoke, was packaging his iron nugget for despatch by drone courier directly to the Mandate-advocate. SiMiYah asked him to send a copy of the despatch manifest to her. Armed with the despatch manifest, SiMiYah contacted the Mandate-advocate and gave him her briefing on Great-aunt BaBaBaBaDah's case. The Mandate-advocate retrieved the contract from the contracts registry maintained by the Global Council of Records. He lodged a petition of Contract Dissolution by Virtue of Irreconcilable Difference.

On hearing that, Quentin said, "Of course. I should have expected that irreconcilable difference is a virtue here." Quentin was happy he was able to add to his list of things to mock the Allundrians for.

As she watched SiMiYah effortlessly tapping over each of their carefully lined-up dominoes, Tracey's helpless admiration for her efficiency mixed with a mounting dismay as they slid back to where they had started.

They left Great-aunt BaBaBaBaDah and, it seemed, a straggly line of others, stretching long into the distance. Those others were in states ranging from quiet contentment to delirious excitement. It looked to Tracey that the contentment and excitement of every one of them had been bundled into SiMiYah as she rejoiced with them in what also sealed her own demise. Tracey was torn between letting SiMiYah keep her celebration and pointing out that she still a problem to deal with, a problem that far outweighed all the petty gripes she had just so deftly dissolved. Empty of any new plan for the looming exile, she left SiMiYah to her own thoughts. Those thoughts were giving her steps a hint of a skip all the way to the resource hub.

At the transport terminus doors, they all stopped, uncertain. Finally, Tracey said it. "Where will we go now? What can we do?"

SiMiYah frowned. She said, "I still don't want to be exiled."

"But now we are back where we started."

"It has all been for nothing?" Tracey's minder was saying, "So sad. Very sad. You feel like you could cry. Don't do it." Tracey said to SiMiYah, "What will you do now?"

"I need to nominate my Mandate-advocate today."

"What if you don't?"

"I will be found guilty without a hearing, of course. It is in the by-laws of the Justice Mandate."

"But you can't get one. It isn't fair. There isn't any time. There must be another way."

"The only other way is for me to represent myself. But that is hopeless. Minder says it, and it will be. Even with all the help of minder, I know I can't do it. Minder says it. Only a Mandate-advocate knows what to say."

"That's it then. That is what you must do. You must represent yourself. There is nothing else."

"They may increase my penalty, even though the exile is the maximum penalty, they might find a way. It is what minder says."

"If it helps, for once, I have to agree with that minder." Quentin had no clue that what he said held not a single atom of help in it.

Tracey jabbed him in the ribs with her elbow. It looked like an accident. She said, "If that is the only way, shouldn't you try? You can't be exiled. It's not right."

"Minder says *not*. But I think … I think I will not listen to minder – this time. Yes, I will nominate myself as advocate. I will do it now." She whipped on her BringSeeDo and a few moments later put it down. "Now my case is ready to be scheduled."

Nothing else to be done, they dawdled into the resource hub. It was quiet, on the brink of long-sleep with few Allundrians about. Tracey's minder was the only sound she heard. It said, *"Doomed? Have you doomed her now? You did it."* Her mind was swaying, waltzing deeper into her minder's words, when she was distracted by a soft light.

SiMiYah's BringSeeDo was glowing on her arm. SiMiYah glanced at it. "Ah, my trial date has been set. Quiet, minder, I am going to look. I will need to eventually." She read the symbols and gasped. "It can't be. Can it be? My trial date is 734-45-42."

Conrad_27-8 said, "That is three years and ninety-seven days away."

Tracey perked up. She said, "See? Now you have plenty of time to find yourself the most excellent Mandate-advocate."

"No. I can't nominate an advocate after the case has been scheduled."

"Well, at least you will have time to prepare. Even time to get some Mandate-advocate know-how."

"Mandate-advocate know-how will be useless."

"Why useless? Even some knowledge will help. You might find some technicality."

"Yes, it will be useless. No, minder, not that. I am saying this means there will probably never be any hearing for my case."

"I don't understand."

"It has been listed with a priority of Extreme Urgent – the lowest. So, no doubt it will be rescheduled several times before it is heard, put back to the end of the queue each time, back to the end of a queue that only ever gets longer. My case will probably not be heard for fifteen or twenty years, or longer, and the trainee Mandate-guide who lodged the case is already old. If he does not testify … it means … it means … I will not be exiled." Relief had flooded in, washed over her, a cleansing gush, sweeping away the burden of fear and gloom that had been crushing her, and then it receded, leaving her mind clear, fresh, except for a vague smudge on the edge of awareness.

Tracey was almost as relieved as SiMiYah. She let go of her frustration at SiMiYah, at SiMiYah's innocuous self-sabotage. "Now everything can go back to the way it was."

There it was – the smudge. "Yes, back to the way it was. We can just go back to our dwellings. I will be able to keep on doing my work, my HearTell integration engineering. It is my place, isn't it? It's like my home, where I belong. So why do I feel as if it's not … not quite enough?"

Quentin said, "This is the problem with coming into contact with relatives."

SiMiYah said, "Wait – it's all good now, isn't it? We can all go home."

Quentin said, to no one in particular, "Sure, everything's just fine." *Fine for everyone. They can all be as happy as a … as an otherwise sensible animal going back to lick up its vomit.* "Let's all just go back to all of those Mandates. Those so, so sensible and so, so helpful Mandates. All that justice that fixes nothing, but is satisfied when it has broken off a few more pieces. Oops. Back to that theory of special equality, the tail-chasing fun of calling different the same and calling the same different. But that's all fine because you can have whatever personal view you like, until you don't like. But it doesn't matter. There's always another one. Back to the warm embrace of those cosy random clans, clans of one thousand embracing arms and one thousand free hands each holding a cleaver, a thousand busy cleavers hacking at the others, a thousand blind hands not seeing they are hacking away at themselves. A bit gory. No need to look at that. Back to where it's safe. Yes, to where you can be safe because you can attack the attackers who are attacking you for the same reason. Back to having everything you want so that you can find you really want something you don't have. Rinse. Repeat. Back to an existence where purpose is a means with no end. Back to baking your well-being pie – the task of making the thing you have never seen from ingredients you don't have. Back to being free. Free to run amok trapped in a loopy world built from madness for the amusement of the insane. And why do they have to go back to all of that? Because if they didn't, they would be in serious danger. In serious danger, that is, of lurching into some horrible pit where logic and clear thinking were somewhere in evidence." He realised that, for once, everyone had been looking at him as he indulged in his quiet rant. He stopped talking.

Kieran said, "A different guide will point to a different direction."

SiMiYah said, "Yes, maybe something a bit different would be good for me. I don't know what I want. I'm not even sure minder knows. I might start by listening to minder a bit less. Hush, you. I just don't know how. Minder is very clever but maybe there are things it doesn't know about. When I try to think about them, it shoos me away. It worries about me wasting my time. Do you think it could be hiding something? Or is it afraid? But there is nothing to hide in me, is there? Of course not, minder, I know. That is silly too. How can something in me be hidden? Who would do that? Is there anything minder doesn't know about? Yes, minder, I know. It is all plain to see, hear, touch – all that. But I do wonder. What is really good for me? What is good?"

Tracey leaped at the chance to work on a prickly itch that had been rankling more and more with each passing visit, one she had not been able to reach until now. She had decided the relationship between these creatures and their minders was not just dubious, it was all wrong, deeply flawed, the *unnoticed-in-plain-view* cause for a plague of nonsensical antics accepted as everyday normal in an otherwise clear-thinking society. The way their innocent trusting hosts gave themselves over to their minder's bent control chafed at her. The way they insinuated their cunning *i-am-only-trying-to-help*, their twisted *it-will-be-good-for-you* perspective into every single thought riled her. Suppressing the fervour she felt, she put it as diplomatically as she could. "I think you are right. Maybe you should be a bit more of your own mind. You know, try to be a little more in your own self." From SiMiYah's blank look, she knew that was too vague. "What I'm saying is, you could be a bit more independent of your minder. That might be a bit different." She felt a fraud saying this, mainly because her own minder was telling her exactly that. "*Hypocrite. Hypocrite,*" it said. She could not refute this because even now, she was listening to it.

"Yes, I do know what you mean," SiMiYah said. "I can't say anything without it hearing. I can't think anything without it knowing. Every branching of this road I am on turns back to itself. I need different help."

Tracey knew she could not give the help SiMiYah needed. Trying to lift the mood, she simply said, "Who doesn't need help? So hard to know what to do. I wish it could be different."

SiMiYah gave her a tentative Allundrian smile. "Yes, there is always something to do. Minder must work very hard to keep me on the right path. It leads me down the ways of the Mandates. A different way to be, you say? Yes,

I want one too. But how? Is there somehow a freedom that does not cling to chains of want, a justice that does not brand all culprit and immortalise every crime, an equality that does not hammer everyone into one hard mould, a clan that makes no outsiders, a safety that knows no danger, a knowing that does not trample truth, a well-being that needs no seeking, a purpose that rests in being? Minder tells me it is dangerous. But – do you know? – something in me *is* beckoning very quietly and something in me is drawn to it. Yes, I need to be careful and stay away. But still, I wonder if there is something else. Something that is not a sweet road to decay."

Then Tracey saw SiMiYah anew, now not face, arm, and leg, now a knowing, for an instant, a deep connection, out of time, a glimpse here and gone and she had no words for it. "There is already something different about you. You are not like all the rest. If anyone can find it, you can."

"The only thing that is different about me is that I know we are all the same. All. If anyone can find it, we all must." SiMiYah turned to order their GoSomes, which had emerged and were moving towards the platform before she had left the SeeDo.

Their return to the resource hub that serviced what they had started thinking of as their home dwelling pod was a quiet one. Tracey felt drained but contented. SiMiYah dared to hope for an unknown, possibly dangerous 'something different'. Conrad-27-8 was working on a formula to determine the probability of a calamitous event befalling them before their arrival. He spent most of the time sending surreptitious glances to Quentin, attempting to fathom the factors that would give him the probability that Quentin would lose control, run amuck, and slaughter one of more of them. Quentin, increasingly annoyed at the coquettish doe-eyed looks he was getting from Conrad_27-8, fumed at the thought of meeting HaaTiToTo again and having to explain to yet another vacuous committee why the research project he had somehow landed had gone nowhere. Kieran was enjoying the scenery.

As they left their GoSomes, sombreness got out with them and tagged along. The walk from the resource hub to the dwelling used by the Allundrian scientists was slow, not slow enough to be a dawdle, but pensive.

SiMiYah said, "I must go to start my long-sleep now. You will be returning to your town to start long-sleep too? It's late in the season. Everything is going into stand-by mode."

"Yes. We will be going. I don't think we will be back again."

Tracey wanted to hug SiMiYah but did not know if she should. In all their visits to Allundria, she had never seen anyone do it. So, she stood very straight, arms rigid, stiff at her sides, in the Allundrian way. She said, "Mandates preserve you."

SiMiYah reflected the farewell posture less stiffly and said, "Mandates preserve you." She turned towards her dwelling.

When SiMiYah was too far away to hear them, Quentin said, "That one definitely needs someone to guide her. How will she possibly get by without you?"

Tracey saw that, in his own way, Quentin was trying. She let out a long sigh and without malice said, "For someone who knows so much, you really don't know anything, do you?"

Quentin was surprised and pleased that, for once, Tracey had acknowledged his expertise.

Tracey watched SiMiYah enter her dwelling without a look back. She did not see SiMiYah stepping lightly to her bed for long-sleep, silent tears rolling down her cheeks to a peaceful smile.

Conrad_27-8's BringSeeDo chimed. He looked at it, and then at Quentin. "We are five hundred and eighty-nine day-parts late. Acting Global Affairs Director HaaTiToTo is waiting in the dwelling to receive your debrief."

Quentin said, "And now comes the part that we really should have concerned ourselves with all this time. I never asked for this mission anyway." He fixed an intent look on Tracey.

Tracey's minder adroitly whisked away her optimistic contented state of mind, setting up in its place a squawking see-saw, guilt and worry rising and falling against each other, an expert team committed to their task, untiring.

As they entered the meal-room, HaaTiToTo was standing, his back to them. They all felt that HaaTiToTo, the Galactic Council's Global Director here, was most likely harmless, but even so, he was not going to be pleased. They would have preferred to escape whatever unavoidable unpleasantness their minders warned them was about to transpire – confrontation, admonishment, disappointment, fingers pointed firmly at failure, future visa issues.

Sensing their arrival, HaaTiToTo turned and spoke first. "The Mandates preserve you."

Because nothing else will? wondered Quentin.

"The time you had for your mission is up. Those who put their trust in you will want to know the results. Those who risked their bodies for your use will rise from long-sleep expecting their rewards. Now we must deal with the repercussions."

Quentin had been in this situation enough times before. He had some proven opening gambits at his disposal. "You need to remember, with any truly breakthrough endeavour, the timing can never be certain."

HaaTiToTo played a non-listening counter that deftly side-stepped Quentin's opening. "Yes, you have had enough time. The initial investigations have been completed, in line with your proposed approach."

"My proposed approach?"

"Your approach – the one for which you are accountable. The engineering of the research instruments was straightforward."

"The research instruments? What instruments?"

"Ah yes, I forgot, you did not see the instruments before they were deployed. The research team were offered your consulting services, of course, but they elected to proceed from your concept-level design, by the Clan, Equality, and Purpose Mandates."

"Clan? Equality? What? I am accountable for something I was not even consulted on?" This looked to be taking a nastier turn than even he had been expecting. In the academic world, repercussions were usually delivered with all the force of a slosh-slap from a soggy tissue. Quentin's ploys for avoidance rarely worked, since all his attempts to play empathetic and contrite ended up turning into an excellent impression of disinterest. And then, afterwards, there were the inevitable half-concealed sniggers from his puerile colleagues, as if he actually had been slapped with a soggy tissue and pieces were still stuck on his nose.

"And you seemed to be out most of the time anyway."

Glaring at Tracey, Quentin said, "She can explain that." Tracey had hoped she was not going to be part of this, even though she knew that it would have to turn to her at some point.

"Anyway, they have the results now."

"They already have results?" Something had been going on. Whatever it was seemed to have ended up somewhere much faster than he could have imagined, leaving him stranded. He tried to buy some time to catch up. "Look, initial results can be misleading. Analysis and reporting must be completed. You must allow time for full peer review. You cannot make any hasty decisions based on preliminary data." He nearly said *hasty funding decisions* but remembered where he was and heard his minder ask why he was even bothering. They could take their mission and excrete it onto their Mandates. Then his minder was moaning about losing his chance, the only chance he was ever likely to get to go to an exo-planet.

"Yes. They have had spectacular results."

"They have had spectacular results?"

"Using your proposed approach."

"The results from building the instruments I proposed?"

"Correct. Beyond what I ever imagined. They are astonished, completely overwhelmed."

"Beyond what you imagined. Astonished. Of course."

"Of course, you knew what to expect, but they had no idea. And to suggest something that could be executed so quickly. Brilliant."

"It was apparent that the ability to execute quickly was always of the essence. Of course." Quentin still had no idea what these melonheads had been up to, but it seemed to have worked out somehow.

"Yes, after you suggested floating some balloons, the engineering was trivial. No need for a guidance system, they decided, or even any ground-based control – not to start with – just the optical image capture devices and radiotelemetry for the image data. There was a lot of scepticism. No one expected to see anything, to tell you the truth. Once the balloon got over the cloud layers (there are four, they found out) – they could not believe the images. They all started coming through at thirty-six thousand spanparts.[9] Those … those images … beyond description – the countless blazing stars, the sun."

At last, it was making sense now. Quentin thought, *Ah, a high-altitude balloon. Yes, that could work. Not for real astronomy, but a start.* He ached to glimpse the pictures. "I wouldn't mind a quick look at those images. Even though I am only an astrophysicist, in a room full of cloud-watchers, I can certainly assist in their interpretation."

"But you don't understand. They don't know what to do."

---

[9] 12,843 metres, Conrad_27-8 told them later.

"I suppose not, since it is totally beyond anything they have seen, or even dreamed about before."

"So, you do understand. No doubt you have anticipated the next logical step."

Quentin knew the step he was talking about would definitely be one he had *not* anticipated. He said, "Certainly, but I would like to hear you explain it," adding under his breath, "by the You-wouldn't-know-logic-if-it-kicked-you Mandate." Then, at normal volume, "And 27-8, don't butt in now, let's see if he gets this right."

Conrad_27-8 had been thinking the next logical step would be to state accurately the altitude of the cloud ceiling. HaaTiToTo had clearly indulged in a grubby approximation. This time, he had not been planning to butt in to share his conclusion.

"They need help. They are desperate. Is there anything you can offer?"

Quentin was starting to know what it must feel like to be a founder of an important new branch of science. "Well, I could suggest an outline of a comprehensive research program. The new science of astronomy will boom. Just like you want."

"No, it won't. It's finished now."

"What's finished? Exactly?" Quentin had to ask, even though he could not imagine getting any answer that he would like.

"Astronomy. All of it."

Quentin scrunched up his face. He stared at HaaTiToTo. "Why?" It was all he could get out.

"There is no Mandate for it."

"No Astronomy Mandate? I can give you one, it'll be great. Far better than the others."

"I don't mean that. Anyway, the Mandates have been fixed for three thousand years now. They cannot be changed. No, the problem is that the scientists don't know what they are looking at, the images of all those blazing stars. They are afraid. They cannot imagine what they are looking at. They guessed at the image of their sun – at what that was. Seeing it clearly, not through clouds, terrified them. Do you know, it is huge, and flames are leaping out from it?"

Quentin was practically drooling as HaaTiToTo described the images. "But don't they want to *know*? You know, discover stuff, like actual scientists."

"They don't know what they are, those things on the images. They don't know what will happen if they send something up again. Remember, no one here has seen beyond the clouds before. They don't know what those dazzling objects are. They only see an unexplained horde lurking beyond the clouds that keep them all safely hidden. The scientists' minders only have questions. Might those things be disturbed if they send something up there again? Could they fall on them? Are they dangerous? They are so afraid of everything out there, their wits have quietly slunk out by the emergency exits. They will not go against their minders. They just want to feel safe."

"Their wits have left? That would be unique around here. To have wits that might go absent, I mean. In that case, I think I can make this simple enough for everyone, even though I am only an astrophysicist. Here's my radical idea: you could explain that all those lights out there are suns, just like their own. Yes? All perfectly safe. Even though they are infernos of nuclear fusion that would vaporise a passing Allundrian in an instant, we are not close enough for that to happen. Not for now, anyway. Probably. Most likely."

Tracey had been trying to stay inconspicuous by pretending to admire a bushy plant profuse with pendulous flowers, white with yellow frills. Giving it a serious look, she said to it, "Too much information, I think."

Quentin was intent on relieving HaaTiToTo of his concerns and did not hear her. "But here's the good thing: those suns are all a long way away. I mean a very, very long way away. Mostly, anyway. Those scientists are completely safe. Unless there's some black hole in the vicinity, or even a neutron star, but there aren't a lot of those. You wouldn't pick them up on your images anyway. If there were one, you wouldn't want to run into it of course, or even get close. Then this whole world would be smashed in the gravitational field."

Still addressing the plant, Tracey took on a mild scolding tone, one she might use to an errant young child. Leaning closer to her wayward plant, she said, "You are not helping now, are you?"

But Quentin was intent on explaining that all the nasty things need not concern them. HaaTiToTo, who, like Conrad_27-8, was originally an aquatic 65535nian and so had only the vaguest notion of stars, was certainly no astronomer, or even just an astrophysicist. Having had no real understanding of stars himself, he wore an expression that had started as mild concern but, with each assurance that Quentin gave, had grown to alarmed dismay.

"Not much else out there to be worried about. Of course, there is the radiation. That could easily be quickly fatal. A silent, invisible killer. Get you before you know it. Obviously, the clouds or perhaps the planet's magnetic field provide protection here. But not out there. Lots of paranoia about it on my planet. Anyone would think that it's contagious."

"Contagious?"

Tracey, picking out one particular flower, said to it, "And you – you may have just ruined any chance you ever had of getting that treat you wanted."

"Sure, down here, it is safe enough. Mostly. You just want to hope your planet is not intersecting the orbit of some …" *no word for comet* "some … hurtling mountain-sized rock. You definitely don't want to be around when you get an extinction event from the impact of one of those. Do you? That could take care of over eighty percent of life on this planet. On the other hand, a good cleanout can work wonders. But don't be concerned about those. We've only had a few of them on our planet."

"Only a few?" HaaTiToTo started backing towards the door. "I hadn't realised. I had no idea. All of this is very good to know. We will issue the appropriate warning notices." He left quickly, almost running. In dismay, Quentin watched him go. A moment later he was back, looking as if he had forgotten something.

Quentin, not hiding his desperation, said, "But I really should see the results. I am sure I can make some suggestions, point out improvements, tell them what to look for." Quentin knew it was almost certainly useless, but he had to try. If nothing else, the star images just might give him some idea of which part of the galaxy they were in.

"It is too late. They are forever archived, access prohibited. It is by the Safety Mandate." HaaTiToTo picked up the serving plate, still with some remnants of fruit on it, held it over his head with one hand and hurried out again.

Their mission was over.

Addressing the vacant spot left by HaaTiToTo, Quentin said, "Well now. It seems we could be about to have a Galactic Council that is afraid of the Galaxy. No doubt any moment now, the order for its destruction will be issued."

Tracey, picking out one particular flower, said to it, "And there you have it – consider yourself lucky if you get plucked off your silly bush and stuck in a vase somewhere, all by yourself. Your friends here would only be dropping their petals on you, anyway."

Quentin said, "Did you say something? I had to try, but those Galactic Council pumpkins just don't have any people skills."

Chapter 21

"I'm confused." As if to prove it, Mist-on-Water ambled around and around a beetle-back tree, the heavy stick she had used on the trail dragging up dust behind her. She did not know what to think. Not knowing vexed her. A failure to be fixed. Making it worse, not knowing had been coming more often of late, more vexing each time. Failure back again, not fixed yet. Failure was to be concealed. Not this time. This time she was ready to accept help. Help from someone who welcomed her questions. Someone whose answers were strange, yes, unproven, yes, but not lines of rote. Someone who did not see her failure but her seeking. Someone who understood. Here she had found someone who understood. She stopped making dust and looked at Sand-on-Stone.

From the blank look she was getting, Mist-on-Water saw that Sand-on-Stone did not understand. She explained, "You have talked to me of many things. But are they true? You are worse than the oracles. At least they leave nice juicy holes in their tales, nice juicy holes and tasty flaws. With them, I am the cute little rodent that has stolen their sweet morsel out of their fat, inept fingers, and I nibble away at it, in my safe little place in plain view of them but just out of reach of their slow clumsy fingers." She stopped to look Sand-on-Stone down and up. "But you, your gaunt crafty fingers are nimble, your nasty tricks too well made. They could be true, your tales. If they are true, they are important. I do not want your confusion, but you have caught me up in it."

"Ah, so I have convinced you." Sand-on-Stone knew he had not. He stopped trying to drip water into the hollows that marked where the purple spot melon seeds were planted. No shoots yet. The bowl he was using had no spout and the water was running down the side, dribbling everywhere.

"Convinced? Not at all. For a start, your guide-in-hiding is an unconvincing hero. It does not rush in, just in time, when all hope is lost, to flail my assailant. It is a rescuer that has made its own answer, not the one I instructed. Time does not master it. When all hope is lost, it is not the hope I want. But yes, it could be that I am your rock sniffling at the moaning wind. I don't think so, but yes, it could be. And so, I cannot fault your pretty, prickly tale." She gave Sand-on-Stone an accusing angry look, fitting for someone who was the cause of everything that called for blame. "Say-I, it is only one of many fantasies that even I could make up, make them with care, make them with cleverness, to explain these deep yearnings, yours and mine, these palling clawing cravings, all of those clever tales enticing, promising profound knowings, announcing astounding hidden answers, revealing the how to every why, and all my tales near impossible to be certain of what part is true and what is not. I only allow your tale, your silly tale that claims witnesses who will testify but that places them where they are not heard, I only allow it because it has found in me a place I knew not, a place it then seemed to call its own. But your answers have just made more questions in me."

"Yes, knowing the route is not taking the journey. But the journey that takes you nowhere is a torment."

"This sickness torments us. None can say why. Is there a reason? Is it all just dust and wind? The folk in the village, they know nothing, old uncle. They move, they dance, they look alive, but they are not; they never lived. They go places and end up nowhere. What use are they? What use am I? What use is anyone?"

He turned his eyes to her, eyes sad and concerned. Staring at the ground, she did not see him. Sand-on-Stone did not want to see Mist-on-Water troubled. He wondered if perhaps he had gone too far. "Say-you. So-be. You could forget it. For now. Just concern yourself with the orchard, wait on the fresh delicate aroma of your next meal, sing the songs of rest to the weary evening. Perhaps it is not the time for this, not for you."

"You know that I cannot do that. Not now. The orchard is not enough. I cannot ungrow this thing you have sown in me. Maybe it was not even you who did the sowing. I refuse to tend it but it does not die. It cries out in whispers, sometimes it gnaws softly in the night, sometimes it springs out to unnerve me as I go about my day. It is a hunger you have awoken in me, a quiet hunger, waiting, patient, a hunger to feed I know not what. It is a thirst, and one that not just I have. I begin to see it in every aunt and uncle, they all have it. They thirst. They thirst, and yet cool clear water has never found their lips, lips cracked with cloying dust. And so that dust, all their lips have known, that is what they think they want. And still they thirst. I see that too." She sat, at last, on the ground. "There's nothing I can do. There is no hope."

"There are two things you can do. You have a choice. And as for hope – all is hope."

"What choice do I have?"

"The choice of what is sane and what is insane. You decide if The Source is insane. The Source who made real the idea that life will not be bound in any way, not by time, not to place, not by form; that no life can fade, but only grow; that all that is, is for all; that no crime is possible, only beauty; that to give is to gain because all life is one with all other life; that everything that is, is known to all; that no life is lesser, nor another greater; that all are together and can never be apart; that joy abides forever within life and is born from it; that meaning is in being and to be is to create." Slowly he poured the rest of his water onto the ground, letting it dribble where it would. "Decide if that is limp-mind – some will say it is – or if it is the ways of this world that are the ways of madness. The madness of calling a clumsy crawl through the dust freedom; of thinking that there is any beauty in a march to oblivion; of saying that the hate in the justice is better than the hate in the crime; of holding high the fallacy that one can be special while declaring all equal; of trying to fill the hole inside with things locked outside; of thinking the child of safety will be born of the flesh of attack; of believing the one whose purpose is to create needs to create some other purpose. Either The Source, or the world made within, is madness. All is hope, or it is nowhere."

"Or. There is no source. And no choice. And hope is …"

"If there is no Source, what is that voice?" He pointed to her chest.

"You are *not* helping. It's too hard."

"What can I tell you?"

"How can I find where the truth is? How long will it take?"

Those questions had no answers, not ones that came neatly wrapped in a small parcel, easily slipped into a shoulder bag, ready to be taken out for inspection at leisure, then put back for later. But Sand-on-Stone felt there was more Mist-on-Water still had to say. It was not like her to have no plan. "Have you thought what you will do?"

Mist-on-Water had come to a decision, one that scared her a little, one she knew would be resisted, one she had decided she would test against Sand-on-Stone first. "I will leave the village for a time."

"Leave. Why? What will you seek?"

Mist-on-Water had herself asked that question a few times already, expecting some good answer. None had come. She paused again for an answer. She let out her breath, slowly. "I don't know. But I will not find it in this village."

"Say-you."

Silence.

In her mind a question was forged, a gift. She gave voice to it: "Why am I here?"

"To take tiring lessons from a dreary recluse?"

"Oaf! I know you are here to make all the mush-minded ones feel better about their mushiness. I mean: do I have some purpose here, in my life? Is it something

I decide? I can decide. Easily. But then … but then I admit it: I am small, still young, *very clever don't you forget*, but just one, just one in a vast world, a no one in a nothing village, a tiny grain blown about on an endless shore. If that tiny grain decides, if she decides to go this way or that, it counts for nought to the sightless wind on that endless shore."

Sand-on-Stone was thinking he should remember that; he could not have put it any better himself. "Is this the first question you do not have your own answer to? It must be noted in the village records."

"I will give you an answer: our purpose here is just to suffer, abandoned. We are good at it."

"Can you say that purpose is true?"

"Can you say it is not true? Where does my purpose come from – if I have one?"

Sand-on-Stone pointed at Mist-on-Water's chest. "That string of green beads you wear is new." Mist-on-Water lifted her several strings of beads to her face, letting them fall one by one through her fingers, until she held one of green agate, a large stone at the centre, flanked in order of size by smaller stones. "Yes, that one. And what happened to the other one you had last time? The blue and white one?"

"The blue and white one was my orchard-novice beads. I don't need it anymore. You know that."

"So much labour in those beads."

"They are just beads. Yes, they did have much work in their making. But they come and they go. Some tell of me. They change with me. Some are just pretty, and I keep them. Until I tire of them and trade them or give them away. Even beads get a purpose given to them."

"Even beads. How much more are you? Here, you hide in your cave of confusion, a cave sheltering you from your purpose first given. Your new purpose here is to learn, to learn to look out on another world, a world where all is well. Your first exercise is in accepting what you are."

Mist-on-Water understood that he was back to his fable of his source again. "Accept what? That other me? That unseen wonder, created out of time, a marvel hidden from itself?"

"What other purpose could there be for this string of soft flesh you wear? Put on for a few dawns and evenings, then set aside or mayhap, as you say, ripped from your frantic fingers."

"So-be. If that is true, why is it so hard? No, wait. How can it be easy to see another world when there is only one to see?"

"No, it is not hard. You always look at that other world – the real one, but rarely see it. When you see it, you do not know it."

Mist-on-Water squinted and keeping her head still, slowly moved her eyes – left as far as they would go, then right as far as they would go. "Only seeing one world," she said as her eyes started moving slowly left again.

"Have you ever gone somewhere, away, to a place, a new place, where there is quietness, and stillness, by the river, or on the top of a hill, and felt the peace there."

"There are places I go. Where it is peaceful. Sometimes I go."

"No. You never do."

"What? *What?* …" It was all she could get out. She jumped up, arms tense, fingers straining hard.

Sand-of-Stone held up his hands, palms facing her. "Please hear me. I say there is no peace in those places. The peace you see, you feel, you know, is what is left *in you* when you come to a place, where nothing there is yours to hold, where nothing is yours to do and where your restless mind rests. Then the beauty, the peace, the oneness, and all the rest you feel so real. They all in you – *in you*, not your flesh, nor any place. Think on it. And they are always in you. Everything is in you. You can invent a world of war in there, or accept the peace, stillness and joy that lie waiting."

She could not refute that but Mist-on-Water said, but was not ready to let him to win. "You have not proven anything. You still want me to seek what I barely see, to ignore what I can touch. This is getting me nowhere. Why should I keep listening to you?"

"Perhaps you should pay more attention to what the oracles say, to what they want." He knew that would not happen. She knew he knew.

"I have been afraid to ask, but I suppose I must: what does your source-with-no-name want from me?"

"Nothing."

"That checks that one off then."

"I mean …"

"I knew it." Mist-on-Water allowed herself a small celebration at her victory in flushing out the admission to come.

"So-be. Just one thing then: The Source wants you to accept what you want. Almost the same as nothing."

"To accept what I want? Say-you. Ah, yes, I see your trick this time. What do I want? An sneaky, slippery, tricking question. Say-I. That is why all of this is so hard, this choosing. I admit it, if I tell it true, I do not even know what I want. Not truly. All I know is that sometimes when I see something I don't have, I want it. Sometimes when I see someone doing something new, then I want to do it. Then when I get it, or do it, I soon find I really want something else I don't have, or haven't done. Does it ever end?"

"So-be, I understand now. You do not know what you want, so you want to find out what that is. So, you will seek it beyond the village. Very good." A pause, brief. "But wait." Another pause, longer. "If you say you will go to find what you want, then of all that you find out there, beyond the village, how will you know when you have what it is that you want? No, don't tell me. It will not be any of the things you don't want. Is that it? You are very clever. Problem solved. So-be."

"You have been warned before about mocking me." She gave him her best glare. "But that is it. Thank you for putting it so as to make my sensible words sound as addle-headed as yours. But it will do for a start: I will go to find what I want. But you will keep that to yourself. If the others hear it, they will say I have been too long with you, and pity me my freshly scrambled wits. Even if I don't know what I want, I will learn."

Sand-on-Stone felt it was not the time to start another round of playful verbal jousting, and silence came. He broke it with, "You will go alone?"

"Apparently not."

"Say-you?"

"Have you forgotten already? Your guide-in-hiding? She will come along with me, you say. As I am going along my path I will creep around and look behind every bush until I see her, then I will go around behind her and yell to make her jump and possibly wet herself."

Sand-on-Stone made a strange sound as he stifled a chuckle. It seemed there was nothing more to be said for now. He took the second bowl of water and poured it into each of the second line of depressions that marked where the purple stripe melon seeds lay, letting it splash hard into the soft soil. Delicately, he pushed soil up to repair a few spots where the water had broken the toe-high banks.

"So-be. Are you finished here, then?"

"What about my armband? Do you bestow on me the token of my graduation from your attempt at teaching me?"

"There it is." He nodded towards an armband hanging by his door, tied up to a peg with some string, polished bronze gleaming softly, bearing a pattern formed with fine silver wire, inlaid with white, ruby, and cobalt enamel.

"That was there on the first day I came here. I could have just taken it then and left?"

"Yes. It has been there for you to take any time you were ready."

"Say-you." Mist-on-Water felt deceived, felt she should have been angrier but did not find it in herself; what had passed, had passed. She decided she would let time judge the value of that. She reached up, took the armband off its hook, and examined the crafting. It was a good one, its design geometric, its lines fine and true, the colours well balanced but hinting at rebellion perhaps, or was it just wild returnings to a beginning?

"What path will you take? What will you do?" Sand-on-Stone understood that even if the destination were unclear, this was no rash mood and Mist-on-Water would have planned what could be planned.

"I will go upriver to start with, for a time, and then I will get a boat, somehow, turn around, and let the river take me where it does."

"And on your journeys no doubt you will be able to tag along with many oracles as they go about their ways. Would they not welcome your guidance, your unceasing supportive insights, in their work?"

"Thank you for the suggestion, so very helpful, but I think a better one is to trade. I know how they do it, the traders. I have my craft. I have some of my own craft pieces that I can start off with. I will take them. And I can buy from one village and sell in another. I know how to barter my profit." She sat, then stood, took three small steps in a circle, then sat again. "But I will see the world. There is much more than this village we have. You have told me many things. I must find out about them. I will meet others, many others. I will speak to all of them. They will speak to me of different things. Or perhaps, the same things. I will see. There will be much more I can learn. And perhaps even find some answers."

A breeze rustled through the leaves. Far off, some birds squawked.

"So-be. Will you come back to the village? Soon?"

"Not soon. Sometime, I think. Who knows? I don't know." Mist-On-Water stood, slowly.

Sand-on-Stone spoke quietly. Mist-on-Water could just hear the words. "I hold you in my heart."

"I will go now. Walk easy." Without pause, she turned with purpose to the track through the forest.

Watching the backs of her legs clomp away, Sand-on-Stone stretched his arm high in farewell. At the edge of the clearing, where the track started, Mist-on-Water looked back and saw him standing, still, arm stretched out, fingers spread wide, and she answered his gesture, swinging her arm barely above her waist, her fingers loose.

The copper enamel-inlaid armband hanging again by the door, it too was giving her small waves as it floated on the breeze. Then she was gone.

Final Note

I nearly have all the observations I need for my report. I even have the conclusion already nicely sketched out in my thought gestation matrix. Essentially it's this: since nothing they are doing is working properly, they should try a completely different way. Just a couple more sessions in this weird anti-idea vortex my fuzzy-brained specimens are all hooked into, then back home. This time I need to make sure I have everything before I go. I am always leaving something behind. (smile symbol).

Chapter 22

Nearing the door of the hospital room, Tracey saw the lights were dimmed. She entered silently and sat on the chair for visitors. Her father lay on his back, eyes closed, the hearty complexion she had always known now pale, sallow. Tracey crossed her arms against the coolness of the room but, even in the cool air, her father's brow was shiny with sweat. She pondered what she would say to best navigate this visit.

Her question still unanswered, her father's eyes opened slowly, barely, closed, and then opened again. As if somehow aware of her silent presence, he tilted his head to where she was sitting.

"Hi, Dad."

Her father's reply was a soft grunt. He straightened his head and closed his eyes for a few seconds. When they half-opened again, he was looking at the ceiling.

Trying to be mildly cheery, Tracey said, "How was your night? How are you feeling? OK?"

"OK? If you mean *are the endorphins swirling between my synapses at adequate levels? Are my serotonins keeping me merry?* then I suppose I've been worse. I get by with a little help from my friendly nurse, Sister Morphine. But I suspect in the end she may be no match for the dastardly gate-crasher, Substance P. JABOC, you know."

Not too bad, thought Tracey, *just a bit of grumpiness for the moment.* What she said was, "Yep, *Just A Bunch Of Chemicals.* Just all those chemicals doing their little dances. A synthesis here, a double displacement there, a split, twirl it all about, everyone jiggling around the dance floor having fun." She sounded like the one who had been left out, standing to the side, to watch, by herself.

"Soon this old bag of chemicals is going to start a different reaction. It's called rapid exothermic oxidation."

"Yeah, I know. At least we'll remember you. You know, how Uncle Fred says Aunt Wilma still lives in his memories." It felt empty and distant. She had not meant it that way.

Her father glared at the ceiling. "Live in your memories, will I? You must be joking. I'm thinking that before you walked in here, you still remembered me. No introductions needed. Your brother may even remember me too, if you show him a photo. Possibly one or two other people too. But that's not me living in those mouldy memories. Your memories don't have throbbing fires in every bone. I live here, not in some creaking leaky memory. And when I die, I won't be living anywhere."

"I wasn't saying that. I just … this's hard." The last, barely above a whisper.

His glare faded. His eyes turned to her. "Don't be sad. I am still here, JABOC and all."

"Just A Bunch Of Chemicals again. Is that true?" Tracey's question was for herself, or the unhearing room, not really for him. Is anything true? According to the Constitution, we all have a bunch of freedoms. We do, do we? Where are they now? No answer. Not here. She felt empty where hope belonged. There's no purpose to this. He's forced into a club no one wants to be in. He doesn't deserve it. It isn't fair. It made her angry. Her anger dropped away to despair.

Her father had not expected her doubt. It unsettled him. He clenched his jaw.

"True? Of course it's true. We have overwhelming evidence for it, and no proper evidence for anything else." He turned his head to look at Tracey. Until now she had always accepted the science, but until now the science had been essentially academic. Now it mattered. Now it was time to accept the hard facts. Of course she did not like them. *But the truth is not a choice. Only accepting it is. She may not want to accept the inevitable. But the inevitable is nothing if not inevitable.* He looked back at the ceiling. He waited, not wanting, but ready to wade through a conversation that would end up being pointless.

Tracey felt she had quite compelling evidence for something else. Carbon, oxygen, hydrogen, and the rest could not go to the places she had gone. But what had, she did not know and, anyway, it was not evidence that would be admissible in this court. So, she said nothing.

Wanting to bring the topic to a conclusion, her father, with an edge of bitterness summoned to cover a surge of sadness, said, "Do you?"

"Not really. What good would it do anyway?" Then a question came to her. Where the question came from, she did not know. *What good? Good?* It surprised her and she repeated it aloud, for herself, not for her father. "But what makes those 'good' ones, you know, *good*?"

Her father's eyes turned back her, narrowed.

She went on, "You know, if those serotonins, etcetera, are really at the bottom of everything we call *good*, and if that Substance P, and whatever else, if they are really at the bottom of everything we call *bad*, and if they're all just chemicals, which they are, what is it that makes some of them *good* and some *bad*?"

"Huh?"

The hazy line of enquiry wavering in her mind came into sharper focus. "I'm just thinking – we all know pain is bad and feeling good is – well – good. Yes?"

"OK." An uncertain glance denied his casual tone.

"But those chemicals are all just chemicals. All the same. It's what you say. There is nothing about some of them that makes them good. Nothing that makes some other different ones bad. They are all just chemicals, they are the same atoms and all that. They don't show up riding white horses or black horses so we can tell the good guys from the bad guys. It must be something else."

"So?" Now he had put on a well-practised, inscrutable poker face. Telling nothing, unless you knew it well. What it told Tracey, was that she might be on to something.

"So, something must know the 'good' ones are good, and the 'bad' ones are bad? What is it that knows the *good* ones are good? If everything is all just a jumble of chemicals. Chemicals don't know things."

Her father gave a grunt, buying time. "Well, it's obvious. Every species evolved to want the *good* chemicals. And those chemicals are not just jumbled up. They have an unimaginably complex order. Every cell is a precise, dynamic, self-replicating structure of many types of carbohydrates, different lipids, nucleic acids, dozens of proteins, and the rest. Then the structures join up into systems and then systems of systems. *Knowing* and *wanting* are in those structures and systems which are too complex to imagine." Even as he gave it, he felt the answer was lacking.

Tracey felt it too, an answer that sounded closer to speculation than explanation. "Mmm. OK. That's clear enough. Knowing good is only a pattern of chemicals in my brain, and wanting or not wanting things is all just another bunch of chemicals. Nothing but a fantastic organic machine. Obviously. Yes?" She nodded her head overeagerly, wide-eyed, gently sarcastic. Then, her voice bitter, "And that's it then. That's all there is. That's all you are and all I am. Objects, not minds. So nothing matters. All the facts, right there."

Her father said, "OK, maybe it's not all the facts, but it is some of them. Despite what some people want, you don't get to choose truth. You can just choose to ignore it." He didn't want to ignore it. He wanted to find it. *Truth? What is truth?* It was all he had ever wanted to know. *Meaning, all the chemicals am I want that. Dammit. They can't want anything, no matter how they are put together. Is it all just an illusion? Chemicals can't have illusions. Double dammit.* "It's all been researched and explained." He knew that was not the truth. There were vast gulfs in what was explained. For anyone who bothered to look, to think. Or for any bunch of chemicals that bothered to, anyway. "No one has any other answer."

She had another answer. She had her story to tell. One that thrilled and scared her. One she would never tell, could barely ponder. "Some people have other … experiences." She knew it was lame. She knew some of her friends had *experiences* that were clearly in fact, just a bunch of chemicals. There was Ravi and Alfred. Too many mornings, she saw those chemicals in their blurry eyeballs, heard them in their slurry words and smelt them in their giggles after lunch. Others were just dreamers. There was Judy, deflecting every hard fact with rainbow fantasies. Waltzing unicorns.

She saw his puzzled look fade, followed by some small nods. As usual, he had found an answer.

"Good? It's just a word. It has a definition. Or maybe a billion definitions – no one even agrees on what it is. It doesn't matter." Then softly, "The same as all the other words." *Words don't matter anymore.*

She still felt there was more. "There's more here than just a word. More than a definition. More than just some chemicals, stuck in some brain stewing together with some other chemicals to brew up a whole lot of different chemicals. Chemicals that learn and think and know. *They know something, Jon Snow.* I think there's more. I *feel* it. I know feelings come and go. Not this one. There's something different about it. After the atom is all sliced and diced, could something still be hidden? Something that does not need any word to exist. Something to do with being aware, or knowing, or feeling. Something never learnt. Something every newborn, even seconds old, has. Yes?" *Maybe.* She did not know. It was all she had. Not enough. *But what is it – that something else, something that tugs, so gentle, so still?*

The conversation had distracted him, the yawn and stretching of intellect had perked him up, but he looked weary again. "No, nothing else. Everyone just learns and remembers. There are structures in the brain for memory. We need to know what is good and bad to survive. We need hunger, pain, yes, even hope. It's what life has evolved to." Voice husky, he said, "Good. Bad. Does any of this even matter? Now?" Despite his words, it did still matter – to him. Or the truth of it, at least.

"Now? Maybe. If there's more to life than death."

"You're not about to go all religious on me, are you? Just because I'll be gone soon."

Tracey had not been about to go all religious. "No." She sighed. She sighed again. "I don't know. I don't know what it is. I don't know what I am talking about."

But he knew. He was not going to admit it. She had told him. *A newborn*, she had said. *A baby.* Her words had taken him back. Back to her birth, and then to her brother's. He had been there. Back then, in that first moment, in the midst of joy, he had been startled. A surprise, a spark. He had seen something there. He had seen something that had no word. He would not use the word miracle. That word angered him. Her. Not just a lump of clay. Her brother. A person. Already. Tiny, yes. Ungrown, yes. But already themselves. He had seen … something, known it. Then. Something not clay. But he could not fit it in. He could not test it, could not prove it. It was all imponderable. So he had discarded it. Every day, as he watched the same something he had seen in that first moment grow and learn and change and every day stay the same. Every day he set it aside – a mystery that could undo everything.

And here it was again, the mystery. Beside him. *Not for long.*

He turned his eyes to her. She was looking at the floor between her knees. He thought of what he had seen then – that first breath – some spark there, some shadow there. Since that first minute, he had seen them both grow with her. That spark that drew her to people, and them to her, that shadow that gathered itself into a mist of self-doubt. But they were not her. There had been something else. *Nearly the end.*

Something else. Something beyond beauty and wonder. From the very first. What had told him that? Some instinct – just a pattern etched into the cells in his brain? *Most likely.* Maybe they were enough to make him care, to want to protect, to want to nurture. That he could accept. But what let him see something beyond beauty and wonder? Not that messy squirming worm. That had not looked nice. Life. Creation. Why could it not stay? He had a thousand answers to that. All correct. Was there another answer he did not have? More correct? Making the others wrong?

She looked at his face. Grim. And sad. "It's not like you to be so moody."

"What? No reason to be blue?" Then a memory, and a smirk at the wit he was about to share. "You know how it goes." He ran a hand down his sheet. Voice croaky, he sang, "My nights in white linen, never ending my groans." He waited for some more words. "Too hard to be here, no one holding my hand. Answers I've always had, to quiet my mind. Knowledge I have now, I don't understand."

He had twisted the lyric, but she knew the tune. A song she had to go past. Too sad. Too feeble the words she had, ones she did know how to send. Her and him. Together apart. Jointly alone. Her, alone with her sadness.

Him, alone with his thoughts. *What is truth? His daughter, the love he had said too few times: just chemicals? Is it nothing in the end? I don't know everything. There could be more. No – if I don't know everything, there is more. But what?*

In the silence she felt she was being crushed. It was not the silence doing it. "You don't know everything."

"OK. I don't know everything."

"But you keep trying."

He smirked. "This will bring the end of that." He brushed his hand over his chest, flicking his fingers away.

Gently, "You don't know that either."

That was true.

After she said goodbye, he remained distracted from his self-consuming body, opening slowly to a new idea, a glimmering dawn of lightness and peace.

As Tracey was walking away, she wondered if it had all been futile and pointless, if everything was futile and pointless. Or … what if nothing was? What then? No answer came, and she had to hurry to make it to Quentin's apartment on time.

When they had returned from their final transfer, Quentin had wanted to do some urgent work on a presentation he was giving the next day. Before Quentin had ushered them all out, Conrad_27-8 had made them agree to meet again for a final debriefing.

Tracey came directly from the hospital and was at Quentin's apartment a little early. She apologised for it.

Quentin said, "How was it?" Tracey had previously told Quentin how hard she found the hospital visits.

"It was OK, actually. I think I found a way to get Dad to consider that there could be more to us than just a bunch of chemicals."

"You did? How?"

"Well, I was talking about how chemicals may not explain everything. Not everything of what we somehow are. It's – you know – all that Conrad stuff. And it's not just us. Loads of people talk about experiences that aren't explained with chemistry. A lot of those guys are obviously just crackpots, or grifters, or maybe just honestly confused. But are they all? Every one? I wonder. Anyway chemicals don't explain what we've been doing."

"But, of course, you can't let on about what we've been doing. Or it would be …" He took a breath, then to the Wizard of Oz tune, "*we're off to see the funny farm. The wonderful farm of fun.*"

"Of course not. Anyway, at least I could suggest there might be more to everyone's existence. Without going down the *you'll-never-guess-what-I've-been-up-to* path. Something more, but what? Maybe it's something good."

"Who knows? I'll admit it. I don't begin to understand what we've been doing – that consciousness transfer bit, I mean."

For Tracey, that brought back memories. "But the mess on SiMiYah's planet – anyone can understand that.

I don't get why they don't see it. Why they don't see the way they live is ludicrous and pointless. Kieran sees it too, I think, and even you do. I feel sorry for them."

"They all seemed to get what they thought they wanted, even SiMiYah."

"Did she really? I do hope she finds happiness."

"In that loony bin? Not a big risk of that happening. Not when everyone is just running around, bumping into one another, falling over, jumping up, rushing off to look for something, shouting out *Urgent! Urgent!* But none of them has any idea of what they are really looking for. They don't even have a word for it."

"No word for happiness? Maybe not. But you surprise me a little. It seems that behind all your one-track haka war-dancing swagger, you do get it."

Quentin rested his head back, closed his eyes, breathed in deeply, let it out slowly, and drummed his fingers on his leg. "All I get is this. I can see my little fingers doing their little dance. I feel them on my leg. I can think it proves how real they are. It all looks solid, but it's not. This stuff, all that JABOC that looks solid, is ninety-nine point nine-nine percent nothing. Tiny electrons and quarks make up those atoms I am seeing as solid. But add their sizes together, if you can make them have a size, which arguably you can't, and it adds up to zero point zero zero zero one percent of that good ol' atom. The rest is nothing. Big, fat, solid nothing. Unless they don't have a size. In that case, those atoms are nothing but crazy vibrations of something I barely understand and can't begin to imagine. The only thing anyone knows is what's in their head. Not what's real. All I get is two things: one is that I don't know anything, and two is anyone else who thinks they do, doesn't. And don't you ever repeat that. Actually, you can forget I said it."

With a shrug of disinterest, Tracey made sure she remembered that, in case she needed to repeat it to him one day.

Quentin shifted the conversation away from himself. "Anyway, clever of you to get your dad to swallow the idea that there might be some bit of him that doesn't turn into worm food." Even now, Quentin himself was actively avoiding thinking through what the implications of that might be. "I suppose this means you'll want to go back and convince your chum SiMiYah about that too."

"No, I don't think so."

"No?"

"I think she already knows."

"A pity. You never got to see me in my ruby slippers."

Addendum

He could not tell her. He wanted to. He thought she wanted to hear. He did not think it could be told. He sat by the fire he had made, a tasty but fibrous bird-claw root softening in the water bubbling in the clay pot on the coals, a page on his writing slate.

He started to write. The words came slowly.

Beyond all word and ken of flesh,
It lives.
Substance of no number and no end,
It is not in time.
It is all.
Knowing all,
It knows no flaw.
It cannot wither or go.
It has no answer –
It makes no question.
Faint here seen, behind shadow in my dream:
All comes from It, departing not.
Everything born from Love is as Love is.
Life.
We, we who are not male, not female, not creature, but being –
We are born of It.
We are as It is.
Together. One.
It is Free.
Free is no want, no ask, no doubt, no wait, no end.
These stars of pebbles,
They are counted.
The numbers for counting have no end
But counting will find an end.
We, the end will find.
We, birthed in dream,
Suckling black imagining,

Unseeable light seeking,
Need not seek.
It abides here yet.

He read what he had written, read it again. Sand-on-Stone lifted the hard-bartered page from his slate and dropped it in the fire.

Hello (surprise) Supervisor!

✌δ☛Ω [incomplete symbology - untranslatable]

Time to come back already?

ΩΩ⩞⌬ [incomplete symbology - untranslatable]

Of course I will bring everything back with me.

Printed in Great Britain
by Amazon

59101599R00212